# THE WRONG'UN

# THE WRONG'UN

CATHERINE EVANS

First published in 2018 by Unbound

www.unbound.com

Second edition published in 2022 by Inkspot Publishing

www.inkspotpublishing.com

ISBN (Paperback): 978-1-7396305-7-7

ISBN (Ebook) 978-1-7396305-8-4

Design by Mecob

Cover image: © Shutterstock.com/Shanina

For Rom Tiddly Pom

*'Sometimes, in jumping to avoid your fate, you rush headlong to meet it instead.'*

Edie Fell Newell

# THE NEWELLS

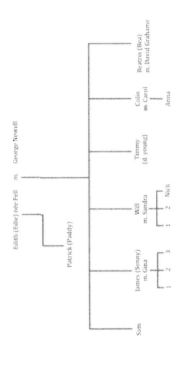

Edith (Edie) née Fell    m.    George Newell

Patrick (Paddy)

Sam

James (Sonny)
m. Gina
1   2   3

Will
m. Sandra
1   2   Nick

Timmy
(d. young)

Colin
m. Carol
Anna

Beatrix (Bea)
m. David Grahame

# CHAPTER ONE

I'm just an old bat now, so it doesn't matter what I think. I'll tell you this though. Things were never the same between me and George after Bea was born. To have a girl after so many boys. 'Oh you must be thrilled!' people said. People don't know what they're on about half the time.

We started our family straight off. He'd sooner have waited for kids, but there was no stopping me. Sammy first, Sonny hot on his heels and him barely three months old before I found out Will was on his way. It was hard, those early days, George scratching a living at Jebsen's Yard before he set up on his own. There never was any question of me working. Not with two little ones and a third waiting to burst in on the world. Another man would have torn his hair out.

Paddy came to us after Will was born. Beautiful. Like a Botticelli angel. He was four when we got him. I'll never make up for those four years. Fair, he was, when the rest of us were dark. He was different in other ways. You know kids. Needy, always looking for attention. Not Paddy. I tried so hard with him. To read him a story or play a game. Paddy liked to look at books by himself and didn't get excited about games. He was just more self-sufficient, more independent. The only person he was interested in was George, and George didn't know what to do with him.

I still feel a lurch in my heart when I think about the one we lost. Timmy. I used to panic I'd forget his little face, as if I ever would. They didn't want me to be the one to dress him for his burial. They said it would be too upsetting for a woman in my condition. Colin was on the way by then, you see, but who else should have dressed him if not his own mother? I don't remember much about that time. Just flashes in the darkness, like the sight of his tiny white coffin, my children's frozen faces, George in a panic looking for Grubby, Timmy's toy rabbit. We'd wanted Grubby to go in with him but in the end he was buried alone. I went through the rest of the pregnancy in a dark fog. Colin was the smallest of our babies. Forced out early by grief and shock. He helped us to heal. It sounds like we forgot about our Timmy once we had a new baby, but I swear it's not true. Colin was supposed to be our last.

My brother was with us when Timmy died, on leave from the Merchant Navy. George liked Jackie, though he drank too much and had an eye for the ladies. I was fond of my little brother. I'd been like a mother to him after our mam was gone. Anyways. Jack never came back to our house after Timmy died.

Life goes on, so they say, even after the worst kind of disaster. I blotted Jackie from my life and got on with the business of mothering.

We had clever children, George and me. Sammy was the first boy from St Stephen's to get into Oxford. He got a mention in the local paper. I cried when I saw it. He ruffled my hair and called me his daft little mam. If I'd known what kind of life it would lead to... being buried in a lab like a gnome. I'm not saying it's not worthy, whatever it is he does, but he should be married with kids. Newell men tend to find a girl and then stick to her their whole life. Things didn't work out that way for me and George, and not for Sammy neither. He lost the only girl he ever loved.

Sonny rose like a rocket at Morgan Stanley before he set up his own hedge fund. He's minted, living in New York, married to a Yank with a couple of kids. He takes very good care of his old mam. Bea too, to be fair, though she can't take credit for her money like he can.

Will's third book will be out soon. It'd be nice if this one wasn't about us. It's a mixed blessing having a writer in the family, let me tell you.

Colin's an accountant. His brothers rib him about it, but they lumber him every January with their tax returns.

I wonder sometimes what little Timmy would have been like as a man, but I find I can't do it. He's frozen in my mind as a babe in arms.

It was hard on Paddy, surrounded as he was by brilliance, but he was just a late bloomer. The neighbours laughed behind our backs when he went to prison for dangerous driving. Under the influence too. To my face they were all tea and sympathy, of course. Paddy swears the boy came out of nowhere. You know what kids are like. No road sense. The child's walking again now. I shudder to think what kind of pressure Paddy was under to start taking that stuff. I never thought I'd say so, but prison did him some good. Like a cold bath. He swears he's off it now. I pray every day he'll never go back to it. I'm thankful he works for himself as it's hard getting a decent job when you've a record. People are quick to sit in judgement. If they knew the strain he was under... people get a look in their eye when I try and tell them.

So coming to Bea. A gifted student, her teachers said. An all-rounder. Jack of all trades, I always thought, but it seemed a bit mean-spirited to say that about your own child. George was like a strutting peacock whenever his precious angel did well. Always blind, he was, where she was concerned. She writes for some highbrow magazine. She does the commentary, the politics, the features, the world's sob stories, the stuff that people skip over to get to the gossip and the fashion. She could have done any number of things if she'd had a mind. She had one true talent, a golden voice with range and strength, and what did she do? She jacked it in. She should have a kiddie or two. Women these days are obsessed with their careers. It's not like David wouldn't support her. He's a diamond, her husband. She's lucky to have him.

There were no more babies after Bea. I loved having

babies. Having their warm, milky little bodies snuggled up against me, the need and the love pulsing from them for me and no one else. It's hard to explain to someone who hasn't had a baby. They grow away from you, get a sense of themselves, then off they go. They start not to need you any more. Heartbreaking. Colin, the next one up from Bea, was walking and chattering away, a proper little man, and I couldn't wait for a new one. I loved the minuscule little fingers and toes, and how the bigger children, even the tiny ones, dwarfed the newborns. I loved their scrawny matchstick legs and their pinched red faces. Just like angry little baked beans. Their bums. How I loved their little bums. Red and blotchy and dimpled, no bigger than my palm.

It was all different with Bea. The last thing I ever expected was a girl. I wish I could remember if the pregnancy was any different, but it was just the same as the others, so far as I could tell.

'A little girl!' the matron cooed before whisking her away. 'Finally! After all those boys.' As if I'd kept going till I'd finally hit the jackpot. After she'd been washed and swaddled, the nurse gave her to George. He gazed at her like she was the Holy Grail. He cried. Cried, I tell you. I felt a tremble in my stomach as I watched him fall hopelessly in love with the wrinkled, wailing creature in his arms. He brought her to me and had just lowered her to my breast when I jerked forward and coughed. I couldn't help it. He was so overwhelmed he didn't clock it, and the baby stopped crying when he put his pinkie in her mouth. My heart flailed within me as I tried to smile, and tears came to my eyes too. George couldn't speak he was that choked up, grinning and misty-eyed, so grateful I'd given him something so precious. As if the boys, each of our beautiful little boys, were somehow worth less than her. He held her till I was settled, till I'd readied myself to feed her.

The boys were so easy. They'd all latched on in a

heartbeat. Each of them had fused with me, and I'd rock back and forth and hum to them while they fed. And it wasn't just me feeding them. They fed something deep within me, that couldn't be reached any other way. But Bea. She wouldn't settle. It was a battle to get her comfortable and the two of us would go through a kind of wrestling match filled with vexed frustration all for a piddling result, as what she finally got down her wouldn't feed a slimming sparrow.

Finally I threw in the towel and borrowed a pump from the midwife. No shortage of takers wanting to feed her. George had that baby glued to him. The boys fought for the privilege. Smothered with love and affection, she was. Not from Paddy, I grant you. I didn't express for long. It all seemed to dry up. I suppose I just couldn't produce in the same way for a machine, but no one can say I didn't try. I switched her to powder.

As for sleeping – the boys fretted in the night from time to time. There was the odd wet bed and sometimes a nightmare. Especially Will. Imagination comes at a price, poor lamb. But Bea... where she found the energy to bellyache the way she did on the rations she took in, I'll never know. With the boys I'd get up and sort them out. Change the bed, give them a cuddle, whatever they needed. But with Bea, somehow George started to do it. He'd get up for Bea in the middle of the night. Even if he'd worked late or had to get up at stupid o'clock. He never did that for the boys. He'd sleep through all their fussing, and I'd get to them before he even woke up. But with her, it was like he was tuned in to the frequency of her crying. Funny, isn't it?

We were going to call the new baby Albert, after my grandad. In my head he'd become Bertie. It sounds daft, but I had to get used to not having my Bertie with me. Fancy missing a baby that didn't even exist. We didn't have any girls' names ready.

George was shaving one morning before work. He was

still at Jebsen's. I was in bed trying to feed Bea. She'd been home from the hospital five or six days and we were still calling her 'the baby'. Sonny was reading Peter Rabbit to Colin at the foot of the bed. Suddenly he stopped.

'What's the baby's name?' he asked.

George laughed. 'Good question, my lad,' he said. 'What *are* we going to call her? Alberta?'

I was silent. Your brain doesn't work right after you've had a baby. I didn't want to give Bertie's name away.

'What do you reckon, Princess?' he asked me again.

'I'm thinking,' I said.

'What about Beatrix?' Sonny asked.

George and me looked at each other. 'Beatrix,' he said, trying it for sound. 'Not many Beatrixes around, that's for certain. I like it.' He looked at me.

'Why not?' I said.

George chucked his razor in the sink and ruffled Sonny's hair. 'Nice one, Sonny,' he said. He kissed me, leaving a bit of foam on my cheek. He cupped the baby's head with his palm. 'Little Beatrix,' he said and bent over to kiss her too.

Colin stood up on the bed. He was still tiny, dressed in red pyjamas, his hair tousled from his bed, looking delicious as a plum. He could normally put a smile on my face. He jumped into George's arms. The three of them giggled like halfwits.

'George, you'll be late for work,' I said. The baby started crying. 'That's torn it! Sonny, go and get ready for school. Take Colin with you.'

'But he doesn't go to school.'

'Just get him out of here. Clear off, both of you.'

The cry was a particularly pathetic kind of mewling.

'That was a bit harsh, Princess,' said George. 'They were only having a bit of fun.'

A flash of heat surged in my chest. I was just about to mouth off, when I got a hold of myself. He was right, but I was the more livid for it. I looked down at the baby, and I longed for Bertie. Like I said, your brain isn't the same after a pregnancy. George quietly turned back to the bathroom and pulled the plug on the water in the sink, no doubt leaving it flecked with foam and stubble as per usual.

*\*\*\**

Patrick Newell sat alone in a cavernous pub on the Holloway Road, two fingers of Kronenbourg remaining in his pint glass. Face-up on the table was a cheap pay-as-you-go Nokia, which he glanced at frequently. He held an iPhone in his hand. His dark cashmere coat was draped over the chair next to him. Snowflakes had melted into water beads on the surface of the fabric. Each time the double doors of the pub opened, a blast of freezing air blew in. People left swaddled against the cold, umbrellas at the ready, or entered pink-cheeked and foot-stamping into the sudden warmth. A couple of overly made-up girls perched at the bar whispering and giggling together. They were looking his way, eyes like crocodiles'.

Paddy was used to the admiring glances of women. In his forties, he was tall and athletic with patrician features. The cast of his face promised strength of character and high intelligence. Perhaps of more interest to the girls was the stamp of money. The fabric and the clean lines of his dark suit bore all the hallmarks of bespoke tailoring.

His iPhone vibrated. Diana. He sent the call to voicemail. Moments later it beeped. He put the phone to his ear to listen to her message. 'Darling, I'm looking forward to seeing you tonight. Pick me up at eight? If the children weren't here, I'd summon you early for... well, it wouldn't be polite to say. Call me. Bye.' Diana, so groomed, so polished, so well-preserved. So fucking tedious. He took the last sip of his lager.

His iPhone rang again. The screen flashed 'Lorena'. He

hesitated, thumb hovering. He took the call.

'Be quick, Lola. I'm busy with Phase II.'

'Come and see me. Tonight. At eight o'clock.'

'I've got a date with—'

'I don't care. Bring me cigarettes.'

'Fucksake, Lorena, you're pregnant.'

'Bring them. If I go out, I may slip in the snow and who knows what will happen?'

Irritation bubbled across his chest. 'Fine. I'll see you later.'

A spotty youngster was collecting glasses. Paddy wanted to signal the boy for another pint, but thought better of it. Dritton had assured him he'd be on time. The Nokia on the table beeped. About time. He put the little phone into his trouser pocket and scanned the room. He made eye contact with a stocky bearded man in a green ski jacket leaving the pub.

He collected his things and extracted a small black umbrella from his briefcase. It unfurled with a snap at the click of a button on the handmade wooden handle. Once outside, he held it low over his face, shielding himself from the weather and from CCTV. Only Dritton's legs were visible, scurrying up the Holloway Road against the wind. Dritton took a left into Drayton Park Road, then turned into a residential street flanked on either side by ugly beige terraced houses. The streetlights cast orange patches onto the snow. Paddy kept his head well beneath the umbrella's canopy. Dritton picked his way carefully through the snow, and placed a lone Yale key onto the gatepost of No. 27 without turning round. He turned right into a side road, disappearing from view. Paddy picked up the key and let himself into the house.

The place was in complete darkness. Paddy tried the switch in the hallway. Nothing. He reached into his pocket for his Zippo. The click was loud in the hush and a faint reek of lighter fuel merged with the damp and stale cigarette smoke.

The hallway was awash with junk mail that had been kicked here and there to unblock the door. Holding the lighter, he put his head round the living room door. It was empty except for a mouldy sofa and a broken TV set on the floor. He wrinkled his nose at the smell of damp and neglect. He tried the light switch. Still nothing.

The galley kitchen had fitted cabinets above a Formica counter on one side. Two of the cabinet doors hung from their hinges and one of the doors was missing, like a gap in a row of teeth. A small wooden table was pushed against the far wall, flanked by two Formica chairs. On the table were a candle and a couple of boxes of matches, blobs of wax and a chipped saucer full of cigarette butts. Spent matches lay in disarray over the tabletop. More burnt matches and the odd squashed butt lay scattered on the floor. Paddy lit the candle and was about to sit down when he stopped himself and reached into his pocket for a handkerchief. He wiped the seat and the back of the chair first.

The front door opened and Dritton came in, quickly shutting the door. He swore softly and blew air from his cheeks like a bellows. He stomped his feet on the floor, scattering snow all over the sea of junk mail. He paused when he saw Paddy's dark shape behind the candle, then made his way into the kitchen. He pushed back the hood of his jacket to reveal thick dark hair that shone in the candlelight. The English winter had touched his olive skin with a pale yellow pastiness. His face was rescued from prettiness by a hooked nose that had been broken more than once, and an ingrained frown line, like a stab in pastry.

'Dritton!' said Paddy. He stood up. The two men gave each other an awkward bear hug. 'It's good to see you,' he went on.

'You also.'

'Nice place you have here, I must say.'

9

'Would you prefer to meet at your house?'

The corners of Paddy's mouth twitched. Dritton reached into his inside pocket and brought out a packet of cigarettes. He offered one to Paddy, who shook his head.

Dritton lit the cigarette in the flame of the candle and took a deep drag.

'In my country a house like this would not go to waste.'

'Still homesick? It's funny. You lot love your country so much you'll do anything for it. Except live there.'

'We're free of Albania now. I'll go back soon.'

Paddy was about to say, 'And I'm the tooth fairy,' but thought better of it. Dritton was touchy about his country, his ways, his people. Inside, he had pasted an Irishman who had said he'd 'fuck his flat-faced peasant grandmother for a penny.'

'I saw Fevze quite recently,' he said instead.

Dritton looked surprised.

'Oh yes. I've done a bit of work for him.'

'What kind of work?'

'You know. Bits and pieces.'

'And you want me to do something for you?'

'Yup. I need you to take care of someone.' Paddy had seen at close quarters over an extended time how meticulous Dritton was. 'I'm trusting you as a friend that you'll be professional about it.'

'Please,' said Dritton, with a pained expression, as if insulted. He dragged so deeply on his cigarette that it crackled. 'Who is it?'

Paddy brought out some photographs from an envelope in his briefcase and handed them over. Dritton studied the top photo, a head and shoulders shot of a man in his fifties smiling directly to camera. The picture could have come from a corporate brochure, despite his weatherbeaten skin. The next picture showed the same man dressed casually, drink in hand. In the third, he was tanned and bare-chested, holding up a large fish by the tail. In all of the photos, he looked happy, despite the lines on his face.

'He saw you in prison,' said Dritton.

'Yes. His name is David Grahame,' said Paddy.

Dritton continued to flick through the photographs, cigarette still in hand. He stopped to study one in particular, in which David Grahame had his arm round a tall blond woman leaning in to him. Dritton narrowed his eyes as he puffed on his cigarette. He looked appraisingly at Paddy.

'Your sister's husband?'

Paddy didn't respond. 'All the information you need is in here,' he said, handing over the envelope. 'Where he lives, where he works, his daily habits. Everything. It could look like a mugging. He walks to work most mornings when it's still dark and it would be simple—'

Dritton put his hand up, as if for silence.

'Do you care how it is done?'

'No. So long as it's not traced back to me.'

'You have nothing to fear. What about timing? It's a problem for you?'

'Within a month. The end of the month would be best.' Lorena had just had her twelve-week scan, but he needed a bit of extra time to sort out one or two loose ends.

'You have the money?'

Paddy picked up his briefcase and brought out a bubble-wrapped A4 envelope. He handed it over. 'Half now and half when the job is done. As agreed.'

Dritton took the envelope. 'I will not insult you by counting, my friend.'

Paddy laughed. 'Go ahead and count. Trust, but verify. It's a good principle to live by.'

Dritton shook his head and stood up, tucking the envelope under his arm. 'The key, please,' he said.

Paddy handed over the single Yale key. 'Is that it, then?'

'Yes. Just one more thing. You must be sure. After tonight, there is no stopping this.'

'I'm sure,' said Paddy. He blew out the candle and sparked up his Zippo to light the way to the front door. The two men were about to leave the house together, but then Dritton turned round and raised his hand. 'I go first. You wait.'

'Hold on. I'm the one paying.'

Dritton shrugged. 'As you wish.'

Paddy slipped out of the door, umbrella at the ready. He took a different route back to the Holloway Road. He flagged a cab down and gave Lorena's address in St John's Wood. He'd pick up the blasted cigarettes on the way.

*** 

After Paddy left, Dritton Zladko waited a while in the darkness. Just as he was about to leave, he remembered that he'd brought new candles. He made his way back to the kitchen, lighting his way with a cheap yellow Bic lighter. He dug into his other pocket and pulled out a new box of white candles and two boxes of matches and put them into one of the kitchen drawers. He took a last look around to see if he'd forgotten anything.

He hadn't thought it possible, but the damp was worse than the last time he came. It was strange the neighbours didn't complain to the council. Perhaps they had. The council was useless. The house was solid, with good foundations and well-proportioned rooms. It could be fixed up nicely and sold for a profit. He shrugged at the waste. In his country every room would be full, all generations thrown together, children falling asleep where they dropped. When he had enough money together, he'd go back. He missed his wife. His sons were growing up without him. His brother had no work. 'I will be a father to your children,' he had told Dritton, as if that were a comfort. His brother was an idiot. His sister's husband had left her with two small children. His mother was getting too old to be much help. What a difference he could make with a little more money. Only a fraction of the cash in Paddy's envelope would come to him. He answered to Fevze, Fevze answered to Almas. Who Almas answered to, he, Dritton, had no idea.

# CHAPTER TWO

Paddy was a special little boy. Different. The others didn't like him much. Their own brother. He found it hard to make friends. The others were with their mates all the time, coming home only for meals, often with some kid or other in tow. Not Paddy. I'm not saying he was my favourite, that wouldn't be right, but he needed someone on his side.

Paddy took against Bea from day one. He'd come to us just after Will was born. Maybe it was having my Paddy back that settled me for a spell, as it was another four years before Timmy turned up. When he did, Paddy played up something terrible. Timmy dying and Colin arriving so soon after made it so much worse. So imagine how he must have felt about George heaping his attention on baby Bea, who well and truly pushed her way up the pecking order. Hard for a boy to see someone nakedly favouring one child. The fuss George made when Paddy dropped her. You'd think he'd tried to kill her.

Before Bea could even walk she joined in the boys' games. She'd sit in the garden in her vest and nappy, digging up worms, unaware she was the old king who had to be defended from a young usurper, or that she was the stone that sheathed Excalibur. They played ball around her, and dodged her as if she were a bit of garden furniture. Sometimes they'd take it in turns to leap over her, and she'd sit blinking like a mole as the boys hurtled towards her, then she'd lift her eyes in wonder, wreathed in smiles to see them sailing in the air overhead. I put a stop to it when I saw them do it, babies' heads being soft as eggs. I did my best to watch them, but I had to keep on top of the meals and the clothes and the house and no eyes in the back of my head.

The boys were always ranged against Paddy.

I remember hearing one of their fights breaking out in the garden. I was edgy that day. Maybe I had the curse. Will and Sam were yelling at Paddy. The other boys all stood around Sonny, who held a crying Bea in his arms.

'How would you like it if I stomped on your hand?' Sonny screamed.

'She was in the way,' Paddy said. 'She's always in the way.'

'She's a *baby!*'

Ganging up on Paddy again. I couldn't bear it.

'What's going on?' I took Bea from Sonny's arms. She kicked off again for my benefit.

'Paddy stomped on Bea's hand,' said Sonny in righteous fury.

'I'm sure it was an accident,' I said. 'Paddy, come and say sorry to Bea.'

I lowered Bea to Paddy's level so he could kiss her. He puckered up but she whipped her head away from him. The others started in.

'That was no accident. I'm telling you, Mam, he did it on purpose,' said Sonny. 'He's always hurting her. And Colin and Will. Anyone smaller than him.'

'You're smaller than me,' said Paddy.

'Yeah, but I can fight back, can't I?' His eyes blazed.

'Enough!' I cried. 'Now. I'm putting Bea down here, out of the way. Play nicely, all of you. Paddy, be more careful with the little ones. And the rest of you stop pointing fingers.'

'But Mam—' said Will.

'No buts!' I said. 'More fighting and I'll make you play inside.'

Sonny muttered something. I rounded on him.

'Sonny, what did you say?'

He glared at me, then looked away. It wasn't five minutes before war broke out again.

'Every time you jump over her, you kick her one.'

'Shut up, twat. It's not my fault she moved.'

I'd told the boys time and again they shouldn't be jumping over Bea's head. Paddy was a bit accident-prone where she was concerned, but all the same. They were always leaving him out. I marched downstairs again. I decided to pretend I hadn't heard Paddy's language. George was always on at him about it. It was a drag on my soul knowing where he'd learned it, and more besides.

'What are you warring over now?' I asked. The boys looked sheepishly in my direction.

'They jumped over Bea's head,' said Paddy. 'I told them they mustn't.'

'*Liar!*' Sonny bellowed.

'Enough!' I cried. 'How many times have I told you *not* to jump over Bea's head? And don't call your brother a liar. I won't have it, d'you hear me?'

I looked at the faces of my simmering brood. 'And Paddy, don't tell tales.' I added lamely. The boys seized on what I'd said.

'Yeah, Paddy you arsewipe,' said Sonny.

I grabbed him by the shoulder. '*What* did you call him? Do you want a mouthful of soap?'

We glared at each other.

'Read my lips,' I hissed. 'I'll not have any screaming, nor any fighting or jumping over the baby's head. Understand?'

'But Mam—' said Paddy.

I rounded on him too. 'I said shut it!' I was hoping they'd be united by being ranged against me. A country at war, and all that. 'I don't want to hear another word.' They glowered at me. I looked at their little frowning faces in turn. Nobody said anything at first. Then Will piped up.

'He likes hurting her,' said Will. 'Why d'you let him, Mam?'

I felt like he'd slapped me. So I slapped him. Right across the face. Bea started bellowing, as if I'd hit her, which set Colin off. Will stared at me, then he lifted his hand to his cheek. I looked down at my stinging palm as if it belonged to someone else. If he'd only cried I could have done something, put my arms round him, said sorry; but he didn't. Sonny stared at me too. He put his hand on Will's shoulder. Sam picked Bea up and tried to shush her and put his free arm round Colin. Colin turned to him and clung to his leg, bawling for all he was worth. Paddy gave nothing away, as per usual.

I stalked back inside. I willed Paddy to stay with the others but he followed me in, marking himself out even more.

*** 

Bea furrowed her brow, chasing the dream that was fast scattering in her head. The wind moaned intermittently through the surrounding trees like a half-hearted banshee. She looked at the clock, which glowed 3.07. The seven morphed into an eight.

She propped herself up on her elbow, trying not to disturb David, a deadweight beside her. Through the half-opened curtain, she saw snowflakes blowing thick and fast against the window. There would be no getting out in the morning.

The house was on a hill, exposed to the wind. It was a ramshackle old Cotswolds farmhouse, with a maze of rambling bedrooms and a huge stone kitchen. The garden sprawled and sloped, blending with the open fields and hills that stretched out into the distance. Their car was no match for the treacherous driveway and they didn't have chains.

Their visits to the old place had dwindled, though David didn't have the heart to sell it. His maiden aunt Lucy had left it to him. She had been his guardian when he was a boy, while his parents were 'living high on the hog abroad'.

'Let's take a chance,' he'd said about the prospect of being snowed in. 'Just the two of us for the whole weekend. No visitors, no kids, none of our dreadful relatives. Just you, me and a cellarful of decent plonk. We can pick up a couple of trash movies and curl up on the sofa together. I'll even do the cooking.'

His offer to cook was not one to be taken seriously. He liked to mix up corned beef, boiled potatoes and baked beans, and slop the resulting mixture on toast. It looked like something that could be found on a pavement on a Friday night, and smelled worse. She'd often had to eat corned beef as a child. Even then, it had stuck in her craw.

There was no way she'd make work on Monday. She was writing a big piece about Sudanese women. Her mother had asked her if she couldn't write about something more cheerful for a change, but the world was chock-full of places where life was cheap and tragedies two a penny. How did you decide which stories should be told? Disfigurement, slavery, rape, murder, child killing. All predictably shocking. Unexpected were the vestiges of warmth, humour, compassion, hope and zest for life that survived in people who had suffered the worst kinds of horror. *That* was cheerful. Humbling. But Edie didn't see it that way.

Her boss, Rob, had been hassling her about the time she'd been taking off. He couldn't understand why she didn't drop everything to travel for a story as she used to. Now she timed her trips to ensure they didn't clash with ovulation or clinic appointments. Rob had given Bea a hard time about conducting an interview over the phone. 'You just don't get the same feel for the person, the connection you get from seeing the whites of their eyes. That kind of cheating comes through on the page.' He'd printed the piece regardless.

If Rob knew about the IVF, he would be sympathetic, she was sure, but it was deeply private on so many levels. She feared that David would be judged, and she keenly felt her failure as a woman. David had told her she was being ridiculous, that their inability to conceive was probably due to his bone-idle old sperm. He'd kissed her, then made her laugh by pretending to be a bored, creaky old sperm cell: 'Oh Christ on a bike!' he'd drawled, rolling his eyes. 'The old bugger wants us to go swimming again.'

She was sure that the fault, if that was the right way to put it, was down to her. He never pointed fingers, even after the first two rounds had failed. 'Darling, it'll happen, I promise. We'll have a baby one day. I can feel it in my bones.' The only grumble he'd ever made was about 'those wretched porn mags at that confounded clinic. It's hard to wank off to 1970s German air hostesses, knowing they're now in Lufthansa's knacker yard. Next time I'm bloody well taking my own.'

She wished she could talk to her friends about it. All she had to do was open her mouth. God knows they'd be sympathetic, and it would feel so good to unburden herself. They'd probably be relieved she had a weakness, that there was a worm in the apple of her perfect life. 'Airing your dirty linen in public,' her mother called it.

Her colleague, Martha, also suffered from infertility, as everyone in the office knew. Even Bola, the Nigerian security guard, was kept informed of Martha's husband's sperm count and the probable genesis of her polycystic ovaries. She never tired of running through the pros and cons of all the options that various doctors, sages and quacks had suggested. Nobody was short of an opinion either, volunteering the triumphs and tragedies of 'my sister', 'my friend', 'my cousin's girlfriend'.

Bea listened intently to these conversations, a mishmash of science fiction and old wives' tales. She tuned in, hoping for some revelation, some nugget that would magically open the door that was barred to her.

She wouldn't be back to leave money on the kitchen

table for Lorena, their cleaner. They'd have to leave double the week after. Bea had offered to pay her online several times, but she had always curtly refused. Lorena made her uneasy. 'Your problem,' David had said 'is that you suffer from lower-middle-class guilt about having a cleaner.' He was right. Lorena had taken the job from her sister, Rafaela, during those awful weeks after Paddy had his car accident. Lorena had been brilliant at handling Paddy, even if her cleaning wasn't a patch on her sister's. He was docile as a child with her. Rafaela had at least been friendly, whereas Lorena was a frosty fish indeed. A frosty fish with a blatant sex appeal. Bea and David's Brazilian cleaning lady became a standing joke among their neighbours, who reported sightings of her playing loud rock as she worked, dancing along in tight jeans and figure-hugging polo necks. She wore Marigolds to protect her perfect manicure. Her clothes looked expensive. Bea didn't understand how she did it on a cleaner's wage.

Bea needed to pee. She lay in bed mustering the willpower to get up. David lay in absolute stillness beside her. She settled on her back, pushing her stomach out to give her aching bladder room to expand, postponing the inevitable for a little longer. She ran her hands gently over her stomach as she listened to the wind keening through the trees. Maybe this time it had worked. Maybe she was, actually, right now, pregnant. She threw up the thousandth silent prayer to her nameless god. She tried breathing deeply.

Her gynaecologist, Damien Lillie, lectured her about taking it easy, about how stress had an adverse effect on conception. It was all very well for him to say that. He had pictures of his four children plastered over his consulting room. There were school photos, the children adorable in their uniforms; a shot of them playing on a white sand beach; another of the children in Disneyland wearing giant sunglasses gathered around Donald Duck and a picture of the littlest girl in full riding gear, down to the hard hat, mounted on a pony, smiling gap-toothed at the camera. It was perhaps a little wanting in tact, nakedly displaying his own rampant virility, especially as all his patients came to him for the same reason. She sighed. She didn't begrudge anyone else their good fortune.

Mr Lillie also had a prominent photo of himself in top hat and tails with his arm round his couture-clad, behatted wife, who was holding onto the reins of a magnificent chestnut racehorse. Racing was his passion, apparently. When David had asked him, he'd said that he owned the horse. 'Now that's what I call wanting in tact,' David had moaned afterwards. 'Parading a hobby like that, while charging like a wounded rhino.'

There was a huge board in his office with pictures of all the babies that had been created in the clinic, the ones that had started out as an oddball collection of cells fused together in Petri dishes, frozen in nitrogen, mixed up in test tubes and squirted through injection needles before finally taking up residence in nice cosy wombs.

The treatment was costing an astonishing amount of money. 'A microscopic drop in a vast ocean,' David had sighed. She had seen the bills rolling in for his three kids, who were in private schools, plus the eye-popping maintenance payments he was obliged to send to Diana, his ex-wife. The country pile surrounding them was free of a mortgage, but the upkeep was staggering, particularly the heating bills. 'You'd never think it, would you? Still colder than a penguin's bum.' Their London house had been described by the estate agent as 'a stunning four-bedroom family home in need of minor renovation.' 'Minor renovation! Try major rebuilding,' David had cried. 'Cheaper to burn the sodding place down.'

They supported his mother, Millicent, who lived in a high-end nursing home. It was the best they could find, but still depressing as all hell. She'd come to live with them for a while, until her Swiss cheese memory bloomed darkly into full-blown

Alzheimer's. She'd required vigilant care, as she developed a mania for escape. Initially they hired carers. The first walked out after less than a week as she was 'fed up with chasing the old bird'. The second person hired to watch Millie preferred watching daytime TV. David sacked her after Millie was found wandering round Hyde Park. Millie became as artful as Papillon. They threw in the towel after Bea received a frantic call from the third carer, who'd just fished her out of the Serpentine. The old lady had forgotten everything else, but remembered how to swim. 'Just like riding a bicycle', she'd said breezily, when asked. The cold water did her no harm, and seemed to restore some of her lucidity, but that evening she tried to get away again, complaining that her room was full of dark shadows spying on her. Bea was desperately sorry for her. There was no escaping the fears that lived in your own head.

It was hard to decide between the breakdown of the body or the disintegration of the mind. Her own father had died the year previously of prostate cancer. It had been a protracted death and none of his children had been with him at the end. He'd had a sudden spell of good health, then died in the night without warning. She and her brothers shared the guilt for his lonely death. There was a piece of the narrative in Will's latest book that she could not read without crying.

She couldn't wait for the loo another minute. The mattress groaned as she slipped out of the covers and felt around for her dressing gown. She couldn't find it, so she tiptoed to the bathroom in the nude, her body fast shedding its warmth. She imagined what she'd look like through the lens of an infra-red gun. A glowing bundle of moving red light, growing dimmer as she grew colder, her life light finally expiring as she ultimately froze to death. She sat on the loo and hugged herself, vigorously rubbing her arms. She shivered. The central heating in the house was dodgy as all hell. The boiler could be relied upon to conk out when most needed. The release of tension in her aching bladder was blissful despite the biting cold.

Fat snowflakes whirled in uneven clusters, the wind spitting them this way and that. The branches of the old yew knocked gently against the rattling panes, outlined in white against the luminous sky.

She saw movement in the corner of her eye and turned her head towards the door. David stood naked in the doorway.

'Sorry I woke you.' She whispered it, although they were alone.

He gazed at her, silent. He seemed half asleep. He bent down to kiss her. He reached for her cold breasts, then tried to hug her.

She wriggled free. 'See you back in bed. It's bloody freezing.'

She rinsed her hands under the sputtering tap and bent to take a sip of icy water. David appeared in the mirror and wrapped his arms round her, pulling her against him. He sank his face into her neck. She turned and dropped a peck on his chest.

'Be quick!' she said, still whispering, and dashed back to the warmth of the bed.

He straightened and let her pass. She turned at the door to look at him again. Still he didn't speak and he seemed oblivious to the cold. His face was shrouded in darkness, haloed by the light from the snow. She scampered back to bed and dived under the covers. She anticipated his return, waiting for the great waves of heat he generated, which she could burrow into like a wintering animal. She lay under the covers, and listened to her heart slowing. Her skin warmed. She lay still in the quiet, drowsy and comfortable, losing herself.

Abruptly, she started upright, not sure if she'd been asleep or not. She was disoriented, with a pit of anxiety in her stomach, as if she'd overslept and missed something of vital importance. All was quiet in the bathroom. David peed like a racehorse. She would have known if he'd come back to bed. The mattress was like a noisy old trampoline, especially under his weight. She glanced towards the bathroom. He was lying right beside her, but there was something wrong. She felt a stab of fright in her chest. She reached out her hand and put it on his chest. He was cold and unyielding.

'David!' She shook his shoulders and whirled round to turn on the bedside light. She fumbled for the switch. In her haste, her wrist became tangled with the cord and just as she switched it on and turned back to look at him in the light, she dragged the lamp over the edge of the bedside table. It crashed to the floor. As it bounced, it cast terrible shadows over his face. For a moment it looked animated, but as the light came to rest, the illusion was over.

'David!' she called, terrified, shaking his shoulders again. CPR. That's what she had to do. He seemed long dead. She couldn't comprehend it. He'd been touching her up in the bathroom not five minutes ago, or so it seemed. He had no pulse. She checked that his airways were clear. She jerked his head back and held his lips together with her fingers, then sealed his mouth with hers and blew hard into him twice. She watched his chest cavity rise. It fell lifeless just as quickly after each breath. Then she knelt by his side and interlaced her fingers and pushed down hard on his sternum with the heel of her hand. The mattress groaned with each compression. It did not give enough resistance. Twenty or thirty compressions? She couldn't remember. She split the difference and did twenty-five. Again she made a seal over his mouth with her own and blew all her breath into him twice before pushing down on his sternum again another twenty-five times. She couldn't remember where she'd left her mobile. She had no idea where David's phone was. There was a landline on his side of the bed but she couldn't reach it. Once she'd done another round of chest compressions, she leapt up. Naked, she straddled David to get to it, ignoring the cold.

She couldn't simply dial 999. The house had a complicated telephone system, installed so they could use two or more lines simultaneously. They'd had grandiose ideas about working together from the house, which had never come off. It was important not to rush it, or she'd have to start all over again. Despite her shaking hands, she pressed the green talk button first, and waited to hear a click. Then she pushed 9 and had to wait for a dialling tone. Then she could dial 999. Her heart hammered in her chest with frustration at the time it took to get a connection. His brain and organs were dying with every second. She pumped more air into his chest while she waited for a response.

'999, police, fire or ambulance?'

'Ambulance!'

'What's the nature of your emergency?'

'It's my husband. He's— hang on!' said Bea and slammed the receiver onto the pillow. She needed both hands to make a seal around his mouth. She blew into his mouth hard twice, then clamped the receiver between her ear and shoulder while she pushed down on his sternum, the mattress creaking with each compression.

'Don't hang up. I'm giving him CPR. Wait!'

She switched on the bedside light on David's side and pressed the speaker button.

'I won't hang up, love. What's the problem?'

'He's not breathing,' she sobbed. 'I woke up in the middle of the night to find he wasn't breathing.' She didn't want to say 'dead'. 'He was fine a little earlier— HANG ON!' and she repeated the routine. It was exhausting. Two strong sharp breaths followed by the chest compressions. Her arms ached and her jaw felt tense, after only three or four rounds. Her back was already sore from bending over in the cold.

'Is it two breaths then twenty compressions? Or is it

thirty?'

'Two breaths and thirty. If you've been doing twenty, don't worry. It's enough to get the carbon dioxide out of his lungs. What's your location?'

She gave the postcode while compressing David's chest. She heard him rapidly tapping. She made a colossal effort to pull herself together.

'Is it The Cedars?'

'Yes! But it's…' in the middle of nowhere, she thought in despair, as she paused to blow and pump. '…it's really difficult to find. Hold on!' and she started the cycle again. She'd given the directions so many times to friends who were visiting for the weekend or coming for Sunday lunch. With all the time in the world it was difficult to explain, and people were forever getting lost. She finished another round of CPR, then gave the directions, closely following the script that she had honed over the years. 'The turning to the house is— Wait!' She'd lost count. She gave a few more compressions, then two breaths. 'The turning's on the left a mile out of town. It's signposted "Woodlands". Then the house is a mile and a half down the track on the left. It has a wooden gate with "The Cedars" etched onto it'. Speaking was dragging her away from keeping her husband alive.

'What's your phone number, love?' he asked.

'HANG ON!' she cried, and repeated the CPR cycle. The feeling of dread within her strengthened. Rob had asked her to do a St John's Ambulance course last year, as they needed a designated first aider in the office, and typically no one else had volunteered. The face of the course leader came back to her. The heavy pouches under his eyes had reminded her of a St Bernard dog. She remembered what he'd said. 'You can continue with CPR until an ambulance arrives, but you need a defibrillator to bring someone back to life. Giving CPR just keeps their brain and their organs alive but it won't bring them round by itself.'

'Are you still there?' she asked the operator. 'You asked me something.'

'Yes, love. I need your phone number.'

She recited the number to him and he repeated it back to her.

'What's your name?' he asked.

'Bea Grahame.'

'Mine's Ken. Is he responding?'

'No,' she said, her voice cracking. She edged herself off the side of the bed and stood over David, so she could straighten up while she pumped his chest. The ferocious cold was beginning to get to her. She thought again of the light emitted by the body through infra-red. David would be merging with the dark. She wanted to weep. There was a blanket draped over the foot of the bed. She stopped the round of CPR to reach for it and wrapped it round herself like a cloak, then continued blowing and pumping. The conviction that what she was doing was completely useless grew within her like a nasty weed, but she didn't dare stop.

'Will the ambulance be able to get here? The driveway is really steep and the snow is so heavy.'

'They'll get to you, love. They're used to out-of-the-way places. Is there anyone else in the house with you?'

'No,' she sobbed, holding his lips between her fingers as she'd been taught.

'I'll stay on the phone with you till the ambulance arrives.'

'Thank you,' said Bea. 'It's not working!'

'You're doing brilliantly, love. Keep trying. Just till the ambulance gets there. It seems bleak now, but you'd be amazed at what a defibrillator can do.'

The image of her first aid course leader's face came back to her. 'Most people think that a defibrillator starts someone's heart again with a jolt of electricity. What it does is it *stops* the heart. It's a bit like when you're having trouble with a computer. You switch it off and then turn it back on again, and it often works just fine again, no bother. It's the same with a defib. It stops the heart, which shuts down the irregular heart rhythms, then you can restart it, and it often starts again, no bother. Not always, mind you. Sometimes you can do everything right, but it still won't work. At least you can be sure you did what you could.'

She continued with the CPR for over an hour, to the soundtrack of the creaky old mattress. She was spurred on by her own desperation, and by Ken, cheerleading as best he could.

'I think I see car lights!' she cried to Ken. 'I hope to God it's the ambulance. How am I going to let them in?' she asked desperately. 'The door's locked. It'll mean leaving him.'

'You really don't have a choice, love,' said Ken. 'Just be as quick as you can.'

'Can't you radio them? Tell them to break in?'

'That'll take longer, believe me. Better for you to just run and open the front door. You'll be quick as a flash, I'm sure.

'Don't hang up, please. I'm going now.'

The sprint across the corridor and down the stairs to the front door took no more than a dozen seconds, fifteen tops. She unlatched the door and peered outside. Gusts of freezing air blew in. She shrivelled in her thin blanket. She took in the empty driveway in disbelief. She'd been so certain she'd seen lights. Hope had made her hallucinate. Maybe they hadn't seen the gate and had turned round. She screamed in frustration. The switches for the outside light, the hallway and the stairway were all on the same pad by the front door. She flipped them all on, and left the door propped open, and flew back to the bedroom. It was difficult to give David his next two breaths as she was crying so hard.

'Bea, love. Take a deep breath,' said Ken. She couldn't answer. Her crying made the strength of the compressions erratic, so she forced herself to concentrate, to slow her sobbing breath.

The paramedics finally stormed into the house, flooding it with light and noise. They rushed upstairs to the bedroom. Bea stepped aside to allow one of them to approach David. Stiff and cold, she straightened with difficulty. The medic made a rapid assessment, checking pulse and airways.

'Defib,' he said, and his colleague stepped forward and attached the pads to David's chest. Bea gasped, not expecting it to jolt him so violently. He jerked like a zombie from a bad B-movie before falling back on the bed, limp as a ragdoll. The medic waited a moment. Bea held her breath for the second jolt, her hands over her mouth, praying and willing David with all her remaining strength to blink, or cough, or sit up and say 'What the eff's going on here?' or laugh and say 'Darling, you should have told me we were expecting company.' When the jolt came, his body spasmed again before falling back against the pillow, forcing another groan out of the mattress. His eyes were closed and his mouth slightly open. His skin was grey.

'I'm sorry,' said the paramedic to Bea, his mouth set in a grim line. 'He's gone. You did everything you could.'

'What happens now?' she asked, her voice hollow. Desolation swept over her.

'We'll take him to the hospital morgue. You should come with us too. You shouldn't be alone.'

'You should be treated for shock,' said his colleague, who stepped forward to put his hand on her shoulder. Just before he touched her he changed his mind, probably when he realised she was naked underneath the thin blanket. Naked and shivering. He scurried to the chaise longue by the window to get David's big blue dressing gown, then scuttled back and flung it round her shoulders like a cloak.

'Could you leave me with him?' asked Bea.

'I wouldn't want to leave you alone here...'

'I just want to be alone with him for a moment.'

The two men looked at each other. One nodded. They gathered their equipment and left the room. Bea gazed at David. She lurched forward and threw her arms round his neck. She began to sob. She clung to the cold, dead thing that used to be her husband until the paramedics gently prised her fingers away.

# CHAPTER THREE

In his last year of junior school, Paddy was sent home early with a letter from the headmaster, Mr Penharris. It wasn't the first time I'd been summonsed to talk about 'Patrick'.

'What have you done this time, Paddy?' I asked, my stomach filled with lead. The last thing I wanted was to see Penharris. Paddy lifted his angel face.

'It was an accident, Mam. I never meant it. It was a dare.'

'A dare to do what, exactly?' I ripped the envelope open, scanning his face.

*Dear Mr & Mrs Newell*

*Patrick is responsible for serious burns to one of his classmates, who has been hospitalised.*

*I would be grateful if you would see me at the earliest opportunity. Until we have agreed appropriate action, please keep him from school until further notice.*

*Yours sincerely,*

*Arthur Penharris*

Paddy had almost been expelled two years before. He'd pinned one of the little boys down and punched him a few times in the face. It was true the poor kid had a shiner on him and a few bruises, but he'd said Paddy had cheated at marbles. Honour was a big thing among the kids.

'Kids get into scrapes all the time,' I'd said to Penharris at the time.

'Mrs Newell, his behaviour is really not normal for a boy his age. He shows levels of aggression that I seldom see even in troubled teenagers. But it's not just that, it's the...' He paused.

'The what?' I demanded.

He weighed his words. 'It's the way he does it. In cold blood. He picked his moment, pouncing when the child was alone. It seems they'd argued at breaktime—'

'He called my Paddy a cheat! Paddy would never—'

'That's hardly important now, Mrs Newell. The fact is, Patrick followed him home and chose his moment carefully.'

That was nearly two years ago. I read the letter through for the second time. I looked at Paddy, trying to see into his soul.

'What happened?' I demanded. 'What did you do, Paddy?' I was grateful the others weren't there.

'They dared me to burn her ponytail off.'

'Saints alive, Paddy, you did *what*?'

'A dare's a dare.'

Hair didn't burn like that. It must have gone up like a puff of smoke to cause burns bad enough for a hospital visit. You'd have thought the girls in Paddy's class weren't old enough for hairspray and stuff like that. He couldn't have possibly known how much it would harm her. As for being egged on by the other boys – if he was a scapegoat, there'd be hell to pay.

I'd pulled a rabbit from the hat last time to keep him from being expelled. I couldn't do it again.

I would have liked to have kept it from George, sorted it myself, like I did last time, but it was the talk of the school.

'Hospital, you say? The poor lass,' he said.

'Yes, I know. I hope it's not too bad. But if Paddy has to go to another school...'

George stared at me. 'Never mind Paddy. There's a little girl in hospital. We should have got help for that boy years ago. He's—'

'Don't even say it!' I hissed.

One evening, I'd run upstairs to find out why George was giving Paddy a hiding. George never hit the kids. We'd had a God-awful row about it after they'd gone to bed. George was shaking and had called him a 'wrong'un'. I'd done my nut. 'The way he was hitting Colin...' he'd said. 'The others lash out in anger and it's forgotten in a minute. But Paddy...' He shook his head, disbelieving. 'He was enjoying it.'

I was furious with him for days.

'Let's not argue,' said George. 'We'll go and see Penharris together. The Ashworth job will have to wait.'

'No!' I said, too quickly. 'I'll go and see him myself.'

'We'll not ignore it, Edie. Not any longer. We need to tackle those demons of his.'

'How do you suppose we do *that*?'

George sighed. 'I don't know. Maybe Penharris will have some ideas. I'd like to find out who the little girl is. See if there's anything we can do for her.'

'But we need the Ashworth money.' I scrabbled for a reason to stop him from coming with me. 'You told me the manager's an awkward devil. If you don't turn up tomorrow he'll never give you the really big job. Rewiring the whole hotel is huge. It'll keep us for a year if not more. The older ones need new uniforms and we've got three birthdays coming up next month.'

George hesitated. 'I don't want you to have to cope on your own.'

'He hasn't murdered anyone. He played with matches and it went bad, that's all. We need the money. I can fight his corner alone.'

I persuaded him in the end, as per usual. The next day I asked my neighbour, Molly, to mind Paddy and the little'uns for an hour or two.

'Not at school today, Paddy?' she asked as I shepherded

the kids into her front room. Bea waddled over to her and crawled into her lap.

'He's a bit under the weather,' I lied. Paddy sniffed loudly, on cue. The news would get out eventually, but I wanted to do my bit to keep it under wraps for now.

'You look lovely,' she said to me as she cuddled Bea. 'That frock is just bee*yoo*tiful. I love a bit of silk. What are you dressing up for so early in the morning? While the cat's away...' She laughed and stage winked at me.

'It's nylon,' I snapped. 'I don't see why I shouldn't make an effort every once in a while.'

'All right, duck. Just having a bit of fun.'

I gave her a tight smile. 'Sorry, Molly. I didn't get a wink last night. Maybe I've got what Paddy's got.'

I tottered to the school and knocked on Penharris's door. He stood up as I went in. He was a very tall man, and towered over the desk as he shook my hand. His fair hair was lit up by a shaft of sunlight, giving the room its only bit of colour except for the pictures of his daughter and departed wife on a shelf behind his desk.

'Come in, Mrs Newell. Please sit down.' He was awkward, all limbs, like a big blond spider. 'Thank you for coming. Would you like some tea?'

'No thank you very much,' I said, sitting ramrod straight in my chair. I waited for him to speak.

'I'm sorry your husband couldn't make it.' I'll bet you are, I thought. 'I was hoping to speak to you both. You know Patrick's been in trouble several times since the incident with the Wilkes boy. I've had experience of hundreds of children over the years, and my own daughter's behaviour was very troubling after my wife died, but this...'

'How is she?'

'She's very well, thank you for asking.' He fell silent.

'She's in my Sammy's class. He says she's a bright one.'

'She wants to become a teacher.'

'That's nice,' I said. 'She's only ten, though. Maybe she'll change her mind.' In those days I believed teaching was a cop-out for those who couldn't think of anything better to do.

'Perhaps. Mrs Newell, we must talk about Patrick's—'

'All kids play with matches,' I said. 'I'll own what he did was wrong. And I feel terrible for the little girl. But he surely couldn't imagine how bad it would be.'

'The girl has third-degree burns on her head and neck, and she burned her hands trying to put out the flames.'

'I can't work it out. I can't think how her hair could burn so quickly.'

'He poured lighter fuel on it first.'

'Jesus!' I said, my hands flying to my mouth.

'He stole it from the janitor's cupboard. There's no easy way to say this, Mrs Newell, but, as I told you before, Patrick requires help. Special help that this school is not equipped to provide.'

'There's nothing wrong with him! He's a born scapegoat, that boy. You should support him, not gun against him. That's what everyone does. Even his own brothers.' If it wasn't so shaming, I'd have told him about Paddy's start in life. Instead, I said, 'Try to walk around in Paddy's shoes. All his brothers are so clever. They make friends at the drop of a hat. His little sister wraps everyone round her little finger. Paddy's more sensitive, and quieter, and doesn't have many friends.' In fact, he had none.

'Oh Patrick's clever all right. He channels his intelligence in a different way. He has a tendency to sniff out weakness and exploit it. He picks on those children with exactly the attributes you ascribe to him. The ones that are quiet, and sensitive with not many friends. It's my job to protect those children.'

'There's already a wall between him and his brothers. His sister too, and she's only a year old. Sending him to a different school will make things worse.'

He looked at me properly for the first time. His pity was infuriating.

'So what do we do? Same as last time?' I said.

He looked down, then redirected those blue eyes at me. 'What happened the last time you came to see me is something I truly regret. It was unforgivable. I only ask that you try to forgive me all the same.'

'I could have got you the sack.'

'Yes. You could.'

I felt another pang. I'm not a liar, to myself or to anyone. I had taken advantage of his loneliness, to do what I could for my poor Paddy. On the desk that separated us right then. Beneath the photos of his daughter and his dead wife. He'd clung to me like a man drowning, and had cried afterwards. If just a whiff of it got out it wouldn't matter who was right or wrong. If George found out that would be the end of us. Penharris was too much of a gentleman to call stalemate.

'Please, Mr Penharris. Paddy's got to live with the other kids. You chucking him out will make his life a misery.' It was the closest I'd come to begging in my whole life.

'I think you'll be surprised,' he said gently. 'I don't think it will affect him as much as you may think. He doesn't seem to care whether he has friends or not, and isn't remotely concerned about the good opinion of anyone, unlike the rest of us.'

'You're making him out to be some kind of monster!'

He sighed heavily. 'It's not that, Mrs Newell. He needs extra help to fit in. To learn the tricks of rubbing along with others, which come more naturally to other children. I suggest you take him to a child psychologist, someone who can help him regulate his behaviour. Who can help him deal with his anger and fit in better with other people.'

I couldn't speak. I stared at my hands, then looked up at

Penharris.

'He'll be branded if he goes. Only weirdies need psychologists.'

'That's not true. Psychologists can help with a great number of human woes. Grief, for instance, and trauma. You're right that there is often an unfair stigma attached to psychological treatment, which is why the sessions are held in the strictest of confidence.'

'I don't know any child psychologists.'

'I can recommend someone who helped my daughter enormously after my wife died.' He wrote down a name and address on a piece of paper.

'If I send Paddy to this person, will you keep him in your school?'

He sighed. 'It's not that simple. It's not only Patrick's welfare I need to think about, but Gemma Purves's, not to mention the half dozen other children he targets on a regular basis.'

'So where is he supposed to go?' I asked.

'Harefield Hou—'

'It's a borstal!'

'It's not a borstal. Far from it. It's a school for children with behavioural difficulties. They can cope with Patrick. We can't.'

'Over my dead body!' I said. Tears threatened.

'I'm sorry, Mrs Newell, but you don't have a choice. I must consider the welfare of all, and it will be better for everyone, Patrick included—'

'How is it better for him? He'll be labelled. As a wrong'un. At his age!'

'If his violence is checked early enough, he may be prevented from actually killing someone,' he snapped.

I stared at him.

'I'm sorry, Mrs Newell.'

Another 'Sorry Mrs Newell', and I'd have been ready to lamp him.

Then he really stuck the knife in.

'I understand this is a delicate matter, but there is also reason to suppose that Patrick may need psychological help for issues other than violence.'

'What do you mean?'

'You and your husband adopted him at the age of four, I believe.'

'He's my son,' I said with heat. '*Our* son, I mean,' I added quickly.

'Please don't misunderstand me. I'm not sitting in judgement as to—'

'So why does it feel like you are?'

'I'm just trying to gently point out that the first four years of a child's life are enormously influential, and as he spent them in foster homes and in care—'

'They have the ruddy nerve to call that care!'

He was silent. I was flustered. Panicked. I barely trusted myself to speak. When I did, it was through gritted teeth.

'We've done all we can to make sure Paddy forgets those four years. We don't speak of it in our house. Our youngest two don't know a time when he wasn't around. The others are young enough to forget.'

'You may find that you're storing up a great deal of trouble for the future.'

'That's not your concern.'

'I'm sorry you see it that way.'

'I see it just as it is. You wash your hands of him and we're left to pick up the pieces. Then there's the money. Have you thought about how tight that is in our house? We can't spare a penny for a boy at Harefield.'

'I will write to the local authority and make a case for financial assistance. There's a budget available for cases such as

Patrick's. There will be a means testing assessment, following which they will determine whatever contribution you as a family will have to make, if any at all.'

'So we'll have complete strangers nosing into our business?'

'I know the Education Officer. He's a very reasonable man and my letter will, I'm sure, lead him to look on your case favourably.'

'So you've got it all sewn up, then. There's nothing more to say, is there?' I stood up. I swayed a bit. My legs were bloodless and I was wearing those ruddy shoes. 'A child at Harefield House. We could just put a sign up outside our front room, that we breed weirdies.'

'I can understand it's a sore trial. People can be quick to judge. It won't be easy for you as a family. But the people at Harefield do sterling work, and Patrick may be taught how to build bridges with other people, which will help him enormously in life. He's not learning that here.'

Nor at home neither, I thought.

I went the back way home so I could cry in peace away from nosy parkers. I fetched the kids from Molly only when my eyes could no longer give me away. I couldn't abide people feeling sorry for me. The next term, Paddy went to Harefield House. Penharris had been right. He made the switch without turning a hair.

***

Lorena wore a pair of thigh-high shimmering stiletto-heeled boots, her legs astride a man lying handcuffed on the floor. Her eyes glittered with malice. Despite the handcuffs, he was trying to touch her. He rubbed the backs of his hands against the soft insides of her thighs. He was gagged with a scarf, but moaned audibly above the background music.

She wore nothing else except for an emerald green silk G-string, a tiny triangle as thin as a cobweb, held in place by two diamante circles, which twinkled at her hips in the half-light. The little garment was not required for coverage. Her pubis was bare as a babe's, except for a thin vertical strip of hair. Her body saved its richness and luxuriance for the glossy mane on her head, as no hair sprouted anywhere else. She'd spent thousands on lasers and electrolysis. She'd never have to shave for the rest of her life. She'd also spent a fortune on skin peels, to eradicate old scars on her face.

His moaning got louder.

'Shut up!' She kicked him in the side. He yelped and cowered, then straightened himself, as if expecting more. 'As if I give a SHIT what you have to say.' Her vowels were flattened. *As eef I geeve a sheet.* She spread her legs wider on either side of him, then slowly lowered herself so that she stood with her legs open to the maximum point, hands on her knees, and hovered for an impossible time above him. He groaned. Beads of sweat formed on his forehead. She began to fondle her breasts.

'You like this?' she whispered, throwing her head back. He nodded like a wagging dog. She lowered her hand to his groin and softly felt the tip of his hard-on. 'You like this?' she demanded. He panted and groaned. She bent to grab his chin, and shook it. 'Shut your mouth! I told you already.' Abruptly she straightened her legs and strode towards the stereo to turn up the volume. She sashayed back towards him, demonic in the half-light.

Bowie was crooning about green eyes.

'Now what was I doing?' she demanded, and fondled her breasts again. His eyes bulged from their sockets. 'You like my tits?' *You like my teets?* He nodded vigorously, and lifted his arms upwards in an attempt to touch them. She began to lick her lips in a vulgar parody of sexiness, and swayed from side to side, keeping her breasts just out of reach. 'Ooooh baby,' she pouted, her reddened lips pushed out in a Jaggeresque pout, and turned round and waggled her backside above him. The back of his hand brushed against her left buttock. She twisted round. 'Don't touch me, you little shit!' *You leetle sheet.* 'I touch you, understand?'

The music was building in tension. Her mobile rang. She usually had it switched off when working, but she was expecting a call. She pointed a finger at her victim. 'Don't move,' she commanded, unnecessarily.

'*Si, caro*,' she said, cupping her hand to her ear to block out the music.

'What are you doing?' Paddy demanded.

'You mean who am I doing?'

'Get rid of him. I want to see you.'

'You will have to wait. Come in an hour.'

'Fucksake, Lorena, I told you already—'

'All things come to he who can wait.' She hung up.

She resumed her position. The fruit of her labour had suffered a setback for the interruption, so she spat into her hand and smoothed the wetness over the tip of his penis. He gasped. She resumed fondling her breasts with her free hand. He was soon as hard as before and back in his puppy dog state. With that fine judgement born of long experience, she saw a handjob was not going to do, as it usually would.

'You are difficult today, no?' she sneered. He nodded eagerly. She tightened her grip on his penis. He squeezed his eyes shut, and convulsed with anticipation. Without breaking her rhythm, she reached for a small box by the side of the sofa and fished for a condom. She broke open the plastic with her teeth and rolled it roughly over his penis. She unhooked one of the diamante circles holding her G-string in place. She had designed and sewn it herself. At least the nuns had taught her one thing that was useful. It allowed her to remove it elegantly without having to alter her position. The small piece of green silk hung limp from her thigh. She lowered herself onto him. She could get herself in the mood if she wanted, but despite what she'd said to Paddy, she was now in a hurry. She released his bindings. 'Feel my tits,' she demanded. It would be over much sooner this way. He tore off the gag and reached for them, just as Bowie's voice reached a crescendo.

'God, Lorena!' he gasped, as he thrust into her. It was over inside of a minute.

She paused a moment, rocking back and forth, then raised herself and reattached the little green triangle. She sauntered to the fireplace and lit a cigarette. She turned the volume of the stereo down. Bowie had done his work again.

'You want one?' she asked. The man gasped like a landed fish. His penis wilted fast within the sodden plastic.

'You know I quit,' he whined. 'It's times like these I regret it.'

She stood naked except for the thong and the boots, the firelight playing with the colour of her hair. Her magnificent breasts were goosefleshed, and her olive skin gleamed, flushed with the glow of early pregnancy. Her stomach was rounded, not yet protruding. She tossed her head back and inhaled.

He gazed at her. 'Lorena, if I were a painter I'd be having an orgasm right now.'

'Another one? Such greed. I have to kick you out now.' *Keek you out.*

'Another appointment?' He laughed. 'No rest for the wicked.'

'Not an appointment. My boyfriend.' She smiled. She liked describing him that way, even though it was a broad use of the term.

'Your boyfriend!' He laughed. 'He's an understanding guy.' Groaning as if in pain, he hoisted himself to his feet, wet condom in hand, and made his way to the bathroom. She heard him clear his throat and run the tap.

'Run the bath for me, *caro*,' she called out. She heard the plug clink against the enamel, water running, then the roar of the boiler firing up.

He was suited and booted within a few minutes. He opened his briefcase and handed her an envelope.

'Richly deserved, as always.' He smiled, and pecked her on the cheek. 'Can you do next week? Tuesday?'

'Sure, why not?'

'I mean an all-nighter. My wife's away with the kids.'

'That will cost you, baby.'

He smiled and raised an eyebrow.

'I almost forgot,' he said. 'Are you done with the blouse?'

'Ah yes,' said Lorena. 'It's hanging in the hallway.'

It was aquamarine silk, exquisitely stitched. It was wrapped in a plastic dry-cleaning bag.

'That is a knockout, baby. She's gonna love it.' He examined it more closely. 'It's got a little label,' he said. '*Lorena C.*' He laughed. 'That is so cute. Let's hope she ain't too curious where I got it from. What do I owe you?'

'Nothing, *caro*. It's my pleasure.'

'You're the best.' He pecked her again. She shut the door on him and counted the contents of the envelope. Five hundred pounds in new twenties. She slipped the cash into her needlework basket. He paid double what the others did. He often brought her gifts. Most brought presents, but his were a cut above the rest. Quality jewellery, pots of Crème de la Mer, theatre tickets, cashmere, silk underwear; once an antique cuckoo clock, of all things, just because he'd been to Zurich and thought she'd like it better than chocolate. Her pregnancy, when it showed, was bound to put him off. Not for the first time, she felt a bitter resentment wash over her. It had better be worth it.

In the bathroom, she unzipped the boots and climbed

into the scalding water, putting her cigarettes and lighter within reach. She lay back, lit another cigarette, wiggled her aching toes and waited for Patrick. *Padreek*. She never called him Paddy.

She was in a green Chinese silk dressing gown when he arrived. Her hair was still wet. It was freezing outside and his skin was cold to the touch, but within seconds he'd shed his coat, scarf and jacket.

'It's festeringly hot in here.'

'I like it. It reminds me of home.'

'Were you working when I just called?'

'Yes,' said Lorena, lighting a cigarette and sitting down. 'So what?'

Paddy looked at her. 'Because it's not good for the baby. You'll not get another chance, you know.' He sounded exasperated.

'Why not?' she said. 'There are four more eggs in the clinic.'

'It's not like a trip to sodding Sainsbury's, Lola. Do you think it's that easy? That it works every time?'

'It did for us,' she said, shrugging.

'People go through round after round and still don't get pregnant,' he said.

'But I did, first time. So why worry?'

'David's dead.'

She stared at him. 'That was quick.'

'He died of a heart attack.'

'You kid me!'

'I kid you not. It seems God has decided to be our accomplice.'

She shuddered, a relic of her Catholic past. She took a deep drag of her cigarette.

'So there won't be other chances. Put that fag out, Lorena.'

Lorena lowered her face and glared at him from beneath her beautifully arched brows. 'I am not a fucking laboratory. Understand? If I want to work, I work. If I want to smoke, I smoke. You don't like it, you find someone else to carry this thing.' Suddenly she laughed. 'You sound like you are the father.' Her accent with him was more muted, her English better. She hammed up her accent for her clients.

'In a manner of speaking, I am,' he said. 'It wouldn't have come into being without me.'

She took a puff of her cigarette, then stubbed it out in a bronze ashtray beside her. 'I suppose that's true.'

She padded over to him. She raised her arms to lift her damp curls and allowed the dressing gown to fall open. She wound her arms round his neck and wrapped her leg round his. 'Not staying, *caro*?'

'I can't,' he said, circling her waist and kissing her. 'I'm having dinner with Diana.'

'Again?' She smirked, and led him to the sofa.

He looked at his watch. 'I really have to go.'

'Fuck Diana,' said Lorena.

'I probably will later.'

'She can wait her turn.'

*** 

Paddy pulled up outside Diana's an hour later. Whatever mysterious quality he possessed, it had worked on dozens of women, starting with his mother. All his life, women had done what he had wanted them to, including Carol, his youngest brother's wife.

Then along came Lorena. It had been a low point in his life. He'd crashed his car and broken an arm and a leg. Ironic, really. That's precisely what it had cost him financially, especially as the kid's family had sued. Broke, with zilch mobility. It was not a good place to be. He'd gone to stay with Bea and David, not having much choice. He'd had to put up his Thameside penthouse as security for bail while he waited for the trial to come up, and was forced to tap David for the rest. The penthouse was on the top floor with no lift, and he couldn't find a carer willing to climb stairs. Fucking Daleks. Of course, his mother had offered to move in. Six weeks of living with Edie. He'd rather be buried alive. He'd chosen the lesser of two evils, and gone to stay with his sister.

Bea and David had gone out to work each day, leaving him to his own devices. He had to work from his bed. He couldn't afford not to. The boy's family was claiming compensation and the lawyers were eating money. It had been hard to focus. To concentrate. There was the pain, but also the itch for the powder. He'd made a decision to stay away from it. He could have bought the penthouse outright with what had gone up his nose. More than that, it had affected his focus, melted his steel core. The accident had almost ruined his life. No one would believe it, but he'd also felt bad for what he'd done to the kid.

A physiotherapist came to the house every day. He was told he'd never get full range of movement back in his leg, but the physio hadn't reckoned on his determination. Apart from the physio, the only company he had during the week was Rafaela, the cleaning lady. Brazilian, thirtyish. Not bad-looking. She wasn't his type really, but flirting with her had been something to do. She had not responded well. She complained to Bea that he'd goosed her. He probably had, he barely remembered, and he'd laughed when Bea told him off. 'Rafaela's a Catholic. You really offended her. We can't afford to lose her, Paddy.' He'd laughed and promised to apologise. Rafaela remained wary, which amused him.

Rafaela did two half days for Bea and David, and also worked for five other households, either full or half days. She made extra money babysitting, for which she was always available provided it didn't clash with her evening classes. She was trying to improve her English and was also studying maths. She needed both subjects to qualify as a mature student for a degree course. She wanted to become a teacher. On average, she made six hundred pounds for a full week of back-breaking work. She sent home a hundred of it, and felt guilty it wasn't more. At his prompting, she explained she was saving towards a deposit on a flat, and she needed money for course fees and books. She wanted to buy something small in East Finchley, or similar. Somewhere not too expensive in Zone 4, which would appreciate in value over time. It was crazy paying rent when you could own your own place, she said. Paddy was both admiring and contemptuous of how hard she worked for such a small, far-off reward.

'So just out of interest,' he'd said to her. 'Do you ever nick stuff? From the houses you clean? I won't tell, honest,' he'd added and winked at her.

She'd bridled, which amused him.

'In the eyes of God, stealing a hairclip is the same as stealing a diamond,' she'd said, eyes flashing fire.

'Are you a virgin, Rafaela?' he'd asked her softly, as he stroked his groin.

She'd picked up her mop and bucket and left the room with a furious blush. When she returned to tell him she'd finished for the day, he said, 'Come on Raffie. Tell you what. I'll pay the deposit on your flat if you blow me. Seriously. I will.'

The next time she was due to work, Lorena turned up instead.

The first time he saw her, she'd looked him over as he lay on the bed. He felt at a disadvantage, a feeling he was not used to. 'My seester is seek of you. I will not put up with your sheet. I work here until you leave.'

Paddy was transfixed.

Both sisters had magnificent bone structure and good bearing. Nature had worked from the same raw material, but a lucky throw of the genetic dice had given Lorena her perfect olive skin, despite two very faint but long, thin scars on her face, one across her forehead and one across her left cheek. Rafaela's face was pockmarked, marks she tried to hide beneath layers of ill-matched foundation. Lorena was a good four inches taller than her sister. They had the same colouring, but Lorena's curls were strong and lustrous, where Rafaela's hair was straight and lank, despite the money she spent on products to give it a little volume. Both lacked formal education, and were equally determined to get ahead. Paddy was amused by the difference in the routes they had chosen.

Paddy had smiled at the glowering goddess at the foot of his bed. 'I won't give you any sheet.'

She did not give a flying fuck about anything. Paddy loved her flint heart. For a cleaner, her clothes were too good. Her manicure too perfect. She had the kind of grooming that only money could buy. Her mobile was always ringing or bleeping. She had a different ringtone for each caller. Unlike her sister, Lorena made the very most of her natural attributes, aesthetically and financially.

He began to long for Lorena days. She never knocked on his door as Rafaela had. She swept in and began to pick his clothes off the floor.

'Only pigs live in their own shit,' she said. In fact, Paddy was obsessively neat, but he liked seeing her bend down.

Her English was much better than her sister's.

'I am more sociable than Rafa,' she said.

'I'll bet you are.'

He couldn't shock her. She'd laughed when he asked if her cunt was also Brazilian.

'Is your prick also useless and broken?'

She barged in one sweltering afternoon. Paddy was

irritable from heat and waiting. She was supposed to work mornings.

'Where the hell have you been?'

Her hair was caught up in a clip from which tendrils fell across her cheek and neck. Her olive skin glowed with the summer heat. She was barefoot. Her toenails were perfectly painted a dark purple. She moved his crutches from the side of the bed to the far wall.

'What are you doing?'

He lay imprisoned on the bed, sweating.

'I work when I want,' she hissed. Her mobile trilled. It was secured to her chest by her bra strap. She dug it out and was just about to take the call.

'Don't answer it,' he said. 'Come here.'

If she was surprised, she did not show it. She glanced at the screen and sent the call to voicemail. She stood at the foot of the bed, knowing he couldn't move. He shifted himself upright and stroked his hard-on. Her face was inscrutable. Some moments passed before she stepped forward, long brown legs gleaming in a patch of sun. She peeled off her top and her skirt, eyes glittering. She unclasped her bra and shimmied out of her knickers, swaying her hips.

'It *is* Brazilian,' he whispered.

She climbed onto the bed, kneeling above him with her legs spread to either side.

'This is going to cost you a lot of money,' she whispered. She took his hand and turned it palm upwards and guided it towards her. She pushed his middle finger inside her. Her wet muscles clamped around it. She leaned forwards to dangle a dark nipple above his mouth. He lifted his head to lick it. She reached across the bed to grab a pillow to prop up his head, then arched her back while he licked one nipple and squeezed the other, his fingers slipping in and out of her. Only when sodden and panting did she finally fuck him.

Lorena did not get much cleaning done that day.

She had no scruples about anything. She was not ashamed of being a whore or behaving like one. When she felt like it, she told him tales about her clients, which he relished. When he was able to tackle stairs, they had sex in more inventive places. They regularly raided David's cellar and sat outside in the garden sipping wine while Lorena bared her breasts to the sun. The heat and the wine made her extraordinarily horny. The garden was not wholly private, but she didn't care a straw for the neighbours.

He was wound up to breaking point on the days that Lorena did not come to the house. She turned up when she felt like it.

It enraged him. Grumbling, he started to do bits of cleaning and nagged her to do a better job. He was afraid she'd get fired.

'What do I care?'

'Why are you doing this?' he'd asked her, meaning the job.

'My sister. She begged me. Until you leave.'

'And you agreed out of the goodness of your heart?'

'She is my sister.'

'That can't be the only reason.'

'She told me about you. She said you were like the devil. An angel on the outside and rotten within. I wanted to see for myself.'

'See me, do me, milk me,' he said, as he handed over a wad of notes. 'You're cheaper than coke, I suppose.'

According to Lorena, Rafaela was not a virgin. She begged forgiveness from the Holy Mother each day in her prayers, as well as on her knees on a Sunday in the Catholic Church of East Finchley. Her best friend's older brother had raped her when she was fifteen. She blamed herself. It was the last time in her life she hadn't been fully in control. She and her friend had smuggled a bottle of cane spirit into a party. Her friend's brother picked them up, and on the way home, her friend had puked out of the car window and passed out. According to Lorena, Big Brother took a detour, to the site of a derelict factory. Little sister was out for the count, and did not hear the teenage Rafaela crying for help, pinned to the back seat of the car.

'That's terrible,' said Paddy.

Lorena shrugged. 'That's life.'

'So how come you're not a good Catholic girl?'

'My mother and my sisters pray to God for my soul. He must be bored with all that begging.'

'I'd like to hear you beg,' he hissed, lunging for her breasts.

They christened each room, David's study included. They combed through his papers. It was like a game. They found Bea and David's joint will. The survivor would get the lot. On the death of the remaining spouse, the estate would be divided equally between any surviving children. David's three children were named, and the wording included any subsequent children born to either of them. As well as the will, they found details of investments, the extent of the wealth and the property, down to every last penny, painting, ornament and stick of furniture. A blue file labelled 'Farrers' contained the details of 'Grahame vs Grahame', including Diana's settlement and maintenance details.

'Half a million tax-free for each year of marriage. Makes you look cheap as chips!' he laughed.

Humour was not Lorena's strong suit.

'Plus three times the CSA maximum in maintenance for each child while they remain minors.' He whistled.

Then there was the children's trust.

If he could get his hands on some of the great pile of cash that David and Bea sat on, his life would be transformed.

Lorena was similarly affected. Sex was not the only appetite they shared.

Bea's bedside drawer contained a host of items. A battered old book of poems by William Blake, odd bits of jewellery, including a pair of antique diamond earrings, pens, a notepad. None of these things were of interest to Paddy. What was of interest was a diary of her menstrual cycle, syringes, swabs, folic acid tablets. A file provided by Damien Lillie's clinic, with records of previous treatment, appointment notes and instructions. An invoice for embryo storage. According to the notes, she'd tried everything from progesterone injections to Clomid and now, IVF. The drawer was a little potted history of her failure to conceive.

Despite the shadow of the trial, Paddy passed the best summer of his life. He couldn't pinpoint the moment the idea had come to him. All of the disparate strands of information he had learned about his sister and her husband swirled around in his head until they crystallised into a scheme. At first it seemed ludicrously elaborate. Broken down into its component pieces, though, it became feasible, especially after seeing the invoice.

He persuaded Lorena to continue working for the Grahame household, even after he was able to return to his own apartment.

His time in jail had put the brakes on. He'd been sentenced to two years. The boy's family were outraged. He'd been released early thanks to overcrowding. There were people who needed locking up more than him, apparently. Rapists, thieves, muggers, terrorists. Killers. Paddy smiled at himself in the driver's mirror and ran his fingers through his hair before walking down the path that led to Diana's front door.

# CHAPTER FOUR – BRAZIL, 1990s

Odolina Carvalho had been forced to leave school at a young age to help support her mother and the younger children after her father died. For her, it was liberation. She hated the nuns with their ready canes and pinched lips, preaching about sin and hellfire. She'd managed to find herself a job in a hotel on the outskirts of Rio as a chambermaid, a position normally reserved for a member of the manager's very large family. 'I guess he liked me,' Odolina said to her delighted family. She lost the job as quickly as she'd got it, accused of stealing a diamond bracelet from a guest. No one was able to prove anything. The last blow job she gave to the manager ensured he did not report the incident to the police. She shrugged off this early hiccup in her career and got a job in the Pasadena, one of the two bars in her home town. The owner, Luis, already had two waitresses, but the place was busy so he welcomed a third. He reckoned Odolina's appeal would be good for business. She had to move back home. That was okay. Her mother had long lost control of her.

Odolina had a conviction that she would not have to try hard to find her destiny. She was certain it would come looking for her. One evening, a group of men visited the bar. As always, she flirted with them, reasoning correctly that that was why she had been given the job. One of them was a photographer, new to the area, who took a liking to her. He took pictures of her as she served the drinks. At first she smiled prettily, but by the end of the evening she was pouting and smouldering, to the baying approval of the crowd.

The photographer, Antonio, came back to the bar the following morning and showed her the pictures. She shrugged. It had been a fun evening, but she had a hangover and work to do. She had always looked good in photos. He offered her the chance to pose for him in a bikini. Her mother had lectured her and her sisters endlessly about men, how ready they were to take advantage, how good girls from good families could be drafted into prostitution and pornography blah blah blah... These warnings bored her rigid, but it seemed they had percolated her consciousness after all. She refused.

He could get her modelling work, he said. He had a client based in Rio who manufactured swimwear, and they were always looking for girls with that certain something. Being pretty was not enough. The world was stuffed to the gills with pretty girls. The camera had to love you. 'Look at these. The camera adores you.'

It was hard to get her excited about anything, but the idea of modelling electrified her. She'd been born to wear glittering garments and lead a life of glamour. She'd look just as good as any of those spoilt American bitches she saw in magazines, on billboards, on TV.

Still wary, she visited his studio. He had a box of bikinis in different colours and styles, all in their wrappers with bona fide tags attached. She recognised the logo. He invited her to try one on. There was no private place for her to change. He turned his back to her ostentatiously. 'How do I know you won't turn round when I'm naked?' He rolled his eyes. 'If you were a boy, you'd be in much more danger.' She laughed, shocked but exhilarated. She'd heard whispers about people like Antonio, but no one had ever been so open before. He took pictures of her in various poses.

So, aged eighteen, Odolina's modelling career began. She was featured in two shoots for the swimwear manufacturers, getting her picture pasted onto the door of a local boutique and onto a few roadside billboards. However, the client was constantly on the lookout for new faces, so her first burst of glory did not last long. She was undeterred. She became a small celebrity in her little town, thanks to Luis, who had a blown-up picture of the bikini-clad Odolina mounted in the Pasadena, earning her cheers and catcalls from the men, and dark looks and mutterings from the other waitresses, Elisabeta and Sylvana. To infuriate them further, she began to be known as 'Odolina, Odolina, the Jewel of the Pasadena.' She liked that it pissed them off. She cared nothing for their opinion. She would get bigger, better modelling jobs, and she could stick a finger up to her home town.

To her mother's horror, she did an underwear shoot, and used the proceeds to send pictures direct to various agencies and companies. It was expensive, and soon ate into her tiny pool of capital and her earnings from the bar. Antonio helped her, putting her forward for a number of other jobs. They wanted something different all the time. The application of the female form to selling products was infinite. As she waited for the perfect job, the one that required a dark smouldering sexpot with generous breasts, her body was changing. Her breasts got bigger and her hips began to fill out. Her teenage slimness was morphing into a voluptuousness that made her irresistible to men, but less suitable as a model.

The nuns had neglected to teach her the rudiments of biology, but she had an innate understanding of genetics, which manifested itself in the bitterness she felt when she looked at her mother. Overused and overweight. Her older sister, Lorena, was fast following suit. Odolina could see how she would end up if she wasn't careful. She would not go the same way as the other women in her family. She did not have to marry the first idiot who asked her, and she could certainly stop herself from becoming a broodmare. Odolina's mother had given birth to eight children. Lorena had just had her second child, and there was no reason to suppose she wouldn't continue to pup for years to come.

The thought of some little creature growing inside her

and sucking at her breasts made Odolina feel nauseous. Before the babies came, Lorena had been breathtaking. She'd even managed to escape Santa Ana. She had worked in Lisbon for two years but had come back to marry her childhood sweetheart. Odolina despised her for it. It was like freeing a plumed bird, only to have it cling to the cage.

Lorena's husband had cried when he saw his ravishing bride on their wedding day. If he had known that in a few short years she'd be wandering around in shapeless tents covered in baby puke, her once-magnificent breasts in constant employment, stretchmarked and leaking, he would have cried even harder. Still, he seemed happy enough. The idiot.

Antonio managed to get Odolina small assignments every now and then. She was often asked to model swimwear and clothing for wholesale buyers. She imagined these jobs would lead to discovery and catapult her to fame. She was quickly disillusioned. More often than not, she had to parade up and down in hideous garments, nobody looking at her, too intent on the clothes, 'the products'.

Antonio's belief in her never wavered. If it hadn't been for him, she would have given up and... what? She couldn't say. She pulsed with unfocused ambition. She began to have anxiety dreams.

She was setting out the tables in the bar when Antonio arrived in a state of high excitement. A company in Rio wanted a model for a TV advert for Oléo Anjo. Angel Oil, a tanning lotion. They were interested only in unknowns. They were looking for athletic, olive-skinned girls with warm colouring who could run in a bikini. Modelling in swimwear and underwear were Odolina's best chance. When she was fully clothed, she sometimes appeared heavy-set. It was a cruel trick of the camera, but it made her appreciate why the most successful models were skeletal. The camera endowed flesh where none existed. Naked, semi-naked or in swimwear, her body was revealed in its full glory. Antonio swore she'd be perfect for the job.

Luis gave her the day off for the audition. It was the talk of the bar. The night before, one of the customers raised his glass to Odolina. Then, he toasted her photo on the wall. The picture was a little raddled round the corners, and had begun to peel away from the brickwork. 'To the Jewel of the Pasadena!' he cried out. He shook his head with a foolish smile on his face. 'You were so hot.' He was drunk and intended no insult, yet she was cut to the quick. Sylvana sniggered. Odolina's eyes smarted and her hands shook as she collected the glasses.

She had to be chosen. It was a matter of life or a living death in that one-horse town.

Antonio did not stop talking all the way to Ipanema. Odolina, silent and sullen, stared at the horizon, narrowing her eyes to the hot air that blew into his clapped-out little car. She breathed in the heat that rose from the tarmac. A sense of foreboding was growing inside her. She had to make it now before her rose was totally overblown. She had never been troubled by dismay or self-doubt, or concerns about the future. She had always been scarcely human in her supreme self-confidence. Now all these strange, unwelcome feelings besieged her at once.

They had been told to arrive at ten o'clock. It was only nine when they got there, but the beach was already swamped with girls. Some had their mothers or other chaperones with them. The air was feverish, akin to the eve of a major battle. The girls sweated and chain-smoked. Some chattered and giggled among themselves. All eyed their rivals, some more brazenly than others. Odolina and Antonio spread towels on the sand in the last remaining patch of shade and settled to wait.

Antonio had told her not to bother with an elaborate outfit. 'A hot bikini. That's all.' He was specific about make-up. 'Waterproof mascara, Odo. A lot of it. Then top your lashes with

Vaseline. Lip gloss with a tint. Not lipstick.'

'What are they looking for?'

'They want someone who looks natural, someone who can run without looking like an elephant or a frog. Without wobbling all over the place.' She was glad of his advice. Most of the girls, wilting like picked flowers, were caked in make-up that had started to run.

'Are you sure about that bikini, Odo?' Antonio asked. 'Did you bring any others?'

She looked down at the hot pink affair that she imagined looked good against her olive skin.

'I like this one the best,' she said.

'Show me the others.'

Resentfully, she dug into her canvas shoulder bag. She pulled out a petrol blue number and the cheap black bikini, which consisted of four plain triangles and a few bits of string.

'This one,' he said, picking up the black bikini.

'It's cheap.'

'It's perfect, Odo.'

'I am not your puppet, Antonio,' she said with heat.

He held up his hands. 'Okay, okay.'

A couple of vans arrived, which set the girls on the beach and their companions abuzz, like a flock of mynah birds. Crew spilled out of the vans, evicting the occupants of the best shade. While they set up, a tiny middle-aged freckled woman with a frizzy bob began to walk among the girls, appraising, assessing. She carried a clipboard. A gun would not have given her more authority. She ordered the girls to stand in line. Odolina sauntered to take her place. There were raised voices and the distinct sound of a slap and a yelp. The heat and the long wait had taken its toll on the collective temper.

'You!' barked the tiny woman to one of the warring girls. 'You can leave now. You also,' she said to the victim. She was deaf to their pleas. Her indifference was devastating.

Odolina mentally tucked the trick away for future use.

There were two dozen girls in front of Odolina. She glanced behind her, astonished to see about a hundred girls, and more still appearing. The woman appraised each one in turn, as if buying livestock. She batted each girl on the shoulder, away from the camera crew. The process was rapid. Suddenly, she stopped to appraise one of the girls and asked her to turn round so she could get a good look and feel of her buttocks. She sent the grinning girl to the crew. The process of elimination began again in earnest. Odolina stood straight and tall and sucked her belly in as she got closer. The girl in front of her stepped forward and was rejected. The woman looked Odolina up and down, and just as triumph began to surge through her, the woman shook her head and batted her on the shoulder away from the crew. Odolina was stupefied. Five years, building up to one moment, over in an instant.

She made her way in a daze to Antonio.

'Come. Quickly!' he said.

He seized her by the hand and marched her behind a dirty yellow pick-up truck. He held up a towel. 'Get out of that pink thing,' he said, and handed her the black bikini. 'Quick! Just do it!' Feverishly, she obeyed. He led her to a freshwater shower, installed for sea swimmers. He shoved her into the cascade of water, ensuring she was drenched. 'Forgive me, cara,' he said, and reached for her breasts, tweaking the nipples between his thumb and index finger until they stood up in protest. 'Now get back in line.' Again, she obeyed. She pushed her wet hair back and stood straight and tall. The black bikini was stark against her voluptuous frame, and her olive skin gleamed, sparkling with droplets in the sunlight. She inched forward. When she reached the front of the line, the woman appraised her for a moment, then nodded and sent her to the camera crew.

Antonio grinned. Odolina was not normally given to

gratitude, but she felt a flicker of it then. She had to get this job. She had to show those bitches in the bar. She had to get out of that town and escape her mother's life.

Odolina was approaching twenty-three, a venerable age for an unknown model. She looked at the other girls who had made the first round, just as they were looking at her. There were seven of them. Only seven from the dozens in line. Every now and then another grinning beauty would join them from the long line stretching to the end of the beach. All were dark-skinned Latinas like her, except for one honey blonde with green eyes. There were so many beautiful girls. So many perfect faces. Perfect bodies. She was pitted against goddesses.

Warily, the girls started talking among themselves. They had a lot of time to kill. The honey blonde offered Odolina a cigarette. Odolina decided to be friendly. The girl told her that her boyfriend worked for Oléo Anjo. This must be why she had been chosen, against type. In Odolina's head, she imagined how the ad would appear if she directed it. A long-legged, tanned Amazon, running across Ipanema beach, the twin mountains and the distant *favelas* behind her, drenched to the skin in a bikini, shaking off droplets of water, like shedding diamonds in the sunlight. There was one in particular who fitted Odolina's mental casting.

Eventually, the little frizzball approached them.

'From that rock,' she instructed, 'run towards the camera, one by one. We will film each of you. Try to look like you're enjoying it. Got it?'

'When should we stop running?' asked Maria.

'Not until you pass the camera. Got it?' she said again.

The girls retreated to the rock. Odolina first dashed back to the shower and stood under the water that had been so lucky for her before. Soaked, she rejoined the others. Surreptitiously, she tweaked her nipples to ensure they stood out. Adrenaline shot through her.

A girl named Frieda was called first. She looked magnificent. Then Maria, the honey blonde. Her buttocks shook visibly as her feet hit the ground, and her legs were slightly splayed. Flor, the tallest of the group, went next. A six-footer at least, she had beautiful muscle tone.

'Odolina!'

Odolina began to run. She focused on the distant horizon to avoid staring directly at the camera. Despite her nerves, it felt good to run in a bikini, the sand underfoot and the breeze blowing against the fast-evaporating droplets of water on her skin. She softened her gaze and the muscles in her face, and felt her limbs and muscles working. She looked amazing. She knew it. Her attention switched abruptly to the knot in her bikini at her neck. She felt it loosening. She finished her run bare-breasted as an Amazon, the bikini top hanging limp from her midriff.

Odolina rectified her top before turning to face the catcalls from the crew. One of them clapped her on the back. 'A special show! Very nice.' Maria laughed and winked at her. Frieda was so intent on glaring at Odolina that she was blind to a man sauntering up behind her. He encircled her waist and lifted her into the air. Odolina noticed an expression cross her features. Fear, maybe, but it was so fleeting that she felt she must have imagined it. Frieda quickly recovered herself and leaned against him. He was big, with dark hair and sideburns. He had draped himself around her, and drew her more closely against him. Odolina turned her attention to the next girl running towards the camera. Her breasts bobbed up and down like flesh-filled balloons. 'She's going to give God a black eye,' said Frieda's boyfriend, laughing.

Odolina scanned the edge of the beach for Antonio. He caught her eye and winked.

There was a lot of waiting around that day. By the end of the afternoon, twenty-two girls had been filmed, out of the hundreds that had flocked to the beach. A handful, including Odolina, were asked to run for a second time. The girls were told to drench themselves in the shower first. Odolina made her way to the shower to take a turn under the water. She was looking forward to it. Even in the shade, the heat was blazing.

The frizzy-haired woman grabbed her by the shoulder just as she was about to step into the water. 'Not you,' she said. Odolina felt a flash of panic. 'This time, you stay dry,' she said.

Her second run felt as good as the first. Her unruly mass of dark curls bounced with each step, not being weighed down by water. A sudden breeze caught her hair and blew it around her face. Without breaking her stride, she swept it aside with her arm, a gesture at once natural and graceful, and she smiled involuntarily for the last fifteen yards, as the crew handclapped her to the finish. It seemed that the devil really did look after his own, as she'd heard often enough from the nuns. She wished they could see her now, those miserable dried-up old bitches.

One of the crew offered Odolina a sip from his Coke bottle.

'No show this time?' he said as she took the bottle. It was gloriously cold. 'A pity.' His colleagues laughed. The crew's response had earned Odolina another killer glance from Frieda, who seemed surgically attached to her boyfriend. The crew were like demigods on the beach, but seemed oddly deferential towards Frieda's gorilla. She couldn't understand it.

Odolina suppressed her returning swagger. She whiled away the time flirting with the crew. Flor tried to join in, and Odolina made an effort to include her. She could afford to be generous. Flor's shoulders drooped imperceptibly and her smile fell short of her eyes. Her air of defeat was self-fulfilling, as the little woman with the clipboard told her she was sorry. It was the first time that day she had sounded sincere.

It was between her and Frieda. The frizzball ordered a series of photos of both girls while the crew began to pack up their equipment. She made furious notes on her clipboard, looking up in Odolina's direction without ceasing her scribbling, then looking down again without so much as a glance at Frieda. Odolina's heart hammered in triumph. She couldn't wait to give some expression to her fierce joy.

The photographer began dismantling his camera. The little woman stood up and approached her and Frieda. Odolina glanced in Frieda's direction. The girl was beautiful. A tinge of doubt made her shiver despite the afternoon heat.

'We will let you know if either of you are suitable for the next stage,' she said.

Frieda nodded at the woman and scurried off to be reunited with her boyfriend.

'The next stage?' asked Odolina.

The woman did not appreciate being questioned. 'We decide if we use one of you. Or we look again.'

'Okay. Thanks,' said Odolina.

'So?' said Antonio.

'So we have to wait. She said it was between me and that sulky bitch.'

'The one with the caveman?'

'Yes.'

Antonio peered over her shoulder at the couple, who had linked arms as they walked. 'She is not nearly as sexy as you.' He looked again. 'Shit! I know that guy. Nuno!' he called out. 'Nuno!' He ran towards him. The man and the girl stopped in their tracks and turned round. The man took his shades off and squinted in their direction.

'Antonio,' he said. He waited for Antonio to close the distance between them and took his outstretched hand. 'What are you doing here?'

Antonio gestured towards Odolina. 'Odolina's my friend.'

The man lifted his jaw in Odolina's direction.

'Who is she?'

Antonio laughed. 'The Jewel of the Pasadena!'

'What do you mean?'

'Oh nothing,' said Antonio, discouraged by the display of extreme unfriendliness. 'Just a bar in Santa Ana. Anyway, it was good to see you, Nuno.'

'You also, Antonio.' They shook hands again.

'Who is he?' she asked after they'd gone. 'He's such an asshole.'

'He's a photographer and he makes movies. You know what it's like. We all know each other. His father's some big shot. They say he's a mobster. Papa's always dating models, so I guess Nuno feels he has to do the same.'

They began the long drive back to the Pasadena. 'What kind of movies does he make?'

'Not the kind you show your mother.'

She laughed. Antonio was the closest person to a friend that she'd ever had. She began thinking about Nuno. He was obviously crazy about Frieda. He had money, and he was happy to spend it on her. She should find someone like that.

She glanced at Antonio, who was drumming his fingers on the steering wheel in time to a song on the tinny radio. Friend or no friend, she should spread her net a bit wider. She resolved to get to know more photographers. Nuno might be a good start.

# CHAPTER FIVE

Colin Newell called his brother Sonny, who was on holiday in San Francisco with his wife and kids.

'Sonny? It's Colin.'

'Hey Col! How are *you*?' Living in America had done odd things to his accent. 'Bloody hell. It's only six in the morning for you, isn't it? Is everything okay? Is it Mam?'

'No. It's David. He died last night.' In the years that David had been with Bea, Sonny had become one of his closest friends. Colin knew the news would hit hard.

'Jesus,' he said.

'I'm sorry, Sonny.'

Sonny was silent. Then he said, 'Bea must be in pieces. What happened?'

'Suspected heart attack. He was dead on arrival. I got a call from the duty nurse not five minutes ago. She said Bea was sedated.'

'Oh Christ. Is anyone with Bea now?'

'No. She's in Oxford.'

'Maybe we should call Paddy. I could call him. It *is* an emergency.'

'Emergency be damned. Shame they let him out of the nick so early. Barely six months for mowing down a young kid while off your face on coke. It's enough to make you spit.'

'Okay, okay. I was just thinking he's the closest to her.'

'I don't want that bastard anywhere near Bea. I'm going soon as I get hold of Carol. It's my weekend with Anna. She could come with me but Carol may have other ideas. You know what she's like. I thought I'd call you before it got too late.'

'I'll get a flight over soon as I can.'

'That'll be good. I'll leave off calling everyone else until I know what happened.'

'You're right,' said Sonny. 'They'll find out soon enough. Shall I ring Mam though, or will you?' Their mother was up early every day of the week.

'Could you?' said Colin. 'I've got to get ready.' He was relieved he wouldn't have to break the news. 'It'll be good to see you, Sonny.'

'You too, Col. I'll text you once I've booked the flight.'

Next, Colin called Carol. No answer from the landline. He tried her mobile.

'Colin,' she croaked. She sounded rough. Evidently, she'd been making the most of her child-free Saturday night. 'What the bloody hell do you want? Do you know what time it is?'

While he paused to consider how to answer, she changed her tone. 'Is there anything wrong? With Anna, I mean?' He heard the rustling of bedclothes and a man groaning in protest close to her. In spite of himself, he was struck by a jealous pang.

'Anna's fine. It's David. He died last night. Bea's in hospital in Oxford and I need to get to her.'

'Oh God. How awful,' she said with a note of contrition. 'Was there an accident or something?'

'No. Heart attack. They're treating Bea for shock.'

'I'm not surprised.' She coughed. 'I hope this doesn't set her off on one of her... episodes.'

'I wish to God I'd never told you about that. It happened only the once, and under extreme circumstances.'

'Don't go off on one, Colin,' she said and coughed again.

He swallowed his anger. 'I have to set off soon. I want to be there when she comes to. I'd like Anna to come with me.'

'She can't,' said Carol. 'She'll miss school, for one thing.'

'She's only nine.'

'Far too young to be around death and funerals. You

know how sensitive she is.'

'She came with us to my dad's funeral. You thought it would be good for her to say goodbye. She *wanted* to say goodbye.'

She paused, scrabbling for ammunition. 'Your dad was a blood relation. David's not.'

'Bea's her blood, much as you'd like to deny it.'

'Kids love anyone who buys them nice presents.'

Again, he struggled to suppress his temper. Where Carol was concerned, it was difficult not to descend to the politics of the playground. He gripped the receiver.

'Bea needs her family round her. David's in the bloody morgue, Carol. Fit as a butcher's dog one minute and dead the next. Life's too bloody short to fight over a week at school...' He paused, as he heard Carol's bedfellow say 'For fuck's sake tell him to...' Carol covered the mouthpiece. He heard a furious muffled exchange.

'Hang on,' she said in an exasperated whisper. He heard more rustling bedclothes, footsteps, then a closing door.

'Who's that?' He hated himself for asking.

'Nothing. Just the telly,' she mumbled.

'Quite a grumpy telly.'

'Shut up, Colin. Look. I just don't think it's a good idea,' she said.

'Carol, please.'

'Fact is, Colin, this is a pointless argument. You can't take her out of school without my say-so.'

For a moment, he was so angry he was unable to speak. Carol never consulted him about any decision involving Anna, despite being legally obliged to do so. After the split, Carol had enrolled her at a school round the corner from her new house, rejecting the school they'd originally chosen when still together, which was a bus ride away. As always, Carol's choice had everything to do with her own convenience.

Incensed, he'd called his lawyer, a hardboiled single mother in her fifties. 'Colin darling,' she'd rasped, audibly lighting up a cigarette. 'I know it's frustrating, but unless her choice is a sink school full of crackheads and pimps with a dealer at the gate, I'd advise you to keep your powder dry. Going back to court will cost a bomb and they'll probably rule in her favour anyway.'

Colin dragged himself back to the current argument. One of the terrible side effects of negotiating with Carol was that the impotent rage he experienced after each lost battle swamped him afresh. The word 'negotiate' implied some sort of mutual agreement benefiting two parties of roughly equal power. That was a bloody laugh. The power was all on her side, and his lawyer and hers had both made certain he understood this. He despaired of ever being free of this dull fury.

'You can drop her off at my place in an hour,' said Carol.

'I'll drop her off right now.' He knew she wasn't at home and wouldn't want to admit it. She hesitated. God alone knows who she was with this time. It wasn't any of his business, but it still caused him pain.

'Wait! I'll come and get her. I'll be with you by seven thirty.'

It was Colin's turn to hesitate. 'Fine. If you're not here by then, she's coming with me.'

There was a long pause. 'Okay. I'll be there. But Colin, if I'm late because of traffic or... whatever, you have to wait for me.'

'I'll see you in an hour.'

Gently, he shook Anna by the shoulder. She was instantly awake. An early bird, like him. Not like Carol. While they were still together, Carol would surface only after he'd taken Anna to the playground, returned with the papers and when the house was filled with the smell of bacon and extra-strength Colombian coffee.

'It's still dark, Daddy.'

'You've to go back to your mother's early, sweetheart. Your Uncle David died in the night.'

Her fists flew to her mouth and her eyes welled up. 'Has he gone to heaven?'

'I'm sure he has,' said Colin, despising himself. He did not believe in an afterlife. He sighed. 'Nobody really knows what happens after you die, but if there's a heaven, then David's in it. Jump up, sweetheart. I've got to start for Auntie Bea's soon as your mother gets here.'

'Can I come?'

'You've got school, pet'

'Please, Daddy.'

'I don't know how long I'll be away. I'm going to jump in the shower. Why don't you start packing for me? I have to leave soon as your mother arrives. I don't want Auntie Bea alone.'

He packed a shirt in dry-cleaning plastic and stuffed a few things from the laundry bin into a plastic bag. He'd run them through the machine at Bea's house. He took his darkest suit, still in a dry-cleaning bag, out of the wardrobe, along with an ironed shirt and a tie for the funeral, which he supposed would take place in the coming week. 'Can I leave you to get on with this lot, pet? I've to pack up my laptop and do a few bits and pieces.'

Colin ran his business from a small study downstairs. He'd left Ernst & Young before Anna was born to set up on his own. A pregnant wife had given him the spur he'd needed to go independent. He provided accounting, financial advice and tax planning services to a few dozen private individuals and a growing number of small to mid-sized companies. His success was no longer a source of joy to him.

He sent an email to his part-time secretary with a few instructions. He cancelled two meetings scheduled for the following week.

He printed off directions to the hospital from the AA website and studied them closely. He packed up his laptop and the files he had to work on that week and slipped them into his briefcase. The printed directions went into a side pocket for easy access in the car. Upstairs, he found Anna struggling with the zip on his suitcase.

'I'll do that, duck. Do you fancy any breakfast?'

'No, thanks.'

'You sure? Egg on toast? Shreddies?'

She shook her head. He glanced at his watch. It was gone seven thirty. He tried not to get anxious about Carol's arrival. The knot in his stomach was turning into a dull rage. She'd had a quickie with loverboy. Why else would she take so long? He wanted to spit.

He put his bag in the car and hung the suit and shirt in the back seat.

'Nothing for it now but to wait for your mam,' he said to Anna. He sat down in the living room, where he could keep a lookout for Carol's car. He patted his knee and Anna crawled into his lap. One day she'd be too big to fit there so snugly. He pushed the thought from his mind.

The minutes ticked by. Colin couldn't bear the wait any longer.

'Up you get, pet,' he said. He was about to tell Anna she'd be coming to London when Carol braked sharply in front of the house. It was just before eight.

'There she is,' he said, his voice measured. 'You've got all your things together?' She nodded. Her weekend bag and school satchel were by the front door. He picked them up along with his briefcase and led her outside. Carol's engine was idling. She rolled her window down. She didn't meet Colin's eye.

'Hello darling,' said Carol. 'Jump in, double quick. Daddy has to get away.'

Colin did not trust himself to speak.

'Daddy! My notebook! I left it by the bed!'

'I'll get it, pet. You stay there—' but she wriggled past him. He stood by the car, wanting to rage at Carol. Instead he unlocked his car and put his briefcase on the passenger seat. The two of them waited for Anna's return. Finally, Carol said 'Colin, I'm sorry I was late. I—'

'Please, Carol. I don't want to hear it.'

'I just—'

It was unlike Colin not to accept an olive branch when offered. 'It's bad enough that you make my life difficult, but could you not have an ounce of compassion for Bea?'

'I drove like the clappers.'

'It's taken you an hour and a half. I could be well on my way by now if you weren't so...'

'Weren't so what?' Her voice rose an octave.

'So unreasonable, Carol. If you'd just said that your new man lives so far away, I could have left Anna with Mrs Beech until you got here.'

'I don't have to tell you anything about my life! I don't want her left with a stranger.'

'She's no stranger and you know I'd much rather have taken her with me.'

'Stop fighting!' yelled Anna, who'd reappeared unnoticed by her parents. Bright spots appeared on the apples of her cheeks. Both adults looked guiltily in her direction. She turned to her mother. 'Mum, I want to be with Auntie Bea.'

'No, darling. It's not a time for children and I don't want you missing school.'

'I want to go.'

'Anna, no means no. Now come on. Your father has to get going.'

Anna glared at her mother. 'Two against one,' she said and tucked her notebook under her arm. She marched up to Carol's car and reached into the back seat for her overnight bag and her satchel. 'I'm going, Mum. Don't try and stop me.' Then she walked the five or six paces across to Colin's car. Her feet crunched the ice on the ground with each step. She strapped herself into the booster seat at the back, leaving the door open. Carol went red in the face. 'Anna, you're to get into the car right now.'

'I am in the car.'

'You know damn well I mean my car.'

'I'm going with Dad.'

'You've got to go to school.' The pitch of Carol's voice continued to rise.

'I've got the rest of my life to go to school.'

'Colin, tell her. Tell her she's got to come with me,' said Carol.

Colin believed in parents showing a united front, but he would choke if he tried to support her.

Carol got out of her car and marched towards Anna, who shut the door and locked it. Her chin trembled. Carol bent down, her face separated from Anna's only by the glass. She jabbed her finger against it. 'Anna. Get out of the car. NOW.' She stood up, deeply agitated. She wasn't wearing a bra. Her nipples tightened in the freezing air. Colin was furious with himself for noticing.

'Colin, tell her.'

Colin lowered his voice. 'I think she should come. I believe it's in her best interests.' Legalese was bound to irritate her. The divorce had infected them both.

'I am so sick of you bleating on about her best interests.' She made no attempt to keep her voice down.

'I wouldn't have to if you thought about them yourself once in a while.'

'What the FUCK do you mean?'

'Language,' he hissed. 'It's not good for her to be kept from my family.'

'Your family are the most dysfunctional bunch of—'

'And yours are the Waltons, are they? Let's not go down that road. We'd be here all bloody day.'

'That's right. Bitch about my family in front of her,' she spat. 'You're such a hypocrite. You accuse *me* of being a bad parent. Look at her! Ignoring her own mother on your say-so. She's unmanageable after she's spent time with you. Encouraging her to skip school—'

'It was okay for her to skip school so you could get a cheap flight to Spain.'

'I am so sick of you banging on about that! On the pittance you—' Carol's mobile rang. She stomped back to her car to look at the display.

'Hi!' she said, her whole demeanour changing. She listened, then visibly relaxed. She injected a breathlessness into her voice that Colin recognised. 'No, honestly, it's fine. I'm rubbish in the mornings too.' She glanced at Colin and walked out of earshot, or so she thought. 'I had such a good time last night. Maybe that last bottle wasn't such a great idea.' She giggled softly. 'Today? That would be great, only... really? It's just that I'll have Anna with me and... no. Her dad has to go to London and my mum's away. Thing is...' She walked further from him. He tapped on the car window. Anna opened the door, tears on her cheeks.

'I'm really sorry, sweetheart. I've got to go. Your mam's doing what she thinks is best.'

Anna sniffed and unclicked her seatbelt. 'I shouldn't have made such a fuss.'

Carol ended her call and came striding back to the car. 'Darling,' she said to Anna. 'You've been crying.' Anna gave her a basilisk stare.

'Uncle David's dead. Auntie Bea's alone. I want to see her.' Carol reached over to touch her cheek. Anna flinched from her.

'Darling, I'm sorry. Do you want to go that much?'

Anna looked suspiciously at her mother.

Carol sighed loudly.

'All right. Off you go. You haven't got much of your stuff with you. Colin, you'll have to take her to H&M or something.'

Anna threw her arms round Carol's waist. 'Thanks, Mum,' she murmured into her mother's stomach. She lifted her head. 'I'll phone you every day.'

'I hope so, darling.' Carol smiled at Colin over Anna's head. It was infuriatingly disarming.

Anna jumped back into his car and strapped herself in. As he locked the front door to the house, Carol said, 'Well, you got what you wanted. Take care of her.'

'So long as you get your hot date in.' He regretted the words the instant they escaped his mouth. 'I'm sorry, Carol.'

Carol laughed. 'At least I have a hot date. You know, you'd make a very good monk, Colin.'

She waved and blew a kiss to Anna before she got back into her car. Before she drove off, she rolled her window down.

'Oh, Colin. Please tell Bea I'm sorry. I really am.'

Colin nodded.

Finally, they set off.

'Daddy, what was that word Mummy used for your family?'

'Which word, darling?'

'It was a long word. Diss something.'

'Oh. Dysfunctional.'

'What does it mean?'

'It's used to describe something that doesn't work too well.'

'Is it true, Daddy?'

'That our family's dysfunctional? We are a bit. Most families are a bit dysfunctional. Mummy didn't mean it, particularly. She said it because she was cross.'

Anna took a moment to digest this. 'Is it dysfunctional to get divorced?'

He laughed. 'You could say that. People get divorced because their marriages haven't worked out too well.'

'Is that what happened to you and Mummy?'

Colin met his daughter's eyes in the mirror. 'What did she say about it?'

'She said you both decided you weren't in love any more.'

Colin almost laughed out loud. He couldn't blame Carol for telling a whopper. Anna fell to silence, staring out of the window. Suddenly she piped up.

'Why doesn't Mummy like Auntie Bea?'

Her job, her friends, her house, her money, her marriage. The last could now be scratched from the list. 'What makes you think she doesn't like her?'

'The way she talks about her. She said that Auntie Bea spoils me. She said she needed children of her own to spoil, instead of someone else's.'

He brooded over the spat with Carol. He supposed that without their combined chromosomes in their daughter, it would be much easier to move on. He hated that expression. Perhaps he was just kidding himself. Even if Anna had never come into being, he'd still love Carol. In spite of everything. He just loved her, despite her many and obvious flaws.

Carol wouldn't be able to get away with her cheap stunts for much longer. Anna had developed a finely tuned sense of justice, and was learning to stick up for herself. He saw in the mirror that she'd fallen asleep, her long fair hair completely curtaining her face.

The drive went quickly. The roads had been cleared and the traffic was light. He stopped to fill up with petrol, and bought tuna sandwiches and a big bottle of Evian. At around 11am, he pulled into the car park of the John Radcliffe Hospital.

Bea appeared to be sleeping. Her face was screwed up, chalky white, the same colour as the sheet she lay upon. She opened her eyes as they approached. He bent to kiss her cold cheek, and took her hand, which was cold, despite the overheated ward. Dehydration and superbugs sprang to mind. Anna was quiet, and looked at her aunt in awe. Grief had made a stranger of her.

'I'm so, so sorry, Bean,' said Colin, using her old nickname from childhood. She whimpered. It was a wretched sound.

'What happened?'

'He just... died. I don't know how it happened.' She choked on more tears. 'He was fine before we went to sleep. We even... and he was fine. I gave him CPR. I was too late. I did it wrong. I just don't know. I'll never know.'

'You'll drive yourself mad thinking that way.'

'I got the number of compressions wrong. I didn't push down hard enough.'

'Hush, now. You should go back to sleep. You look all done in.'

'No!' she said with surprising strength. 'You've to take me home.'

'Is that a good idea?'

'I don't want to stay here.'

'Well, if you're sure. I'll help you pack up. Not that you've brought much. Is this it?' He gestured towards the clothes on the chair. 'Where are all your things?'

'Back at the house. We'll have to go back there before we drive to London.'

'Where are your keys?' he asked.

'The house isn't locked. Help me up, Col.' Bea's voice gained in strength when she was upright. 'Tell the nurse that I'm going while I get dressed.' Anna stared at her, then with visible resolution she approached her aunt and patted her shoulder awkwardly. Colin felt guilty. Maybe Carol had been right. This was no mission for a child.

The nurse was filling in forms. She held a plastic cup of tea in her left hand and ticked and crossed boxes on a form rapidly with her right. She was a round little woman. She took off her glasses as Colin introduced himself.

'You're her brother, are you?' she said in a soft Irish brogue. 'That's grand. She'll be needing her family.' She peered around him to look at Bea.

'She's had a huge shock,' the nurse said. 'I understand from the ambulance crew she gave mouth to mouth and it didn't work. She kept at it for hours. She's got the grief, but likely guilt as well. She kept saying she didn't want to live any more before we sedated her. We've got to take these things seriously. She did all she could and more besides, and it's important you persuade her of that.'

'I will,' said Colin.

'I'm sure you will.' She glanced around him again at Bea. 'I'm very sorry to have to ask but I'm obliged. Does she have any history of mental illness?'

Colin hesitated. She'd been just fifteen. It was twenty-odd years ago, over half her lifetime. Losing your husband was a crippling blow for anyone, sudden or otherwise. Bea and David had been lucky to find each other. He thought he'd found his life's partner in Carol, but she'd had other ideas. Grief was the terrible flipside of loving another person so intensely. Bea would be strong enough to withstand it, surely? She wouldn't try anything like that again. People survived these things all the time. People lost husbands, wives, siblings, parents, even children and lived through it. Not for the first time, he shuddered at the thought of losing Anna. Having a child made you vulnerable, a hostage to fortune. The little nurse gave him a shrewd look.

'No,' he said.

'And she's never tried to harm herself?'

Again, Colin hesitated. The capacity to survive was immensely strong, even in Bea. He was sure of it. She had her family. She had friends. She had their mother. Even if Mam and Bea hardly saw eye to eye, the sense of family was strong in them both. She would recover. Of course it would take time. She was young enough to find love again. She'd never do what she'd done again, he was certain.

It was something they never referred to in the family. At the height of his love and trust for Carol, he'd told her what Bea had done, something she'd given him plenty of opportunities to regret. He was not naturally paranoid, but he had an aversion to giving such information away. He had no idea how it could be used against her, but who knew? His mind raced with the possibilities. He didn't want it stored anywhere, even in a dusty file in a hospital archive. Supposing he told this kindly-looking nurse what had happened; it would not stop Bea from jumping off a bridge, a cliff, taking pills or hanging from the end of a rope if that was what she was minded to do.

'No,' he said finally. 'As you said, she's had a huge shock. But we'll take care of her.'

'I'm glad to hear it,' the nurse said gently. 'All the same, it would be just as well to encourage her to have some sort of counselling. Grief counselling, you know.'

'I'll talk to her about it,' he promised. 'Do I have to sign anything?'

'No. Just don't let her get behind the wheel of a car before the sedation wears off.'

To his surprise, the nurse's eyes became moist. She shook her head and took a gulp of tea. 'It fair tore my heart to hear her crying for him last night. I'm glad she's got family who love her.' A lump came to his throat. He touched her shoulder.

'Thank you for looking after her,' he said.

Bea leaned on Colin to get to the car. The storm of the

previous night had vanished, and the sun shone brightly on the glinting snow. The harsh light forced another rush of water into Bea's eyes. She squinted and shaded them with her hand. Colin settled her into the front seat and asked Anna to get a blanket from the boot. He shook it out and tucked it round Bea's legs and shoulders. Bea gave a trace of a smile before her mouth resettled in its new line.

Colin caught Anna's eye in the mirror and blinked at her in silent solidarity. As they got closer to the house, Colin sensed a tension building up inside Bea.

'Do you want me to get your things?' he asked. 'You can wait in the car.'

'No. I want to go in,' she said. They had to park on the road. There was no getting up the hill without chains. The driveway was a foot deep in snow. David's car was completely covered. The snow blanketed the surrounding countryside and hung in great clumps from the tree branches. A perfect day for a winter walk. None of them wore shoes with a suitable grip, so they held on to each other as they made their way to the front door. The house looked bereft and yawningly empty. Bea's eyes streamed.

'My stuff's upstairs,' she said. 'Why don't you go into the kitchen where it's warm. I'll not be long.'

'I'll come with you,' said Anna.

'Go with your daddy, sweetheart. You can help him look for David's phone. It's in the kitchen somewhere. Mine too, I think.'

No sooner had they set foot in the kitchen than they heard the trill of a mobile. It vibrated angrily on the wooden table. The screen flashed 'Hilly'. David's daughter, Hilary. Colin was torn. He did not want to be the one to tell her that her father was dead. On the other hand, he couldn't bear to think of her unquestioning certainty that her father was still alive. He let the call go to voicemail. A text message popped up a moment later. He saw that there were also thirteen missed calls.

'Who was that, Daddy?' asked Anna.

'It was Hilary, duck.'

'Why didn't you answer it?'

'Because I can't tell her her father has died. It should be Auntie Bea does that.'

Anna ruminated.

'Daddy, if you died, I'd want to know. I'd want to know straight away. I wouldn't care who told me. I'd just want to know.'

They both jumped when the house phone rang, piercing the quiet. It rang four times. The answering machine kicked in as Bea came downstairs with an overnight case and her handbag. A scratchy recording of David's voice pierced the quiet. 'Hello, you've reached the Grahames. Please leave a message and we'll ring you back. Thanks. Bye.'

A pang tore through Colin at Bea's stricken face. There was a tutting sound, then Hilary's plummy voice echoed around the kitchen. 'Daddy. Bea. Where the hell are you? You'd better not be snowed in, or you'll miss my play tomorrow night. Can you call me, 'cos if you miss it I'll...'

Hilary ranted on. Bea stood stock-still for a moment, then dropped her case and ran to the phone. She hesitated and let Hilary continue: '...and if you don't make it, I'm going to be seriously peed off. Anyway, call me once you've finished frolicking in the snow or whatever else you're doing.'

The three of them stared at each other.

'Oh God,' said Bea.

Colin hugged her. 'If you've got all your stuff together, let's get to her straight off. Much better to tell them face to face.'

'It is *not*!' said Anna, her colour up. 'Ring her back and tell her right now. I couldn't bear it if you were dead and nobody bothered to tell me.'

Bea crumpled into a chair. 'You're right. You're absolutely right. I just need a minute. Then I'll do it.'

Anna put her arms round her aunt.

'I'll put the kettle on,' Colin said, feeling humbled. He'd been right to bring Anna.

\*\*\*

Sonny wore an eye mask, and he'd wedged in some earplugs, but nothing would drown out the din coming from the little girl to his right. Her mother, a beautiful Sikh of thirty or so, was doing her best to calm her. Sonny had plenty of experience of flying with his own kids. He loved them more than his own self, but they could be a colossal pain in the arse.

He had a foolproof method of tackling transatlantic travel. He ate dinner in the executive lounge, popped a couple of sleeping tabs with a stiff whisky, then passed out on a first-class flatbed the second the seatbelt signs were off. This time, he'd arrived at the airport too late for dinner and had left his tabs behind. First and business had been solidly booked, so he was wedged into a doll's seat with Little Leather Lungs next to him.

He hadn't had to turn right on an international flight in years. He was a platinum member. He'd clocked a million airmiles. Fat lot of good it did him now. The flights were oversold. They were bumping people off, the woman at the desk said. If he wanted to go to London, he'd take economy or nothing.

He was eaten up with grief, with worry for his sister, and was dog tired besides. He and Gina had carted the kids back to New York on the earliest available flight from San Francisco. He'd taken a shower, packed a fresh bag and got a cab straight back to JFK. He had to be there for Bea. Although Sammy and Paddy were technically older, the role of eldest had always fallen to him. Sammy's head was jammed in the clouds, and nobody in their right mind would want Paddy having any kind of sway over them.

It was a bad time to be leaving the office. Equity markets were in freefall. Most fund managers were happy to take credit for top-drawer performance in rising markets, convinced it was down to their own brilliance, whereas losses were down to 'The Market'. He had no patience for that kind of thinking. There was always something doing well. If the world descended into chaos, he'd invest in guns and baked beans. Sonny had a talent for gauging how fear and greed would affect the markets. In 2008, he and a handful of others had made a killing by betting against sub-prime mortgage debt.

Anyone would think he'd had access to information procured only by weird voodoo magic, denied to the rest of the financial and political community. In fact the writing on the wall had been plain for anyone who cared to look. Sonny had written numerous investor letters, countless articles for the financial press, given interviews and spoken at conferences to warn of the signs of the advancing crash, but had been roundly ignored. Political cynicism, banking greed, investor delusion and the stupidity of the regulators and the ratings agencies had created the perfect environment for him to make millions for himself and for his clients. One of his biggest private clients had been David. That would all be split between Bea and the children's trust. Then there was her own pot of money, independent of David's. Bea would never have to worry financially. She should have her bum in the butter for life, as their dad used to say.

His fears for her were wholly different. He was concerned about her state of mind. He remembered what had happened the night his parents split. Neither he, nor any of his siblings, understood the root cause of the schism or what had pushed Bea to do what she did. Right up to his death, George had been as tight-lipped as Edie.

The endless discussions among the siblings over the years had failed to come to any satisfactory conclusions. Their parents had been rock-solid, then all of a sudden they'd crumbled. Their dad, George, might have spilled the beans eventually. God knows, sometimes it seemed as if he'd longed to talk. He was dead now. That left Edie. She'd never crack, not under torture. He smarted at the memory of asking her.

He'd taken her to her favourite Chinese, long before George was dead. They'd had some wine and they'd set to talking. Proper talk, not just idle chit-chat. It was a prickly topic, but he felt he might never get another chance, so he'd taken the plunge and asked her. Her face had changed.

'It's between your dad and me. Let sleeping dogs lie, pet. Raking up what happened years ago does nobody any good.'

'Mam, it's important. It's not idle curiosity.'

Edie's colour flew up. 'I'll not have any of you poking your nose in where it's not wanted.'

'It's not—'

'That's the end of it, Sonny. If your dad's said nothing, I'll not be drawn on it. I'll thank you not to bring it up again.'

Know when you're beaten and move on. It was one of the more valuable pieces of advice he'd plucked from his enormous library of self-help books. An army of gurus believed persistence was the key to success, citing Thomas Edison and Papillon as proof that it paid off. Never, never, never, never ever give up, Winston Churchill had said; but then he'd never met Edie.

# CHAPTER SIX

Bea gazed at the clothes hanging in David's wardrobe. The shirts in white, pastels and stripes, all on hangers with starched collars. The suits. Lights and greys and darks and pinstripes and linens, all neatly facing one way as if queueing. The empty suits filled her with an unbearable pain. His ties, dozens of them, coloured, plain, patterned, spotted, stripes. Shoes, jumpers, golf shirts, shorts, boxers, socks, trousers, handkerchiefs, T-shirts, an old leather jacket from his student days that no longer fitted him, which he'd refused to throw away. All his things reduced to a giant haul for a charity shop.

Sandra, Will's wife, gestured to the wardrobe.

'Do you want some help going through all that?'

Bea shook her head.

'There's no rush. You'll know when the time's right. Maybe Dan and Harry can help you. They may want to keep some of it.'

She wasn't ready to let his things go.

Bea remembered loafing around on a Sunday with the papers, reading an article about obscure last wishes. 'I don't really give a rat's arse,' he'd said. 'Stick me under the rose bushes if you like. They're looking a bit seedy this year,' and continued with the crossword.

Now he was dead, though, it seemed terribly important to get everything right. To have the right readings and to play music that was significant to him and meaningful to those gathering for his final farewell. *Desert Island Discs* for the dead. They weren't churchgoers, yet she wanted the service in a church. David would have laughed at her. 'The only people who have grand funerals nowadays are royalty and East End gangsters.'

Her house was filling up. Colin and Anna came first, then Sonny, followed by Will and Sandra and their youngest son, Nick.

'Soon as the funeral's over, why don't you come and stay with us?' asked Sonny. 'Long as you like. We'll take care of you, me and Gina will. It'll be good for the kids to spend some time with their auntie. They're growing up so fast.'

Bea had a moment of vertigo, where the next forty years stretched into a void that she had somehow to fill.

'I just can't imagine what you're going through. It's awful, like,' said Sandra. She had always been demonstrative. It had taken Bea some time to get used to it. Geordies were supposed to be hard as rocks. Sandra reached over and pulled out a tissue from the box by Bea's bed and dabbed at her eyes.

'So what do you think you're going to do?' she asked.

'How do you mean?' asked Bea.

'Well, after the funeral, like. Will you stay here?'

She thought about it. She had total freedom. Nothing and nobody to consider. She could rot in this house like Miss Havisham. She could sell it and set up home somewhere else. Wherever she wanted. She could quit her job. She could become a hermit, a recluse; she could up sticks and set up an orphanage in Kinshasa or Timbuktu. A boundless freedom that was utterly unwanted.

Sandra patted her leg. 'Why don't you come for a walk in the park with me and Nicky?'

'Didn't Colin take him this morning?'

'Aye, he did, but it'd be good for you and me to get out for a bit. I haven't left the house since we got here. Colin's taken Anna to see Carol's sister. He's good like that. Considering what she did, he doesn't seem to hold it against her family.'

'Do you mind if I don't, San?'

'C'mon, Bea. The fresh air will do you good. God, I can't believe I just said that. I sound just like me mam. You'll be gathering cobwebs soon. Let's go. Even if just for half an hour.'

Ten minutes later they were outside.

'Me and my big gob,' said Sandra as they fought against the wind. It was freezing, despite the sun shining with a glare that forced them to squint into the biting wind. Bea pulled her coat tight against her. They marched to the playground in the park and released Nick from his pushchair. He was so swaddled in layers he could barely move. He watched a little girl go down the slide. She hesitated at the top. Her father stood by the side of the slide and gently encouraged her down. Eventually she went down, holding his hand all the way.

'Well done, Sienna,' he said when she reached the bottom.

Nick wanted a go. He whined to be free of his coat.

'No, my lad. It's too cold,' said Sandra. He bellowed. 'Oh all right then. Come here. I don't know why I bother,' she said to Bea. 'I should just give in straight off and be done with it.'

Freed from his bondage, he ran to the slide. The little girl was standing at the bottom, about to go back to the top. Nicky barged past her.

'Nicky!' said Sandra. 'That wasn't very nice. You should've let the little girl go first. Sorry,' she said to the girl's father.

'That's quite all right.' He smiled. 'She's already had a go.'

Nick had to stretch his legs to maximum capacity to gain purchase on each rung. Sandra tried to help him but he shook her off. He launched himself from the top, his bottom making contact with the slide with a thud about halfway down.

'Nicky!' cried Sandra and rushed towards him.

'Gosh,' said the girl's father. 'That was a bit gung-ho.'

Nick blinked with surprise at the bottom, as if deciding whether to laugh or cry. He turned expectantly towards his mother and his aunt and grinned, and for an instant looked so much like her father that Bea sucked in her breath. George's eyes. George's smile.

'Well done, Nicky,' she said. Her eyes watered. The little boy was the living repository of her father's genes. His blood. Her blood. Maybe she would— She banished the thought. She picked him up and cuddled him close. The little boy laughed, then struggled to be free for another go.

'A bit more careful this time, pet,' said Sandra, rolling her eyes.

After fifteen minutes they bundled him, protesting, back into his coat and power-walked back home, frozen to the bone. After a hot bath, Bea was so exhausted that she lay down on the bed. She tried to resist sleeping. The nights were long enough as it was. But she couldn't stop herself, and fell asleep.

Will woke her up.

'It's seven o'clock, duck,' he said. 'Sandra's made pork chops. D'you fancy one?'

Bea shook her head. Will sat on the bed beside her.

'I thought I'd better wake you or you'll not sleep tonight.'

She nodded. 'The nights are the worst.'

'When I can't sleep, I don't even try. To keep marital relations smooth, I get up. Read a book, watch the telly.'

'What is it keeps you awake?'

'Sometimes I can't stop thinking about things.'

'I didn't think anything ever got to you.'

'Sometimes I get the wisp of an idea, and the harder I chase it, the more... sorry. You're not bothered by all this.'

'No, I am. Honest. Tell me.'

'They come when I stop chasing them. Easier said than done, though. It's like trying to ignore something stuck in your teeth.'

'You mean your ideas?'

'The ideas aren't a problem. The problem is separating

them from memory. Whenever you think you've got an original idea, other stuff forces its way in.'

'Stuff?'

'Yeah, to do with us. You know, the family. Mam still hasn't forgiven me for writing about Dad.'

'Did you ever tell Dad about it? Before he died?'

''Course. He said I should write what comes naturally. He said if he'd known he was to be a character in a book he'd have tried to be a better man.'

'He couldn't have been a better man.'

Will nodded. 'He was writing something himself. Just before he died.'

'You never told me!'

'He asked me for a notepad. I tried to teach him how to use my old laptop, but he never got the hang of it.

'Have you got it? The notepad?'

'No. I asked the nurses but they denied all knowledge. I wonder if they didn't just chuck it. By the end his writing was like a drunken spider crawled out of an inkpot. Maybe they couldn't make head nor tail and just tossed it.'

'Did he give any idea what it was about?'

'I never pressed him. I wish I had now.'

Bea stared at the ceiling taking this in. George, at the end of his life, writing something. She was filled with longing.

'Do you think he wanted us to see it?'

'Yeah, I do. That's why I never pushed him. I thought... well, I thought we'd all be reading it sooner than we wanted.'

Bea nodded. 'I wish he hadn't been alone at the end.'

'I think about it all the time. I wanted to throttle the nurses for not calling us. I felt bad afterwards. They seemed as shocked as we were that the end was so sudden.'

'Tea's ready!' Sandra called.

'We'd best go down,' said Will. 'Chops don't eat themselves.'

\*\*\*

'I want it back, Dritton,' said Paddy.

'I warned you,' said Dritton. 'You cannot change your mind.'

Paddy laughed. 'I haven't changed my mind. But you didn't fell the tree, did you?'

There was silence on the other end of the line. Eventually Dritton said, 'I have never heard of this.'

'In all conscience, you can't keep the cash since you did nothing to earn it.'

'You don't understand. I have given it to Fevze. He – these are not people you wish to upset. For your own peace of mind—'

'If I wanted peace of mind I'd enter a monastery. Drits, you're a mate, you really are. But it's not my style to pay for stuff that's not been done. Tell you what. Just remind Fevze what I've done for him. Anything happens to me, a USB stick gets delivered to the coppers.'

Dritton was silent.

'Don't be like that, Drits. I copied the files just in case I needed to protect myself. If Fevze's got a problem, then tell him to pick it up with the man upstairs.'

'The man upstairs?'

'You know, the Big Man upstairs.' Paddy laughed. 'He was the one who did the job. For free.'

\*\*\*

Damien Lillie's mobile phone rang. It was his wife, Stephanie.

'Hello darling. Are you busy?' she asked.

'My next appointment's due any minute.'

'It'll only take a sec. I'm on the Val website and I've

found a fantastic chalet with a sauna and Jacuzzi. Ski in, ski out…
it looks amazing. I just wanted to double-check dates. I want to
book it now for the week over Easter. It's bound to go really
quickly.'

'Sweetheart, isn't that the most expensive time?'

'Well yes, but it's the only week we can do with all four
of the children. Oliver's got his school trip to Greece the first
week of the holidays, and I don't want him missing out.'

'How much is it?'

'Fifteen thousand euros for the week.'

'Fifteen thousand! Is the Jacuzzi gold-plated or
something? That's just ridiculous.'

'Don't make such a fuss, darling. We'll be sharing with
the Dickinsons.'

'What, fifty-fifty?'

'Well, no. They'll be coming without their kids, so I
thought we could ask them for two or three thousand.'

Lillie felt a spike in his blood pressure. 'So we'll be
subsidising their bloody holiday for the second year in a row!'

'If we ask them for more, they won't come.'

'Which surely tells you something, darling.'

She huffed. 'When we stayed in Le Hameau last year it
was a thousand a night for the three rooms and we agreed it
would be cheaper to rent a chalet.'

'Yes, but darling,' he said, trying hard to inject calm into
his voice. 'Fifteen thousand makes Le Hameau look cheap. I
mean, there has to be something more reasonable, surely.'

She was silent. Then she said, 'It's the chalet the Kerrs
stayed in. D'you remember they were telling us about it?'

'What, the eight-bedroom place at the foot of Belier?'
He struggled to control his exasperation. 'There's no way on
earth we need as many rooms as all that, even with the sodding
Dickinsons.' He exhaled shortly. 'Darling, the Kerrs stayed there
at the beginning of the season with three other families. Be

reasonable, sweetheart. Look, I have to go. My ten o'clock's here,' he lied. 'Have another look. I'd rather go back to Le Hameau than pay through the nose for rooms we don't need.'

'But Damien, I—'

'Got to go. Love you, darling. Bye! Bye!' He made a loud kissing noise before cutting her off, then brought his arm careering down as if to smash the phone onto the desk. At the last second, he gently replaced the receiver.

He thought back to their last skiing holiday. The two older kids had outgrown all their ski gear, and rather than pass it on to the two youngest, Steph had given all of it away. Top-quality down jackets at two hundred quid a throw and North Face salopettes that had only been used for one season. 'But darling, Phoebe didn't want to wear blue or yellow. She insisted on pink, and it seemed unfair to buy her new stuff only to make Miranda wear the cast-offs.'

It was impossible to make her understand.

He thought sourly of the Dickinsons. No wonder they loved tagging along on Lillie holidays. They paid a quarter of each restaurant bill. 'There are six of us and only two of you,' Steph would coo, ignoring the fact that the children ate only spaghetti with cheese and ketchup, while Bill and his wife Caroline guzzled rivers of booze, and routinely ordered seafood, always massively overpriced at the top of a mountain.

'Don't make such a fuss, darling,' Steph said whenever he privately grumbled. 'You know we're much better off, and besides, Bill said he'd do Phoebe's braces for free.' That was something, he'd supposed at the time, although of course it had never happened. Steph had taken her to a top-flight orthodontist on Harley Street, on the say-so of one of the Yank yummy mummies at the school gates who had more money than sense. Those braces had cost six grand so far and the bills still rolled in every quarter.

He put his head in his hands. He didn't begrudge Steph

her shopping trips, he really didn't. He liked having a well-dressed and glamorous wife, and he liked her to be happy. But there were shopping bags emblazoned with the labels of Beauchamp Place boutiques in the corner of their enormous bedroom that weren't emptied of their contents for weeks. Four children at private school was a crippling expense as it was. You'd think at that price they'd actually get an education, but Lillie was constantly shocked at the extent of their ignorance, and to add insult to injury, Ollie needed extra maths lessons at forty quid an hour. Then there were the pony club fees, the ballet classes and the music tuition. Phoebe couldn't join a violin class like the other kids. Oh no. She had to have individual attention. Steph had blown four hundred quid on a violin, congratulating herself it was second-hand. Again, he wouldn't mind if his daughter actually possessed a smidgeon of talent or if she put the hours in. Listening to her screech through her practice was as agonising as nagging her to do it in the first place.

The mortgage, the school fees, the holidays, the cars, the credit card bills. The kitchen table groaned with brochures from rural estate agents. Steph had started nagging him about buying a weekend cottage in the country. 'Somewhere pretty, where the children can roam around and play Pooh sticks like I did with my brothers when I was little. Where we can invite our friends to stay.'

Of course, only Oxfordshire or Hampshire would do. He couldn't imagine any of the kids wanting to roam free, surgically attached as they were to Nintendo. Playing Pooh sticks seemed a bit tame compared with *Grand Theft Auto*, and inviting their friends to stay meant asking ghastly people that Steph wanted to impress. Or the bloody Dickinsons. When he thought about it all, his heart started palpitating.

Deep within himself, he knew the source of his trouble was not his profligate wife or his spoilt children. The clinic was a goldmine despite the premium location, the staff and the top-notch equipment, which cost a fortune to service and maintain. It was extraordinary how much money childless couples were prepared to part with to realise their dream. It was a growth business. Infertility was on the rise. The rich were insensitive to price, and even those of modest means were prepared to sell or mortgage their houses, take out loans with crippling interest rates or hand over their life savings in order to hold their own baby in their arms.

Steph knew all about the horse, of course. She'd been totally behind him. Owning a share of a racehorse was fantastic, she'd said, such a hoot, such fun. She loved dressing up for the races. Being able to invite people to Ascot and Goodwood was social nirvana for her. What she didn't know was the extent of his losses. He just couldn't bring himself to tell her. He'd had a terrible streak recently. When he forced himself to think about it, he hadn't had any luck since a rank outsider called Tin Pan Alley had completed his trifecta, and even then, he'd blown the winnings on a guaranteed sure-fire winner, which had trailed in second from last. He was ashamed of the feeling now, but at the time he'd been seized with a savage desire to snatch the whip from the jockey's hand and flog the wretched beast himself. That was a year ago. Since then, financially speaking, he'd sprung a major leak. Logically, he knew each new race was not the answer to his problems, but he couldn't seem to stop himself from throwing good money after bad.

He had once seen himself as debonair, swashbuckling, carefree, reckless, but losing money you couldn't afford was pathetic and seedy. He didn't like to think of himself as a loser, but even that he could just about handle.

What he couldn't cope with was another situation, also one of his own making. He had been blind, stupid and greedy enough to break the ethical code he had sworn to uphold. Not to mention the law. The money Patrick Newell had offered had seemed like the answer to his prayers. Instead, he'd allowed himself to be snookered, blackmailed. He couldn't do a damned thing except pay, and pay, and pay. Otherwise his house of cards would crash to the ground.

***

Sonny, as David's executor, set probate in motion. Colin helped Bea go through David's in-box and address book, and started making calls. Will pitched in too when he arrived. Sometimes the three brothers were on the phone simultaneously, creating a kind of low-pitched hum in Bea's living room, like the droning of bees. They all developed a patter. 'I'm sorry to have to tell you...' 'I'm ringing about Mr David Grahame...' 'I'm afraid I have some bad news...'

'Bloody hell,' said Will to Sandra when she came in with mugs of tea. 'It's like working for the gloomiest call centre in the world.'

Colin related his conversation with the nurse. Sonny frowned. 'We can't be doing with all that again. We'd better do as the woman says and fix her up with a counsellor.'

Colin and Will looked at each other.

'I know, I know. Oh ye of little faith. You may think it's New Age bollocks, but it'll help her.' He googled a psychiatrist named Kaye Borthwick. 'Oh good. She's still practising. Still in Lincolnshire, too.'

'Who's she?' asked Colin.

'She's a shrink who helped Paddy when he was a kid. You were too young to remember.'

Colin's lip curled. 'And you want a recommendation from *her*?'

'She worked wonders with Paddy. Mam told me about it.'

'Wonders,' said Colin, shaking his head. 'I'll take Anna

for a kickabout in the park. Would Nick like to come?' he asked Will.

'Yeah. I'll get his trainers on.' While Colin and Will got the two children ready, Sonny called Kaye Borthwick's office. He was put straight through.

He explained who he was.

'I remember your family very well,' she said.

'My family? I thought you only saw Patrick.'

'An individual is often representative of the whole.'

'I'm not sure Paddy entirely represents us,' said Sonny. 'But he's not the reason I'm calling. It's about our sister. Her husband died.'

'Oh. I'm terribly sorry.'

'Thank you. I was hoping you'd be able to recommend someone for her to see.'

'I'd be delighted to see her.'

'I mean London-based.'

'Oh.' She sounded disappointed. 'Does she need psychiatric help?'

'No. Not as extreme as all that.' He hoped it was true. Bea had been fine for years. He had stopped worrying about her because of David. He'd loved her. Made her happy. 'I'd like to find her a good grief counsellor. She's taking it very hard, as you'd expect, but... the thing is – well it was years ago, but when she was a teenager she tried...' Sonny paused. Silence on the subject had been hard-wired into them.

'To kill herself,' Borthwick prompted.

'Yes,' said Sonny. He found himself disliking her. After a few words over the phone. It was irrational.

'I'm sorry, Mr Newell. That sounded terrible. The grapevine in a small town is very efficient.'

Sonny shook his head. Gossip. Of course.

'It was a long time ago,' she continued. 'but I remember it particularly clearly because of the connection with your brother Paddy. He'd moved on by then, of course.'

Sonny remembered Paddy 'moving on' only too well. Paddy had left home on the day he'd written his last A level exam. It had been terrible for their mother. And Paddy being Paddy had made sure it was terrible for everyone else too. She'd planned a surprise family dinner for him after his last exam. Mam had been so excited, rushing around with banners and balloons. She'd made Paddy's favourite dinner. Steak, chips, mushrooms, peas. Sirloin steak for a family as big as theirs cost the earth, but she'd really pushed the boat out. She'd made his favourite pudding too. Baked Alaska, something like that. Something complicated that took a lot of trouble. Quite fitting, really.

Their dad had come from work early. Mam had asked him to bring some lager home, and a couple of bottles of wine. It was probably total shite, the wine that he'd bought, but nobody knew any different then. Sonny the student would have been flabbergasted at what his adult self was prepared to shell out for a decent bottle. Being allowed a drink was the mark of manhood in their family. They waited for Paddy to come home. Colin came back without Bea, who was about eight at the time. She had some sort of after-school thing, singing or piano. Must've been piano, as Bea never sang again after the nativity. Sonny remembered there had been a bit of a tussle about whether she could skip it so she could be there to surprise Paddy with everyone else. As always, Edie's will had prevailed.

They carried on waiting. Dad even cracked open some of the lagers. He gave one to Sonny and another to Sam. Will and Colin were allowed a sip each. Mam was fretting they'd have supped the lot by the time Paddy came home.

Finally Bea turned up in a right old state. Paddy had lain in wait for her. He knew all about the party, he'd said. She was to go home and tell them they could stick their steak dinner. He was done with school and done with the family. He'd taken a packed bag with him to school that morning with everything he wanted. They could burn the rest. He had a train ticket out of town.

'Where's he going?' asked their mam, ashen-faced.

'He wouldn't say,' said Bea.

'You must know!'

'I don't, I swear!'

'If she knew she'd tell us,' said their dad. 'He's gone to London, I reckon. It's all he's ever wanted to do.'

'You should've found out!' said their mam to Bea. 'Why did you come home without finding out? How will we find him?'

'Leave her alone!' Sonny had yelled. 'You're always laying into her. We're better off without him.' Things had really gone downhill from there. Paddy was the cause of so much misery, as per usual, and Bea got the blame. There were some terrible ructions in their house that day. Nothing new there. No wonder this woman remembered Paddy so well.

'Mr Newell?'

'Sorry! I was miles away. So do you think you can recommend someone?' He wanted to end the call without being impolite.

'I do know of one exceptionally good therapist practising in London. I've known her for years. She's highly respected in family trauma, breakdown and bereavement. She's written papers, books, articles, speaks at conferences, you name it.'

'That sounds just the ticket,' said Sonny. He felt he'd been a bit harsh in his initial judgement of Ms Borthwick. 'She's not too... up herself, is she?'

'What do you mean?'

'Bea needs someone patient-focused.'

'We call them clients these days. I assure you Rebecca has her feet very firmly planted on terra firma. She has to keep her hand in on the practice side. Otherwise she'd have nothing to write about. Theoretically speaking, of course,' she hastily added.

'What did you say her name was?'

'Rebecca Gladwyn. Her office is in Marylebone. She's very busy, but I'm certain she'll find a window for Bea if the referral comes from me.'

'You even remember her name. My sister's, I mean. Considering that it must be thirty-odd years since you saw Paddy. Longer, even.'

'I remember your sister very well.'

'Do you? How?'

'As a matter of fact, I saw her sing. At a school nativity.'

'Not *the* nativity?'

'Yes. Not something you forget in a hurry. Her distress was very painful to witness.' She sounded sincere. He wondered why he'd responded so badly to her during the early part of the call. He supposed it was a reaction to talking about something so deeply buried. It was like stirring poison that had settled a long time ago.

'Did you have a kid in the play?'

'Oh no, er... I don't have children. I've never been married.'

'Why would someone without a child sit through something as painful as a junior school nativity play?'

'It was all a long time ago now, but I do remember Paddy telling me I shouldn't miss it. Anyway, I must let you go. I'll email you Rebecca's contact details. Be sure to tell her that I referred you.'

'Hmm? Yes, I will. Thanks.'

Sonny was thoughtful as he put the phone down.

'What did she say?' asked Will.

'She recommended someone. It's funny, she still remembers Paddy and all of us.'

'Why wouldn't she? He's a shrink's wet dream.'

'Yeah, I guess he is. We all are.'

'Speak for yourself, mate.'

'Oh come on, we've all been scarred in one way or another, especially Bea. We just deal with it in different ways. Now David's gone, she needs this more than ever. Talking to someone professional will help her process her feelings,' he said.

'Makes her sound like a factory,' said Will.

'Bottling up your issues...'

'Her husband's just died. You could say that's a bit of an issue.'

'You know what I mean. David dying is going to bring a whole lot of buried stuff flooding back to the surface.'

'And how much is this emotional plumbing going to cost?'

'Sixty quid an hour. Of course I'll...'

'Flamin' Nora. I'm in the wrong sodding job.'

# CHAPTER SEVEN

Odolina fizzed each time the phone rang in the bar. Her mind drifted. She confused the orders, or forgot them completely. Luis whispered in her ear while she rubbed the same spot on one of the wooden tables with a damp cloth over and over: 'You think if you rub hard enough you'll see your face in that wood, Odo?' He clapped his hands in exasperation.

The Pasadena closed when it closed. It depended how many paying customers remained in the bar. It was astonishing how long some people could eke out a drink. Odolina was usually happy to stay until closing, but that evening her head ached. The bar was still jumping. Luis was pouring tequila into shot glasses.

'Luis, I'm sorry I've been distracted,' said Odolina. 'I've been a prima donna, no?'

He winked at her. 'You okay?'

'I'm tired. I want to go home. I'll come in early tomorrow.'

'If you stay another half-hour, I'll give you a ride home.'

'I want to go now.'

'Okay, *cara*. See you tomorrow.'

It was a fifteen-minute walk home. Her mother nagged her not to walk by herself at night, advice she'd ignored for years. She kept her wits about her. Body language. She'd read in a magazine that the fearful are targeted more frequently than the confident. This made sense. It was only human nature to exploit weakness. Violent crime was bad in the cities, but rare in her small town, except for drunks fighting. There was not much else to do. There were people in that town who would give their eye teeth to work in Luis's bar. Most of Santa Ana made their living from sugar cane, in the fields or the factory.

The streets were deserted. She crossed the road to pass Bebo's, the other bar in town. There were a few people outside. Even the most dedicated barfly stepped outside once in a while to escape the foetid smokiness of the bar. She did that too at the Pasadena. She'd go outside and stand on the verandah for a smoke and watch the men playing cards. They'd summon her to stand behind them to bring them luck, and she'd comply if she was in the mood.

Her white T-shirt glowed in the moonlight, and her long legs emerging from her denim mini attracted a few calls. She ignored them. She continued along the narrow street past the grocer's. The crescent moon lit the way clearly enough once she was out of town. She headed for the shortcut home, a dirt path on the edge of the sugar cane fields.

As a child, she'd often hidden in the cane, usually to escape a beating. The cane was off limits, but the children in Santa Ana were feral and persisted in daring each other. Snakes, rats, spiders and other such creatures made a home for themselves in the dark between the thickening stalks. There came a point in the growing cycle where the top of the cane plants formed a complete canopy, blocking all light to the ground. The leaves entangled themselves into an impenetrable jungle until the crop was burned just before the harvest.

Odolina loved seeing the cane fields on fire. At dusk the red flames met a red sky and she felt a bittersweet yearning for a different life as she listened to the crackle of the perishing leaves. Cane rats as big as cats scuttled out of the edges of the fields in a high panic, some with terrible burns. She had eaten plenty of barbecued cane rat. It tasted like murky chicken. There was a certain irony in the creatures escaping a field on fire only to end up on a skewer.

Out of habit, she checked the road both ways, despite the quiet. People rode bikes with no lights and freewheeled their cars to save petrol. As she turned her head, she became aware of a shadow in her peripheral vision, and saw the glowing red of a cigarette tip. She sucked in her breath. 'Who's that?' she asked in a clear voice.

The shadow took a deep drag from the cigarette, then flicked the butt. It spiralled in the air before being swallowed by a patch of long grass. Odolina's eyes were accustomed to the dark, and she could see the whites of an enormous pair of eyes.

'Chico, is that you?' A regular in the bar, Chico was fond of playing practical jokes. Scaring her half to death on her way home in the middle of the night was exactly his idea of fun. The shadow moved closer. Terror struck Odolina when she realised those white eyes were painted on a mask.

She did not scream. She saved her energy for flight. The shadow blocked her way back into the town. She sprinted across the road. Once on the other side, she had two choices. She could run down the path towards home. She was a good runner, but any reasonably fit man would outclass her, especially over distance. Or she could run into the cane.

The cane was between six and seven feet tall, about half its full potential height. It was still possible to run between the rows. Odolina kicked off her flip-flops and dived down a random row, running through the leaves for around fifteen feet before she cut across two rows, forcing her way between the thick stalks. She was terrified he might be right behind her. It was still possible to run at speed, although she was forced to use her arms to protect her eyes and face from the long cane leaves that hung in tangled clusters from either side. Like long paper swords, they cut into her skin as she flew through them. She dropped her bag. Her white T-shirt advertised her position. Still running, she pulled it over her head, but kept it around her arms as protection from the cutting leaves. She heard the snap of a cane shoot close behind her. A surge of fear spurred her on.

She sprinted down the rows. She cut across rows to the right at random, keeping her eye out for gaps in the cane. The leaves hid her from view but they betrayed her position with their furious rustling. The noise was too loud for her to judge how close he was. She did not dare stop to listen.

She kept moving on the diagonal. Each cane field was a hectare in area, separated by a gap big enough for a tractor. She aimed to emerge close to the north-east corner of the cane field at the intersection. With enough of a head start, she could run into any one of the other three fields. She'd go in far enough to be hidden from view. Then she'd remain stock-still. He would be forced to search for her. First, he'd have to pick the right field, and while he was thrashing through the leaves, she could edge silently away. Even if he picked the right field, he'd have to be lucky to pick the right row.

She emerged into the open. She was too far from the intersection. It was a good forty feet away. She could not resist the urge to turn round. She heard him thrashing around in the cane. Too close. She darted for the cane field in front of her. Her foot caught against an irrigation pipe. She hurtled forward. Her stomach lurched as she flew into the air. She raised her arms to break her fall. Pain seared through her shoulder, ricocheting to her elbow, but she scrambled to her feet and propelled herself forward in an almighty effort to pick up speed. She heard him yell out. She couldn't breathe for panic. She dived back into the cane. He would see her point of entry. There was nothing she could do about it. She had to keep going. She had to keep ducking between the rows until she could elude him. He was bound to get tired. She ignored her own exhaustion.

He gasped and roared behind her. She was slammed to the ground, landing flat on her chest. His weight forced all the air out of her lungs. He lay on her back, gasping, allowing himself time to regain his breath. She could not draw air into her lungs. She felt his heavy breath against her ear and his hot and heaving sweatiness against her bare back. The strength ebbed from her limbs. The pain in her shoulder was intense.

Struggle was useless. She may as well have been nailed to the ground. She grew weaker and weaker from lack of air. Then she felt the pressure in her chest release, as he raised himself onto his elbows above her. She took in a great gulp of air. A wave of nausea hit her. She wriggled in an effort to turn to fight. He raised himself further, allowing her to turn. The mask hung askew from his face. She heard him curse as she reached up to gouge his eyes. It was a feeble effort. He grabbed her flailing wrists and pinned them to the ground above her head. She cried out as the pain jolted through her shoulder. He let go of her wrist and punched her hard across the jaw. She tasted blood and felt the gravel of a cracked tooth in her mouth. He punched her again, smashing her cheekbone. Her ears rang. She no longer used her free arm to attack. She held it up against her face in a pathetic effort to ward him off. He hit her again. Each time it hurt less. The fourth time didn't hurt at all.

# CHAPTER EIGHT

The doorbell rang. Ten o'clock sharp, and Sam must've expected me to be waiting, in my hat and coat, clutching my handbag, suitcase at the ready. I took the stairs slowly, holding on to the banister. It's just as well to pay attention at my age. The kids have been on at me to get a stairlift, but I won't hear of it. I'm not a cripple.

'Come in, duck, I'm not quite ready,' I said after he'd pecked my cheek. 'Who's that in the car?'

'A friend of Bea and David's. He's coming down with us.'

'Do you want to ask him in?'

'He'll be all right,' said Sam. 'You'll not be long, will you?'

'Give me a minute or two.' I pointed to that morning's *Daily Mail*, still unopened. 'Paper's there if you want a read.'

It's a horrible want of manners being late. I don't drive, so I hate to keep people waiting, but I was torn about what to wear to the funeral. I'd read a piece recently in the paper that said black was no longer the thing. People change things for change's sake. It's ruddy irritating. I was tempted to wear my purple suit. It's a dark, muted purple, more like aubergine really, but I couldn't bear it if it turned out to be wrong. Some of David's family are ever so... well. I'd hate to show myself up.

I had to decide. I fixed on the purple suit but decided to also take my long black coat to wear over it. If the suit was wrong, I could always keep the coat on. Churches were chilly at the best of times. It would be fine for the big day. I chided myself for using that expression.

I wondered at David having a church funeral. He and Bea hadn't bothered with a church wedding. They hadn't even got engaged. They'd sneaked off to Thailand on holiday and come back, bold as brass, married. I'd assumed the patter of little feet couldn't be too far away, but no. I felt a bit deprived, I must say. I never got the chance to be Mother of the Bride at a swanky ceremony. God knows I've been Mother of the Groom often enough.

I quickly flicked through the wardrobe for the coat. It was hanging over a sky-blue silk suit I'd last worn to Sonny's wedding. I don't know why I've still got it, in truth. Should have got rid of it years ago. I'd thought it perfect for a smart London wedding, but then I met Gina's parents.

Gina was from Nantucket, but she and Sonny had both been working at Morgan Stanley at the time they got married, so they'd decided to tie the knot in London.

Gina's father was white-haired but tall and good-looking, and he'd worn an immaculate morning suit with a sprig in his buttonhole. Her mother wore an oyster silk dress that draped so perfectly around her it looked as if it had been specially made. Her strappy high heels flaunted her perfectly painted toes. I'd never wear open-toed shoes, to a wedding nor anywhere else.

Gina's father took his wife by the hand and twirled her towards him. 'You look cuter than a bug,' he said, and she laughed. So glamorous, the pair of them, and so together that the whole day was ruined for me. They were far too polite to ask why George and I were at opposite ends of the top table. No doubt the bride had briefed them. She'd had her finger on every detail.

I draped the coat over my arm and called down the stairs to Sam.

'You couldn't come up and pick up my suitcase could you, duck? Save me from dragging it down myself.'

"Course, Mam,' he said, and bounded up, taking the stairs two at a time. I was forever telling the kids off for doing it when they were little as it made such a racket. Now the house is like a tomb.

When we got to the car, a tall, blond man got out and introduced himself. Gordon Something. He offered me the passenger seat, but I settled in the back.

'We'll be going straight to Bea's then?' I said, rooting around my bag for my compact.

'Actually, Mam, you and I are going to Sonny's. Colin and Will are at Bea's. Sandra and Nick, too, so she's got a bit of a full house,' said Sam.

'That still leaves a room free,' I said. 'She needs her mother with her.'

'I think she's got one or two staying from David's side as well,' Sam mumbled. He coughed and leaned over the steering wheel. 'We'll go round soon as we've dropped our stuff off at Sonny's.'

I wanted to say something about the arrangements, but I didn't like to with Gordon in the car. He seemed nice enough, but I felt he should have made his own way to London. This was a time for family.

'Were you at school with Bea?' I asked.

'No. I met her and David on holiday in Spain a few years back. I was with my mother and her boyfriend.'

'Boyfriend?'

'I know, it's a silly word to use to describe him. He's almost eighty.'

'Why do they not get married?'

He laughed. 'My mother's been married a few times already. Perhaps the novelty's worn off.'

'And do you like him?'

'Alfonso? Yes. Very much.'

'And he and your mother are friends of Bea and David?'

'Oh yes. She and Bea have become quite close.'

'Close?'

'Yes. They see each other quite often. My mother's

terribly fond of her.'

I took this in.

'Do you live near Sammy, then?'

'No, I live here. Same as you.'

'Never!'

'I work in Sutton Bridge, not too far away. I'm an engineer. I live in the Old Vicarage. I'm Bea's tenant. Have been for a while now. It's a lovely house.'

I did not like to be reminded that Bea owned that house.

After a while I closed my eyes, pretending to be asleep. Not that it bothered Sam or Gordon. They seemed to know each other. Why this bothered me so much, I couldn't say.

After a couple of hours' driving, we stopped off for a bite to eat. Gordon and Sam split the bill between them, and wouldn't let me chip in. I had a glass of wine with my fish and chips. It perked my mood up a bit, so I made a bit more of an effort to be friendly.

After we'd dropped Gordon off at his mother's, a smart white house off Gloucester Road, we were let into Sonny's by his housekeeper, Aditi. Her husband, Jamling, carried my case up to my usual room, the one overlooking the garden. I loved staying at Sonny's, but I should have been at Bea's. What were people to think at me being kept at arm's length like that?

Jamling's a Gurkha. He used to be in the army. I know it's awful how the Gurkhas have been treated after all they've done for our country, but Jamling and Aditi are on to a very good wicket, let me tell you.

Sonny doesn't like staying at hotels every time he's over, so he doesn't want to let the house, and he doesn't like leaving it empty between times. An empty house is just asking for trouble. Jamling and Aditi get the basement flat in return for taking care of the house.

If you ask me, the basement flat's too good to let folk

you hardly know live there for free.

'They won't be living there for free,' Sonny said. 'They'll be taking care of the house. Jamling's a good maintenance man. Aditi's a fabulous cook.'

'What if they have dozens moving in as soon as your back's turned? I've read about people like that in the paper. Squatters' rights and all that. You want to be careful, Sonny.'

'That'll never happen.'

'How can you be so sure?'

'They've got honour.'

'Now there's an old-fashioned word. Well don't say I didn't warn you.'

I have to admit Gina's done a good job of doing the house up. I dread to think of the money that's been spent on it. Not that it's any of my business.

I couldn't help thinking I'd missed a trick when we were all under one roof so many years ago. So much brown and beige. I'd never given a thought about nice colours and space-saving like people do these days. God knows we could have done with a bit more decoration and a lot more space. Instead, I'd put up and shut up without even thinking about it and now I'm on my own it hardly seems worth the bother.

Jamling's good-looking with a cheeky smile. I have to admit that he's loyal, and he seems to work hard.

As for Aditi, she's addicted to daytime telly. She gets quite worked up and yells at the people on Jeremy Kyle. Sonny and Gina think it's hilarious. Nobody complains, so it's hardly my place. Mind you, she's good with the children, and she cooks like a dream. Her butter chicken is like tasting a little piece of heaven. I asked her to show me how she did it. Mine wasn't the same. I suspect she skipped some vital ingredient, even though I was watching her like a hawk.

I love foreign food. Me and George had never had the money to eat in restaurants. Then little places started popping up: Indian, Bangladeshi, Chinese places that weren't too expensive and once I'd been pushed into going, I loved them. Eating veg I'd never heard of cooked in ways I'd never imagine. I remember my first taste of sweet and sour pork. Those little pineapple chunks in the sauce. Who'd have ever thought it? Now people take it for granted that they can eat whatever they want whenever they want it and can buy things like avocados from a supermarket in the winter. I'd never heard of an avocado when I was a girl.

No matter how good her cooking, I'd not want someone not family living in my house. They've been handed everything on a plate. Gina's sorted their British citizenship, they get sent home to Nepal to visit their grandchildren every year, they don't pay a single bill and they get paid a decent whack on top. Sonny calls it a retainer. And to add insult to injury, Jamling does outside work too. Building jobs, plumbing and mechanical work. Sonny encourages it! 'So long as they take care of us and the house is in good nick, they're free to do whatever they want.'

Gina says they're part of the family. It niggles at me. Let's face it: blood's blood, and that's the tie that binds.

# CHAPTER NINE

Bea woke with a pain in her ear as she'd squashed a pair of headphones against her pillow. She'd been listening to David's iPod, the soundtrack to his life. The batteries were dead. The silence was filled with the creaking of the mattress in her head. The sound would stay with her for the rest of her life.

The room was in darkness except for a sliver of light coming from the doorway. Will must have left it open. She had a raging thirst. She'd slept in her clothes and they stuck to her. She picked up her watch and turned it towards the light. Twelve minutes to six. Time was ticking. Her mother would soon be in London. Her brothers let her be, but that wasn't Edie's way.

She pushed the duvet back. Her skin prickled in the sudden cold and she felt a rush of blood to the head. She caught hold of the bedstead and shut her eyes for a moment before she padded to the bathroom. She drank from the tooth mug, filling it repeatedly. Back in the bedroom, the walls seemed to close in on her. The room had taken on a strange aspect. It wasn't their bedroom any more. She'd intended to strip and get into the shower, but her energy deserted her and she lay back on the bed staring upwards.

There was a knock at the door. It was Sonny. He came in with a cup of tea and put his hand on her forehead, as if she were an invalid.

'Bean, I got the details of a counsellor. Someone you can talk to. If you're all right with it, I'll make an appointment for you.'

She continued to gaze at the ceiling. She had no desire to see anyone.

'It's to guide you through the process. That's what it is. A process. A journey, if you like.'

'It's not a process! It's...' She tried to form the words.

'It's terrible seeing you in such pain.'

Her anger evaporated. What made her so bloody special? All over the world, right at that instant, people were suffering as she was. People lost their children, their families, their homes, their livelihoods, their status, their identities, their way of life. Some had to watch their children starve. She was spoilt beyond belief.

'I hate the thought of speaking to a stranger.'

'Maybe you are Mam's daughter after all. Look at it this way. She won't be a stranger for long. Not once you've told her your life history.'

'She?'

'Yeah. I got a recommendation. For someone who specialises in bereavement and family issues. She's based in Marylebone. She can see you the day after the funeral.'

To talk to someone she'd never seen about things she never discussed. A woman paid to listen, to probe into her life and tell her when her hour was up. Another rich bitch with nothing better to do than lie on a couch and whinge.

She had an attack of vertigo. Panic seized her. She gripped Sonny's arm.

'Steady, Bean,' he said, and put his arm round her. She clutched at him as if she were drowning.

'I can't bear it,' she said.

He held her to him. 'You have to, but you don't have to do it alone. Let us help you. Let this woman help you. What have you got to lose?'

*** 

The night before the funeral, she lay awake in the dark. David's last night replayed itself in her head. She lifted her head and smacked it against the pillow to drive out the sound of the squeaking mattress.

She put on her dressing gown and a thick pair of socks and padded downstairs to the living room. She turned on the light and looked around. She wasn't sure what to do. The telly might wake the others up and she didn't want her ears assaulted by noise. Reading was not remotely feasible. She lay on the sofa, trying to appreciate the sensation of being awake when everyone else was asleep. She'd always loved having the night to herself, but that was Before.

Someone whispered, 'Oh it's you.'

She gasped in shock and sat bolt upright.

It was Will. She put her hand on her heart to steady it.

'You frightened me half to—' She stopped herself.

'Sorry, Bean. I didn't mean to scare you. I was working in the kitchen,' he said, still whispering. 'It's warmer in there.'

She followed him. His laptop was on the table, glowing in the semi-darkness. A sentence caught her attention. *'Why's the baby so still, Mam?'* Her spine prickled.

Will fetched the milk from the fridge and poured some into a pan.

'Want some cocoa?'

'Yes please.'

He poured more milk into the pan and fired up one of the gas rings. He adjusted the heat before putting the pan on to boil.

'Are you writing about Timmy, Will?' she asked.

He glanced at her in surprise. 'He died before you were even born.'

'I know. But I grew up with him all the same. The idea of him, anyway. Do you remember him?'

'Aye, I do. I remember when he died. Paddy found him.'

'I didn't know.'

'I can still hear Mam screaming.'

Bea put her hand to her mouth.

'It was terrible. Our Uncle Jackie was looking after us. Mam had gone out. He fell asleep, Uncle Jackie did. Sammy and me used to tickle his moustache and he'd gurn in his sleep. We thought it was the funniest thing ever. Anyway, Mam was narked with me about something and dragged me upstairs. There he was. Timmy, dead.'

Bea shuddered. 'I thought you said Paddy found him?'

'He did. He told us Timmy was dead even before Mam came back, but we paid him no mind. He was always making stuff up. Anyways, the book's not about Timmy at all. It's about a girl who kills her baby sister.'

'So it's totally fictional?'

'Everything I write is fictional.'

'Mam's not going to like it.'

'Mam never likes anything.'

\*\*\*

The night after Paddy got expelled, George asked me to go with him to the Purves' place. He wanted Paddy to come with us to say he was sorry. We were to ask for permission to visit the girl in hospital. What George meant is that Paddy should apologise for being a monster, and we should apologise for having a monster as a son.

I wouldn't go. Don't get me wrong, it's not that I didn't feel for the little girl. I did, more than I can say. I was Paddy's mother though, and he needed to know I was on his side. George stalked out of the house on his own, clutching a present for her, a doll. He said it was just as well he wasn't taking Paddy as it was so bloody obvious he didn't give a tinker's cuss about what he'd done. We'd never rowed in front of the kids before. Bea kicked off, and she set the others in motion. The older boys skulked off to the room they shared upstairs. The only kid not affected was Paddy.

I tried to explain to George that just because someone isn't bleeding doesn't mean they don't feel pain, but he just shook his head.

The kids were all in bed by the time he came back. He told me the girl's parents had been very decent. He said the little girl had been shy at first, but they were soon playing noughts and crosses. She was a lovely little thing apparently, and had loved the doll.

By the time we went to bed that evening we weren't speaking. It wasn't enough for me to know she'd been badly burned. I had to also know that she'd always have a scar on the back of her head and neck, and there was a big patch where hair would never grow unless she had a skin graft. He was almost crying as he said it. He wasn't just rubbing salt in my wounds, he was cutting them deeper first. I asked him if he wanted Paddy's severed head on a platter.

Things were pretty cool between us for a few days. The kids were miserable with us not speaking, and tiptoed around like a bomb was about to go off. I was damned if I was going to make up with him. It was always George who threw in the towel first. It was just a question of waiting.

We had Sunday lunch in silence. Normally it was hard to be heard in the din of chattering. George turned to Will and asked him how he'd enjoyed Sunday School, just for something to say.

'It was okay. Did you know that if you're bad God will punch you?'

Everyone started laughing, even Bea and Colin, although they didn't understand. George's eyes met mine over the table. We never said anything, but that night George reached for me and things got back on track again.

It's a funny thing, life. Sometimes the thing you fear most turns out to be for the best. Harefield House was the making of Paddy. He discovered computers, and was hooked. I always knew he was clever as the others. Just needed something to sink his teeth into. Something that really grabbed him. Computers fired him up in a way I'd never seen before. Paddy got into the odd scrape at Harefield, but on the whole they knew how to keep him in check. Things got better at home. I'd been convinced Paddy going to a different school, one for 'bad boys', would be a disaster, would bring shame on us and push him and the other kids further apart.

I should have let Penharris expel him first time round. It sounds like a joke, doesn't it? The mother who'd do anything for her child. George never suspected a thing. In a thousand ways that's worse, betraying the trust of someone who trusts you. The day it happened, George kissed me when he got back from work, as per usual. All through dinner, I couldn't look him in the eye. That night, he pulled me towards him in his sleep. He always was a heat-seeking missile. I lay in the dark with my eyes wide open and my lips pursed together to keep from crying. My punishment was to live with the knowledge that I did what I did with Penharris for nothing.

*** 

I've never seen such a mishmash of people at one funeral. His mother, strapped into a wheelchair and away with the fairies. Hadn't the faintest idea who Bea was or any notion that David was dead. A small mercy, I suppose. It's not right burying your own child. She'd been a tall woman, and I remember David describing her as 'formidably intelligent'. She's just a poor scrap now, with no sense in her head.

Diana was there, his ex-wife. Bea should have barred her. Anyone would have thought she was the widow in that Cruella de Vil get-up. Those poor kids. David's, I mean. My heart went out to them. How their mother could show them up like that. No matter how posh your voice or fancy your clothes, breeding will out. She was making eyes at my Paddy. Made a beeline for him soon as the service was over.

Hilary read out a poem. Something about being master of my fate, 'I am the captain of my soul'. Her voice rang out clear as a bell even though she nearly broke down in the middle. Bea's told me she's in all the plays at school. You could tell, believe me. It was a sock in the eye to her mother when she sat next to Bea in the church. Good for her.

As for that awful Dorothy woman, Lady Something or other, with her funny old Spanish fancy man and that horrible little dog. Bringing a dog to a funeral, I ask you. It escaped her handbag and jumped on the coffin, yapping and wagging its tail. People laughed. Can you believe it? Some gangly man had to chase after it. When he turned round I realised it was Gordon.

Dorothy brought a hip flask. I saw her passing it to Bea, I'm sorry to say. David's stepsister thought Dorothy was Bea's mother. No wonder, the way she hovered round her, sucking up the limelight. Some people are ghouls around death. Foul-weather friends. I stepped forward to be introduced. I told her I'd always wanted to meet all of David's family, but was sorry it took such a terrible occasion to make it happen. She must've welcomed a bit of dignity. Thank heavens Bea didn't blub in the church. She's done enough of that at home.

David's stepsister asked if I was staying with Bea. It put me on the spot something terrible. I said I'd be staying a few days afterwards, once everyone had left. In my defence, I thought it would be a good idea even before I said it. All I had to do was cancel the milk and papers.

The wake was at Sonny's house. Bea's boss came along, not only to the funeral, but afterwards as well. It was decent of him. A couple of other people from her work came along too. Another bloke, I forget his name, and a Martha or Mandy. She got tipsy and told me all about her troubles having babies. The things people are happy to discuss with complete strangers.

Diana didn't come to the wake. If she'd had the cheek to even try, I would have given her a piece of my mind. How someone like David could marry a mare like that defeats me. He really was one in a million. He could charm the knickers off a nun, as my dad would say. A first from Oxford, a scholarship to Harrow, a charmed existence – all wiped away in a flash.

I never got much of a chance at education. I did well at school and was forever being told I was clever. My teachers said I could do really well for myself. Become a legal secretary or a PA. I know now, years later, how funny it must seem that we aimed so low; for all we were told it was the stars. Nowadays, I'd have gone to university or been a presenter on the telly. I could have done anything. I probably wouldn't have had so many babies. Well, people don't any more, do they? Mind you it was pretty unusual even then. People thought we were Catholics. They didn't stop to think how much each one could be treasured and loved, no matter how many you have. If I had my time over… well. No good comes from dwelling on what might have been.

# CHAPTER TEN

'Mrs Newell?' said Rebecca Gladwyn. She hoped her smile conveyed compassionate understanding. *She looks a lot like Paddy*, thought Rebecca. It had been years, but she remembered those few weeks that Paddy had stayed with her when he first got to London only too well. At her husband's insistence, Rebecca had had to throw the boy out. Bloody Kaye and her pet projects. The sister was good-looking, like her brother, although grief and rage came off her like static.

'Call me Bea.'

'Oh, sorry... I meant Grahame. Newell's your maiden name, isn't it?' They shook hands.

'I use both.'

'There's no lift, I'm afraid.'

Rebecca led her up two short flights of stairs, conscious that her bottom wobbled with each step. These days her trousers had elasticated waists. Especially necessary after blowing her diet at the weekend. Her husband had disappeared with his golfing buddies to Marbella, so she had taken the train to Lincoln to stay with Kaye, who was a feeder. A feeder and a booze enabler. Halfway up the stairs, she had to pause for breath. She tossed her grey bob to one side and addressed Bea over her shoulder.

'Did you find it okay?'

'My brother drove me here.'

'Ah yes. The one who made the appointment.'

'No, that's Sonny. My brother Colin brought me.'

By the time they got to the top of the stairs, Rebecca was puffing like an asthmatic walrus. Her attempts to hide it made it worse.

'Are you all right?' asked Bea.

'Thank you, yes. Terribly unfit, I'm afraid.' She preferred not to tell her patients about the emphysema. She wished she'd never told Kaye. Kaye fussed over her enough as it was. She'd be insufferable if they actually lived together. Rebecca was perfectly content with weekends every now and again and the odd holiday. Her husband's love of golf gave her plenty of opportunities to fit Kaye into her life. Their liaison had continued undiscovered for thirty-eight years.

Rebecca's therapy room doubled as an office. Her desk, computer and phone were in one corner. The room was dominated by a large salmon pink sofa and a matching armchair by the window. The walls were sea green, supposedly a calming colour. Between the sofa and the chair was a small coffee table, on which stood a box of tissues and a bottle of water with two clean tumblers. A large green perspex crate stood in the far corner, overspilling with toys.

Rebecca flopped into the armchair. The sunlight streamed in from the window behind her. Bea had to squint at her.

'Would you like the blinds down?' asked Rebecca.

'Let me do it.'

Rebecca was glad not to have to get up again.

'I'm terribly sorry about your husband,' she said, unable to suppress a cough.

'Thank you,' said Bea, blinking rapidly. Rebecca gestured towards the box of tissues.

'You're lucky to have family who care about you. It struck me very strongly when I spoke to your brother.'

'What did he tell you?'

Rebecca hesitated. 'He told me a bit about your family background and your early life. I'd like to hear about it directly.'

'It doesn't have much to do with losing my husband.'

'It gives me a sense of what has shaped you, and the extent you've had to deal with loss in the past,' she said. She was conscious she sounded airy. She softened her tone. 'It gives me an idea of your resilience, your inner resources, what kind of support you have to rely on.'

'Oh,' said Bea, clearly unconvinced.

'Bea, you're radiating grief like heat from a fire. You have to find a way to channel it. You have to endure it, and in time it will lessen.'

'I wasn't looking for a shortcut,' said Bea.

'You're probably familiar with the stages of grief? Denial, anger, bargaining and finally, acceptance,' said Rebecca. She did not know why she listened to Kaye. Kaye had assured her that Bea would be fantastic material for her current book.

'You will thank me,' she'd said.

'The poor woman needs help, Kaye,' she'd replied. 'She doesn't need to be research fodder.'

'I don't see why you can't work with her and take what you need at the same time. You've done that to me for years.'

Rebecca had been forced to admit that Bea was in a unique position to discuss the effects of birth order and favouritism, given the family dynamics as Kaye had described them. It was plain she didn't want to be there though. 'It sounds very clear-cut, doesn't it?' Rebecca continued, 'but the point is you may not go through the stages in that order, and some of them may take more time to work through, and even then you may skip and regress between them.' Rebecca was aware she sounded wordy and theoretical. Up her own arse, her husband would say. 'Before we go into all that, I think it's quite important to establish the possibilities and limitations of the therapeutic process. What are you hoping to achieve from it?'

'Nothing, really. I'm here because of Sonny. He nagged me to come. He's worried about me. They all are. They think I...'

'Yes?' said Rebecca, after a pause. Of course, Rebecca knew about Bea's early suicide bid. Kaye had filled her in on everything.

Bea was silent.

'Are they worried you may harm yourself?'

Bea's colour began to rise and her chin trembled. She mastered herself after a few moments. She stood up, looping her bag over her shoulder. 'I'm sorry to have wasted your time. There are things I prefer not to discuss.'

'Repressing—'

'Repression is underrated!'

Rebecca laughed, in spite of herself. 'I'm sorry. I'm laughing because if everyone took that view, my profession would be wiped out. Please don't leave. Let's start all over again. The last thing I wanted to do was antagonise you. How about we have a cup of tea and we can talk? About nothing in particular, if you like, and you go ahead and leave after that if you feel like it. How does that sound?'

Bea hesitated, then perched on the edge of the sofa.

Rebecca picked up the phone on the desk. 'Priyanka? Two teas, please. Thanks.' She replaced the receiver. 'Now how should we do this?'

'Why do you do this for a living?'

'I've always been fascinated by people and what makes them tick. I love being able to help people reach their full potential. Whether that's helping them to work through negative emotions to achieve stability or peace, if you like, or helping them change behaviours or thought processes that are unhelpful and that prevent them from being as happy as they can be.'

'Do you think grief is a negative emotion?'

'That's an interesting question. Grief is certainly unpleasant...'

'Unpleasant,' said Bea flatly.

'Yes, but necessary. Sometimes the pain seems unbearable. But people who go through the grieving process often achieve very hard-won wisdom and insight, and the best outcome is that they arrive at a point where they can remember the person they've lost without experiencing pain.'

At least they were having a conversation.

'I read once that psychotherapy only works on intelligent and articulate people who are motivated to change,' said Bea.

'I presume you're implying that if you possess those attributes then you don't need a therapist?'

'I suppose so.'

'I don't want to upset you again, but can I ask why you're so reluctant to talk about yourself?'

Bea paused. 'I was brought up that way. *We* were brought up that way. Cracks are to be papered over and forgotten. Loose lips sink ships. Least said soonest mended.'

'So both parents were like that?'

'My mother. My father went along with it. For an easy life, I suppose.'

Now we're getting somewhere, thought Rebecca.

'Your brother, Sonny, obviously takes a different view?'

'Sonny's gone through years of therapy. His wife cajoled him into it. She's American, and her family share everything. Not like ours. Anyway, now he's the King of Self-Help. Will ribs him rotten.'

'Who's Will?'

'Another brother.'

'How many do you have?'

'Five.'

'Five! My goodness!' said Rebecca, knowing perfectly well.

'There was a sixth, but he died young, before I was born. A cot death. My mother doesn't really talk about it.'

'Are you close to your mother?'

'She always preferred the boys, especially Paddy. I always felt she didn't want me around. I was always much closer to my dad. Until suddenly, when I was fifteen, he upped and left home.'

'That must have been intensely painful.'

Bea reached for a tissue. 'You could say that. I'd always been so certain of him, then suddenly he left. That's how I felt about David. So certain of him. And now he's left me as well. For good.'

***

Bea got the tube home after her session with Rebecca. Clumps of dirty snow clung to the pavement. The temperature was still below freezing, but the sky was cloudless and the streets were bathed in wintry sunshine. She'd taken a wodge of tissues from the box in Rebecca's sea green room. On top of her constant crying, she felt herself coming down with a filthy cold.

Bea recited 'Invictus' under her breath on the way home from the tube. Hilary's reading had almost pushed her over the edge. Her throat constricted at the memory. Hilary had started the reading with a resonant power, but her voice had wavered. She had come close to cracking and was forced to pause. The collective will from the congregation had spurred her on, and she'd ended the reading with her voice vibrating with angry heartbreak, as if shaking her fist at fate.

'Did you say anything in church?' Rebecca had asked.

'Yes,' said Bea. 'Sonny also said a few words.'

'Did people stay afterwards?'

'Yes. Everyone went back to Sonny's place. His housekeeper had cooked up a storm. Sonny opened up his cellar. It was a brilliant party. Missing only the guest of honour.'

Edie had protested at the number of cases. 'We'll sup the lot,' Sonny had told her. How right he was. A good number of the guests staggered out by the end, absolutely plastered.

Diana had swanned into the church, swathed in dark

cashmere. Both sons in tow, she had taken one of the pews near the front reserved for family. Bea was forced to admit she was family, in a way that she herself could never be to David. Unless... Better not dwell on it. Diana had settled herself into the pew and sat serenely with her sons. It was difficult not to admire her chutzpah. Her brass neck, as Edie called it. Harry sat next to his mother, eyes hollow and red-rimmed. Dan sat with his girlfriend, Serena, who had her arm round him. Possession masquerading as care. Bea had forced herself to approach Diana. Diana quickly composed herself. She got to her feet and took Bea's outstretched hand. The two women embraced.

After her reading, Hilary had climbed down from the lectern and sat next to Bea in the left-hand pew, taking Bea's hand. Hilary was drawn to her, as someone who felt as wretched as she did.

After the service, she saw some of David's old friends air-kissing Diana nervously, glancing guiltily in her direction. Bea linked her arm in Hilary's, and led the girl over to her mother.

'We're having a few drinks at my brother Sonny's house,' said Bea. 'Would you like to come?'

'Thank you,' said Diana. 'I won't. I'll take Harry home.'

Harry's eyes were as pink as a rabbit's. Bea felt a fresh constriction of her heart.

'I'm going with Bea,' said Hilary to her mother. 'I'll see you later.'

'All right, darling. Don't be late, though, will you?'

At Sonny's house, Hilary had flitted round like a bird, talking, kissing, hugging her father's old friends. She had eaten nothing, drunk far too much and had thrown up in the kitchen. She was like a firework, burning with brittle brightness, then crash-landing, broken to the ground. Bea had forced her to sip water and had led her upstairs to lie down. She gave her a glass of water and smoothed her hair back.

'Well didn't I make a total tit of myself,' she'd said,

cheeks streaked with mascara. 'Fuck! Fuck fuck fuck, why did he have to fucking die?'

Dan and Serena had also come back to Sonny's house, Serena like a praetorian guard, not leaving his side, answering all questions put to him. 'Fucking limpet,' said Hilary to Bea. 'I wish I had someone like that. Fuck, Bea! What am I going to do?'

Her family were having a last lunch together, then everyone would disappear in their different directions, except for Sandra, who was staying a few more days. She had a guilty sense of relief that her mother would soon be going home. Paddy had conveniently declined the invitation to lunch. The church was the first time he and Colin had been under the same roof since Paddy had taken a wrecking ball to Colin's marriage.

As a child, she had always been afraid of Paddy. She was still not easy with him as she was with the others. She had tried hard to build bridges with him since his accident and his spell in jail. There was an undercurrent in Paddy that was sometimes almost tangible.

'He's a wrong'un,' David had said.

'He's my brother!'

'Sorry, darling, but he is.'

David had helped him nonetheless, for her sake.

She approached the house just as Colin was returning from the park with the children. He carried Nick on his back. Anna was beside him carrying a football. The trips to the park had become a daily event. Even in a crisis, people developed routines. Nick looked at Bea's red and stricken face with bewilderment.

Sonny came down as they opened the front door. Hot savoury meatiness wafted from the kitchen. Sandra did a great line in comfort food. It felt wrong to be hungry.

'How did it go?' asked Sonny in a low voice, as Colin trooped past them with the children into the dining room.

'Fine,' she said. 'She's a strange woman.'

'How do you mean?'

'I don't know. She seemed interested in the oddest things.'

Sonny considered. 'Maybe she takes a holistic approach.'

'I didn't mind. It was easier than talking about David.'

'Stick with it, Bean,' said Sonny. 'It'll really help you.'

Will came thundering down the stairs. 'So was it worth it?' he asked.

'I used up a lot of tissues,' said Bea.

'What, sixty quid's worth?' said Will, winking at her.

Bea laughed. It was like a cool spring shooting up in a desert. Will grinned, pleased at himself. She caught sight of a photo of her and David in Thailand on their wedding day. She wore a white bikini and flowers in her hair. He was in black swimming trunks and had tied a shoelace in a bow round his neck. Tears sprang to her eyes.

'Look what you've done now, Will,' said Sonny.

'He hasn't done anything,' said Bea.

Will ignored Sonny in any case and led Bea into the dining room, where the table was set for lunch. She caught the tail end of Edie opining on 'this therapy business.'

'Why spill your guts to a therapist when you can repress everything in The Comfort of Your Own Home?' said Sam. It had been the title of Will's first novel.

Edie bridled.

Sandra dished up great dollops of mashed potato onto hot plates, which were passed around the table. Will served up the stew.

Nick sat between Bea and Sandra and stared up at his aunt. He had never seen an adult cry. He came close to toppling off his chair in an attempt to pat her arm.

'Whoa, Nicky,' said his mother, steadying him. She

handed him a spoon. 'It's hot, darling. You need to wait, or blow on it a bit.' Nick shovelled a wodge of stew into his mouth, then went red in the face and began to shake and pant. 'I told you, Nicky! You have to blow on it. Drink this, darling.' She gave him some water. 'Wait for everyone else, sweetheart. It's good manners and will give it a chance to cool down. Anna, have you got enough there, pet?'

'Yes, thank you, Auntie San.'

Sammy poured Bea a generous splash of red wine. She took a careful sip, then eyed the food in front of her.

'It'll do you good,' said Edie. 'You're looking thin as a lath.'

Bea said nothing, but tried a forkful of mash. It was delicious. Buttery and not over-smooth. She reached for the black pepper.

'I'm starving,' she said.

'You want to take better care of yourself,' said Edie. 'Eat well and sleep well. That's all the therapy you need.'

'Don't be a Doubting Thomas, Mam. You should try it some day,' said Sonny.

Will rolled his eyes and leaned over to pick up a bit of mash that Nick had dropped on the table.

'You must be joking,' said Edie. 'Telling a complete stranger all the ins and outs of your life. For a whole hour! I'd struggle to find things to say.'

'We talked about the funeral,' said Bea.

Edie put her fork down. Her hand flew to her chest. 'What a funeral it was too,' she said. 'And the party afterwards. You did him proud.' Bea looked up at her mother in surprise, then realised she was talking to Sonny. 'I can't believe we went through all that wine. I thought you'd gone way over the top.'

'I knew it wouldn't go to waste,' said Sonny.

'Those mountains of food. I don't mind admitting I was wrong. Just one sandwich crust and a couple of sausage rolls left by the end.' Edie sipped her wine. 'That Hilary. She brought a tear to my eye. "My unconquerable soul". She'll go far, that one.'

Sandra nodded. 'It was David all over. Did you choose it, Bea?'

'We both did.'

'I can't believe that Diana turning up. You should never have let her in, Bea,' said Edie.

'Mam, it was a funeral. There isn't a guest list,' said Colin.

'Or bouncers on the door,' said Will.

'What about David's little'un?' said Sam. 'He needed his mother.'

Edie sniffed.

'This stew is smashing, San,' said Sam.

'Do you fancy a bit more?' she asked.

'Mmm. Don't mind if I do.' He held his plate towards her.

'Anyone else? Edie?'

'Just a tiny bit,' said Edie.

'When's your flight, Sonny?' asked Sam.

'Six. What about you lot? What time are you planning to set off?'

'About three, I reckon,' said Sam. 'All right, Mam?'

Edie shifted in her seat. 'I thought I might stay a few days. It's not right me going back to an empty house when Bea needs company.'

'Oh!' said Sandra. 'But Nick and me are…'

'You should get back to your boys. I don't need to rush home.'

'I called them this morning,' said Sandra. 'They've hardly noticed we're gone, have they, Will?'

'Nope,' he said. 'Give us another spoonful, love.'

Bea battled to compose her face. She took in a breath.

'Mam, it's kind of you—' she began carefully.

'So that's settled then. I'll get the train back Wednesday. Sandra can get back to her kiddies.'

'You've never taken the train. Not ever,' said Will.

'I'm not helpless, you know. First time for everything.'

Sandra glanced at Bea, then back at Edie. 'That's nice of you, Edie, but I'm staying until next week whatever. I've got it all sorted out with me mam.' She took Bea's hand under the table. 'I'm looking forward to spending a bit of time with Bea.'

'Well,' said Edie, 'there's no need for you to shoulder everything yourself.' She looked at Bea expectantly. Bea felt a terrible tension rising in her chest. Silence fell over the table.

'Mam, I wouldn't want to put you out...'

'My own daughter's husband dead and she's worried about putting me out! All I have to do is cancel milk and papers.'

Bea's chin trembled again. 'Thanks, Mam,' she said in a strangled voice. She pushed her chair back, making a graceless exit to the bathroom. Sonny and Colin half rose out of their chairs, then both sat back down again. The brothers all looked at each other and shrugged. Sam shook his head at their collective impotence.

'Well,' said Edie.

'Is Auntie Bea going to be okay?' asked Anna.

'She's going to be sad for a long time, duck,' said Sam, ruffling her hair.

'Nana?' said Anna

'Yes, duck?'

'Daddy and I are coming back here next weekend. Why don't you stay with Auntie Bea until then? Then she won't have to be alone at all.'

'I'll have to get back before then, love.'

'But you said—'

'I don't expect a little girl to understand,' said Edie. 'But there are people who depend on me.'

'But—'

'Wednesday it is and that's that. Sandra, you can drop me off home, can't you? It's only an hour out of your way.'

'If that's what you want, Edie...'

'It is what I want.'

'Do you fancy a bit more stew, duck?' asked Colin to Anna.

'No, thank you, Daddy,' said Anna. She put her fork down. 'Thank you for the lovely lunch, Auntie San.'

'Aaah,' said Sandra. 'You've got beautiful manners, darling.'

'Most of the time,' muttered Edie.

***

I had to lie down after that lunch. Sonny told Bea he'd bring Gina and the kids to see her in the school holidays. He called it the school recess and Will took the mick. Sam drove back up north without me and Colin had to get Anna back to her mother. Anna put me on the spot a bit asking why I couldn't stay with Bea until the Friday. She'll only be alone two days. She'll have to get used to it sooner rather than later. I didn't like to say that I have my bridge mornings Thursdays. It wouldn't have sounded right. I don't like to let the others down. They live for bridge mornings. We used to rotate and take it in turns to visit each other's houses, but now we always go to Tracey's, as she finds it so hard to get about.

It was lovely having all the kids together, even if it was for a funeral. Bar Paddy, of course. All his life he's been excluded, and since that... that business between him and Carol, it's ten times worse. I hope Anna doesn't grow up to be like her mother.

My head throbbed a bit when I got up. I found Bea sat on the rug in the front room playing trucks with Nick.

'What colour's this one, Nicky?' she asked him.

'Boo.'

'Clever boy! And what about this one?'

'Owange.'

'Good. And this one?'

'Wed.'

'So how many trucks do you have? One... two...'

'Fwee!' He giggled as she tickled him.

She clocked that I'd come in and started to get up.

'Don't stop on my account,' I said. 'They're a great comfort, aren't they? Especially when they're so little. Such a lovely age.'

'Would you like a drink of anything?'

'Oh, no! That's why I had to put me head down this afternoon. I'm not used to wine at lunch. Goes straight to my head.'

'A cup of tea instead?'

'No, you're all right thanks. Where's Sandra?'

'Having a soak.'

'She's been run ragged these past few days by the looks of things.'

'She's been brilliant.'

'She should've gone home. She should be with her kiddies.'

'It's only for a few days. They're not babies any more. Even Nicky here's not a baby any more.'

Nick began to make a low growling noise, and drove one of his trucks across Bea's thigh. As he drove it over the cliff of her knee, he made a crashing noise. He smiled gleefully.

'You're right. They grow up so quickly.' I sighed. 'You're good with him.' She didn't say anything. Sometimes Bea is devilish hard to talk to. 'Pity you and David never had any of your own. It would help you focus on something other than...' I hesitated.

'Other than myself, you mean?'

'All I meant was that you'd be a good mother and it's a shame you don't have a kiddie or two. I suppose with David having three already, and your career...'

Bea's hair fell down over her face. She picked up one of Nick's trucks and started opening and shutting the little toy door as if it were the most fascinating thing in the world.

'Not that it's too late,' I said. 'You're still young. You could always meet someone else.'

'He's a week gone, Mam!'

Nick looked up from his truck, startled.

'You know what I mean. It's just that you shouldn't write yourself off. You're still a young woman.'

'I don't want to talk about it! I don't even want to think about it.'

Nick looked at me, then at Bea. His chin started to wobble and his face turned red. 'Oh Nick, I'm sorry,' said Bea, and pulled him onto her lap but he wouldn't be quieted. I got up from my chair and held my arms out to him. He stared up at me and howled. I was surprised. He's usually very fond of his nana. Bea used the side of the sofa to pull herself up from the floor, Nicky still in her arms. She paced back and forth on the rug. I offered to take him again.

'It's all right, Mam. He'll be fine in a minute.' He was. He quieted right enough after a bit. Sandra came in a moment after I'd sat back down. She was in a dressing gown, hair wet and cheeks flushed.

She came up close to Nick and rubbed noses with him. He giggled. She held out her arms to him for a cuddle.

'Ah that's nice, that is,' I said and laughed. 'Sometimes only Mammy will do. Isn't that right, my little duck?'

I didn't mean anything by it but Bea always was touchy. She left the room in a right old huff and we didn't see her again until dinnertime.

***

'I don't know why she's decided to stay. She doesn't want to be here any more than I want her here.' Bea lay on the bed propped up by pillows.

'She's not an easy one, your mam. It's only for a few days. She means well.'

'If it weren't such a dreadful thing to say of anyone.'

Sandra giggled.

'She makes me feel two inches tall. I don't think I can take her for four more days,' said Bea.

'Maybe you'll have a chance to talk to her. She's lost a husband too. It could be good for both of you.'

'It's not the same. They hadn't spoken to each other in years. She's a closed book where Dad's concerned.'

Sandra sighed. 'Well, if it gets too much, we can always leave Nick with her and go for a drink or something.'

Bea sat up suddenly. 'Sod it,' she said. 'I'm going back to work Monday.'

'Don't rush into it.'

'Would it put you out if I did? Go back to work, I mean? I'm so grateful you offered to stay. You could go back early. On Monday, say. Mam's right that you shouldn't be away from the boys. She could go back Monday as well. You lot can't stay on widow watch for ever.'

'Widow watch!' said Sandra and nudged her. 'Get away with yer.'

'Hilary's going back to school on Monday. If she can launch herself back in, then I should too.'

'You're barely eating or sleeping. You look exhausted.'

'Other people don't have an option.'

'But you do. Give yourself time.'

'I've got forty-odd bloody years. I may as well just go

back.'

'Well,' said Sandra. 'Whatever you decide, I'm here till Wednesday regardless.'

'Thanks, San,' she said. 'Mam and I alone are like two ferrets in a sack.'

'I have my uses. I'll go and put the dinner on. I'll feed Nick first and put him to bed.'

'Don't go to any trouble, will you, San? We could have the rest of the stew and mash.'

'Between the lot of us, we finished up every scrap. I'll do us some mushroom omelettes. Are you up to that?'

'Thanks, San.'

Bea called Rob to let him know she'd be in on Monday.

'Are you sure you're ready?' he asked, but she could tell he was pleased. He detested paying freelancers. Rob was convinced the magazine only survived because he was as 'tight as a gnat's chuff.'

'Definitely.'

'Quite right too,' he said in a soothing tone. 'It'll take your mind off things. Get straight back into the saddle. Doesn't do any good to brood. Right, well,' he said, sounding embarrassed. 'I've run out of platitudes. See you Monday.'

She put her phone down and pulled a tissue from the box by the bed. The soft paper brushed against the cardboard, sounding like the tearing of sinew. In her new state, even innocuous sounds were imbued with violence. She smoothed the bed, straightened a few things on her dressing table, then brushed her hair. She wandered into the bathroom and filled the tooth mug with water and drank it slowly. She became aware that she was procrastinating and steeled herself to go downstairs. Sandra was right. She should try to talk to her mother. One day it would be too late.

She thudded a little harder than usual on the stairs to give some warning of her approach. She didn't want to catch her mother talking about her.

'...best thing for her, I reckon. Good for her.'

'What's that?' asked Bea as she walked in. Sandra was mixing eggs, while onions, mushrooms and garlic fried in a pan. Edie was sitting at the table peeling cooking apples.

Edie looked up. 'I was just saying that going back to work shows a bit of backbone.'

'Thanks, Mam,' Bea said.

'Have a glass of wine and give me and your mam a top-up,' said Sandra. 'Not too much left in that bottle.'

'I'll open another,' said Bea and picked one from the wine rack.

'I wasn't sure which ones were for drinking,' said Edie. 'David did love his wine. I know he had some special bottles kept aside.'

'Help yourself,' said Bea. 'It doesn't matter which ones you drink.'

'You say that,' said Edie. 'But you may be sorry later.'

'Trust me, Mam. I couldn't care less.'

For once, Edie did not press it.

'It was lovely having you all together for lunch,' she said. Two positive statements from her mother in two minutes. Maybe she'd resolved to make an effort. 'Bar poor old Paddy, of course.'

'I invited him,' said Bea. 'The only person who excludes Paddy is Paddy himself.'

'He didn't fancy getting the evil eye from Colin, I expect. Do you think he'll ever let bygones be bygones?'

'I don't know,' said Bea.

'She always was a fast one, that Carol.'

'Fast one!' said Bea. 'Paddy seduced her, then dumped her the minute she left Colin.'

'Why are you taking her side?' asked Edie. 'She never was a friend to you.'

'Maybe not, but she gave up her marriage for Paddy, then look what he did to her.'

'The person you should feel sorry for is Colin,' said Edie.

'I do, Mam. She broke his heart. But I also feel sorry for her. Paddy targeted her. She'd just had a baby. Colin was distracted with the new business and Paddy saw his moment to strike. She fell in love with him, and he was just toying with her.' Edie's lips had disappeared into her face. Bea sat down next to her at the table. She took a chance and put her hand over her mother's. 'I'm sorry, Mam. It must be terrible, being stuck in the middle.'

'I'm just surprised you can be so bloody even-handed. You and Colin always were thick as thieves,' said Edie. She didn't pull her hand away.

'That's true,' said Bea. Her hand on her mother's began to feel awkward. She lifted it to pick up her wine glass.

Sandra poured the egg mixture into a pan. 'You two are more alike than you know,' she said.

Edie and Bea both looked at each other, and both said 'No' at the same time. The three of them laughed. Bea had a glimpse of an alternate life, a life where she was at ease with her mother. She'd felt these flashes before, these tiny openings, and had learned not to force them.

'Pity Will had to go home,' said Edie. 'Couldn't he work here?'

'He's giving a lecture tomorrow and he's being interviewed on Wednesday. On the radio,' said Sandra.

'Fancy that!' said Edie with pride.

Sandra put the omelettes on the table.

'Don't wait. They get cold in two ticks.'

Edie began to eat. Bea eyed the food on her plate. It felt so wrong to eat when David was dead.

'Mmm,' said Edie. 'This is lovely. There's a bite to it.'

'I put in a pinch of chilli.'

'So what's Will's new book about then?' asked Edie. 'I almost dread to ask. Anyone reading his books must think our kids should have been taken into care.'

'It's fiction, Edie,' said Sandra with a smile. 'Stephen King writes about vampires. Nobody thinks for a second he's got first-hand experience.'

'You know very well what I mean.'

Bea's pulse fluttered. She knew her mother would find out eventually, but she didn't want to be there when she did. 'He likes to keep his books close to his chest until they're finished,' she said carefully.

'Not really,' said Sandra, not picking up the hint. 'It's about a young girl who commits a murder.'

'Murder!' said Edie. 'Well at least we can't be blamed for that.'

Bea remembered what Will had said about them finding Timmy. A picture came into her head, unbidden, of her mother screaming while rocking him close. She shuddered and put her fork down.

'Had enough?' said Sandra.

'Thanks, San,' she said in a coarse whisper. She had to leave the room quickly. She just made it to the bathroom in time to heave on nothing.

# CHAPTER ELEVEN

The night before her return to work, Bea lay in bed unable to sleep. A car engine backfired on the street, piercing the air like a gunshot. She was gripped with panic. Her heart raced. She forced herself to take in slow gulps of air. She would have welcomed some sort of disaster. For the house to cave in, or explode. For some cataclysmic external force to put an end to the grief. She lay on David's side of the bed breathing in the smell of his pillow. She felt the grief stripping the inside of her chest, as if she were bleeding internally.

She was fathoms deep when her alarm went off. She struggled to surface. She opened her eyes and felt a new blow to the stomach at the realisation that he was gone.

She shuffled to the en suite bathroom. She brushed her teeth and showered in the dark; she didn't want the extractor fan to come on. The noise sounded like a death rattle. The water encouraged the tears to flow. An objective part of her brain marvelled that she hadn't wrung herself dry. She'd left her towel on the radiator in the bedroom, so she padded across the wooden floor naked and dripping to get it. David would never moan about her wet footprints again.

She dried herself quickly, as the air was cold. She looked truly terrible. Hollow, red-rimmed eyes. Gaunt, haunted. Stringy wet hair 'all over the shop' as her mother would say. She rifled through her hanging clothes, and stopped abruptly at a forest-green velvet dress. A bridesmaid's dress that had never been worn. That she'd kept all these years. *Oh Clare...* Thinking about Clare would only set her off again.

She chose a grey dress that used to be figure-hugging and was now a size too big. All her adult life she'd been convinced that the secret to looking her best was to be five pounds lighter. She was wrong. She dug around in the chest of drawers for a bit of colour, and found a dark-red wrap cardigan. She had a lot of shoes. David had loved her in high heels. 'High heels and nothing else'. She knelt down to burrow for a particular pair of stilettos from the mound of shoes in the wardrobe. She found the left one and began to dig around for the right. David had bought them for her in Seville after they'd eaten a fabulous lunch in front of the cathedral. They'd sat outdoors at a trestle table and ploughed through an enormous sea bass, filleted in front of them by a waiter with caterpillar eyebrows.

The fish was caught only that morning, the waiter had told them, baked in salt and needing only a tiny squeeze of lemon so as not to drown the taste of the sea. Potato medallions fried in olive oil and herbs with some spinach on the side, gently steamed with garlic and lemon. Glasses of chilled Alborinõ that glinted pale green in the sunlight, the bottle in a bucket of ice beside them. David chatted to the waiter, exercising his talent for extracting a life story inside of five minutes. The man was from Kosovo. He'd lost his wife and children in the war. He had married again, a Spanish woman much younger than himself. They had a two-year-old daughter. Theodora, Gift from God. They'd ordered a second bottle. After he cleared their plates, he brought them grappa on the house. David toasted the waiter's little girl.

They'd meandered back to their hotel afterwards. The streets were lined with orange trees. Bea threw her head back to fill her lungs with the citrus scent wafting from the leaves. Better do that quickly, David had said, before someone lights up another fag. They'd wandered in and out of the shops, bought the shoes and a belt, then had an espresso at a pavement cafe, deciding that Spaniards must be born with cigarettes in their mouths, agreeing that they were both just jealous as it would have been the perfect moment to light up.

Three years later, alone, on her bedroom floor looking for a shoe, Bea longed again for a cigarette.

Back at the hotel, she'd collapsed onto the bed, caving into that special drowsiness that follows a magnificent lunch, wine, warmth and the luxury of a whole afternoon stretching ahead with nothing in particular to do. She'd had no horror of time then. David drew the curtains and joined her on the bed. She lay against him in the darkened room, and was on the brink of sleep when he began kissing her neck. She stiffened, close to nodding off, then yielded. She had recently come off the pill. Sex had taken on an added erotic thrill. Infertility had not yet begun to haunt them.

He tried pushing her dress up to her waist, but it was too tight so she turned to allow him to unzip it and wriggled to help him pull it over her head. She arched her back to let him unclasp her bra. She treaded her knickers down her bare legs and turned lazily to kiss him back. Then the fire alarm had gone off.

'Ignore it,' he whispered. 'It'll stop in a minute.' His hard-on pressed against her naked thigh. Above the shriek of the fire alarm, she heard raised voices in frantic Spanish coming from the direction of the lifts, and the sound of fists banging on doors. 'Bloody hell,' David groaned. 'We'll roast on the fire of our own passion.' Then a thumping on their door. *'Fuego! Fuego! Todo el mundo fuera!'*

'You know what the Spanish are like,' David grumbled. 'So hysterical about everything. They'd sound excited watching moss grow.' She'd pulled her dress back on and scrabbled for her knickers. She couldn't find her left shoe, so she grabbed her handbag and fished the new black stilettos out of the shopping bag. She tucked them under her arm and left the room barefoot, pulling David towards the fire escape. They joined several others descending the stairs. They ran down from the seventeenth floor, and on the fourteenth they slowed behind an elderly woman leading a little dog, a white chihuahua, a frantic ball of yapping excitement. The woman's movements were halting, and she grimaced each time she took a step downwards. Her white hair was pulled back behind a blue Hermès scarf. Her skin was thin and pale as paper, and covered in liver spots.

'*Posiblemente le podamos ayudar?*' David asked, offering her his arm. She stopped and leaned against the banister, taking the opportunity to breathe in great gulps of air, rasping as she did so. Her knuckles were white with the effort of gripping the rail. Her head slowly turned on its axis, reminding Bea of a tortoise emerging from its shell. She looked balefully at David and said, 'No speako dago.'

'My Inglese is much better than my Espagnol,' laughed David.

'Oh thank the Lord for that!' she said. Her vowels were strangulated. Thenk the Lawd for thet. 'Someone who speaks English. Don't just stand there. At this rate the whole shebang will be razed to the ground. You,' she said, pointing her arthritic claw at David. 'I suggest you carry me. And you,' she said to Bea. 'You may carry Pepe'. She handed over Pepe's lead.

David held her in his arms like an elderly bride and began striding down the stairs. Bea put her shoes on the floor and edged her feet into them, then gathered the little dog up in her arms. The tiny beast turned and nipped her in the arm, like a striking cobra.

'Ouch!' she yelled. The dog wriggled out of her arms and yelped for all he was worth.

'Don't mistreat Pepe!' the old lady said, as if Bea had bitten the dog.

'He just sank his teeth into me!' said Bea.

'He doesn't like strangers. Can't you be a bit more gentle?' The fire alarm increased in volume as they descended. The woman continued to audibly hector Bea, who did not bother to reply.

They smelled burning. Pepe began to hyperventilate with panic. His little bug eyes looked ready to pop out of his head. He nipped Bea again and she yelped with pain.

'Bea darling,' said David. 'just hold his jaws together. It can't be hard. He's so tiny.'

'You bloody try it then,' she said. She put her index finger over his nose and looped her thumb under his chin, intending to apply gentle pressure above and below to hold his jaws together. He was too quick for her and managed to whip his head round and nip her again, this time drawing blood from her wrist.

'You little *bastard*!' Bea yelled.

'Don't you dare swear at Pepe!' said the old lady. 'Pepe darling, don't listen to such terrible language.'

Bea ignored her. 'No more bullshit from *you*,' she hissed at the dog. This time, she grabbed him firmly by the scruff of the neck, disabling his ability to move his head. Pepe had made no further protest, beyond a constant low growling through his white bared teeth. The din was so loud that Bea could no longer hear him, but she felt his tiny body vibrating with fury.

Eventually they emerged into daylight. Outside, pandemonium reigned. The manager and various members of his staff were trying to count guests and staff, all of whom were screeching at each other in unintelligible Spanish. David gingerly set the old lady onto her faltering feet.

'Are you all right?' he asked her. She set her hair and scarf to rights and smoothed her blouse. David held his hand out to her. 'David Grahame. This is my wife, Bea.'

'Charmed,' she said, and took his proffered hand.

'Why don't I lead you over to yonder bar? Perhaps I can get you something hot and sweet to drink,' said David.

'I'd prefer something stiffer.'

He offered her his arm. 'You're quite right. Perhaps a

large brandy is exactly what the doctor ordered.'

'Not my fucking doctor,' she said. 'If he had his way I'd live on weak tea and water. Oh look, the fire brigade's just arrived.'

The area outside the hotel became ever more chaotic.

Suddenly the old lady began looking in all directions. 'Where's Pepe? Pepe! Pepe, darling, where are you?'

'He's right here,' said Bea between clenched teeth. 'I'm afraid to let go of his neck in case he takes my arm off.'

'Come to Mummy,' the old lady cooed. 'Is she being horrid to you?' Bea laughed in outrage at her spectacular rudeness. She handed the little creature over. He promptly yapped and snapped at Mummy. She began to feel some sort of kinship with the dog.

'Pepe, Pepe, that's very naughty,' the old lady said soothingly, and held him gingerly to her breast. Bea noticed that she too held him surreptitiously by the scruff of the neck. David led the old lady towards a little bar on the other side of the road. Bea tottered alongside, getting used to her new shoes. She felt unaccountably guilty, as if they were leaving the scene of a crime.

Before they closed the distance to the bar, the hotel manager grabbed David by the arm, gushing forth a torrent of Spanish. Bea's Spanish was strictly phrase-book. David tried to explain that they were just going for a drink, and if the manager needed their names and room numbers to check off against their list, he'd be happy to supply them. He dug into his pocket for some paper, found a restaurant bill and wrote their names and room number on the back of it. 'Let me write down your name and room number too,' he said to the old lady.

'No need,' she said. 'I'm not a guest. I'm the mistress of a guest.'

David grinned. 'And what has happened to your inamorato? Did you leave him to roast in the hotel?'

'If I did, it would be no more than he deserves. But no, as a matter of fact he had to go out on some errand. It was most inconvenient.'

The manager looked from one to the other, not understanding the exchange.

'Oh, I beg your pardon,' said David. 'Beatrix and David Graham, room 1707.' He offered the manager the scrap of paper. The manager stared at it in incomprehension, and a black cloud descended on him. He began yelling at David as if the restaurant bill conveyed a deeply obscene personal insult. David again tried to explain in Spanish that they just wanted to go for a drink until they could get into the hotel again.

'Please understand, Signor,' he said, sotto voce. 'This lady is very frail and needs to sit down.'

'I'm not dead yet, young man,' she said. 'Although I will be if we don't get a bloody drink pronto.' She turned to the manager and tapped her finger threateningly on his chest.

'Io. Guesto of Alfonso. Count Alfonso. Biggo Shotto Count Alfonso.'

The manager looked at her, incredulous, then backed off, holding his hands in front of him in a placatory gesture. He turned to survey the chaos around him, looking on in fury as more of his guests sneaked off, like naughty children hiding from Nanny at bedtime.

All of a sudden he spotted a boy of about eighteen, wearing charred chef's whites. The manager strode menacingly towards him like a villain in a Disney cartoon, shouting and gesticulating. The boy's tragi-comic expression reminded Bea of Pierrot, particularly as his eyelashes had been singed off.

The manager's shouting fit ended as abruptly as it had begun. He shook his head, raised his eyes to heaven, then gathered the boy to his chest. The young man cried with relief, and David clapped and cheered with the best of them.

'It was worth missing out on a shag for all this,' he

stage-whispered to Bea, and roared laughing.

Remembering that laugh brought back a thousand memories. She wanted to weep that she'd never hear it again.

The old lady had looked disapprovingly at the furore around her. She kept a firm grip on the scruff of Pepe's neck.

'Such melodrama. You're only encouraging the national hysteria,' she said.

'Let's get a drink,' said David.

'Hear, hear,' said the old lady, brimming with impatience.

They got a table outside, overlooking the hotel. The old lady introduced herself as 'Lady Fellowes. But you may call me Dorothy.' David gestured to the waiter, who smiled in recognition, as he and Bea had stopped by several times; but his face fell when he saw Dorothy, and when he cast his eye on Pepe, he looked ready to reach for a crucifix.

'No dog,' said the waiter, waving his finger from side to side in the air.

'But the place is stuffed to the gills with dogs,' said David, pointing to a poodle and an Alsatian.

'Not zis dog. He not allow.'

'You don't like chihuahuas?' asked David.

'Such a fuss about nothing,' said Dorothy. 'He gets nervous among crowds. He was a bit undisciplined.'

'He shit on table,' said the waiter.

'Really,' said Dorothy. 'The fuss they make over a bit of poo-poo.'

David persuaded the waiter to let Pepe stay, assuring him that he'd remain in Signora's handbag.

The bar bulged with other exiled guests crowding around the bar and the terrace, watching the activity around the hotel. David ordered a bottle of Rioja. Dorothy asked for the first of a series of very large, stiff pink gins. The Spanish were niggardly with the bitters, apparently, so she carried her own bottle of angostura in her roomy handbag. She dug under Pepe's bum for it. He nipped her again.

'Pepe darling. That's very naughty.' To properly root around every nook and cranny for her Dunhill Thins, she put Pepe momentarily on the table. If he were a ticking bomb, David and Bea would not have watched him more closely. Cigarettes located and Pepe back in the bag, she lit up, leaned back in her chair and inhaled deeply, closing her eyes. She held her breath, allowing the nicotine to do its work. Eventually two streams of smoke emerged from her nostrils, giving her the look of a dozy dragon. She settled further back into the chair and took a large slug of gin.

'Well, that's better, I must say. Down the hatch.' She clinked her glass against Bea's, then David's. Her smile transformed her face, which must have once been beautiful. The cheekbones and the fine grey eyes remained, but the rest of her features were ravaged by time and pink gin.

Dorothy was a widow. Her most recent husband had died in a hunting accident, leaving her a flat in South Kensington, the lifetime interest in his house in Hampshire and a considerable amount of capital. 'Not bad for a marriage of five years. Poor old Piers. Of course his daughters can't wait for me to kick the bucket. Then they get their grasping mitts on the lot. Not that I don't have a certain amount of sympathy. They probably felt safe as houses having him over for Christmas, sending him a birthday card and the odd picture of their beastly children. It must have been infuriating for them to have me swan in, marry Papa and swipe the lot.'

'They sound awful,' said Bea.

'Oh they are, my dear.' Alcohol had softened her stance towards Bea. 'Perfectly ghastly. He was far too much of a gentleman to admit it, but he knew he wasn't overly blessed in the daughter department. Their neglect suited him down to the ground. They're so fucking dull. Alice bands, tweeds, flats, tartan skirts. Not an ounce of glamour. No sense of style. Both have insisted their husbands go double-barrelled. So middle-class.'

'Do you have any children of your own?' Bea asked.

She sent her eyes heavenwards. 'Yes. Gordon. He's here with me in Seville.'

David laughed. 'I thought you were visiting your inamorato.'

'What a charming word.'

'You seem too... dignified to have a boyfriend.'

Dorothy snorted. 'You mean too bloody ancient.'

'Not at all. A veteran sex kitten.'

'David!' said Bea.

Unperturbed, he asked, 'So you're visiting your lover and you brought your son along?'

'It was Alfonso's idea. He's throwing a party tomorrow night for his seventy-fifth birthday, and has invited his whole family. That's half of Andalusia. Then he's invited his close friends, the other half. *My* whole family amounts to Gordon.'

'He sounds a very decent fellow.'

'Alfonso? Yes, I suppose he is'.

'As he's a local, why the suite at the hotel?'

'The plumbing at his town house has gone and packed up yet again. He doesn't stay there very often. He disappeared after lunch to see about it, leaving me to face the inferno alone. He took Gordon with him. Gordon's terribly practical.'

'Where does he usually live?'

'He has a finca in the countryside.'

That sounds lovely,' said Bea.

'Oh it is. But I prefer to stay away, especially when his daughters are around. They disapprove of me,' she said complacently, and took a large gulp of gin.

'Stepdaughters seem to be a recurring problem for you,' said David.

'It's a Catholic thing,' she said, airily waving her hand. 'They probably suspect I'm after his money, but they're far too well-bred to say so. If my Spanish were good enough, I'd tell them straight. I gave up marrying for money years ago.'

'Do have another gin.' David smiled. 'Why don't you marry Alfonso?'

'David!' said Bea. 'Sorry, Dorothy. He's so nosy.'

'Oh don't apologise. Alfonso's a perfect dear and I'm not against the idea at all.'

'So why don't you?' asked Bea.

'To annoy my stepdaughters.' David and Bea both laughed.

Several gins later, the hotel reopened, so they escorted Dorothy back. The fire had destroyed the kitchen, so the restaurant was out of commission and room service was suspended. Bea invited Dorothy to join them for dinner, but she refused.

'Thank you, but I suppose I'd better wait for my boys.'

They found a tiny restaurant with no menu where they were served chicken, chorizo and chilli stew with rice.

After dinner, Bea would have preferred to go straight to bed, but David persuaded her to have a nightcap. The manager insisted on giving them their drinks on the house, especially as they were friends of Count Alfonso.

'Who?' asked David.

'You know, Dorothy's boyfriend,' said Bea.

David began explaining they'd never met him. The man looked confused.

'That's very kind of you,' said Bea, cutting in.

David laughed. 'How right you are, darling. Gift horses and all that. I'll have a Campari and soda, please. What about you, Bea?'

'A glass of Rioja for me, please.'

The manager glided off to get the drinks just as Dorothy

arrived, arm in arm with an elderly Spaniard.

A tall, gangly fair-haired man wearing a cream linen suit followed them into the bar. Pepe was asleep in his arms.

'Ah, there you are,' said Dorothy. 'Alfonso darling, this is the scrumptious pair who saved me and Pepe from the flames. David and Bea...' She cupped her ear ostentatiously.

'Grahame,' said David, standing up and offering his hand.

'This is Alfonso,' said Dorothy. She waved vaguely towards the tall man in linen. 'And this is my son, Gordon.'

'How do you do,' said Gordon. He was about to shift Pepe to his left hand in order to free his right.

'Don't wake him up!' said Bea.

Gordon laughed. 'So you've met the great beast.'

'Would you like a drink?' asked David.

'Please,' said Alfonso. 'You saved my darling Dorothy. Let me...' At this, Gordon rolled his eyes at Bea and smiled.

'We only carried her down a few stairs,' said David.

'Seventeen floors,' said Gordon. 'That's got to be half an Eiffel.'

The manager steered the group towards a cluster of four empty chairs that were more comfortable than the bar stools. He put the two drinks down on the table and brought over an extra chair for Gordon. Dorothy asked for the inevitable pink gin and Alfonso for a glass of Rioja.

'Is that a Campari?' asked Gordon, pointing at David's glass. 'I'll have the same.'

'I don't know how they stay in business,' said Bea.

Gordon smiled and arranged his long limbs in the chair gingerly so as not to wake Pepe. The gesture reminded her of another very tall, rangy blond man from long ago. She put the thought from her mind.

Alfonso invited them to his birthday party.

'We'd hate to impose,' said David.

'Oh, you could just about squeeze them in, couldn't you, Alfonso?' said Gordon airily.

Alfonso laughed. 'My family is very... extended. After seventy-five years I have acquired a few friends. And my neighbours would be mortally offended if I did not invite them. We will have a lot of people, but please come. It will make me very happy.'

She'd remember Alfonso's party as long as she lived. The food, the champagne, the wine, the music, the company: the glitterati happily rubbing shoulders with peasants in the dusky beauty of the Andalusian hills. Dorothy had been charm itself, and over time had become a real friend. It had annoyed Bea sometimes, David's efforts to find out about people, to get under their skin. Especially on holiday, when she wanted him all to herself. People opened up to him like oysters.

Bea stood up with the shoes in her hand, picked up her bag and crept down the stairs. She blinked rapidly. She'd put waterproof mascara on, but she needed to take control of herself. She edged her feet into the shoes. Wallet, notebook, pen, phone, purse, lipstick. Tissues.

Keys. She needn't bother double-locking as Sandra and her mother were there. She supposed she should get reinforced locks, something by Banham or Ingersoll, especially now she was on her own. They had been meaning to get round to it since they'd moved into their 'ravishing money pit', but had never found the time.

As she was about to leave, Sandra padded into the kitchen in her pyjamas. Her dark hair was matted and clumped.

'You look smashing,' she said. 'Want a cup of tea before you go?'

'No thanks. I want to be in early.' She had a horror of walking into a full office and having everyone turn to look at her.

Sandra put the kettle on.

'Sure you won't have a quick one?'

'No. I'll pick up a coffee on my way in.'

'All right, pet. What time will you be home?'

'Not sure. Around six. Maybe earlier. Oh God, I nearly forgot. It's Monday. Lorena comes on Mondays. I haven't got any money on me.'

'She'll forgive a bit of forgetfulness from you right now.'

'Not sure about that.'

'How much does she need?'

'Fifty quid. Oh, and another fifty for last week.'

'Don't fret yourself. I'll get it from the cashpoint and pay her.'

'Thanks, San. I'll give it back to you tonight.'

'Anything particular you'd like her to do?' said Sandra.

'Lorena always does what she wants.'

# CHAPTER TWELVE

There comes a time when you have to forgive yourself for things. My hair shirt's not done me any good. Kids need rearing, meals need cooking, clothes need washing, houses need cleaning and husbands need fussing over, in bed and out of it.

By the time he died, we hadn't said two words to each other for years, but we were still like two halves of a well-oiled machine. In all the years since we split, we lived in the same small town. Town is a generous word for it, too. We never planned it in advance, but we soon started living around each other without having to come face to face. It was like a dance. For instance, I'd go to the post office for my pension on a Thursday morning. He went in the afternoon. All direct debit now, of course.

I don't like to do a lot of shopping all at once. I go to the supermarket on Mondays, Wednesdays and Saturdays. George went once a week on a Friday in his car. I never did learn to drive. Before he died, you would not catch me in the Co-op on a Friday, not for love nor money. If I ever needed anything, I'd send one of Molly's grandkids. Now I can go to the Co-op whenever I choose, and my world's the poorer for it.

We never went through the malarkey of a divorce. The kids got used to us not being together, and the grandkids have never known any different. Neither of us ever told them why we split. George kept mum for Bea's sake, but I like to think it was loyalty to me too. Maybe he felt a fool. Some men are funny like that. For whatever reason, I'm grateful that he was protective, sentimental or proud. The shame would have killed me.

Things started to go downhill when Bea started school. George made a big fuss of her on her first day. Wanted to take her picture in her uniform by the front gate and all that. I really wasn't much in the mood for it all. I had a headache or something. I'd sent so many kids off to school that it was hard to summon up that much enthusiasm. I walked to St. Stephen's that morning with Colin and Bea. Will was at secondary with the bigger boys.

Colin peeled off to his classroom. Bea clutched my hand, a bundle of nerves and excitement. Her little blond head was turning this way and that, drinking it all in, when who should come striding towards us but Penharris. He froze when he saw me, then got a hold on himself and managed a 'Good Morning'. Then he saw Bea. He got down on his haunches and held his hand out to her. She hid behind my legs.

'Hello there. Are you the youngest Newell?'

Slowly, she came out from behind me and put her hand in his. He talked to her in a soft voice.

'I'm Mr Penharris.'

They shook hands. He held her gaze, and held on to her hand.

'I'm sure I'll be hearing wonderful things about you soon, if you're anything like your brothers.'

'We'd best get on,' I said.

'Of course,' he said, and let her go. When I glanced backwards, he was still gazing after her.

\*\*\*

Bea's colleagues did not know what to say to her. They didn't know how to behave. Conversation would suddenly hush when she appeared. People put their heads down. More than once someone stifled their laughter with a 'Sorry, Bea'. It was like having a disease. They wanted to be sympathetic, but not false, considerate but not patronising. Rather than attempt this impossible trick, it was easier to avoid her altogether.

Martha hugged her. 'How are you holding up?' she

asked, and without waiting for a reply exclaimed, 'What a top party! I got absolutely plastered. I love your mum, Bea. She's great.'

Martha had finished the piece on the Sudanese refugees.

'Don't thank me, Bea. It's the least I can do. You did all the groundwork and the research. All I had to do was tweak it here and there. I should have made sure they credited both of us.' She bit her lip and lowered her chin. 'You're not annoyed, are you?

'No,' said Bea.

'You are, aren't you?'

'Honestly, I don't care.'

'Don't be like that. You've got a million serious pieces under your belt. All I've got is gossip and shopping. You don't begrudge me one article, do you?'

Rob took Bea out for lunch. She would have preferred a sandwich at her desk. She hoped he wouldn't turn on his awkward brand of sympathy. She needn't have worried. Beyond a cursory 'How are you bearing up?', he discussed work throughout. She preferred it that way.

She was a widow. Such a soft word for such a harsh reality. To her, widows were old crones, scheming murderesses, poisoners, power-crazed gold-diggers, flint-hearted killers of stepchildren...

Children. She stroked her stomach beneath her desk. Perhaps one of them had taken. Perhaps they both had. She was superstitious about doing a test before her period was due.

\*\*\*

I had no baby to take home with me once Bea started school. Of course there was no shortage of things that had to get done. An endless cycle of cleaning, and washing, ironing and folding, shopping and cooking. I'd put on a bit of music or listen to the wireless while I did it. Amazing the snippets you can pick up from the radio. George did his best to spare me. He bought me a washing machine once he'd won the Ashworth contract. I remember the Pope stirred up a hornet's nest by saying that the single biggest thing that has liberated women over the centuries has been the washing machine. Well I reckon he was bloody right.

The next family drama hit us when Mrs Jackson picked Bea to be the Star of Bethlehem for her school nativity. She was to sing a showstopper, 'Ave Maria'. I was as gobsmacked as anyone. Bea was as shy as a rabbit. People had to say pardon to her all the time, her voice was that hushed, and she'd started to stutter. It got on my nerves something terrible. But Bea had an amazing singing voice. She couldn't s-s-string a s-s-sentence together without s-s-stuttering, but get her to sing and she could do it with no breaks no pauses no bother. She was puny, but she could carry a note, and she had a real oomph to her voice.

We had a rickety piano at home, and we'd often have a singalong, George tinkling away. Bea singing at home was one thing. Bea singing in front of the whole school was a right old turn-up for the books.

After the Angel Gabriel had said his piece to the shepherds, Bea was supposed to sing 'Ave Maria' solo, and lead the shepherds and the three kings to the baby Jesus.

As the night of the play got closer, Bea got more and more agitated. She practised every night with George at the piano. She sang when she was in the bath, when she played outside, just before going to bed. 'Ave Maria' ran in my head all the time. I wasn't the only one. George and the boys would hum it or sing it under their breath at odd moments. Even now, so many years later, when I hear it on the wireless or on the telly, it throws me back thirty years in a heartbeat.

The night before the nativity, I was getting the dinner on, listening to George and Bea at the piano in the front room. She stopped in the middle of the piece.

'What is it, duck?' asked George.

'I f-f-forgot the words. I n-n-need to see the sh-sh-sheet. What if I f-f-forget them on the day?'

'You won't, sweetheart. Something will take over you, you'll see. It's a magical thing happens to people when they're on stage.'

'But what if I do?'

'Just carry the tune, you know, la-la-la until the words come back to you. Nobody speaks Latin any more, so they won't know any different.'

I threw down the knife and stormed into the front room.

'Bea,' I said. 'We all know the ruddy words we've heard it so many times. You won't mess it up, will you?'

Bea buried her face in George's chest, as if taking refuge from me.

'Leave her alone,' he mouthed in silent fury.

'Don't let her bottle it,' I mouthed back.

The two of us smouldered all through dinner, both dying to stuff the kids into their beds so we could really let rip. Paddy ate his dinner, cool as you like. He was never touched by conflict, not like the other kids. Soon as dinner was over, George took Bea off to bed. He was with her for ages. I tucked Colin in and the others drifted off one by one. I paced up and down. By the time he finally came down I was wound up to breaking point.

'She's like an open nerve,' he said.

'You're not going to let her off doing it, George. I don't care what you say.'

'Princess, I...' He held his hands up and brought them down slowly, like a conductor quieting an orchestra. Like he was the reasonable one, and I needed controlling. It wound me up even more.

'You'd never let the boys get away with it!'

'She'll not do it because you've forced her!' he barked. Even now, after everything we went through, I can count on the fingers of one hand how many times he raised his voice to me. 'She'll do it because I've spent an hour telling her she'll be brilliant. Something she could do with hearing from you once in a while, rather than threats of hellfire if she lets us down.'

'You'd never make that kind of effort for the boys.'

'None of the boys have ever had to sing Ave bloody Maria, solo, to the whole school.'

I had to pick the scab right off. 'It's like she's our only child to you.'

I thought he'd choke with red fury. Then he said, 'There's none so blind as them that won't see, Edie.'

I was cut to the quick.

The next morning, George was at the table with the kids at breakfast thanks to the blessed nativity. On a normal day I fed him first, as he had to get off to work way before the kids left for school, leaving me about half an hour to iron shirts while a big pot of porridge simmered for the kids. I liked sending them off with a good breakfast. I did a bacon butty for George, with lashings of butter on bits of bread like doorstoppers, and tea that was sweet and stewed. When the kids came down I'd spoon out hot porridge for them, and put down a huge plate of bread and butter, which was snatched up in seconds, every last crumb. I was forever telling them not to eat like they'd escaped from the zoo, but they were growing like the clappers and it was jungle rules.

It was a different story with Bea. She ate slowly, always the last to finish. She'd take a slice of bread and butter, then tear off a tiny morsel. She'd spread a little honey on it, then would feed it to herself neatly, putting her knife down between mouthfuls, sometimes delicately licking honey from her fingers like a Siamese cat. The boys left the table like a war zone, but wherever Bea sat there was hardly so much as a crumb that overspilled her plate. I'd like to say she got it from me, but I didn't get a chance to eat at table very often. I usually had to feed myself standing up while I was boiling this or stirring that and dishing up for everyone else.

George was going into work late that morning as he wanted to come to Bea's nativity. He upset my routine a bit. He was in no hurry to get out of bed, so I was in a rush to get his breakfast done as well as make porridge at the same time for the kids.

The boys all wanted bacon butties like their dad, when there wasn't enough to go round. I decided to cook up all the bacon that was left, which could make up five decent-size butties. One to George, and half a butty for everyone else, plus their lot of porridge.

Because George was there, I decided not to make Bea eat porridge. He'd think that any dig at Bea was a dig at him. Bea hated porridge. I hated the stuff too, as it happens, but it was cheap and filling and the boys loved it. I put some in front of her every day, and wouldn't let her have her bread and honey until she'd finished it. Always a performance. I knew very well the boys sneaked spoonfuls of it whenever my back was turned. Sometimes I told them off, other times I pretended not to see. I didn't really care if she ate the ruddy stuff or not, but if you let kids do what they like, then where will you be?

George was reassuring Bea about her song, that she'd be brilliant. It was like listening to a stuck record. I ran the iron over the kids' shirts, a bit slapdash as we were running late. I gave Bea's tutu a last going-over. I'd borrowed it from Moll's granddaughter. The bodice was fine, as it stretched over her chest, but the little skirt was a nightmare of tulle and gauze, a devil to iron. I picked it up and held it against the light to make sure it was spotless. It looked all right, although there was a white fluff all over it. I gave it a shake and a good pat. The fluff came off easily enough. The spangled tights were also covered in fluff. A good shake put them to rights. I put the tutu on a hanger and draped the tights round the neck and covered both with one of George's old shirts so they'd not get mucked up on the way to school. I hung it off the back of the kitchen door, then grabbed the porridge pot and started dishing up for the kids while the bacon was crisping.

'Please M-M-M-Mam,' said Bea, looking up at me with big sad eyes. 'D-don't make me eat p-p-p-porridge today. I feel s-s-sick.'

Well. Like I said, I wasn't going to give her any but something in the way she said it made me see red. It was the weariness in her pitiful voice. Like I forced the stuff down her throat. Like she was one of them stuffed French geese. Like she was a long-suffering martyr. All for George's benefit.

He pinched her nose. 'It's good to have a few nerves. Otherwise you wouldn't do your best.'

'Bea,' I said. 'You're not the Star of Bethlehem in this house. Eat a bit. Like always.'

George rubbed noses with her. 'I'll help you, duck.'

Saving her from big bad Mam again. I swear it took all my strength not to dump the whole pot on top of their heads. I plonked a dollop of steaming porridge into her bowl, dished up for the rest of the kids in silence and went to see about the butties. I gave one to George, then divvied the rest up between the kids.

Bea took a tiny mouthful and made a face, as if she were sucking lemons. She was the same colour as the porridge.

'Bea, don't touch that butty 'til you've polished that off.'

Paddy ate his butty with a little smile on his face. He was nearly seventeen by then. Tall, blond, so handsome. He'd asked to skip morning classes to see his sister sing. It showed he was part of the family. That Borthwick woman was always going on about how he needed to learn cooperation. This was proof he was doing it.

He reached across and took a spoonful of Bea's porridge. George winked at him. Paddy was usually the last one to help Bea out, and I was always trying to build bridges between George and Paddy, and honest to God I don't know what made me so hell-bent on making a point. I stormed over to Paddy and snatched his spoon away from him. I threw it down on the table, splattering porridge on his shirt. Cool as you please, he stood up, unbuttoned it, pulled it off and held it out to me. Like I was his maid. I can't begin to tell you what was going through my head. Rage at Paddy. Yes, Paddy. The one I was always shielding. But I ask you. The cheek of it. The sheer want of respect. Then there was George. Lording it at the table. Laughing with Bea and the boys. I was fuming at myself. For not keeping my big cakehole shut. For forcing a big scene. Bea had George on her side. George, who'd always been on my side.

I snatched Paddy's shirt from him and flung it on the floor. I glared at George, then picked up the spoon and cast my eye on Bea. Her eyes were darting between me and Paddy, face like a skittish ghost. I gathered up a big dollop of porridge, then forced her mouth open. I pushed the spoon between her puckered-up lips and shoved the porridge down her throat. George stood up. His chair screeched against the floor.

'Edie, that's enough,' he said.

I went cold. I forgot all about Bea and the porridge when I saw his face. He was looking at me like I was a monster. It was too much. I pulled the spoon out of her mouth. It was that quiet in the room I heard it clank against her teeth. George and I were locked together in a look, like if one of us broke away that would be the end of us. I was warring with him but more with myself. Then I heard a rumbling, like distant thunder. The next thing I knew the table was covered in sick and the boys were all gasping in shock. Will grabbed the bread and butter plate away in the nick of time. George picked Bea up, sick and all, and carried her to the bathroom. He cast me a look I'll never forget.

I was a jumble of feelings. Not wanting to be angry any more, but I was. Not seeing why I should feel guilty, but I did. Not knowing why I felt so… stupid, but I did. I wanted to cry but didn't know what for. I wanted to make amends but didn't know how. I would have happily swung right then for George, for Paddy and for Bea.

I couldn't face the mess on the table. I picked up the milk jug and plonked it next to the sink. I wrapped up the plates, food, crumbs, sick and everything else in the tablecloth, gathered the corners together in a loose knot and dumped it outside in the back garden to see to later. I had to get a new shirt sorted for Paddy and clean up what had spilled on the floor.

When Bea came downstairs, she had some colour in her cheeks.

'I'm s-s-sorry, M-M-Mam.'

George kept all expression off his face.

'S-s-sorry I m-m-made a mess. I feel b-b-better now.'

I patted her back awkwardly. I felt wrong-footed. I thought about hugging her, but it might have come off false. I wanted to tell George I was sorry, but I couldn't find the words. Even if I'd tried they'd have come out wrong. I'd make amends, I thought. I really would. I'd always been able to get George back on side.

God alone knows what he'd said to her, but she was like a different child. Full of beans and yammering away, compared to the ghost at breakfast not five minutes ago. As if the p-p-puked-up p-p-porridge had p-p-purged her of all worry.

She lifted her eyes to mine. A shaft of sunlight broke

through the window, and lit up her blue eyes so they shone like stained glass. It happened from time to time, the shock of fear I'd get when I saw them. It was like looking at Penharris's eyes. I gathered her up in my arms to get her out of the sunlight. She gasped and stiffened, then shut up smartish she was that surprised, then slowly she stole her arms round my neck.

I held her tightly to me, afraid to look up. When I did, I saw George had a tear in his eye. He melted like butter on a boiler. We may not have been good at the hearts and flowers in our house, but I felt forgiven. It was hard to push the tears back. It wasn't a performance and yet it was. The tears were real, all right. It's just that I was crying for something else, something George would never understand. He took it as a sign of love for his precious little angel and I wasn't going to tell him any different.

# CHAPTER THIRTEEN

A cane hand found Odolina in the morning. She had regained consciousness, but lay in the grass under the early morning sun summoning up the will to get to her feet. She could barely see, as one eye was swollen shut and the other watered copiously. He gave her some water from his flask. She wanted to guzzle it down as her thirst was raging, but her mouth refused to move properly, so he had to give it to her slowly, in tiny sips, cradling her head in the crook of his arm. He carried her home.

Odolina's mother was sweeping the porch when he appeared with her broken daughter in his arms, followed by a small rabble of excitable children. Her screams attracted more children, and her neighbours. Someone ran for Sergeant Lopez. He lived nearby and his shift had not yet begun. His hair was still wet when he arrived to the chaos of the Carvalho household.

Odolina was laid out on a sofa. Her mother knelt by her side, a heaving bulk, sobbing into a faded floral cushion. Women bustled about, trying to take charge, bossily attempting to calm Odolina's mother down, fighting for space at the stove where all four rings were in use; pots were on the boil for cleaning the casualty's wounds and for making coffee. Children ran amok, everywhere underfoot, crying, confused, working themselves up to fever pitch. Rafaela, who was then fifteen, had her sister's head in her lap, and was helping her to sip water from the side of her mouth that was not slit and swollen.

Lopez had seen some things in his time as a policeman. Nevertheless, the sight of the girl affected him. This was the daughter of his dead friend, a girl he had watched grow up. He had always known that she was trouble, but no one deserved to be cut up like a chicken.

'Maria!' he barked. 'Get these brats out of here. Bianca,

get your husband's camera. Now! Be quick. Salome, don't clean her up until I can take pictures.' Indignant, Maria shooed the children out as if they were hens. Bianca was forced to cede the stove to Salome, who was delighted to have control of the pots. 'Lucia, go and call the clinic. Tell that fat fool Garcia to move his backside. She'll probably have to go to hospital in the city. That eye looks bad.'

He patted Odolina's mother on the shoulder. 'Sarita, go and lie down. Salome, give her coffee with lots of sugar. Get her out of here.'

Rafaela continued to help Odolina drink water. Tears rolled silently down the younger girl's cheeks, but she made no sound. At last, he thought. Someone who wasn't hysterical who was doing something useful. He turned his attention to Odolina.

'Odolina, *cara*, who did this to you?'

Her hoarse croak was drowned by the sound of sizzling as water bubbled over on the stove.

Quiet!' he yelled at Salome. Resentfully, she took the offending pot off the boil.

'Tell me again, *caro*. Did you see who did this to you?'

'Nuno,' she coughed. 'His name is Nuno.'

'Was he at the bar last night?'

'No. Ask Antonio.'

'I can't hear you, *cara*.'

'Antonio knows him.'

'The one with the camera?'

'Yes.'

It did not require enormous penetration to work out that her attacker was Nuno. She'd seen enough of his face. The shape and weight was Nuno's. He hadn't raped, mugged or killed her. He'd just disfigured her, to leave the way clear for Frieda to become the Oléo Anjo girl.

The tally of injuries was long. She had a broken cheekbone, a broken jaw, a detached retina, two smashed teeth and a dislocated shoulder. Nuno had deeply scored her left cheek and forehead with a knife. He hadn't bothered with her right side, as he had split the skin over her smashed cheekbone.

Nuno was not a slick criminal. He insisted he'd been at the movies with Frieda on the night of the attack. He couldn't name the movie or the actors, or relate the theme or plot. When questioned, Frieda could not lie even if she'd wanted to. She had been at her aunt's birthday party, one of fifty other guests, then had gone home with her sister.

Nuno was a stranger in Odolina's home town, yet half a dozen people confirmed they'd seen him in Bebo's that evening, sitting on the verandah facing the Pasadena. Although they respected Lopez, the locals did not usually willingly cooperate with the police, but this time, feelings ran high. She was one of their own. Nuno's arms were marked with cuts from the sugar cane leaves. He hadn't disposed of the knife and hadn't bothered to clean it very well. He'd dropped the mask next to the scene of the crime. It was one of the cheap plastic ghoul's faces sold in shops all over the country for fancy dress or Halloween. It still bore the price sticker with the name of the shop he'd bought it from. The shopkeeper remembered selling it to him.

The call Odolina had been so anxiously awaiting came two days after the attack. Luis cried as he broke the news. A representative of Oléo Anjo visited her in the hospital. One look confirmed that Odolina would not be selling lotion for them, or anything for anyone else.

It was a month before Odolina could get back to work at the bar. Luis had taken her picture down. Often his eyes watered when he looked her way. He gave her a ride home each night. Odolina shrugged. Who was going to touch her now?

The story captured the attention of the press. A small-town girl getting herself attacked was not especially interesting, but a young woman disfigured by her rival's lover to snare a TV modelling job was electrifying. Two beautiful girls and a handsome young man, the pathos of three young lives destroyed. Before and after pictures of Odolina. The stories exaggerated her early success to highlight the devastation of her ruined future.

Frieda was given a shot at the Oléo Anjo job, but was dropped. She had no sparkle on screen. Odolina shrugged. She had started to do that a lot. The cuts on her face were aggravated when she spoke or smiled, so she kept her face as still as a mask. In any case, she was dead inside.

The press began to focus on Nuno's colourful family background, especially the dealings of his father.

Antonio sold his photos of Odolina to several sources. They paid handsomely. He gave the money to Odolina. He arranged for her to be interviewed by newspapers and magazines. After a blizzard of phone calls, a dentist in Rio agreed to fix Odolina's teeth for free.

Her new teeth improved her looks dramatically, but the scars remained, inside and out.

Antonio tried the same with dermatologists and cosmetic surgeons. The best result would be obtained when the subcutaneous tissue was completely healed, which would take time. The best surgeons were in America. He hoped to scrape together enough from the photos and the interviews to send her to the US for treatment. He worked tirelessly, knowing the story would not remain current for long.

One night in the bar, Odolina was called to the telephone.

She didn't recognise the voice.

'You stop talking to the press. You say nothing to nobody. You remember nothing. You don't talk to your friends. You keep your mouth shut, you understand? Or next time you will get cut up by someone who knows what he's doing.'

Luis insisted she call Lopez.

'Odolina,' Lopez sighed heavily. 'I just got back from Rio. These are ugly people.'

'Nuno will be convicted if I talk or not. What difference does it make?'

'Nuno will not be convicted.'

'What are you talking about?' For once, her indifference was breached.

'I've been taken off the case. The evidence will disappear.'

Luis drove Odolina home with Antonio to get her things. The two men sat in the front and discussed her escape. Antonio would buy her a plane ticket to Lisbon. He had an uncle there who could look after her and help her find a job. Luis said he had some money. Not much, but something.

'I have no passport,' Odolina said. She had never left the country in her life.

The two of them turned round to stare at her. Luis dragged his eyes back to the road and smacked his hand on the wheel in frustration.

The two men feverishly began plotting how and where she could hide until they got her a passport. Then Odolina spoke up.

'Lorena has a passport. She doesn't need it anymore.'

She could easily pass for her sister. A flicker of excitement uncurled in her chest. Lisbon. A new life, one that Lorena had not had the courage to embrace. A new name. She hated Odolina. She turned to look out of the window. The tips of the cane leaves brushed the moonlit sky. Despite the aggravation it caused to the wound on her cheek, she smiled to herself in the dark.

# CHAPTER FOURTEEN

We trooped off for the nativity smartish. We all looked a bit crumpled, but that couldn't be helped. I'd had no time to do my hair. My mind was bound up with how I was going to be a better mother, a better wife, a better person.

'The tutu!' I cried. I'd left it hanging on the kitchen door. If Bea was a no-show, George would hold me to account for it.

'I've got it, Mam,' said Paddy.

I brimmed with relief. My heart sang for my beautiful boy. To think I'd been that close to wringing his neck. I was never religious, not in any serious way, but in that moment I sent a prayer of thanks up to heaven. Paddy was showing cooperation, something the Borthwick woman said he was lacking in. She said he needed to be taught to 'emulate' it for the sake of smoother relations with others.

We got to school with seconds to spare.

'I thought you'd got cold feet!' Mrs Jackson cried.

Bea gave a wobbly smile. An attack of the nerves was not far away. I was surprised to see Penharris's daughter backstage. She was pinning tails onto sheep.

'Clare will help you into your costume,' said Mrs Jackson.

I thrust the costume towards Clare. Bea threw her arms round my waist. I patted her awkwardly. 'Do us proud, Bea,' I said, and left her to it.

Mrs Jackson started shooing the kids onstage. I sank into my seat next to George. We'd made it. I had nothing to do for nobody until the show was over. I dropped my handbag on the floor in front of me and unbuttoned my coat. I smoothed my skirt over my knees. The lights went down and George took my hand in his. I felt I was glowing in the dark.

Paddy was on my other side. His eyes were burning. To think that he could get so worked up about his little sister.

Arthur Penharris stepped up to the spotlit lectern.

'Ladies and gentlemen,' he said, 'welcome to St Stephen's nativity play. This year's cast have worked incredibly hard to bring you first-class entertainment and to remind us all of the true spirit of Christmas in an increasingly commercial age. Without further ado, I give you the St Stephen's Primary School Players!'

The curtain came up on shepherds and kings and farmyard beasts, standing around the holy family in the centre. Mr Conway, the music master, played the opening bars of 'Ave Maria'. Usually, he had to crash away, trying manfully to lead a bunch of kids into carrying some kind of tune, but this time he had a lightness of touch, as if tuned in to something divine. The stage lights went down and a spotlight shone on Bea.

She stood in her white tutu and spangled tights, her hair covered in tinsel with a big silver star at the back of her head, like an Elizabethan collar. She looked like a little silver sun. She clutched a wand, a little baton topped off with a silver star. I sneaked a look at George. He was choked up with pride.

Bea turned two slow pirouettes while Conway finished the introductory bars. She took in a deep breath, too early, like she was trying to calm herself down. She shone whitely under the spotlight. The anticipation of her singing was sending goosebumps down my neck. She managed to get her breathing back on track. We'd heard her sing it a thousand times, but as her voice rang out in that hallway, rising up so strong and so true, I closed my eyes to let the first long 'Ave Maria' fill up my head.

'Gratia plenum.' The pleasure of it spread through the hall like a holy blessing.

'Benedicta tu in mulieribus.' Her voice wavered. I thought she was going to bottle it, but she took a deep breath and her voice gained in strength again. *'Et benedictus fructus ventris, Tui Jesus...'* There was a natural pause while Conway let the piano ebb, so we could anticipate the pleasure of the quiet being filled again with that voice. She was shaking, as if she remained on stage by dint of sheer willpower.

Again, she took in a deep breath too early. I willed her to control herself. Conway paused to match her pace. Her voice rang out again, true and clear. *'Sancta Maria, Mater Dei.'* She had just a few more lines to go. Her voice deepened when Conway changed the chord. Oh, it was beautiful. *'Ora pro nubis peccatoribus.'* Pray for us sinners. *'Nunc et in hora mortis nostrae.'* Now and in the hour of our death. Then the last, slow *'Amen'.* She'd found the strength from somewhere, though her eyes were wide and her face pinched and haggard as no eight-year-old's should ever be. Conway looked up from his music in triumph. His face changed when he saw her. There was a collective hush from the audience, as the last note from the piano slowly died in the air.

The place erupted as the room stood to applaud her. Eyes wide as footballs, she gave a kind of whimper and turned to run. She tripped over one of the sheep, then scrabbled to her feet. She ran towards the wings, but Mrs Jackson blocked her, ushering her back onstage, wanting her to lap up the applause. Bea ripped off the tutu, and was having a go at the tights.

Conway stood up. The clapping turned to gasps and whispers. George got to his feet and edged past those in our row. 'Excuse me,' he said. 'Excuse me.' Bea writhed on the stage screaming. She looked boiled alive. Angry red patches, big as poppies, had sprung up on her skin. She ran naked towards one of the wings, right into the arms of Clare Penharris, who scooped her up in her arms. It was like seeing Bea in the arms of her older self. For the second time that day I felt a stab to my soul.

George reached Clare and took Bea from her arms,

covering her with his coat. Bea squirmed and struggled, clawing at her skin. She whimpered and cried like a pup with leprosy. People were abuzz, shocked, whispering, talking, giggling.

I marched to the stage. Sonny and Will followed. Paddy had a feverish look about him, like he didn't know whether to laugh or cry.

George headed for the exit, Bea squirming and squalling in his arms. Without George's coat she'd have caught her death it was that cold outside. Me and the boys followed. People parted before us like the Red Sea. Once outside, I had to run to keep up with him. Sonny, Will and Paddy were hot on our heels. Paddy was laughing. A nervous reaction, like as not, but I didn't want George to hear. I hissed at him to get off to school. Suddenly I remembered the tutu.

'George!' I called. 'The tutu!'

'The what?'

'Her costume.'

'Leave it. Let's just get home.'

I had to get it back to Moll. I ran back to the hall. The kids on stage were mangling 'Little Donkey'.

I crept round the side of the curtain. The tutu lay mangled on the floor backstage, the tights not far away. I slung them over my arm and slunk back down the side of the stage, shrinking in the darkness. As I came down the steps on the side of the stage, I made for the gangway fast as I could without running. I felt someone's hand on my arm. It was Penharris.

'Mrs Newell,' he said. 'I must speak to you.'

I panicked. 'I have to get home.' Good God, I thought. Not him. Not now. Yes, I did an awful lot of praying that day. I wrenched my arm from him. Outside in the bright daylight I breathed in great gasps of air. Penharris was hot on my heels.

'Mrs Newell, I have to—'

'You're wrong!' I spat. 'Whatever you're thinking, you're wrong and you're not to think it!'

He was pale as the puked-up porridge waiting for me at home. I felt weak, like I could barely stand. He had a haunted look on his face. For the second time that day I saw bright blue eyes lit up by a winter sun. He made a strange sign with his hands, like he was begging or... or praying.

'Please. She's—'

'You're to leave us be!' I said. 'I've got to go home.'

'She's mine, isn't she?'

'She's ours. Mine and George's.'

'She's so like Clare. When I first saw her—'

'She looks like Paddy. You'll not be claiming him in a hurry, will you?'

'Mrs Newell, if she's mine I want—'

'She's no more your daughter than I am. He's her father, not you.' It was no lie. In every way that mattered, George was Bea's father. I turned round at the gate. He was rooted to the spot staring after me. God only knew what he would do. Pray God he wouldn't try to talk to George. I couldn't bear to think of it.

\*\*\*

I got a letter from George's solicitor before he died. George had been paying money into our joint account for years. It was what I lived on. The letter advised me to open an account in my sole name, explaining that if we maintained a joint account, there was a danger it'd be frozen on his death. 'As you are no doubt aware,' it said, 'your husband is in frail health, and has instructed me to so advise you, in order to avoid any distress or inconvenience to you.' I cried on reading it. It went on to say I had the right to remain in the 'marital home' for the rest of my life. Where else was I supposed to ruddy well go? Lastly, it said George had put 'a sum of money' into a trust that would pay me an income until my death, but he was leaving the house and the capital to the kids.

George was tidying me away. I was one of the chores he had to deal with before he died. I'd always nursed a dream that he'd give in, that we'd be together at the end. That letter was a bucket of ice water chucked into my face.

Paddy was with George when he died. There's a bit of irony for you. The boy he'd always rejected was with him right at the end. Paddy told me not to say anything to the others. Said he'd burned what George was writing.

'What writing?' I asked him.

'He'd written some stuff for us kids, Mam. Why you and him split.'

I had to sit down.

'Don't you worry, Mam. It's burnt and I'll never tell.' He winked at me.

'What did he write?' My voice trembled.

'You know. Stuff about me. Where I came from.'

'What do you mean?' I trembled.

'Oh, don't worry. He was just speculating. And there was stuff about you and Penharris. You're a naughty girl, you are, Mam.' He laughed. As if I'd done it as a wanton.

'It wasn't like that!' I cried.

'Like what?'

'I did it for you!'

'How exactly did you have sex with another man for my benefit?'

'Don't say it like that!' I put my hands over my ears like a child.

'Don't you worry, Mam. I'll not tell.'

With Paddy you can never be sure about anything.

Bea never sang on stage again after the nativity. She gave up her place in the choir. She was deaf to George, Clare, Conway her music teacher, her brothers. Even Penharris had a word with her, as I found out years later. Stubborn as a wart she was.

I never did find out what caused that rash of hers on the stage. She said it was like itching from the inside out, right through her, where she couldn't reach. Stage fright, probably. Amazing what the mind can do to the body.

I was jumpy for days after Penharris's ambush. I'd promised myself I'd be softer with Bea, but the bald fact is she nettled me just by existing. I was terrified Penharris would turn up and shame me, that he'd risk everything to claim her. Since they've been living in caves, men have put cuckoos into other men's nests. Up and down the centuries, legions of kids have been ignored by their rightful fathers... just my flaming luck that Penharris was the honourable type.

Sammy got sweet on Clare Penharris. He'd never have had the gumption to ask her out, but let's face it, a boy chases a girl until she catches him. She came round to ours the day of the nativity to see Bea. I'd left her with Sammy to nip to the shops, and when I came back, I found Bea cuddled up with Clare on the sofa. I felt funny looking at them. Bea's skin had settled down thanks to calamine, which had dried in great white whorls all over her.

'Hello, Mrs Newell,' said Clare.

'Hiya Mam,' said Sammy. 'Want a tea?'

'Aye. Thanks, love,' I said. He leapt up for the kitchen. I perched on the edge of an armchair.

'I came round to see how Bea is,' said Clare. Bea felt awkward with Clare's arm about her, I could tell. She always did clam up whenever I was near her. It got on my nerves.

'Right as rain, as you can see. Were you skipping your lessons this morning to help out backstage?'

Clare laughed. 'I had a double free, and I knew Helen needed help.'

'Helen?'

'Mrs Jackson.'

The use of the first name put my back up a bit.

Sammy came back in with a mug of tea for me.

'Is this the dregs of the pot?' I asked.

'I made it not five minutes ago,' he said.

'I like it fresh and scalding,' I said.

'Sorry, Mam, I'll—' and he started to get up.

'Never mind. I'll do it,' I said, glad to get out. I put the kettle on. I collected myself. I popped my head back round the front room door. 'Would you like a fresh cup, Clare?'

'No thanks. I'm still drinking this one.'

'I hope you don't mind if I have mine in the kitchen,' I said. 'I've got to get the dinner on.'

'Don't fret about me,' she said, smiling. 'I'm fine with Bea and Sam.'

I started peeling spuds and carrots. I was just about to call Bea in to help when I stopped myself. I didn't want Sam alone with Clare. Sam sidled into the kitchen.

'What's for tea, Mam?' he asked. As if he'd ever been bothered his whole life about what he put in his mouth. So long as I dished up food, Sam ate it.

'Lamb stew.'

'Is it okay if Clare stays?'

'Isn't her dad expecting her back?'

'She says he'll be fine.'

'I don't know if we have enough.'

'Come on, Mam. She's a girl, not a horse.'

What could I say? The three of them helped with dinner. Clare and Bea peeled spuds, and Sammy started to chop onions. He cut the onions in half from the top to bottom, then cut along the layers one way then the other, so they crumbled into small chunks.

'Where did you learn to do that?' I asked him.

He laughed. 'By watching you!'

I wasn't sure I liked the idea of my boys cooking. I liked

feeding them myself. I liked them rushing to the table with rumbling tummies, eager to mop up what they found there. It wasn't just food I was giving them.

The lamb was already cubed so I started on the gravy. Some stock, a bit of Bisto, some dripping, mustard, a dash of Worcester sauce and a touch of flour for thickening. With the meat juice it'd be grand.

'Shall I get some rosemary from your bush outside?' said Clare. 'It's fantastic with lamb.'

My gravy wouldn't be bettered by her sticking her oar in and I wanted to say so. It was one thing her being in my kitchen. It was another her stamping her mark on the food. It got on my wick. I was tempted to make a little joke, but I couldn't trust how it would come out. 'Where's the harm?' I said.

'I'll get it,' said Sam.

'Just a couple of sprigs,' she called after him. 'Do you have a pot for these spuds, Mrs Newell?' I bent down to get the biggest one from the cupboard under the counter. People laughed when they saw the mountains of food I made for each meal, but there were seldom any leftovers.

Clare put the peeled and cut potatoes inside it and rinsed the grit off them at the sink. Once they were clean, she covered them with cold water and put the pot on the counter.

'Where will I find the salt?' she asked.

I passed it to her. She put a good pinch of it into the water.

'Can I do anything else?'

'You're all right,' I said.

Sam came back in with the rosemary.

'She said a couple of sprigs. Not the whole bush,' I said.

Clare laughed.

She broke off what she wanted and dropped it into my gravy. 'We can yank it out just before it goes on the table.'

I picked up a sprig and put it to my nose. Of course I

knew that rosemary went with lamb. It's just that I cooked the way I cooked and that was the end of it.

'How did you learn to cook, Mrs Newell?' Clare asked, sitting back down.

'My mother died when I was nine. I had three brothers. My dad couldn't boil an egg, and the boys were useless so I just got on with it.'

It sounded so clean, but grief's a messy thing. I became like a mother to Jackie, who was only five. I remember hearing my dad crying in the night. I'd lie in my room aching with sorrow, longing for my mother to come back, to fix us all. He didn't stay in his bed alone for long.

I don't like thinking of my father.

I looked at Clare and wondered if she'd had to do the things I had, would it show? Had anyone looked at me and known? Had my older brothers? Jackie had known. I didn't like thinking of Jackie either. I hadn't seen him since Timmy died.

'That's terrible,' she said.

'Oh, I don't know. I had the odd disaster, but I soon got the hang of it.'

'No, I mean losing your mother at nine,' said Clare.

'You know what it is to lose a mother young,' I said. I forgave her for interfering in my kitchen. She could cook because she'd had to learn, same as me.

'I still miss her,' she said.

I didn't like people talking about their feelings. It made me shift inside my skin.

'How did she d-d-die?' asked Bea.

'She had cancer,' said Clare, picking up my mother's cookbook. It was like she had a sixth sense for what would disturb me the most.

'That's old, that is.' I've still got that book. It's a thick old fibre hardback, threads showing. The picture on the cover is long faded. Even then, the pages were brown and dog-eared and some of them had worked their way loose from the spine.

'I'll be careful,' she said. I could see her reading the inscription. '"*For my dear daughter Ellen, on her wedding day. Your loving mother,*" she read out loud. 'Was Ellen your mother?'

I nodded.

'What a lovely thing to have. Like a link between the generations. I expect you'll pass it on to Bea one day.'

Well. Giving the book to Bea had never crossed my mind.

Clare watched me stir the gravy before adding it to the fried chunks of lamb. It was only half five. Time enough for the meat to tenderise over a couple of hours, to stew with the onions and carrots and mushrooms in the gravy. Clare's spuds sat in the big pot on top of the oven in the cold salted water, waiting to be boiled and mashed.

'Do you have any red wine?' asked Clare.

I was shocked. 'Tea not good enough for you?'

Her cheeks flushed pink. 'Sorry, Mrs Newell, I didn't mean to drink. I meant for the gravy. It gives it a lovely flavour.'

'My children will be eating this stew. Maybe in your house your dad lets kids have alcohol,' I said, 'but I'll not have it in mine.'

Bea went white under her calamine.

'The heat of the cooking process burns all the alcohol away, Mam,' said Sam gently.

I slosh wine into all sorts of things these days, but I didn't do it then. My cheeks burned.

I was saved by George coming home.

'Hello, hello,' he said when he saw Clare. 'This is a turn-up for the books.'

'I came to see Bea.'

'That's nice of you.' He smiled. 'Staying for tea, I hope.'

'I probably should be heading for home,' she said,

cheeks still burning.

Sam and Bea both begged her to stay but she stood up to go. I felt bad. All she'd done was try to impress me. I'd catch it from Sam later.

'Clare, please,' I said. 'We'd be glad if you stayed for tea. It's been a rough old day on us, and it'd be a treat for the kids.'

She hesitated. 'Thanks, Mrs Newell.'

George smiled. He turned to Bea. 'How are you faring, then?'

'I'm f-f-fine, Dad.'

'Good lass.' He picked her up, groaning. 'You're getting too heavy for this, ducky. That was some performance. You got through it though your skin was on fire. That's courage, that is. Don't you think so, Princess?'

'Shame we didn't see the rest of it.' Over Bea's head, George gave me a look.

'All I mean is that Clare here and Mrs Jackson went to a lot of trouble putting the show together, that's all.'

I put a cup of tea in front of George.

'Ta, Princess,' he said. 'So how did the rest of it go?' he asked Clare.

'It was lovely.'

'Who filled in for Bea?'

'She'd done her bit.'

Do you have any idea about what happened?' George asked her. 'I've been racking my brains all day. Bea, when did you start itching?'

'S-s-soon as I put the t-t-tutu on.'

I stiffened. 'There was nowt wrong with the tutu.' I said. 'I washed it and ironed it myself, and no one else had touched it before I gave it to you.' I meant Clare. 'No one else.' It was Paddy who'd taken it out of the house. Of course I wasn't about to tell them that. The fluff. Could he have... but what on earth could he have done?

'Where is it?' asked George.

'Where's what?' I said.

'The tutu.'

'Soaking in the bathroom sink. I've got to give it back to Moll.'

'Oh right,' said George, deflating. 'Paddy had it, didn't he?' Like a dog with a bone he was sometimes.

'He picked it up from behind the kitchen door after we'd all left the house without it. Good job too.'

'It's all right, Princess,' he said. 'Nobody's suggesting anything.'

Clare looked a bit uncomfortable, and said, 'Bea, why don't you show me your room?'

Bea didn't need telling twice. Once they'd gone upstairs, Sam said, 'Mam, Dad's not blaming Paddy. He's just trying to work out what happened.'

'I wanted to take a look at that little frock,' said George.

'Why?' I asked.

'Our daughter strips naked as if being burned alive and you wonder I'd like to know why?'

'Everything goes wrong round here gets blamed on that boy,' I said.

'I wanted to take a look, that's all.'

'It needed washing. Things need doing around here, and I do them. For all the good it does me. I didn't know you wanted to play Sherlock bloody Holmes, did I?'

'Simmer down, you two,' said Sam in a furious whisper. 'We've got a visitor in case you hadn't noticed.'

George sighed. He closed his eyes and shook his head. 'Sorry, Princess. It's just that it's a rum thing when it's something she's worked so hard for, something so big, for a girl of her age, a shy girl at that.' He shook his head. 'To have it ruined like that. It could scar her for the rest of her life.'

'For pity's sake, George. It was a school nativity, not the ruddy Albert Hall.'

'For her it may as well have been the Albert Hall,' said Sam.

'That's exactly right,' said George.

There was no sense talking to that soft pair. I checked on the stew. It was bubbling nicely. I put the potatoes on to boil and put plates in the oven to warm.

Clare and Bea were still upstairs when the other boys came home. Paddy came in last, as per usual. He had to get two buses home.

'Where's Bea?' he asked. He had a little grin on his face, guaranteed to put George's back up.

'Good as new after a bath and a rub-down with calamine. How was school?' I asked, hoping to lead them off talking about the wretched nativity.

Paddy wouldn't be led. 'Well,' he said. 'She wanted to make a splash, and she did. No one's likely to forget that in a hurry.'

George narrowed his eyes.

'George, you should've seen Paddy this morning,' I said. 'He was crying when it happened. He was! Nobody was more upset than him.'

'Don't go on, Mam,' said Paddy.

'Let's say no more about it,' I said. You boys lay the table. Lay an extra place. Will, go and get Clare and Bea. Soon as I've mashed this lot, we can eat.'

'Who's Clare?' asked Will.

'She's in my class,' said Sam, cuffing his brother lightly on the shoulder.

Clare sat between Bea and Sam. The likeness between the two girls shone out like a beacon.

'How's your father?' said Paddy to Clare, glancing between her and Sam. Paddy couldn't half show us up when he had a mind.

'Very well, thanks for asking,' she said. Me and George both glared at him.

'He never liked me. He kicked me out of the school.'

Clare shifted in her seat.

'Paddy lad,' said George. 'You kicked yourself out of that school.' He turned to Clare. 'So what were you doing backstage this morning?'

'I love working with the little ones,' said Clare, dragging her eyes away from Paddy. 'Any free time I've had I've helped out with the production. I want to be a teacher when I leave school. I'd like to teach literature and drama.'

Bea looked up at her like a devoted puppy. Sam too.

'We've always set a great store by reading in this house.'

'Oh, you can tell. Sam's always been the brainiest in our class.'

Sam didn't know where to look.

'They all taught each other,' said George. 'All the older kids read stories to the little ones, and they just picked it up. Sam read to Sonny, and Sonny read to Will, and so on. Edie and me hardly had to lift a finger.'

'Speak for yourself!' I said.

'What about Paddy?' she asked.

'Oh I was adop—'

'Paddy taught himself,' I said loudly over him and glared his way.

In the four years he was in care, nobody had read so much as a book to him. The older kids watched terrible things on the video machine, so the younger ones, even the tinies Paddy's age, had seen horror, violence and God knows what else. When he came to live with us, he didn't know what a book was for. I wept for Paddy's lost years.

Sam walked Clare home after we'd eaten. I couldn't

wait for her to leave the house. She hugged Bea before she left. A shadow came over me when she did it. There was a world between me and my own self of the morning.

'She's got heart, that girl.' said George after she'd left.

'Hmm,' I said.

He laughed softly and stroked my cheek with the back of his hand. 'Sammy with a girlfriend. You'll get used to it.'

'He's only fifteen. It's a passing fancy, no more,' I said.

'Maybe. But look at us. You were only twenty when we married, and here we are, still together. With six kids.'

When I remember that moment, I think maybe I could have told him. If I'd told him then, when he was soft, when no one was knocking on our door, when the kids were in bed, when no one was pressing on us.

'We had seven kids, George.' Soon as it was out of my mouth, I wanted to bite the words back.

'I've not forgotten, Edie,' he said. He took his hand away from my face.

The time stretched out like dough. I wanted to say I was sorry, but couldn't find the words. He must've known I regretted it. He held his hand out to me.

'Come on, Princess. Let's go on up to bed.'

'I'll come up in a bit,' I said. 'I'll wait up for Sam.'

'That's barmy.' He laughed. 'He's a young man courting. He won't want his mother waiting up for him.'

'It's not right for him to come home to a dark house.'

'Leave the light on for him, then.'

'I want to wait.'

George shook his head and went up alone.

Sam and Clare stuck together for the rest of their time at school. I waited for the split when they went to university, but not a bit of it. He went to Oxford, she to Durham, and they faithfully wrote to each other while they were at far-flung ends of the country, and would save up all their money for train tickets.

They both worked at the William IV pub in the holidays, and made sure they had the same shifts. Sam had a full grant, of course, but that didn't stretch too far, not once he'd paid for his digs and his living expenses. We hardly saw him, as more often than not after he clocked off he'd go back to her place, and not come home of an evening. I can't say I approved. Her dad did nothing to stop it. Whenever Sam came home, Clare was in tow.

I know things are done differently now from when I was young, but nowadays kids are always jumping in and out of bed with each other. Don't get me wrong. It's not that I've forgotten what it was like to be young. It's just that with George and me it was different. We waited until we were married. 'Who's to say they won't get married?' he said. The thought of it gave me the shivers.

'Don't tie yourself down,' I said to Sam. Plenty of time for all that later.'

'Leave off, Mam,' he said.

I'd tell him to think of his future, his studying.

'I don't want to hear it, Mam, I love her.'

I pointed out that if she'd let him into her bed before marriage, then it mightn't be an exclusive club. It was hard to rouse Sam to anger.

'Don't you ever say anything bad about her. We love each other. Do you even know what that means?'

I was a bit insulted. He said it like I didn't understand what it was to be young. I was two pins from asking him where he thought he came from. The ruddy stork?

'Mam, if you could just hear yourself,' he said. 'She's funny. She's clever and she's kind. She's beautiful. I love her. Why have you taken against her?'

'I just don't want to see your future in ruins.'

'How exactly do you think she's going to ruin my future? She's got ambitions of her own. She wants a career. Do you want me to be a monk?'

I was frosty with her. I couldn't help it. She tried, ever so hard, but I was immune to her. Polite, but that's as far as it went. When she phoned, I'd not pass the message on if I thought I could get away with it. I'm ashamed of it now. In any case it didn't work.

God's got a sense of humour all right and the joke was on me. My child and Penharris's together. Each time he went back to Oxford, I prayed he'd meet someone else. What were the chances of two young people spending all that time apart and remaining faithful to a pipe dream? Fickle they are, the young, I told myself, but the two of them stuck together through time and distance.

I could see she was a pretty girl, and clever, and kind-hearted. I could see all those things, and more. It was that by her becoming family, we'd be closer to Penharris, and I was so afraid of things unravelling. Sometimes, in jumping to avoid your fate, you rush to meet it instead.

Sam's suitcase sat in the hallway on his last day home after the holidays, a deadweight on my spirits. He'd put his train ticket on top of it so he'd not forget it. The suitcase coloured my heart a little darker. All the time he spent with her was time she'd robbed from us. Her and her blasted father.

The phone rang.

'Hello, Mrs Newell. It's Clare. Is Sam there?' He'd only left her that morning, for crying out loud.

'He's gone out.' He'd taken Bea with him. I didn't tell her he'd tried to ring her.

'Oh. When's he back?'

'He didn't say.' He'd said he'd be back by eleven.

'I promised him I'd come and see him off. He was supposed to ring with the exact time of his train.'

'Let me see,' I said and picked up his ticket. The time on it was 14.00. 'It says four o'clock.'

'Four o'clock? Oh good. I've got time to get him a present. Don't tell him, will you?'

'I won't.'

'Tell him I'll be there in plenty of time.'

'In plenty of time for what?'

'To take him to the station. To say goodbye.'

I could still tell her the right time. I could've blamed it on my bad eyes.

'Rightio,' I said.

Sam and Bea came back from the shops together, breath steaming in the cold. I let them in before Sam had time to use his key. Sam had bought Bea a *Bunty* and a quarter of pick'n'mix from Woolworths. Bea and Clare... he was always spending money on the pair of them.

'Clare rang for the time of your train.' I told him. 'She said she'll be here in plenty of time.'

'Smashing,' he said.

I couldn't leave it alone. 'Once you get stuck into your studies, you'll forget all about—'

'Don't say it, Mam. I'll not, you know.'

A tear came unbidden to my eye. 'It's just that I'm so proud of you, Sammy.'

He put his arm around me. 'My daft little mam.'

Time ticked on, with no sign of Clare.

'You'll miss it if we don't go now,' said Will.

'Something must have come up,' said Sam. 'Another two minutes. Maybe I can get a later one,' he added weakly.

'That's just mad, that is,' I said. 'Paying for another ticket when you've spent good money on this one.'

'You told her the time of the train?' said Sam.

'I told you I did.'

He sighed heavily and picked up his suitcase.

'Mam, tell her I'll write to her. Tell her I love her.'

His eyes were pinched around the edges. I started to

feel a bit bad.

I was putting my coat on when Sam planted a kiss on my head and off he went with Will, leaving me and Bea alone. I was proper put out, as I'd wanted to go to the station to see him off.

I started to dread the knock at the door. It came at two on the dot, when Sam was long gone.

'Hello Mrs Newell,' she said brightly, and came in holding a package. 'Where is everyone?' she asked.

'Sam's gone to the station.'

Clare's face fell. 'What do you mean?'

'He couldn't wait any more.'

'What's he gone off without me for?'

'His train left at two,' I said.

The blood rushed to her face.

'Two? You said four.'

'Fourteen hundred.'

She frowned in concentration. She had good features, strong ones. She wasn't just pretty. It was like everything on her face did what it was supposed to do and more besides. I watched those features crumple. I started to feel proper bad. What a stupid thing I'd done. I'd tried to stop water finding its own level.

'Fourteen hundred. How stupid. How stupid I am.' Then she slumped on the sofa. I patted her shoulder. She turned towards me. She put her arms round me. It made me feel a bit awkward. What could I do? I stiffened. She clung to me and started sobbing. I patted her on the back.

'I love him so much,' she said. 'He'll think I don't care.'

'Shh now. Shh,' I said. 'He'll think no such thing.'

I heard Bea come down the stairs. Clare was crying on my shoulder as if her heart was fit only for breaking. Bea stared at us. It made me feel peculiar. I couldn't explain why, but I wished she hadn't seen us like that. She was always in the wrong place at the wrong time.

'I'll make you a cup of tea.'

She was very agitated. 'Is he still at the station, do you think? If I get in the car and drive like mad, do you suppose...'

'No. I'm sorry, duck. He's gone. You only saw him this morning. Did you not say goodbye then?'

'No. Not properly. I said I'd see him off.'

I touched her shoulder. 'The time'll fly by. What with both of you being so busy and all.'

She stood up, a wild look in her eye. 'I'll drive to Oxford now. It'll only take three hours. I can be back first thing tomorrow in time for the Durham train.'

'You'll not be doing any such thing,' I said. 'You'll do yourself a mischief. You stay put. Have yourself a cup of tea and write him a letter instead.'

Now, years later, I can see that fate has a funny way of cornering you, and doesn't let you get away with anything. It was like stuffing an octopus into a box. No sooner do you push one tentacle down than another comes shooting out.

I never stood in their way again. Clare and Sam were a fact of life.

She started dropping in for a cup of tea and a chat, even when Sam wasn't about. I became friendly with her. Imagine that.

Things between me and George settled down after the nativity, as they always did. George wasn't one to hold on to bad feelings. He wasn't the sort to take what he wanted from me without giving his love and affection in return. I was lucky. There are men aplenty who are very good at keeping the two things apart. If I'd only told him. In a quiet moment, say, when things were good between us. But I didn't, and I've spent the rest of my life paying.

I started to look forward to Clare's little visits. She came home on the odd weekend to see her dad. She never stayed long. She'd have a cup of tea then go on her way. Don't even ask me what we talked about. She became like a daughter to me. She was a comfort to me in those dark days after Paddy left. Even now, years later, I still feel the pain of him going.

They were seven years together when they decided to get married. Sammy was still studying, but Clare had just qualified. She got a job as a junior school teacher in Oxford, and would start in the January term. They were getting married in the Christmas holidays. They were mad, we said. Why didn't they wait until Sam was finished? Until he'd done his internship? When he had a comfortable job as a GP? But they wanted to be together, and that was that.

The fear of my secret coming out had lessened. I was tired of being afraid. We'd even had Penharris over for dinner a couple of times with Clare. He was about to become family, after all. To the world, Clare and Bea were just blond girls of a type. Just goes to show what a guilty conscience does to you. Covering up a lie is a worse punishment than taking the truth on the chin. You have to live for a long time to realise that.

The wedding was to be a small one, but Clare had a sense of style and wanted it to be an occasion. Bea was to be bridesmaid, along with Clare's friend Betty. Bea was fifteen by then, thin and gawky, in the middle of a ferocious growth spurt. She and Betty had chosen long fitted frocks in forest-green velvet. They looked like nothing on the hangers, but the girls filled them out beautifully.

After two years in train-track braces, Bea had finally had them removed. She'd be brace-free for the wedding. Her whole face was different without those braces. The way she carried herself changed. She stood up straighter and smiled without putting her hand to her mouth.

We got home from the dentist's late afternoon. Clare and her friend Betty were waiting for us. Betty worked at the local beautician's, and Clare wanted a trial run before the wedding. I've never been one for make-up. I had one lipstick, Rose of Cairo. If you find the shade that suits you, you've no need to buy another. I sometimes wore a bit of eyeshadow. I was lucky. I had good skin and George said I looked better natural without 'that muck' on my face. Still, I'd reached that age, so I agreed to let Betty loose.

'Give us a smile, then,' said Clare to Bea. 'Doesn't she look lovely, Betty?'

'Yep, she does.' said Betty. 'I had braces when I was a teenager. Wouldn't go through all that again if you paid me. Being a teenager, I mean. The braces were the easy part.' I smiled at someone so young sounding so world-weary. Betty and Clare were half my age.

I made a pot of tea. Betty's vanity case burst with brushes, powders, tubes and pots.

'You could be Clare's sister, not Sammy's,' said Betty.

I didn't mind people commenting any more. Like I said, people thought they were two girls of a type.

'Who should I do first?' asked Betty. She was pretty, but her blonde hair stood up in spikes and she wore more eyeliner than Cleopatra. She had a stripe of blusher down each cheekbone like an Indian brave and her lips were painted such a dark purple they looked black. It was all very well trying something new, but the result would be recorded for ever on the wedding pictures. She read my mind.

'Oh, don't mind me, Mrs Newell. I can do subtle, believe me. Shall I do you first?'

'You better had. I've got to get the dinner on.'

She patted the space next to her on the sofa.

'Don't look so scared, Edie,' said Clare, laughing.

'If you don't like it, you've just to say, and I'll do something different,' said Betty. Gently, she took my chin in her hand and turned my face towards her. Her hands were cool and dry. 'Don't look until I'm finished. Okay?'

'Rightio,' I said.

She rummaged in her case for a small bottle of liquid foundation.

'I never wear foundation,' I said. 'It's too heavy.'

'Not this stuff,' she said. She dabbed a few dots of it and blended it into my face. 'That doesn't feel too bad, does it?'

I shook my head. Next she asked me to look up while she lined my lower lids. I had to blink furiously to stop my eyes watering.

'You should do this every morning, then you'll get used to it quick enough. It gives the eye a beautiful definition. Don't worry, it's not as stark as mine, promise.'

I closed my eyes while she applied eyeshadow. I wasn't sure about the colours she'd chosen. She said I'd just have to trust her.

'This is the trickiest bit.' She held her breath as her face was so close to mine. I could smell the mint off her chewing gum. She touched my lashes with a light coating of mascara. She took her biggest brush and dabbed it on a round bronze dish of compacted powder. She gently blew on it, then swept it over my cheekbones in a broad motion, then she gave my lashes a second coat. The aspect of the room changed. My eyelashes felt heavier, and the edges of my vision were outlined in black. I felt glamorous, like one of them heavy-lidded ladies in a black and white movie. Without even looking at myself. She dabbed a touch of foundation on the end of her finger and rubbed it into my lips.

'You'll make my lips disappear,' I said.

'It's a base for lipstick. Makes it last.'

'Oh. I didn't know that. Bea, pass my handbag. My lipstick's inside it.'

'What is it?' asked Betty.

'Rose of Cairo.'

'It won't go with the eyeshadow,' she said carefully. 'Let

me choose a colour, and if you don't like it you can go back to this one.'

I couldn't argue with that. She outlined my lips with a light brown pencil, then filled them in with a pinkish bronze. She took a step or two away from me.

'Ta-da!' she said.

'Honestly, Edie,' said Clare. 'I'd walk straight past you in the street.'

'Mam, you look lovely,' said Bea. 'Those colours really suit you.'

I walked over to the mirror that hung above the fireplace. I looked like me, only ten times better. I didn't look painted or false. Nothing like it. My features looked sharper, defined. She'd made up my face in shades of bronze and brown. Even the eyeshadow was dark brown and radiated outwards in bronze and browny pink. Rose of Cairo didn't belong to my new face.

'Who'd have believed it,' I breathed. 'I always wear blue eyeshadow.' I suddenly realised I'd been missing a trick all those years. I'd always thought of lipstick and eyeshadow as something to finish off an outfit, like decorating a Christmas tree. I'd never seriously thought they could enhance your looks. I'd always believed that good features will out and it was wishful thinking you could hide bad ones. George called it 'that muck' and no wonder, the way I used to slap it on.

I had a rush of sadness when I stood before that mirror in our front room, looking at the reflection of the three young girls behind me. Clare on the cusp of marriage, Bea emerging from her shell, metal mouth a thing of the past, her bright blond head bent over the case of lotions and potions, about to wear her first grown-up dress for her brother's wedding. Their whole lives ahead of them. I felt faded. Empty. What had I ever done except have babies? What did babies do? They grew up and left you. Colin was in his last year at school. Soon I'd be left with just

Bea.

I was struck with longing for Paddy. I hadn't seen him in five years, since his last day at school. I'd abandoned him, and he'd abandoned me. It was my punishment.

'Are you all right, Edie?' asked Clare. Bea looked up.

I had a tear in my eye. I said, 'You've done wonders, Betty.'

Clare got up and put her arm round me. 'What is it, Edie?'

'I was just thinking about Paddy. Wondering what he's doing. He's going to miss the wedding. It breaks my heart.'

Bea and Clare glanced at each other.

For my sake, Clare had tracked Paddy down. She'd made a plan to borrow Betty's car, drive to London, meet Paddy and persuade him to come to the wedding. Clare found out where he was living from the Borthwick woman. Kaye Borthwick had counselled her after her mother had died. Paddy had kept in touch with her. With her, and not his own flesh and blood.

She did it for me. If she'd only let sleeping dogs lie. Paddy would have come back to us in his own time.

George and I were settled in front of the telly when the phone rang. Colin and Bea had gone out to a youth hostel disco. George grumbled; *Blind Date* was on and he had a thing for Cilla Black. It was Betty, in a right state. George had to tell her to slow down. Clare was in intensive care. Sam was on his way to Finchley Memorial Hospital to see her. In London.

'Finchley!'

'Aye. She was driving back from London.'

'What was she doing there?'

'Well, I don't rightly know,' he said.

'Does Arthur know?' Penharris had long since become 'Arthur' to us.

'Betty said he was on his way.'

'What shall we do? Should we go?'

'No, Princess. Her father's going, and Sam. We'd best just wait for more news.'

'Should we ring the hospital? We should be there. For her and for Sam.'

'Princess, we can't do owt. You sit down and I'll bring you a cup of tea.'

'Why did the police call round to Betty's?'

'Clare was driving her car.'

'They wouldn't call round unless it was bad, would they George? They oughtn't to have to start with Betty.'

'I don't know, Princess,' he said, running his hands through his hair.

I made George call the hospital. They were cagey about giving him news. For God's sake, he said, she's my daughter-in-law. They gave in and told him she was critical.

Sam made it to the hospital an hour before she died. I like to think she knew he was there. Penharris was too late.

Clare's death blighted a lot of lives. It's a terrible thing when someone dies young. Against the natural order.

Paddy came to the funeral. He said Clare never showed up. He waited for her over two hours before giving up, assuming she'd got lost or stuck in traffic. Nobody had mobiles in those days. He'd found out about her death from the Borthwick woman, apparently. Sounded about right to me. She'd have loved passing on news like that.

Clare had jumped a stop sign on the North Circular and been hit by a lorry. According to Betty, she'd left bright and early, promising faithfully to have the car back that night. She must've gotten lost. She was a sensible girl, Clare, and a good driver, but the lorry driver swore she'd come out of nowhere. Sometimes there are no answers.

Clare should have given us a clutch of grandchildren. She'd have been a wonderful mother. It was an evil trick God played by taking her. Sam has never got over it. I wanted Sam to stay home for a spell, but he wouldn't. He went straight back to work a few days after the funeral, and his work's been his dry bride ever since. Home, hearth, family, children. The only things worth living for. Everything else is ashes.

Bea took it so hard she made herself ill. She stopped eating and spent all her time in her room crying. Always on the slender side, she was soon skin and bone. The shadows under her eyes were pitiful. I wanted to shake her.

There was standing room only at Clare's funeral. A young, beautiful girl with everything to live for was dead.

Betty couldn't stop snuffling, leaning in to her mam, who passed her one tissue after another. Penharris was not a young man, but he'd always had a kind of military vigour, an inner energy, a natural dignity that he must've done his best to foster over the years, being a headmaster. All his inner fire had gone now. His blue eyes were tinged with pink, and ringed with grey shadows. His cheeks were sunken and his clothes hung off him like he'd been chopped in half. Sam sat next to him in the church. It was hard to picture a sorrier pair. His eulogy was heartbreaking. 'I thought thy bride-bed to have deck'd, sweet maid, and not to have strew'd thy grave,' he said, and the church heaved with sobbing.

Paddy came back home for the funeral. I could barely stand to let him out of my sight. I kept squeezing his hand in the church. To prove to myself he was really there. I had my boy back. I had to keep telling myself not to smother him. Bea was on the aisle end of the pew furthest away from me, thank heaven, as her sniffling was getting on my nerves.

As the last phrase of 'Amazing Grace' died in the air, Penharris and Sam turned to file out. Everybody stood. Penharris always was a mountainous man, tall, rangy, touched by loneliness, but now he was a great weight of dead matter in a dark suit. It was hard to think of him as the same man of years ago, the man of flesh who'd come alive at my touch. I was ashamed of myself for remembering that in such a holy place. He was like a man in a walking coma.

He stopped when he saw Bea. A light dawned in his eyes as they settled on her. He took her chin in his hands and lifted her head. He bent to kiss her cheek. I drew my hand from Paddy's. My palms had come out in a cold sweat.

# CHAPTER FIFTEEN

Sandra needed Bea's help to get Nick into his car seat. He had made an eel of himself. Bea bent to kiss him. Still resentful at her part in his confinement, he whipped his head away from her.

'Saints alive,' said Sandra. 'It's a struggle with him every time.'

Edie emerged from the house lugging her suitcase. Bea took it from her. 'Can I put it in the boot?'

Edie nodded. 'I have all I need in here,' she said, patting her enormous handbag.

Bea helped her mother into the front seat.

'Bye, Mam,' said Bea. She leaned towards her mother. Their cheeks touched. It was as close an embrace as they ever shared.

Sandra hugged Bea tightly, as if to make up for Edie's lack. Bea seemed insubstantial, as if her bones were hollow.

'You take care of yourself,' said Sandra. 'Come and see us soon. I'll come back down when I can. Oh, Bea. Maybe you've thrown yourself back in too soon.'

'It's for the best.'

Sandra got into the driver's seat and anchored her mobile phone into the hands-free kit. She waited while Edie settled herself, then leaned over to help her with her seatbelt.

'All ready?' she asked, as Edie fidgeted with the blanket on her lap.

'Ready.'

Nick, rancour forgotten, twisted in his seat to wave back at Bea. Sandra looked anxiously at the diminishing figure in her rear-view mirror.

Edie leaned back in the chair and exhaled loudly. 'Well,'

she said. 'That's that.'

'What's what?' asked Sandra.

'Just thinking out loud.'

'I'm worried about her,' said Sandra.

'How d'you think I feel? I'm her mother.'

'I feel bad leaving her.'

'I feel bad about it too. But like it or no, she's on her own now.'

Sandra was silent. She looked at Nick in the mirror. He gazed out of the window at the passing traffic. He liked to keep a lookout for lorries and motorbikes.

'All I mean is that it's a fact of life, if a hard one. Her life's down here and ours is up there. She opted to go back to work. Nobody pushed her.'

'Lowwy!' said Nick, pointing out of the window.

Edie continued. 'No amount of hand-wringing will bring David back. I've been on my own all these years. It's just a case of getting used to it. We can all get used to anything. She's still young. She's bound to meet someone else.'

'I hope so. But it doesn't seem to be the Newell way.'

'How do you mean?'

'Newells mate for life, like albatrosses. Clare died long before I was on the scene, but Sam's never looked at anyone else. Colin still loves Carol, for better or for worse. Wouldn't it be lovely if Colin met a nice girl?'

Sandra glanced at her mother-in-law. 'You and George never did fix on anyone else. Leastways—' She stopped, aware she was on treacherous ground.

'Leastways what?' Edie snapped.

'It's nowt to do with me, I know...' said Sandra.

'You're right there,' said Edie. 'The kids can't leave it alone. And now you.'

'You ought to tell them why,' said Sandra, unusually vehement. 'You and George splitting up was devastating to them. The one thing they were sure of when they were growing up was how rock-steady the two of you were, until suddenly you weren't. Not a word of explanation from either of you. There's usually something concrete to hang your hat on. If George had run off with somebody, if you'd been involved with another man—'

Edie twisted as far as her seatbelt allowed. 'Who said anything about another man?'

'Bike!' said Nick from the back.

'Nobody. That's just the point. If there'd been another person or cruelty, or neglect, or violence, the kids may'nt have liked it, but they'd have understood. No matter how awful, there'd be a reason, and no constant wondering. It's not idle curiosity. It's affected them all. Knowing leads to understanding, that's all I mean.'

Edie folded her arms and stared sideways out of the window. Captive as she was, with three more hours in the car, it was the closest she could come to storming off.

'They weren't little kids any more,' she said. 'Only Colin and Bea were left.'

'I know,' said Sandra. 'It would've been a lot worse if they were younger.'

'What are you trying to do? Make me feel bad?'

'No, I—'

'I'll not have you asking me about it any more.'

They drove on in silence. Sandra couldn't believe she'd lit the touchpaper so quickly. God knows her mother-in-law was not easy, but Sandra was naturally so pacific they had never locked horns. She tried to think of something to say to smooth things over.

'Mo'bike!' said Nick from the back. A minute or two later he crowed "Nother mo'bike!'

Sandra felt Edie fuming.

'Yellow lowwy!' Nick exclaimed.

'He'll be asleep soon,' said Sandra. She was then annoyed with herself for apologising for a two-year-old who was amusing himself harmlessly in the back.

'*He's* all right,' said Edie.

Sandra felt another stab of annoyance. This was exactly how Edie manipulated her children into compliance. She'd seen her do it time and time again. As she drove, she recalled the dozens of instances when Edie's passive aggression had extracted a predictable reaction from her children. Only Will occasionally showed flashes of defiance, and even he always drew back from open warfare. He sharpened his knives on the written page, where Edie could not bully him. The others seldom stood up to her. She was a nasty, embittered old woman with no love in her, she thought. No wonder George had left. She immediately felt ashamed. Maybe Edie was sour because George had left. People split up all the time these days, but Edie's generation had suffered stigma on top of heartache. Maybe she was as mystified by his decision as the children were, and couldn't admit it. She was old and lonely. No one should end up like that. She was provoking, yes, but she deserved some understanding.

Sandra glanced in the mirror and saw that Nicky had fallen asleep, his mouth open. Here one minute and gone the next. She reminded herself that Edie had lost a child. Looking at her own son, Sandra's heart constricted. She shook her head to banish the thought. She sighed. It must have been audible, as Edie gave her a look. Sandra waited for Edie to speak. No such luck. She could maintain a silence longer than a Trappist monk.

As she merged on to the motorway, Sandra resolved to break the deadlock.

'Traffic's good,' she said brightly. 'Look at that. A lovely clear road.'

Edie sank further into herself.

'Edie, I'm sorry. I really am. The last thing I wanted was

to upset you. I don't even quite know how the subject came up. One minute we were talking about Bea meeting someone else, and the next... well, you know how it is. I'm sorry.'

Edie said nothing, but she seemed to relax.

'Do you fancy the radio on?' asked Sandra.

'You're all right,' said Edie, sounding weary.

'You sure? It's just past ten. *Woman's Hour* will have started.'

'Go on then.'

The presenter was interviewing a woman who ran a shelter for abandoned girls in India.

'Tsk,' said Edie. 'Terrible what people do to their children.'

Sandra said nothing, grateful that the tension in the car seemed to have dissipated.

The discussion focused on the low status of women in India.

'Those poor children,' said Sandra. 'I'd love to have a daughter.'

'Maybe you will,' said Edie.

Sandra laughed. 'We had Nicky because I wanted a girl. Can you imagine any little boy less like a girl than him? Not that I'd change him. Soon as he arrived, I found I didn't mind. I just loved him, bits and all. Will tried to warn me that Newell girls were rare as hen's teeth. We won't bother trying again.' She said the last with a mixture of decision and resignation.

'Pity in a way. There aren't enough kids in good families. Far too many in bad.'

'True enough,' said Sandra, keen to keep Edie from a discourse on what could improve society. 'Will persuaded me that we could have a whole football team before a pink one turned up. I've accepted now I'll never have a daughter. Strange, as I grew up with the idea that one day I would.'

Sandra wanted to ask Edie how she felt about finally

having a girl, but she sensed the question would not be welcome. Edie and Bea did not share the relationship that Sandra had always imagined she'd have with a daughter. Not for the first time, she wondered what had gone wrong between the two of them. 'They were never close,' Will had told her. It was hard to imagine anyone being close to Edie. Perhaps it was just that simple. Edie was hard to know, hard to talk to. Almost any topic had the potential to stray onto touchy territory. She thought of ways to steer the conversation, but to her relief Edie spoke first.

'Who knows. Maybe there's a good reason why you and Will didn't have a girl. Nature has a funny way of deciding these things.'

'That's very philosophical of you, Edie,' said Sandra, smiling.

Edie shrugged. 'Nothing ever turns out the way you expect.'

They continued for a way in silence.

'There are a few benefits to sticking at three,' said Sandra. 'Nicky'll be going to nursery soon. I'm looking for a part-time job.'

'Whatever for?'

'I'll have some time on my hands. It'd be nice to do something constructive with it. Join the land of the living. You know, talk to tall people who can string a sentence together and clean their own bottoms.'

Even Edie smiled at this.

'Seriously, though, didn't it drive you mad being at home all the time? Of course, you had a much bigger family,' she added, furiously back-pedalling. To her relief, Edie answered without rancour.

'No, duck. I never wanted to work. I was at my happiest looking after everybody. I was needed. I miss that.'

'You're still needed, Edie. You're a great nan.'

Edie smiled wanly but didn't press it. 'Of course, it's different now. You girls are brought up to expect more.'

'It's not just about expectation. The money would be useful. People imagine that authors make a fortune, but once you consider the time each book takes to write, Will works for less than minimum wage.' Sandra laughed again. 'Still, he's been approached by a film producer who wants to buy the option on *Comfort*. They're ironing out the details. The option will earn more than the book sales.'

'It's going to be made into a film?' Edie looked at Sandra anxiously.

'There's no guarantee it'll ever amount to anything. But they pay well.'

'So if it goes ahead, you'll not need to go back to work?'

'It'll be good to go back, for lots of reasons. Before I lose all my confidence. I would have thought you were all for it. Didn't you say Gina should think about going back to work? Her kids weren't much older.'

'That's different,' said Edie.

'I don't see how.'

'She has a housekeeper, a nanny and a cook. It seems wrong somehow that anyone should have so much free time.'

Sandra laughed. 'Edie, that's crazy. Gina's one of the busiest people I know. It's true she has a lot of help, but she only has a cook for the dinner parties. You can't blame her for that. They have people round so often, and a lot of them are Sonny's clients. She cooks most of the family meals herself.'

'When they're not eating at restaurants.'

'They live in New York, Edie. It's part of the culture. You can't begrudge them that.'

'I don't begrudge anyone anything!' Edie snapped.

Sandra rolled her eyes.

'She spends a lot of time with the kids. She's always ferrying them around. She's decorated both houses and runs them like clockwork. She looks after the staff like they're family. Look what she and Sonny have done for Aditi and Jamling. It was Sonny's idea to hire them, but it was Gina who did all the legwork behind their visas. She's sponsoring her nanny in New York through nursing school. She's on the PTA of both schools. Last time I spoke to her she was organising volunteers to fix up a run-down youth hostel, and she's decided to enrol in a postgrad course in psychology. On top of all that, she always manages to look immaculate. The only time she has a hair out of place is after her spinning class.'

'It still seems wrong to me. She's got a full-time nanny, a cleaner that comes every day and an army of babysitters. She even hired a night nurse when the kids were newborns.'

'I had a maternity nurse when Nicky was born.'

'That was different. You'd just had a Caesarian and the whole lot of you came down with flu. I was poorly, and your mother was in hospital having her hip done.'

'I remember only too well.'

'That's just what I mean. It was special circumstances. Gina had no such excuse.'

'But Edie, don't you think that that's the whole point of having money, to make your life easier? Because she wasn't exhausted and frazzled, it meant she could enjoy her babies. Why do the grunt work if you can afford to get someone else to do it?'

'I suppose so.'

Sandra did not press the point further. Edie was as resentful towards Gina as she was towards Bea. She seemed affronted by their wealth and seemingly glamorous lives. Edie seemed to be much more forgiving towards her, Sandra. She could scrub up when required, but even when younger, she'd always been a jeans and jumper girl. She had a degree in modern languages, and got a reliable laugh out of Will by speaking French in her Geordie accent. After university, she'd decided on nursing, a nurturing profession suitable for a woman in Edie's eyes. Edie could relate to her, a full-time mother with limited funds. Getting a job, even a part-time one, would put her out of Edie's reach.

She glanced in the mirror at Nick, still fast asleep. They'd get home around noon, then she'd have just a few hours to wait before the two older boys finished school. She'd collect them herself. She wanted to see the look on their little faces. She smiled to herself in anticipation.

She'd do chicken and pesto pasta for tea. It was easy, and the boys loved it. A salad on the side and some garlic bread. A nice bottle of something. It'd be lovely to be under the same roof as all her boys. To be in the same bed as Will tonight. She thought of Bea alone, and counted her blessings.

'Services in a couple of miles,' she said to Edie. 'Would you like to stop for anything?'

'No, you're all right, duck. If we stop, we'll wake young Nicky up.'

'If we skip this we won't be stopping until we get to yours. You sure now?'

'Sure, duck.'

Sandra's phone rang. It was Will.

'San?' he said over the speaker.

'Hello, pet,' she said. We'll be home in an hour. You okay?'

'Fine. I'll be on air in a minute.'

'Oh God! I nearly forgot. It's live, isn't it?'

'Yup. You should be close enough to hear it.'

Sandra didn't want to miss Will's interview, but wasn't keen to listen to it with Edie.

'The reception may not be too good,' she said doubtfully.

'It should be fine.'

Edie was going to find out what he'd written about

sooner or later.

'We'll tune in. Sorry I forgot.'

Will laughed. 'No worries. I'd better go.'

'I can't believe it,' said Edie, grinning. 'My boy on the radio.'

Sandra was touched. Edie was proud of him, despite regarding his writing as a personal judgement.

Sandra tuned in to Radio Leeds. The eleven o'clock news was winding up.

'Next, we have Sam Logan interviewing local writer Will Newell, author of *The Comfort of Your Own Home* and *The Silent Singer.*'

A few bars of jaunty music introduced the programme.

'Sam's a friend of ours,' said Sandra to Edie.

'Top of the mornin' to all of you listening,' said Sam Logan, 'and a big welcome to *Book Review*. I'm delighted we have Will Newell with us, and before we even start, I feel duty bound to confess that Will's a pal o'mine, and I'm a fan o'his. So if you're expecting me to do a Paxo on him, you'll be sore disappointed. Will, thanks for joining us.'

'Thanks for inviting me.'

A slow smile spread over Edie's face. Sandra turned the volume up.

'Will, you've had two books published now, and you're working on a third. Your first two books are all about family dynamics. Fairly dysfunctional families, it's fair to say.'

'Is there any other kind?' asked Will. 'I never really agreed with Tolstoy when he said that all happy families were alike, but he was spot on when he said that unhappy families were all unhappy in their own peculiar way.'

Here we go, Sandra thought.

'Do you not believe in happy families?'

''Course I do. My wife and I have three children, and I like to think we're happy. Maybe years from now our boys will need extensive therapy and will say that Philip Larkin was right, who knows? The reason I don't agree with Tolstoy is because even happy families, unless superhumanly lucky, are touched by misery, and it can come in many forms. I grew up in a big close-knit family, but we had our fair share of tragedy and drama.'

Edie couldn't complain about that, thought Sandra.

'It's always interesting to readers to find out how far writers take their own personal experience. How far would you say those experiences have shaped you as a writer?'

'Very far, no doubt, but fortunately, you don't need to experience trauma to write about it. Otherwise we'd all run out of things to say pretty damned quick. That's the great thing about fiction. You can make up a whole reality. All writers steal other people's experiences, whether they're conscious of it or not.'

I'm looking at the blurb at the back of *The Silent Singer*. The *Daily Telegraph* critic has written, "The book stayed with me for weeks".'

'Makes it sound like a cold. Or a social disease.' The two men laughed.

'Much of *The Silent Singer* is concerned with illness, old age, regret and death,' said Sam Logan. 'Not particularly chirpy subjects. In fact, it sounds like a day trip to a gulag, but I can assure you, listeners, a lot of it is downright funny. How did you get the balance right?'

'I wrote a lot while my father was ill with cancer. He was in constant pain, but he could still have a laugh. He bantered with the nurses, and he kept an interest in what was going on in the world. He tried to write a memoir, even though sometimes the pain wouldn't let him hold the pen. It was a debilitating, undignified death, but he laughed at himself much as anything else. I don't go all out to lace my books with laughs, but it's nice to know some of it makes it to the surface.'

'Did he know you were writing about him?'

'Oh yes. He always said I should write what comes from the heart.'

What inspired the title?'

'Something that happened to my sister as a kid. She could sing, really sing, but she decided to shut up. It's about wasted opportunity. It relates to the last conversations I had with my father when he was dying. The regrets he had when he looked back on his life. There were certain things that he did, decisions he made that I think he wished he'd done differently.'

Edie sucked in her breath and leaned back against her seat.

'You all right?' Sandra asked.

Edie nodded, and leaned forward again, to indicate that she was listening.

'So tell me about the book you're writing right now. I understand it's loosely based on a family tragedy.'

Sandra held her breath.

'Very loosely, yes. My younger brother died when I was about six.'

'So you were old enough to remember him,' said Sam.

'Absolutely. His death has stayed with me all my life.'

'Does it have a title yet?'

'*The Hush*. He was always making some kind of racket. He'd yabber to himself, even if no one else was around. Babbling, talking gibberish, banging his toys. Even asleep he'd snuffle and snore. He was a cheerful little lad. After he died, my parents were... my... us kids... well, it's hard to talk about it. *The Hush* is the quiet after the baby's gone.'

Sandra glanced at Edie, whose skin had gone parchment-white.

'He died of Sudden Infant Death Syndrome, I understand,' continued Sam.

'Yes. SIDS, or cot death as it was known then. Mercifully, it's becoming less and less common. Timmy was unusually old to be a SIDS victim. It set me to thinking – there have been some terrible travesties of justice, where the parents have been accused of suffocating their children. There was never any question where my parents were concerned, thank God, but it set me to thinking of a scenario – imaginary of course, but what if a sibling, just a child, did such a thing? I wanted to explore the idea of a person doing something while young that hangs over them for the rest of their lives. Kids do stupid and wrong things all the time, but it's unusual for them to do something so bad that it affects them for the rest of their born days. Like Mary Bell, or the boys who killed little James Bulger. So I'm writing about a child, Marianne, who kills her little sister and gets away with it. The assumption is that the baby has died of cot death. Marianne grows up knowing what she has done, knowing the unbearable pain she's inflicted on her parents and the shadow she's cast on her other siblings' lives. When you're your own judge and jury, you can never really be free. When I first started writing, I painted Marianne as a kind of psychopath who wasn't affected by what she'd done at all, but I realised the other path was more interesting, and more believable.'

Edie's hand covered her mouth.

'Edie, are you all right?' asked Sandra.

Edie didn't answer. She shut her eyes and breathed heavily through her fingers. Nick chose that moment to wake up.

'Mumma,' he said, blinking.

'Hello darling,' said Sandra, trying to keep the note of urgency from her voice. 'Edie, do you want me to stop?'

Edie shook her head. Sandra was horrified to see tears spilling from her eyes. Her ashen face was rigid.

'Mumma!' said Nick. 'Need to poo.'

'All right darling,' she said, cursing his timing, the first time Nick had ever given her any advance warning. She was supposed to praise him for his growing awareness of his body's needs. She prayed that his bottom would miraculously suspend activities. Edie's distress was terrible to see. Sandra turned the radio off.

'I'm driving, pet. Can you wait for a minute?'

By way of answer, the car was filled with the acrid smell of shit. Nick started to cry.

'It's all right, sweetheart,' said Sandra. She tried to sound soothing, but she could not keep the note of panic out of her voice. 'Edie, I'm sorry. I'm going to have to stop.'

Edie didn't seem to hear. Sandra pulled the car to a stop on the hard shoulder. With traffic roaring past her, she changed Nick's nappy on the back seat. He sensed her anxiety, and did not wriggle or kick as he usually did. The car rocked each time a car sped past. She strapped him back into his car seat. For once, he made no protest. She tied up the dirty nappy in a plastic bag and chucked it into the boot. She waited for a lorry to pass before climbing back into the driver's seat.

Sandra was supposed to take a detour east to get Edie home. Instead, she kept on the M1, heading north to Leeds. If Edie noticed, she didn't say anything. The rest of the drive was silent, except for Edie softly crying. Sandra was at a loss what to do or say. Nick sat quietly in his chair, a worried frown on his face. When she got home, she saw Will's car was parked on the road. He'd left her the space in the driveway. Edie's eyes were closed, but Sandra knew she wasn't asleep.

'Edie, we're home,' she said, just as Will came out of the front door.

She got out of the car and grimaced at him, gesturing towards Edie.

She swiftly kissed him, then murmured: 'Your mam's upset. Really upset. You get Nick out of his seat. I'll help her into the house.'

Edie was trying to swing her legs out of the car.

Normally she waited for help.

'It's okay, Edie,' said Sandra gently. She picked up Edie's legs and gently swung them round so they landed on the floor, giving her her arm to lean on, minding she didn't knock her head on the roof of the car. She took Edie's bag from her and led her into the house slowly, their arms linked. Edie leaned heavily on Sandra, stopping only to blow her nose. Once inside, she went straight to the bathroom.

'What is it?' asked Will.

'She heard you talking about Timmy on the radio and hasn't stopped crying. It's like her heart's breaking. It's terrible.'

Will filled the kettle and put it on to boil. 'I'll talk to her. Leave the rest of the stuff in the car. I'll get it later. Why don't you get Nicky settled? Put a Disney on or something.'

Sandra nodded. Nicky was soon in Neverland.

When Edie emerged from the bathroom, she shuffled towards the kitchen and collapsed into a chair. She dabbed at her reddened eyes with a tissue. Will put a cup of tea in front of her. She reached for it with a shaking hand.

'San told me you were upset by what you heard on the radio.'

Edie gathered her forces. 'Upset!' she said, at last. 'Is that what you call it?'

'I'm sorry, Mam,' he said. 'It's not what I wanted.'

Edie's eyes welled up again. When she spoke it was between ragged breaths. 'Why did you rake it all up then? Twist it like that. Murder!'

Edie's sobbing got louder. He stroked her back.

'I know what happened, Mam,' he said.

'What do you mean?'

'I know what happened to Timmy. I've always known.'

'Known what?' asked Sandra.

Will did not reply. Edie stopped crying for a moment. Her trembling became more violent, then the sobbing started again.

'Shh, Mam. You'll make yourself ill.'

'What's going on?' asked Sandra.

Will said nothing. He rubbed his mother's back. Edie could not stop crying.

# CHAPTER SIXTEEN

Saturday. Colin was coming to see her. She did not want to do anything, or see anyone, even Colin. Changing her position in the bed seemed like too much effort. The bright winter sun streamed in through the open curtain. The cold clear spell showed no sign of coming to an end.

She forced herself to get to her feet. He was arriving in time for lunch. She had nothing in the fridge and did not want to go out. She opened the freezer and scanned the shelves. There was a tub of frozen curry. Beef. David's favourite. She ran the hot tap over the back of the tub and turned the reddish brown block into a pot with a little water and put it straight onto the cooker. The dormant spices slowly came to life.

'Smells fantastic,' said Colin when he arrived.

'It's from a batch I made months ago. I hope you don't mind.'

'What doesn't kill fattens.' He smiled.

'Would you like something to drink? There's a bottle open in the fridge. Not sure how old it is.'

'Just a cup of tea, thanks. Have you heard from Will?'

'No. Why?'

'Seems Mam's not well.'

'Anything serious?'

'He was a bit vague. I asked to speak to her but he said she was sleeping.'

'We could ring her later.'

'We should. So how have you been? I've been worried about you. We all have.'

'I'm getting through the days. Thank God for work.'

'One day at a time,' he said.

'That's what everyone says.'

'Sorry.'

'It's okay,' she said. 'No one knows what to say, so they come out with platitudinous crap.'

'I suppose so.'

'How's Anna?'

'She wanted to come, but Carol... you know what she's like.' His tone was light, but Bea guessed he was thinking of Paddy.

'It was funny seeing Paddy at the funeral,' said Colin. 'He looks very... together. Is he off the coke?'

'Not sure. I think so. The accident was a huge shock. He only got his licence back recently.'

'Is he working?'

'He never seems to be short of work. You should see his place. He wasn't keen for me to go at all, but I had to get some stuff for him while he was staying here.'

'Just as well he works for himself. He's unemployable.'

Bea got up to give the curry a stir.

'He's not good at keeping regular hours, I suppose, and with his record...'

'Is he seeing anyone?' Colin asked.

'He hasn't said anything. He never talks about his love life.'

'That's a misnomer, if ever I heard one. There's no love in him.'

'You know what I mean. He's never really been one for relationships,' said Bea.

'Just as well, really. He'd throw some poor woman into a living hell. God forbid he ever has a child. Some people are childless for a bloody good reason.' Colin took a sip of his tea, then saw Bea's stricken face. 'Oh God, Bea, I didn't mean...'

'It's okay, it's okay. You're right. It's hard to imagine Paddy as a father.'

Paddy had never shown a desire for children, but there

was nothing to suppose he wouldn't be as virile as his brothers. She was like a dead branch on a flowering tree. She blinked back the tears.

'Bea, I'm so sorry. I could smack myself.'

'It's not you,' said Bea when she was able to speak again. 'It's the smallest things that set me off. My brain plays tricks on me. For seconds I forget, minutes even, then I get a punch to the stomach when I'm forced to remember that he's gone.'

Colin sighed. 'After Carol left, I wanted to die. It was only Anna kept me going. I worked like a dog, so I wouldn't have time to think. I was the most efficient I've ever been. I took on every new client that came my way, even the tiddlers. I responded to emails as they came in, I answered letters by return of post, then filed them straight away, I—'

'You've always been like that,' Bea said, smiling in spite of herself.

'I could help you with your pile of mail. I couldn't help noticing stacks of it in the hallway. I hate to nag, but you've got to keep on top of it. There'll be legal letters regarding probate, and you don't want any delays.'

'I just can't cope with them right now.'

'We can look at them together.' He went to the hallway and returned with an armful of envelopes and flyers. 'Can I?'

She nodded. She watched him work from the top, starting a pile for probate, another for bills and another for cards and letters. The fourth pile was for junk and dead envelopes.

'Sonny's executor, isn't he?'

'Yes. I should be fine once all's sorted. He left a trust for the children, and I won't have to worry about money.'

He put his arm round her. 'That's something. It's better to be miserable with money than miserable without, let me tell you. Sod the tea. I vote we start on that bottle. We could both do with a drink.' When he handed her a glass, she resolved to have only a sip or two, just in case. She took in a deep breath. 'You know, Col, the children's trust isn't just for his kids. It was supposed to be for ours too. The provision is for his kids and any children we may have had. Our future children.'

Colin waited for her to elaborate.

'I'm a week overdue.'

He looked at her, astonished. 'Are you saying you're pregnant?'

'Not necessarily,' she said. 'I have PCOS. Sometimes I go for months without a period. And the IVF hormones play havoc with your cycle.'

'IVF? I had no idea.'

'Nobody knew.'

'Have you taken a test?'

'I'm afraid to. Having David's baby was all I ever wanted before I lost him. Now I'd sell my soul to have him back and I'd be happy with what I had. But this… I'm afraid if I take a test I'll jinx it.'

'Isn't it better to know?'

She shook her head. 'I don't want to know that I'm not pregnant. I like thinking I might be. Just the thought of it is like a little patch of colour in my life.'

'Sod that,' he said. 'Put your coat on. We're going to the chemist's. If you're up the duff, we'll crack open some champagne. You can even have a glass. Just one, mind. And if you're not, you can drink the whole sodding bottle. Either way, we're finding out now.'

Bea shivered with a superstitious prickle. There were six fertilised eggs suspended in nitrogen in a lab in Lillie's clinic. Technically, whatever the result, she still had a chance of being the mother to David's child. She took the curry off the heat and put on her coat as instructed. Now she'd spoken to Colin about the faceless baby, she couldn't bear not knowing a moment longer.

***

Lorena was wearing jeans and a black polo neck. Paddy was struck by how very un-pregnant she looked. He took his coat off and looked around. If she'd been entertaining any of her blasted clients that day, there was no sign of it.

'Did you go to the house today?' he asked.

'Yes,' she said. She was deeply agitated, pulsing out waves of ill-will.

She reached for a white object on the coffee table in front of her and stuck it in his face. It was a used pregnancy test with a blue cross in the window.

He was confused. 'Yeah, so what?'

'This is not mine.' *Thees ees not mine.*

'What do you mean?'

'It's from your sister.' *Your seester.* 'I found it in her bathroom. In the little dustbin in her bathroom.'

Paddy could not help laughing. From what Lillie had told him, Bea was a lost cause fertility-wise. Well. Didn't this fuck up their careful plan.

'Did you check out her diary?'

Lorena rolled her eyes. 'She is so happy. So sad. So full of joy and sorrow... it makes me want to puke.'

She lay back in the armchair and slapped her stomach with the flat of her hand.

'I want to get rid of this.'

Paddy got onto his knees in front of her and reached for her hands. He rubbed them inside his own. 'You don't mean that.'

'I do mean it.'

'The hard part's done, Lola. So she's pregnant. She's miscarried twice. She's gone through three fucking rounds of

IVF. My bet is her chances are slim. If she keeps it, which is unlikely, all it means is that the pie is split five ways instead of four. It's still a fortune. Just think of the money.'

Lorena did not answer.

'At least wait until you've met the lawyer.'

Paddy tried to read Lorena's expression. He'd have to keep an eye on her. He was not surprised at her lack of maternal feeling. What surprised him was his own reaction. He had an interest in this baby that was not strictly monetary. He couldn't explain it to himself. Paternal was probably not quite the right word. Proprietary. That was closer to it.

\*\*\*

Bea felt swollen with secret knowledge, which she hugged to herself.

'You should tell Mam,' Colin had told her.

'No! Not yet. I've got to get used to the idea first.'

She was at the office, trying to research a Syrian charity, but her mind was overloaded, racing with plans. No doubt it was her imagination, but she felt that already her clothes were too tight. Under her desk, she undid the top button of her trousers and pushed her stomach out, to give her little passenger room to grow. She glanced out of the window. The sun glinted against the windowpane. She suddenly felt as if the air around her did not contain enough oxygen. She redid the button and stood up. Her stomach once again felt concave. To her disappointment, there was plenty of room to spare.

'I'm going out for a bit,' she said to Martha, who waved vaguely in acknowledgement. She wrapped up against the cold and walked to the park. Even on a weekday, there were a lot of fathers, pushing prams, carrying toddlers on their shoulders, feeding ducks, kicking footballs... and her baby's father was dead.

She bought a paper cup of tea at the Serpentine, and held it in her gloved hand as she walked around the water. She started to feel hungry. Since David's death, she had resented the feeling, but now she had to take care of herself. She needed to feed the microscopic bundle of cells that was dividing and growing inside her. She felt herself bloom in the weak January sunshine like a winter orchid.

She was circling the Round Pond when she felt a sharp pang in her side. Her heart palpitated. She sat on a bench and stroked her stomach. She couldn't lose this one.

She called Colin.

'I had a pain in my side.'

'What kind of pain?' asked Colin.

'A sharp stabbing pain.'

'Do you still have it?'

'No. It's gone, but I'm so worried.'

'It's probably just a round ligament pain. You usually get them in the second trimester, but it's very common for it to happen earlier. It just means everything's stretching.'

'Are you sure?'

'Carol had them with Anna. Just think how much your body has to expand between now and September.'

'September?'

'That's when it's due, isn't it?'

'I suppose it is.' She smiled.

'Every day you'll notice something happening. Make an appointment with your GP. The sooner you're in the system the better.'

She leaned back on the bench. She just had to last out until September. The time stretched before her like a vast open highway.

\*\*\*

Lorena sat in Henry Armstrong's waiting room wearing a discreet skirt suit and heels. She had taken some trouble over her appearance, overseen by Paddy.

'Not too much make-up. Gloss. Not that red.' She'd wanted to wear her grey skirt suit. She wore it for one of her clients who liked her to pretend to be his secretary.

'It's Prada, for fuck's sake. You're supposed to be a cleaning lady. Earning six hundred a week scrubbing floors.'

'I can say he bought it for me. He would give me gifts, no?'

'Jewellery, yes. Money, no. After all,' he said, deadpan. 'You're not a prostitute.'

Her sense of humour had not worked well that morning.

'Better scrag those nails up a bit,' Paddy had said. She had snatched her hands away from him. They'd compromised on cutting them shorter. 'That's not short, sweetheart,' he'd said, taking the scissors from her. She'd watched resentfully as he'd butchered her nails. He was disapproving as she filed and buffed them afterwards.

'Even a cleaner has some pride,' she'd said.

'I suppose if you looked a complete drudge no one would believe he'd shagged you.'

He'd helped her tie her hair back in a French twist, loosening little tendrils here and there.

'Anyone would think you were gay,' she said.

'How do you know I'm not?'

She looked at his implacable face in the mirror and shrugged. Nothing about him would surprise her.

'You can't give this address,' he'd said. 'Give your sister's. In fact, it may be best if you go and stay with her for a while.'

'No way!'

'Some private dick might come sniffing around. A two-bedroomed flat in St John's Wood will raise a few eyebrows.'

'What will I tell her?'

'Tell her your boiler's bust. I don't know. You'll think of something.'

'So I make the sacrifices. And you sit back and watch me swell up like a whale in that shithole of my sister's.'

'You can't fight four billion years of evolution. Look at it this way,' he said, kissing her. 'If this unravels, you're just an incubator. I'm the one who will bear the full brunt of the law.'

'Don't say it,' she said. 'It is like tempting the devil.'

'It's good you're nervous,' he'd said. 'You'll be more convincing.' Paddy had picked the lawyer with care. Henry Armstrong's speciality was divorce.

'This is not a divorce,' she'd said.

'Of course it is,' said Paddy. 'We're divorcing Bea from her money.'

'Why do you hate her so much?'

He'd paused, giving the question full consideration before answering. 'I just do.'

Lorena paged through *Vanity Fair* while she waited, her eyes gliding off the images on her lap. The waiting room floor was polished oak. The magazines were spread on a small antique table resting on a Chinese carpet. The chairs and sofa were a beautiful soft leather. Italian, if she had to guess. She knew nothing about art, but she saw that the abstracts on the wall were originals, the sort that sold for thousands in sparse galleries in fashionable pockets of the city. The divorce business was clearly booming. The main office door opened, and a middle-aged woman emerged. Her line-free face held a tension beneath the moisturised skin that make-up could not hide. She switched her Gucci bag from one arm to the other while she pulled on a camel cashmere coat. Lorena's nerves constricted.

It was scarcely believable they had come this far. Paddy had talked her into pregnancy. She had long ago promised herself that she would never sacrifice her body in such a way.

She enjoyed being a whore. She answered only to herself. She made good money. Yes, her expenses were high. The clothes, the shoes, lingerie, cosmetics, endless treatments, gym membership. All expensive, but all so pleasurable. She spent a lot on special outfits, on toys: dildos, vibrators, arab straps, handcuffs, restraints. On lubricants, oils, masks, costumes. She made a lot of the clothes and costumes herself.

Her clients appreciated her and treated her well. They paid for an hour here, two hours there, sometimes a whole evening, sometimes overnight. She did not stipulate a set rate. If they offered an amount she was unhappy with, she was evasive about committing to a second meeting. She was good at managing the men.

'Nice clock,' one of them had said. 'Is it an antique?'

'Yes. A present from my oldest client.'

The next time he visited, he brought her a pair of sapphire earrings.

She wore them each time he visited for a few weeks, then sold them online. She was never called upon to explain.

New clients had to supply a work email address. Before their first visit, she would send a bland, professional email confirming the time of their appointment, requesting a reply. She reasoned that an email trail would discourage any thought of violence, and it gave her leverage. She had one self-employed client, taken on only because an established client vouched for him.

The men loved her because she had an appetite impossible to fake. She lacked any kind of craving for affection and commitment. Instead, she demanded sexual adoration, which she got in spades.

She had perhaps ten years remaining to earn at the same level, more if she submitted to Botox, Restylane or other procedures. She had no wish to be an old whore. She'd have to work for twenty years to earn what Paddy had promised her. It was a riddle that had bothered her since she'd embarked on her rewarding career: how could she maintain her standard of living once past her prime? She should have been more prudent with her money. She was not like her sister, squirrelling away every penny. Her dilemma had pushed her into submitting to the procedure in Damien Lillie's clinic.

Lillie was a fool. He'd allowed Paddy to manoeuvre him into an impossible position. She feared that Paddy had done the same to her. Nine months was a long time to harbour stolen goods so visibly.

It was not too late to get rid of the child. She'd done it before. Her younger brother sprang to mind. She'd watched her mother give birth to him, sweating, panting and moaning like an enormous cow. After a monstrous heave, a slick head had emerged from that cavernous body and he'd slithered out like a pink seal. She had been repulsed. Then a second baby came, followed by an indescribable detritus that she now knew was the placenta. The younger twin was not breathing and could not be resuscitated. No wonder, she had thought, living among that filth. She shuddered at the memory.

Her mother had suckled the surviving baby, crying all the while for the one that died. She had watched the baby greedily at work on her mother's nipple. The whole business was disgusting.

'Miss Carvalho? Please come this way,' said Armstrong's receptionist. Lorena gathered up her coat and bag.

Henry Armstrong held out his hand.

'Now, Miss Carvalho. Why don't you take a seat just here,' he said, indicating a sofa against the wall. He sat in an armchair opposite. 'How can I help you?'

Lorena was willing to bet that the cashmere-clad Gucci-lover who had just left had at least been offered a coffee. 'You represented Diana Grahame in her divorce.'

'Yes, I did. Do you know her?'

Lorena battled to remember the script she'd practised with Paddy.

'I'm pregnant,' she blurted.

'Congratulations,' said Armstrong, settling back in his chair. He waited for her to continue.

'The father of the baby. He is dead.'

'I'm sorry,' he said.

Lorena was silent, as she remembered her lines. 'He has left all his money to his three children. And to the second Mrs Grahame.'

Armstrong showed a flicker of interest. 'You mean Diana Grahame's ex-husband, David? Must've missed his obituary. Did he know you were pregnant?'

'Yes,' said Lorena through clenched teeth. From her, it was more believable than tears.

'What was his reaction?'

'He was surprised.'

'I'm sure he was, Miss Carvalho.'

'He was surprised, but he was happy.' Lorena allowed her voice to drop, and she cast her eyes to the floor. 'He was planning to leave her to be with me.'

Armstrong got up from his chair and picked up a pad and pen from his desk. 'How did you meet him?'

Lorena's eyes smouldered as she raised them to his. 'I was his housekeeper.'

A corner of his mouth twitched.

'You laugh all you want,' said Lorena with heat. 'I would not be here if it were not for this child.' The script was coming back to her.

'I'm sorry, Miss Carvalho,' he said. 'You misunderstand me. Can you tell me what your duties were? As his housekeeper, I mean?'

'I cleaned their house. I still clean the house for her. I have no choice. I need money. I clean her house and six others.

It is not right that she lives in that house while I live—'

'Yes, where do you live?'

She reeled off Rafaela's address. 'Once the baby gets bigger, I can no longer do this job.'

He appraised her.

'Who will take care of us when I can no longer work? His children go to expensive schools, and do not have to worry about a roof over their heads.'

'Well,' he said. 'Let's come back to that. I'd like to find out a little about you.'

'What do you need to know?'

'Your background. How you came to live in this country. How you met the Grahames, how you and Mr Grahame... began your relationship.'

'I have nothing to hide,' said Lorena.

'I'm sure you haven't, Miss Carvalho. It's just that if I understand you correctly, I presume you've come to see me as you wish to make a claim against Mr Grahame's estate, and you wish me to represent you.'

'Yes. That is right.'

'You realise you will have to undergo a test? To prove the baby is his?'

'Of course. I am not stupid.'

'I'm not implying for a moment that you are.'

'We should not suffer because he is dead. If he had lived, he would have taken care of us.' She drew both hands to her stomach in the protective gesture she'd rehearsed with Paddy.

'Yes, if the child really is his, he certainly would have had an obligation to do so.'

'Are you saying that I lie?'

'Miss Carvalho, please don't take it personally. I'm a divorce lawyer. I can assure you that only a fraction of what I hear is the truth.'

***

'So did he say he'd do it?' asked Paddy when she got back home.

'He will think about it. He said it was not his usual line of work.'

'That's the problem with lawyers. They've got no imagination.'

'If he decides not to do it, he will refer me to someone else.'

Paddy wanted Armstrong. He liked symmetry. He wanted the same person who'd gone after David in his divorce.

'Did he believe you?'

Lorena shrugged. It was an infuriating habit.

'Did you convince him?' he asked again.

'I don't know!' she said. She reached for her cigarettes. He had to restrain himself from slapping down her hand. He did not want the child to come to harm. It wasn't only because the child was an investment. It was because he was wholly responsible for its existence. He'd never been in that position before. He started to imagine himself as part of the child's future. It was a strange feeling.

***

Henry Armstrong was thoughtful for a long time after Lorena had left. David Grahame, servicing his cleaning lady. She was attractive, there was no denying it. He wondered if she would go to seed once past forty. Those exotic types often did, but there was something very steely about this one.

He was staggered by how far David Grahame had gone against his own interests. Enduring the expense and misery of divorce with Diana, only to marry again and cheat on the new wife with the woman who scrubbed his floors. Of course, he'd escape the furore. Being dead had certain advantages.

'Does Mrs Grahame know about your relationship with her husband?' he'd asked Lorena.

'No.'

'Do you think she had any suspicions?'

'No. All she could think about was having a baby. He said she was obsessed. Nothing else mattered to her. Some women do that. They get married and they forget they have a man to take care of. I think that is why he turned to me. He could talk to me. We fell in love. He felt that I loved him just for himself, not for his ability to make a baby.'

'Which is a little ironic, in the circumstances.'

'I did not mean to get pregnant. But when it happened, we were both happy. His first wife has a big house and money from the divorce. Now the second is left another big house and a fortune, even though she has no child. And me? I have nothing except the child, who will have nothing unless you help me.' Lorena had worked herself up into a righteous fury.

'How long has Mr Grahame been dead?'

'Two weeks.'

'When did you tell him you were pregnant?'

'Two months ago.'

'So he had six weeks to make some sort of provision for you and the child in the event of his death.'

Lorena's colour flared up. 'He was going to do it! He was going to leave her for me. For us. He did not know he was going to die. Why should the baby suffer just because the father is dead?'

'Why indeed, Miss Carvalho?' he'd sighed.

'So will you help me?'

He looked up from his writing pad and took his glasses off.

'I don't know. I'm going to have to think about it.'

'What is there to think about?'

'This isn't my usual area of expertise. I don't normally deal with estates or legacies.' 'This is just like a divorce,' said Lorena, parroting Paddy, 'except for the fact that the petitioner is dead.'

Armstrong could see her logic. She'd seemed perfectly willing to undergo tests to confirm the baby's paternity. If the baby was indeed David Grahame's, then the Carvalho woman would have the full backing of the law in suing his estate.

He wondered at his own reluctance. He made a living out of love turning sour. He did not usually shy away from a fight. He was often accused of stoking the flames, but he did so only in his clients' interests. There is no enemy more deadly than one who has once been promised undying love.

Whichever side he fought for, there were two things the divorces in which he was involved had in common. The first was that the warring couples had a huge pot of assets to fight for. The second was that he always came out a winner.

Acts of vengeful spite undertaken by his clients during the divorce process were no more than expressions of deep and abiding pain. He had a talent for painting similar behaviour from the other side as intimidation, abuse of power, misogyny or emasculation, providing confirmation of unreasonable behaviour. His ability to side wholeheartedly with his clients formed the underpinning of his success. He could not afford to see things in shades of grey. At the heart of all the battles he was involved in was the knowledge that the other side, at the very least, had the chance to defend themselves. He started from the assumption that any declaration about assets from the other side was a lie. In the majority of cases, this assumption proved to be correct. Yet there was something about this Carvalho woman, something about what she had told him that just didn't fit.

David Grahame had accurately reported his assets. The

expensive forensic accountant that Armstrong had hired had found no money salted away, no hurried gifts to relatives, no hidden accounts or secret offshore funds. Diana Grahame received approximately seventy per cent of the joint marital assets at the time of the divorce. She'd received the required half, plus Armstrong had successfully argued that a net present value should be placed on his contracted future earnings. Plus, David had been obliged to pay for Diana's costs, including the astronomical bill submitted by the forensic accountant. The couple had been awarded joint custody, but the sole burden of ongoing maintenance had fallen on him. Diana Grahame had come out of the courtroom as an eye-wateringly wealthy woman. It must have hurt to write that cheque, but David Grahame had done it. As the saying went: 'Divorce is expensive, but that's because it's really, really worth it.'

Grahame had no opportunity to defend himself now. Armstrong wondered why that bothered him so much. If the woman Carvalho was happy for her child to submit to a test, and it proved positive, then that was that. He spared a thought for the new wife. It was one thing finding out your husband has cheated. It was another to have your nose rubbed in it after you'd just buried him.

\*\*\*

Bea was at work when her mobile rang. It was Lorena. Bea couldn't remember Lorena ever calling her before. She usually stuck to texts and scribbled notes on scrap paper.

'I need to see you,' said Lorena without preamble.

'Is anything wrong?' asked Bea.

'I want to talk to you.' Her tone was aggressive.

'Lorena, you may not have heard, but my husband is dead.'

'I know.'

Bea waited for an attempt at condolence. It did not come. 'Why are you calling me?'

'It is about David.'

Bea prickled at the way she said his name. Like a purr, a caress. She waited for Lorena to elaborate. Most people would have felt the need to fill the conversational void. Not Lorena.

'I don't see what—' Bea began, then stopped herself. She felt a stab of anger. Doubtless it was nothing important, yet Bea felt demeaned by asking more. 'What about him?'

'You won't want to hear it over the phone.'

Lorena's insistence on mystery was irritating. The idea that this woman could tell her something about her own husband aggravated her. 'All right, Lorena. I'll be home around six this evening if it's so important.'

'I'll be there,' said Lorena.

'Bring your keys. I want them back.'

'Okay. I guess I won't need them any more,' she said, and hung up.

Bea immediately googled emergency locksmiths servicing Kensington. She made an appointment with the first one available and told Rob she was taking the rest of the afternoon off.

*** 

Lorena stepped through the ticket barrier at High Street Kensington tube, rehearsing in her mind the confrontation she was just about to have with Bea Grahame. She and Paddy had set this thing in motion and it was time to see it through. She was irritated that she was nervous. She skulked behind a lamp post a few doors away from Bea's house and lit a cigarette, inhaling it as if it were a breathing aid. She smoked it right down to the butt, then viciously ground it out on the pavement. She marched to Bea's front door and, seeing that the locks had been changed, hammered on it with the knocker.

Lorena was used to letting herself in and out of the house. The new lock engendered an unjustifiable peevishness in her, which gave her the stomach for the fight ahead. Bea had finally recognised her as an enemy.

Bea and David were never at home when she came to clean and snoop. She seldom crossed paths with either of them. She hadn't seen Bea for months, and was taken aback at the sight of her. Her face looked thinner, older. Shock, grief and lack of sleep had pushed her eyes deeper into their sockets, as if she were seriously ill. Well, she was in for another shock, Lorena thought grimly.

'Your keys, Lorena please,' said Bea. Lorena slapped the keys into Bea's upturned hand. 'What do you have to tell me?'

'You want me to say it on the doorstep?'

'I don't want you in my house anymore.'

'All right. I guess it won't take long. Your husband and I, we were lovers.'

Bea gave a staccato laugh. 'I hardly think so.'

Lorena's natural prickliness spiked to a peak. 'It's good that you find it funny,' she hissed, narrowing her flashing eyes. 'Humour is supposed to help in strange situations.'

'How else should I react? It's ridiculous.'

'Is it also ridiculous that I am pregnant?'

'Congratulations. That has nothing to do with me.'

'The baby is David's. Your husband and I, we made this baby.'

Lorena watched blood suffuse the pale cheeks. It was like a corpse coming to life.

'I don't know what kind of sick joke this is, Lorena. Get off my doorstep and don't come near me again.' Her voice trembled with rage.

'You don't believe me? We made love very often in your bed. Also on the sofa in your living room. The armchair in the study, we did it there a lot.' Lorena recounted all the places in the house that she and Paddy had coupled. It gave her words a convincing edge. 'He liked it there because of the big mirror. He liked to see us fucking. Feeling sometimes was not enough.'

Bea leaned forward. 'If you come anywhere close to me again I'll get a restraining order.' She slammed the door in Lorena's face.

Lorena hammered on the door. She bent to open the letter box and crooned into it. 'I know you are there. I know you are listening. You will be hearing from my lawyer, *cara*. Of course I will be happy to take a test. To prove that the baby is David's. Did you hear me? The baby is David's.'

# CHAPTER SEVENTEEN

I swear to God I wasn't lying. I hadn't forgotten. You never forget a thing like that. I didn't forget, I just remembered it differently. I couldn't keep what happened in my mind without changing it, else I'd have gone mad. Now Will's taken my blinkers off, and I can't stand the pain of it.

They say I can't go home, the state I'm in. I'd sooner be alone. In my own bed. Sandra says I'm ill. She says I've got a temperature. It's not right, making me stay. I've got no fight in me, though, no fight at all.

Will keeps telling me he's sorry. 'I thought you knew,' he said. Now I really do know, and the ache in my heart will stay with me until I die.

They've put me in his study at the top of the house. 'Away from the noise of the boys.' The boys are all right. I can hear Sandra telling them to be quiet when they get a bit lairy. I'd tell her not to bother if she was within earshot.

It's a single bed I'm lying in. Will's desk is on the far side of the room in front of the window, looking out onto the garden. 'The far side of the room' makes it sound like it's big. It's not. The desk is only a few feet away. He's taken his computer with him. It's one of them portable ones. He's working downstairs, so I can have 'some peace'. As if I'll ever know peace again.

The floor's covered with a red-and-gold fitted carpet, and the wallpaper has a red cherry blossom and green leaf pattern. It's textured. The wallpaper, I mean. I can run my hand across the wall and feel the stipples, rough against my palm. They've not got round to decorating in here yet. They've done the rest of the house. Ripped up carpets, torn down wallpaper and made it all white and bare with wooden floors. This room is a reminder of what the house was like when they bought it. They keep saying as soon as they have a bit of time and money they'll change this room into a copy of the others. Pity people can't leave things alone.

There are some black and white framed photos on the desk. There's one of me when I was young, and another of George. There's that lovely picture of the two of us on our wedding day, in the days when I believed with all my heart it'd take death to part us. There's another, a copy of one I have at home. I'm sitting at the centre, holding Timmy. George stands behind me, with Paddy and Sammy on either side of him, and Sonny and Will are on the floor cross-legged at my feet. All the kids are wearing their Sunday best, with side partings like their father. George has his arms round Paddy and Sammy. Anyone looking at that picture would think George loved Paddy the same as his brothers.

Timmy died before Colin was born. So sad there's no picture of all my boys together.

Every picture taken since he died has a hole in it. The photos and the cherry blossoms on the wall start to blur up because I can't stop crying.

There's a picture of Timmy on his own. I haven't seen it for years. George took it with him when he left. It must have come to Will after he died. Timmy's grinning toothlessly, sitting among a pile of coloured bricks. He's wearing nothing but a nappy, holding a brick up in the air. I want to look at it closer. I want it beside me. I want to look at that dear little face. It's an effort to get up, and as I stand I have a headrush so I have to sit down again until it clears. It's getting dark. I try again and make my way towards the photos, and I pick the one of Timmy off the wall and hold it against the dying light coming in from the window. Such a dear, cheerful, happy little face. My heart wants to break free of its moorings. The sadness of a lifetime weighs it down and I am so truly sorry. Sorry for a hundred things, but mostly for leaving my Timmy alone.

The things that happened that day have hidden behind a cloud in my head all these years. It's all clear to me now, though. Will's made sure of that.

It was the summer holidays. George was at work. My brother Jackie was staying with us. He was at home from sea for a spell. He'd never married, Jackie, and he liked to come and see us for a few days each time he was ashore.

It was a hot afternoon. Jackie had got up late after a night on the tiles. I'd fed him and the boys sausages in rolls with a bit of salad. He was unshaven and reading the paper in the kitchen with his shirt off. Every now and then he'd read out something from the paper. It was nice having a bit of adult company. My dress was sticking to me while I did the ironing, and I felt uncomfortably full. I was six or seven months gone with Colin and already a martyr to heartburn. Timmy was in the kitchen with us, playing on the floor with a few cars and bricks, chirruping like a little bird. The older boys were outside having a kickabout with their mates. Not Paddy. The younger kids were playing on the street. I wasn't happy about it, but there was no park nearby, and it was better than having a swarm of kids in the house. Endless cars nowadays, all driving like the clappers, but it wasn't like that then.

Paddy was playing swingball by himself in the garden. Normally, I made the others include him, despite the 'Aw Mams', but that day I'd kept him in. He'd thrown a stone at an old mutt that belonged to one of our neighbours. He was forever tormenting that poor creature. The boys loved that dog and all wanted one of their own, but I put my foot down. There were enough of us crammed into that house without chucking a pet into the mix.

Timmy's eyes were drooping. He wanted his cot. Jackie yawned over his paper as he sipped his tea, and even I felt drowsy. It was quiet except for the odd shout from outside, the rhythmic whacking of the tennis ball by Paddy, and the buzz of a bumblebee, beating its wings against the windowpane.

'I'm going to do a bit of Egyptian PT,' said Jackie, draining his cup and settling into the sofa.

He was like a big teenager. He drank in the evenings, slept in the mornings and had a kip on the sofa most afternoons. Fair do's, I thought. He worked hard. He deserved a bit of R&R, as he called it. I switched the iron off and picked Timmy up. He griped as I lifted him, reaching for Grubby, his stuffed rabbit, then tucked the toy under his arm and nestled against me. He never fought sleep, not like the others. I was half thinking of having a lie-down myself.

I put Timmy down on our bed and curled up around him. I was just getting to the point of no return myself when I thought of the iron. I couldn't remember turning it off. I was sure I had, but I had to check. I got up, careful not to wake him, and crept down the stairs.

Of course the sodding thing was off. Being pregnant puts your brain on rations. I decided to put the iron and the board away before one of the boys knocked them over. You had to watch it with so many kids about.

Next thing I knew, there was a commotion outside from the street. Will barged in.

'Mam! Mam! It's Sammy! He's been knocked over!'

I ran outside, heart hammering. A distraught-looking woman was kneeling next to Sammy.

'What have you done to my boy?' I screamed. His eyes were open and he was blinking at the sky. His forehead was bleeding.

'He came out of nowhere,' she said.

I ignored her. 'Sammy! Sammy talk to me.'

He tried to get to his feet.

'Don't you move, Sammy. Tell me where it hurts.'

I clocked that Jackie was next to me. Jackie gave Sammy

the once-over.

'I'm so sorry,' the woman bleated. We all ignored her.

'Can you move your arms and legs, old son?' Jackie asked Sammy. Sammy nodded. 'Wiggle your fingers and your toes for me, there's a good lad.'

Sammy did as he was told.

'Where does it hurt?'

'My head,' croaked Sammy.

'Follow my finger with your eyes, lad,' said Jackie. Sam did it, though he was squinting into the sunlight.

'How many fingers am I holding up?'

'Four,' said Sam.

Jackie held Sammy in his arms like a baby. 'He'll want stitches. Probably needs checking for concussion, but he seems all right.'

'I can take him to the hospital,' said the woman.

We looked at her.

'I'll go with him,' said Jackie, and carried Sammy towards the woman's car.

'No! I'll go,' I said. I wanted to be the one holding him.

'You sure?' Jackie said.

'Sure. Just mind the kids for me, Jackie. Timmy's asleep on the bed upstairs. Can you put him in his cot? He'll want feeding when he wakes up. There's some leftover cottage pie in the fridge.' I realised I'd not got shoes on. I ran inside and slipped on a pair and grabbed my handbag. I got into the back of the woman's car and left my Timmy to it.

She offered to wait with us at the hospital, drive us home after. I told her I'd take a taxi. She offered to pay for it. Blood money. I said no. I wanted her gone. Are you sure, she kept saying. It drove me mustard. I told her I could take care of my own son, no thanks to her.

'I was driving slowly. All the other kids got out of the way. He came careering out on to the road chasing a football.'

'Mam, it's true,' Sammy said. 'I'm sorry,' he said to her, which made me see red.

Then she cut up nasty. 'Maybe you should think twice about letting your kids play on the road.'

I told her I had no need to answer to her and marched into the hospital in a fine old temper.

They cleaned Sammy up, stitched him together, checked for concussion and the like. He was no worse for wear and was excited about having a scar on his head 'like Frankenstein'.

We waited a bit for the taxi, but were away from the house two hours tops. Sammy barged in ahead of me, dying to show off his stitches. The others were in the garden. Jackie was passed out on the sofa. Paddy was sat by himself under the apple tree. They didn't like him joining in, but that never stopped him trying. He was playing with Timmy's rabbit. He had a funny little smile on his face.

Sammy swaggered over to his brothers to show off his wound.

'Where's Timmy?' I asked them. Paddy swung his head round to look at me.

'He's still sleeping,' said Will. I noticed he had some dirty grazes on his arm.

'What happened to you?' I said.

'Nothin', Mam.'

'How did you get those?'

'I fell over.'

'On the road?'

He was unwilling to say, probably sensing that the road's days as playground were well over. He didn't want to put the seal on it. He said nothing.

'Come with me, lad. I'd better clean you up.'

'Aw, Mam. Can't we do it later?'

'Now. We don't want that to go bad. You're filthy, you

are.' They all were. Every night they bathed two or three at a time before we sat down for tea, and the rings in the tub after had to be seen to be believed.

I frogmarched him upstairs to the bathroom, where I kept the TCP. Our bedroom door was open. The two of us stared at Timmy on the bed.

He lay on his back, his one arm outstretched, the other across his chest. One leg dangled off the bed. He was frowning. His eyes were open. And he was still. So still.

'Mam,' whispered Will, as if afraid of waking him up. 'Why's he so quiet, Mam? He's not moving.'

I hurtled to the bed and picked him up. It was like holding a ragdoll. I cuddled him to me and rocked him back and forth. Those fat little arms and legs dangled lifeless against me. No breath, no sound. No snuffling, chattering, babbling, prattling, no gurgling. I shook him. Nothing. I laid him face-up on the bed and tried blowing into him. I picked him up and shook him again.

'Jackie!' I roared. 'Get Jackie!' Will tore down the stairs yelling for Jackie at the top of his voice.

Horror, confusion and darkness. That's what it was like. I haven't lied, except to myself, and I swear I hadn't meant to do that. I just couldn't keep what I saw in my head without changing it, as the pain of it skewered me. A pillow was lying on the floor. With Timmy so still, and his rabbit with Paddy, a bell started clanging in my head.

Jackie and the boys came clamouring. I couldn't stop screaming. I held Timmy to me, holding his little head against my shoulder, stroking his hair, and crying, crying, I couldn't stop. Like now. The wound's reopened, ugly and gaping.

Jackie could do nothing for him. My little man was dead. It was hot that day, but Timmy wasn't warm any more.

Timmy'd be nearly forty by now. He'd have a family of his own.

Jackie tried ringing George but he'd already left work. He came home to the horror of it all. Someone sent for the doctor and an ambulance crew turned up. Like I said, I don't remember much, except for George, eyes streaming, arms round me as the doctor sedated me, telling me he was sorry, so sorry as he helped the doctor prise Timmy away from me. So far as I could tell, the ambulance crew took him away to be poked and prodded in some morgue far away from his mother.

'She's seven months gone,' I remember George saying while I lay paralysed on the sofa. They'd sedated my body, but could do nothing for my mind. 'The baby'll be all right, won't it?'

'This one's a fighter,' he said after he examined me. 'It'll be a comfort in the days ahead.'

'What happened?' George asked.

The doctor sighed. 'Cot death, it's called. It's thought their systems are so immature, they just forget to breathe. The heat won't have helped him. It's rare, though, Mr Newell, thank God, especially for a baby his age. That's no comfort to you. I'm truly sorry.'

I took to my bed. I wanted to die. Why did I not let Jackie go with Sam? Timmy would have been safe asleep in my arms. I'd blinded myself to the horror living among us.

I couldn't cope with what had happened, so I changed it in my mind. A mother's protection shifts from the dead to the living. Paddy was my living breathing son. I could do nothing for Timmy anymore.

Will kept looking at me, those days after Timmy died. His face was white and pinched, and he held himself rigid, like a toy soldier. I didn't know what to do about what he'd seen. He was only little, but sharp as a tack.

George accepted the doctor's verdict, backed up by the coroner. Why not? It was in black and white on his death certificate. I'd have believed it myself, had I not seen the look on Timmy's face. The pillow on the floor. Paddy with Grubby in the garden. Paddy since. The other kids were clingy, tearful, shocked, withdrawn, *something*. Not Paddy. He was the same as usual, cold to the chaos around him.

George brought chicken soup and bread up to our room one evening. He and Jackie kept a routine going for the kids. I couldn't bear to be with them.

George helped me up, put the tray in front of me.

'Princess, you've to eat. If not for yourself, for the baby.' He put the flat of his palm against my belly.

I picked the spoon up, dipped it in the soup and held it to my lips. Spoon in soup, spoon in mouth. Spoon in soup, spoon in mouth. I ignored the bread.

George held it together in front of the kids. Alone with me, he was as much a fountain as I was. He stood by the white-painted cot that had seldom been empty in the years of our marriage, gripping the two corner knobs, leaning against it, head drooping low. His shoulders shook with sobbing.

I wanted to go to him, but I didn't have the strength. I could only watch him cry through my own tears.

He sat next to me and took my hand.

'They asked if we wanted him home before the funeral. I told them we did,' said George. 'They'll bring him home tomorrow morning.'

I wanted him home too.

He continued: 'The funeral's tomorrow. I arranged it all with the vicar this afternoon.'

'Why didn't you tell me?'

'You were sleeping, Princess. I'd not wanted to wake you. I've got his coffin sorted.' His crying started up again. 'It's that small, it's...' I tried to put my arms round him. It was awkward, as the tray lay between us. 'We'll bury him with Grubby.'

That's so right, I thought. Timmy couldn't bear being without him. I blanked out of my mind where I'd last seen

Grubby. It's clear as a Hollywood film to me now though.

He sniffed and ran his fingers through his hair. 'I can't stay from work much longer. Jackie's offered to extend his leave on compassionate grounds. It'll be good for you and for the kids.'

'The hell it will!' I snarled, and swept the tray to the ground. The bits of bread went flying, and soup spilled on the bed, the floor and over George's trousers.

George was too gobsmacked to speak.

'If he'd put Timmy in his cot like I'd said...'

'What difference would that have made?'

I couldn't explain. I was gripped by an urge to blame and destroy. I leapt from the bed, surging with hatred. George caught my arm. 'It was no fault of his!'

I shook myself free and thundered downstairs in a righteous fury.

'Get out of my house,' I screamed at Jackie. 'I'll not have you playing nursemaid to my kids.'

'Jackie, she doesn't mean it,' said George, hot behind me. 'She'll be all right, you'll see. Princess, come back to bed.'

'He left our baby alone to die.'

'Have you gone mad, Edie?' asked Jackie, his voice full of pain.

'He's your brother, closer to you than anyone,' said George.

'Lazy and feckless, that's what you are. You couldn't do the one thing I asked.'

'Seeing as we're laying our cards on the table,' hissed Jackie, 'I've a good mind what happened.' He looked at Paddy. 'He's always been a wrong'un. And little wonder, when you think on where he came from.'

'What are you saying, Jackie?' asked George.

I screamed to stop him answering. 'You'd throw blame on Jesus himself if you had to. Our baby dying is on your head, same as if you'd killed him yourself.'

The kids were crying.

'You should never have taken him in. Unnatural devil's spawn—'

'Steady on, Jackie. He's just a child,' said George.

Will, mute for days, chose to pipe up, 'You saw what happened, Mam. Same as me. It was—'

'Don't you say a word, Will!' I grabbed his hand and dragged him up the stairs. I needed to put the fear of God into him inside of a minute.

I sat him on our bed. I knelt in front of him and clamped my hands on either side of his head. He tried to twist free, but I held him fast, locking his eyes on mine.

'Will. Timmy died in his sleep. Do you understand?'

He tried to shake his head, still held fast in my hands. Cautiously, I let go, as if he were a wild animal about to bite me.

'It was Paddy, Mam. He told us he put a pillow over Timmy's head. He's always telling lies so we didn't listen.'

'Timmy died in his sleep,' I said through clenched teeth.

He shook his head. His face was screwed up, distorted with confusion and fear.

'If you say anything different, they'll come and take you away. All of you. You know that? They'll say we're not fit to look after you. They'll take you away and you'll never see us again. Do you understand? Do you?'

He trembled. What could I do? What would happen to Paddy if the truth came out?

I heard George coming up the stairs. I clasped Will to me so tightly that George couldn't see his face. He was stiff in my arms, like he'd gone into some kind of shock.

I heard the front door slam shut.

'Is that him gone?' I said, feeling strangely calm.

'How could he stay?'

'It was only the truth.'

'The truth hides itself well in this house.'

If I'd had any fight left in me, I'd have asked him what the ruddy hell he meant. I rocked Will quietly back and forth. George didn't push it. Maybe it would have been better if he had.

George got back in touch with Jackie after we separated. I've seen Jackie in the odd photo, and some of my grandkids talk about him, they don't know better. So many years have gone by but I can't even begin to make amends for what I did that day.

# CHAPTER EIGHTEEN

Hours after Lorena had gone, Bea remained at her kitchen table in her silent house, turning Lorena's surrendered keys over and over in her hand, just as Lorena's words fermented in her head. Fury and grief had raged within her for precedence, and now she was empty and devastated, like an abandoned battlefield after the killing is done.

Bea wanted to kill Lorena, make her cry out with pain. It could not be true. She would have known. She would have felt it. The rage had eclipsed her grief. She could not get rid of the polluted pictures that Lorena had planted in her head; Lorena and David in her bed, Lorena and David on the sofa, in the study... *'He liked to see us fucking. Feeling sometimes was not enough.'*

Apart from her intuition, there was the question of practicality, of logistics. When would he have found the time to fit in an affair? She had cut her travelling over the past year, the period that Lorena claimed covered their great love story. She and David were together every evening. On the rare occasions they went out separately, they still ended up together in the same bed. They both worked during the day. His days and nights were accounted for, of that she was confident, except for an hour here and there. She could not imagine someone like Lorena being content with such crumbs.

But no amount of logic could stop a jealous worm from stirring. The wronged partner was always the last to know.

Despite Diana's claims in the divorce court, David was adamant that he'd never cheated on her during their sixteen-year marriage.

'Not in any serious way, anyway,' he'd said.

'What does *that* mean?' she had asked.

'I snogged a girl in a pub after a rugby match once. I was drunk. She wanted me to go back to her place, but I had the sense to go home. I regretted it afterwards.'

'Because you felt guilty, you mean?'

'Of course I felt guilty. Seedy, too. A middle-aged man groping a young woman in a pub. It's just wrong.'

'Was that the only time?'

'In all the years I was with Diana, I never slept with anyone else. But...' His voice had died.

'But what?'

'I fell in love with someone.'

'Really?'

'Maybe that's a bit melodramatic. I was lonely. I felt neglected, and I met someone who seemed to be the answer.'

'Who was she?'

'A lawyer we hired to do some work on the European business.'

'Did she feel the same way?'

'Oh yes. We were instantly attracted. Like I was to you,' he'd said, and kissed her.

'What happened?' They had been lying in bed together. She had felt utterly secure with him. With David, her demons lay dormant for long stretches. At that time, his past was his past and she was his present and future.

'We had an early-morning meeting in Luxembourg, so we took an evening flight together and stayed in the same hotel.'

'And?'

'Anyone who saw us at dinner must have supposed we were lovers. The air was crackling. We had a bottle of wine with dinner, then went back to her room.'

'Oh, God!' said Bea. 'I thought you said you hadn't cheated.'

'I didn't. Not in the conventional sense. You see, she

was also married. She loved her husband, and I still loved Diana, at least I thought I did. We raided her minibar and talked about my marriage, her marriage. She said her husband trusted her. That she couldn't betray him, even if he never found out. God, I was jealous as hell. Then she asked me if my wife trusted me. I couldn't answer. It seemed irrelevant whether she did or not. Diana just didn't care about us anymore.'

'And?'

'I kissed her goodnight and went back to my own room. Afterwards, I fantasised about what I'd do differently. You know, be ˙ more Errol Flynn about the whole thing – but whatever, I missed my chance.'

'Do you still think about her?'

'When someone mentions Luxembourg, I think of her. I don't think I fully got over her until I met you.'

'I wonder if she still thinks about you.'

He'd laughed. 'I doubt it.'

Bea wasn't so sure. An unfinished love affair, stifled before it had begun, was more disturbing than a relationship that had run its natural course. David had sensed her uncertainty. He'd kissed her again. 'Don't even think it,' he'd said. 'I have you now.'

She had believed every word he'd ever told her.

When they had met, he was separated from Diana, renting a small flat a few streets away from the family home. It was a car accident that gave him the push to leave. He'd just dropped Dan, his eldest, off at boarding school. It was the boy's first time away from home. David had felt morose driving back to London. The memory of the small figure waving at the car, blinking back tears, had tugged at him and he wondered, not for the first time, whether they were doing the right thing.

'Just because we went to boarding school doesn't mean we have to pack our own kids off,' he'd said to Diana.

'Boarding school isn't all gruel and cold water these

days.'

'What about loneliness, bullying, isolation?' he'd asked.

'You aren't close to your parents. I wasn't close to mine. How could we be when we were packed off for eighty per cent of the year?'

'It's like a holiday camp now,' she'd said. 'He *wants* to go. All this worrying is pointless.' He supposed she was right. As he'd driven back from the school, the idea of going back to her that evening depressed him. He couldn't remember the last time they'd had a laugh. They weren't affectionate with each other. They had intermittent, perfunctory sex, always initiated by him.

'Did you ever tell her how you felt?'

'Twice. The first time she told me I took things too seriously. It was only natural for a couple to grow apart over time, she said. It was one of those things and we should make the best of it. It's not as if we're at each other's throats, she'd said. You don't beat me. We don't cheat on each other. We're both busy. Honestly, David, she'd said, I wonder why you fret so sometimes.'

'And the second time?'

'The second time she was furious. She said I was making her anxious about nothing. There were couples she knew who were deeply unhappy. I was looking for trouble where it didn't exist. We had a huge row about it. Once we'd both calmed down, she suggested we take a trip together. We could farm the kids out and go away, just the two of us, somewhere we'd never been before. It never happened.'

'And the accident?'

He had dropped Dan off and was driving home. The house would be so quiet without him. His spirits were low. The September evening shadows had started to lengthen and merge. He punched the CD button. Deep Purple. He was tempted to floor it to cheer himself up, but he already had three points on his licence, and the road was littered with speed traps. He kept his right foot in check.

Bea visualised it as if the memory were her own.

He was cruising at seventy, and saw a Renault Clio parked on the hard shoulder, a woman frantically waving at the passing traffic, her face a caricature of panic.

David pulled over. Distressed damsel, hairy trucker, bearded hippy, David would have pulled over. Her child had been stung by a wasp and his whole throat had swelled up. The boy was grey, gasping for breath, his mother helpless, trying not to scream.

David recognised anaphylaxis. He had an epinephrine pen in the car. Diana was allergic to shellfish. She carried an EpiPen in her handbag, another in her coat pocket; two shared shelf space in the fridge alongside the eggs, there was another in the glove compartment of the car. She was diligent about replacing them before their expiry dates. He ripped off the packaging and plunged the needle into the boy's thigh, right through his trousers. The effect was immediate. His airways opened, his face relaxed and turned pink with the sudden flood of oxygenated blood. The boy closed his eyes and gulped the air, like a drunk in a whisky barrel. 'Thank God it was fast,' David had said when recounting the story to Bea. 'He wasn't going to last much longer.' His mother had called an ambulance before she'd flagged David down. He waited with her for its arrival.

He put his hazards on, and settled into the passenger seat of the little Renault, sitting sideways with his legs out of the car. She sat in the back, the boy's head on her lap, stroking his hair, mopping his brow with a scarf. She was elated, giddy with relief, as was David. The two of them were high on the impossible odds of him being on that stretch of road, at that particular time, with an EpiPen. 'And you stopped! No one ever stops. You stopped and you had what he needed. It's the kind of thing that makes you believe, in spite of everything, that there is a God,' the woman had said. They both laughed, luxuriating in their luck. She had been so certain that her child was going to die, and he'd been given back to her.

'I knew exactly what she meant. The God bit,' he told Bea. 'I felt this glow inside me. The whole thing was a fluke, and I hadn't done anything even vaguely heroic, but I felt singled out by providence that I'd been able to do that for the little chap, and for her.'

Then David's Audi smashed into the back of the Renault.

'Jesus!' the woman had screamed. The boy was jolted wide awake, and began bawling. David leapt out of the car. A battered Citroën had rammed into his Audi and propelled it forward into the woman's car. He saw a girl lying on the ground, her arm stretched out and her face turned to the side as if she were swimming front crawl. David didn't need to touch her to know she was dead. She had flown through the windscreen of the Citroën on the near side. The car had hit the Audi at an angle, and the rear end of the Citroën stuck out into the slow lane of the dual carriageway, angling for more casualties, like a deadly domino.

The driver was a boy, about twenty. A thin stream of blood trickled from his forehead where it had hit the steering wheel. David helped him out of the car. He was conscious, but dazed. His seatbelt had saved his life. He was stoned. 'Totally blazed.' David guided him to the side of the road. He saw the girl and screamed, gathering her into his arms. Even with the roar of the passing traffic, David had said, his screams were terrible. The mother of the boy held her son in her arms, cradling his head to protect him from the sight of the dead girl and the screaming boy.

David turned the Citroën's hazard lights on, to ward off oncoming cars. The car stank of weed. 'The boy and I could have picked up the back of the Citroën easily, and dragged it out of harm's way, but he was in no fit state to help me, and I couldn't do it on my own.' David called the police. The ambulance arrived and took away the woman and her son, the weeping boyfriend and the girl. David stayed with the cars until the police turned up, followed by a tow truck. The Renault would need a bit of bodywork, but David's Audi was a write-off, as was the Citroën.

The policeman took him back to the station to make a statement and he waited there for Diana to pick him up.

'I was shell-shocked. The coppers gave me endless cups of tea and couldn't have been nicer. Diana was pissed off. She tried not to show it, but I'd wrecked her evening. I can't remember what she had on. Book club or PTA, I don't know. I followed her to the car in silence. She hated driving, so I offered to take the wheel. "After what happened today? You must be joking," she said, as if I was to blame. Her questions were perfunctory, as if she felt a duty to make conversation. I tried to explain the terrible sense of deadness inside of me.

When I told her what had happened, she had snapped: "Why didn't the mother carry an EpiPen?"

"I don't know. Maybe he'd never been stung before." She was judging someone she hadn't even met.

'I tried to talk about the girl dying. Pointlessly, arbitrarily, stupidly, just because her boyfriend was whacked out and she hadn't been wearing a seatbelt. It was all churning around in my head.

'That night, I couldn't sleep. I felt sure that the woman would be haunted by the boy driver crying out the dead girl's name, as I was. I felt a stronger connection with a stranger that I'd never see again than with my own wife.

'Diana sensed I was still awake, and started to rub my back. I felt heartened that she was being kind. I started to think we'd bridge the rift just by being kinder to each other. Maybe she'd been right about putting things into context. Maybe the girl had an appointment in Samarra, and nothing, short of bending the universe, would change it. Perhaps I should bloody well appreciate what I had, and not take it for granted.

'I remembered Diana as the young girl I'd fallen in love with so long ago. She was still there somewhere. I turned in the bed and took her in my arms. I kissed her. We hadn't been as close to each other for the longest time. This woman was my wife, I thought. I was an idiot to let us wander away from each other. I kissed her again, which had rather predictable results. I wanted us to seal our new closeness, to bond with each other again. She stiffened. It's been a long day, David, she said. Clearly, you feel a whole lot better. You got me all worried about nothing, she said, and turned over.

'After the accident, I think I slumped into a kind of depression. I got up, I went to work, I helped the kids with their homework and started driving at the weekends to Dan's school to watch his rugby matches, all the usual stuff, but I carried this deadness around in me. Eventually Diana tackled me about it. I tried for the last time to explain it to her, but she had no patience with me. She said she didn't see how "that whole miserable incident" should still be affecting me. Her EpiPen saved a boy's life, she said, blah blah and some junkie smashed into the back of our car and yes, it was very sad that a girl died. But people die all the time, David. Just take a look in the bloody papers. If you're going to go into a decline about strangers dying, then you may as well slash your wrists right now. Shit happens, David! I'm sick of living with a zombie.

'I said some pretty unforgivable things back to her. How cold she was. Colder than a fridge and less giving. "That's your trouble, David," she'd said. "You confuse sex with affection." Anyway, to cut a very long story fractionally shorter, I was soon looking at flats.'

Bea was convinced he'd left Diana because he felt trapped, neglected, unloved and alone. Despite that, he hadn't cheated on her in any meaningful way. Bea was conscious of employing the same phrase that he'd used himself. Maybe she'd been an idiot to blindly accept his version of events. What did it mean to cheat in a meaningful way? Why had she accepted so unquestioningly what he'd told her? She'd always felt that Diana deserved to be left. She'd neglected David and taken his love for granted. Maybe things were not that simple. He'd run around kissing girls at rugby matches and fallen in love with other women on business trips.

She tried to tell herself that things between them were different. He would have absented himself, in body and in spirit. He wasn't that cold. He hadn't been cynical enough. Unless the man she mourned was someone she hadn't known at all.

*** 

Lorena stared in mutiny at Paddy. Her eyes glittered from beneath her black, shaped brows. She itched for a cigarette. He would leave for Diana's soon enough. Then she could puff away in peace.

'That's annoying,' he said, referring to the keys. 'It was handy being able to get into the house. Her diary's a real source of inspiration.'

'The hard part is done. This,' she said, thumping her stomach. 'This is the hard part. You don't need to do any more.'

Paddy kissed her and stroked her stomach. 'I have a plan for my sister.'

'A plan? Beyond the money what more do you want?'

'She always was close to the edge. This might tip her right over.'

'You want her to kill herself?'

'Don't be so melodramatic. No, not at all. I like her miserable, not dead.'

'I almost feel sorry for her.'

Paddy looked at Lorena.

'Are you all right?' he asked.

'I hate this... thing inside me.'

Paddy was alarmed. The money meant little to him. Money was a tool, nothing more, a means of achieving other aims. The idea of Lorena flaunting David's baby at Bea had been exquisite to him. Now the consideration of revenge was slowly receding. The baby was more than a weapon.

Something was going on inside Paddy. Ever since the child had become a reality, strange feelings had stolen over him. Feelings that were utterly new to him, which strengthened daily. The child was wholly his creature. He could not wait for it to be born. Could not wait to see its face, to hold it in his arms.

'Lorena. Listen to me. You won't do anything dumb, will you?' Her eyes met his, and he saw all too clearly that she had already considered the possibilities open to her.

'Think of the money,' he said. The muscle in his cheek contracted. 'Think of the money if you think of nothing else. You'd have to suck an awful lot of cock for half a million.'

She reached for her handbag and got out her cigarettes.

'Don't fucking smoke, Lorena.'

'I smoke when I like.'

He fought the urge to snatch the cigarette from her hand.

'I'm sorry,' he said. She raised her brows. Those words did not often escape those lips.

He sat next to her and kissed her. He took her swelling breast in his hand. She pressed herself suggestively against him.

'Consider it your pension fund,' he said.

It was an unfortunate thing to say. Her eyes flashed in fury. She stood up and sucked on her cigarette so hard her cheeks concaved.

'Oh come on, Lorena. Don't be like that,' he said. 'You know what I mean.'

She pushed him away as he came closer. 'Get away from me. Don't you have a sister to destroy? A Diana to do? Your games mean nothing to me. It is only the money I want.'

He laughed, and gathered up his coat.

Just then his cheap phone tinkled tinnily from his pocket. It was Fevze.

'I'm guessing that you're calling only because the message hasn't sunk in,' he said.

'Dritton has told me that the woman in the pictures is your sister.'

Paddy digested this. A whole realm of possible outcomes suggested themselves. Fevze's voice was heavy, laden with doom. He assumed Paddy cared for his sister's safety and well-being. That was the thing about other people that he found hard to understand. They made themselves vulnerable by giving a damn.

Fevze thought it would upset him if he set his gorillas loose on Bea. He had plans of his own for Bea, but he loved a wild card. Lorena could sue the estate with or without Bea.

'Fevze, you listen to me,' he hissed into the telephone. 'You leave my sister alone, d'you hear me? Don't go anywhere near her. She's pregnant.'

He hung up. Whatever happened next, it was bound to be interesting.

# CHAPTER NINETEEN

A couple of days I've been here in Will's study, alone with my ghosts. Timmy, Clare, Penharris, George, all wronged, all long dead. I've wronged the living too. Jackie. Bea. I've had some time to think about things. I remember listening to some idiot on the telly saying that there was no such thing as mistakes, only 'learning opportunities'. Maybe he could explain to me how it was a learning opportunity to leave my baby alone to die, to blind myself to the true colours of my son, to set him loose among my children, to betray my husband, to falsely accuse my brother, to fail my daughter. Yes, as if my list of crimes wasn't long enough, I have to tack that onto the end. When I think of her as a baby, it makes me want to weep. She was a lost little soul, floundering and helpless without the love of her mother. What I wouldn't do to have my time with her again, to gather that pale little scrap to me, and not turn my back on her like I did. What was wrong with me? Nothing I can ever do will make up for the lack. I long for both babies, for Bea and for Timmy, the living and the dead. Bad enough that she lost her dad, but she's no moorings left now that David's gone.

I've started to think about other things. Things I didn't want to dwell on too closely at the time. Paddy turned up for Clare's funeral. For years we hadn't seen hide nor hair of him. Why would he come to her funeral? At the time I didn't give it any thought. Now I think about what Paddy might have done all the time.

After Clare's funeral, George visited Penharris. Everyone was talking about him. How sorry they were for him, wondering if he was all right. Honestly. If only people could hear themselves. Of course he wasn't all right. First his wife, then his daughter, in a few short years. Some people must feel cursed.

Sam stayed with Penharris the night of the funeral. I wanted him with us. To take comfort from his family; but he said that it wasn't right that Arthur should be alone. George agreed, said I had to let Sam be, that he must do things his own way. My poor Sammy. His skin was grey and he slumped like he was being crushed by an unseen weight.

Sam's never found anyone else. What Sandra said was true. We don't have it in us to love twice.

It was less than a week after the funeral when Sam came to the house to pick up the rest of his things. He was going to stay at Penharris's one more night, then go back to Oxford.

'What else can I do, Mam?' he'd asked when I'd begged him to stay.

'It's not right carrying on as if nowt's happened,' I said to him. 'It's not right not staying with your family.'

'Bugger what's right! Nothing's right, nor will be, ever again.'

I wanted to tell him he was still young, that he'd find someone else. A voice in my head warned me to button it.

'He knows we're here. He must deal with it in his own way.' What I wouldn't give to have George's arms about me once more.

George took to stopping at Penharris's each evening before he came home. Penharris had been alone with George way longer than he'd ever been alone with me.

'The grief's killing him, Princess,' he said. 'Sometimes I think he forgets I'm there. I invited him round for tea, but he didn't want to budge. It's like he's given up. January term starts soon. He's given no sign that he's ready to go back to work. I was thinking of having a word with Mrs Jackson.'

'It's not up to you to interfere, George,' I said.

'If I lost everything, and my whole world fell apart, I might be grateful for someone interfering. If you saw him, you'd understand. Seeing him's enough to make a stone melt. He's a broken man. We've lost a child, but we've got each other and our other children, thank God. He's got no one. No one at all. I wonder you don't have...'

'Don't have what?'

'A bit of compassion, Edie.'

I had ruddy compassion and more to spare, but I couldn't explain how afraid I was. The way Penharris had kissed Bea... at bay for so many years, my old fear was back.

I resented the time George spent with Penharris. I wanted him out of our lives. He'd been a plague on me long enough. I said nothing, but my feelings spilled out of me, like it or no.

'It'd be nice if you came with me, you know,' he said softly in bed one night.

I shook my head in the dark and said nothing. He sighed and rolled away from me.

It was a miserable Christmas. Sammy didn't come home. I begged him, but he said he was joining a group of students and lecturers who were alone at Christmas due to distance, divorce or death. He preferred to spend time with a crowd of loners rather than his own family. George had invited Penharris for Christmas lunch. I was seething. I did not want him at my table.

Bea, as always, made things worse. She'd taken to visiting Penharris. I could hardly stop her. She was fifteen years old, and would backchat me when I tried.

She came in one afternoon, cheeks pink with the cold, holding a book.

'Want a tea, Mam?' she asked, putting the kettle on.

'No ta. How is he?'

'Awful.' Her top lip quivered.

'Why do you go if it upsets you so much?'

'It's not seeing him that upsets me, Mam. Clare being dead upsets me.'

'It's a hundred times worse for Sammy.'

'I know that, Mam. I'm glad to go. He understands.'

'Meaning that we don't?'

'No! That's not what I mean. He loved her so much.'

'What do you expect? She was his only child.'

She stared at the kettle, frowning. 'He'd have loved her just as much, even if she wasn't an only child.'

'If she'd had brothers or sisters it would have been a consolation for him.'

She turned her blue gaze at me. 'Why do you not go and see him?'

I was fed up with people asking me. 'I've not the first idea what to say. I mean, what on earth do you talk about? Your father's never answered me straight.'

'It doesn't matter. I read him poetry. He likes to close his eyes and listen. He gave me this book. He said it was one of hers.'

I looked at the book. *Songs of Innocence and Songs of Experience.* I remembered it from school.

She picked it up and fingered the cover lovingly. 'I love that we can talk about things like this. I couldn't do that with anyone else.'

I prickled. I pictured the two of them in earnest discussion about poetry. Maybe he'd tell her. Maybe he'd blurt it out. Bea knowing would almost be worse than George knowing.

'Instead of bothering that poor man you should spend a bit more time on your homework.' She'd be taking her mocks in January.

'You've never shown the slightest interest in my homework before. Why now?'

'Don't get mouthy, Bea.'

'You call it mouthy if you like. I call it a fair question.'

Then came New Year's Eve.

'Princess, it's just a drink. He's not a leper. Do it for me. All I want is to drop in for one drink, then we can come home and see the New Year in together at home, like always.'

What choice did I have?

Bea and Colin were going to a New Year's Eve party at the youth hostel. Bea hadn't wanted to go.

'Do you think she'd want you moping round here? Go on, love. You can raise a glass to her at midnight,' said George.

Nothing is more mawkish than a teenage girl. I wanted to give her a good clout. I was angry all the time. At Clare for dying, Sammy for shutting himself off, at Penharris for making puppets of my family, for their constant nagging at me.

We took a bottle of sherry with us.

'Just one drink, George,' I said. 'Promise? Then home to see the New Year in.'

'If I stay awake that long,' he said, yawning as we trudged up the hill to Penharris's house. A thin cold rain was falling. I held the sherry in the crook of my arm, and he held an umbrella over us both. 'It means a lot to me, you coming tonight.' He put his arm round me and pecked the top of my head. That was the last kiss.

Penharris lived in the Old Vicarage, a big detached house on a corner of the main road leading out of town. As we walked down the gravelled driveway, we saw him through a large pair of bay windows. He stood with his hands in his pockets staring into the fire. The light played across his drawn face. Once inside, it didn't feel much warmer in than out. He led us to the room with the fire, which was big and draughty with oak-panelled walls. He closed the door to try to keep the warmth in, but the heat went straight up the chimney.

We sat in blue-patterned wing-backed chairs and a sofa around a walnut coffee table. The room smelled of tobacco and leather. I was surprised to see an ashtray on the table, with a couple of ground butts in it. Perhaps he'd had a visitor, I thought. Then I saw that there was a packet of Woodbines on the mantelpiece above the fire, and a box of matches.

'Thank you so much,' said Penharris, accepting the sherry. 'Can I take your coats?'

'You're all right,' I said. 'I'll keep it on while I warm up.' I didn't intend to take it off.

He put the sherry on a drinks cabinet that was clustered with bottles of different shapes colours and sizes. Penharris had never struck me as a tippler. He took three tumblers from the shelf above the bottles and poured a generous measure of sherry into each.

The glasses were crystal or cut glass. They were the sort of thing I'd normally have commented on to make a bit of conversation, but it didn't seem right.

He held his glass up to us.

'It's kind of you both to come.'

The firelight showed up his face. Grief had left a terrible mark. He seemed more spindly than ever. He seemed to have no flesh on him at all. Haggard, that's the word. He wore a dark green woollen jumper that hung off him, and some dark trousers. I don't think I'd ever seen him out of a suit before, except... well. He and George did all the talking. Whatever I thought of to say sounded false in my head.

He felt in his pockets, then looked about the room, before his eyes settled on the cigarettes. He offered us the packet, but neither one of us had ever been smokers.

'I hope you don't mind if I do,' he said. We both said no, and I think I even said something about liking the smell, which was a lie.

'It's a filthy habit,' he said. 'Clare used to nag me about it when she was a child. Then when Anne was diagnosed with cancer, I gave it up. But now, it hardly seems worth keeping off them.'

'Whatever gets you through the days, Arthur,' said

George.

We should have all been united in a common feeling, our love for Clare, and shouldn't have had to sit there like maiden aunts, clutching our sherries, pretending it was a nice social occasion. As George said, we'd lost a child ourselves. Of all people we should have understood that nothing could make Penharris feel better.

'Sam sends his love,' I said.

'Yes, thank you. He called me today.' Which gave the lie to my words. He didn't seem to mind, though, and gave a wintry smile at the effort. 'Sam's been wonderful. He calls me every day.'

He never called us every day. His own family. No news was good news, so far as George was concerned, but he wasn't their mother.

'He knows better than anyone else what I've lost in Clare.' To my horror, tears came to his eyes and rolled down his cheek. He did nothing to check them, and showed no sign of shame. I was astonished. It may sound unfeeling to you, but people were different in those days.

George leaned over and touched his shoulder. 'They made each other happy.'

Penharris got a hankie out of his pocket and blew his nose. He took another deep drag of his cigarette.

'That's something, I suppose. She always was a happy soul. Except when her mother died, of course. Those were hard times. I thought I'd never go through anything like that again.'

Finally I found something I could say. 'She told me about that. When I first met her.'

He stubbed his cigarette out. Almost immediately, he lit another one.

'She liked talking to you, Edie. She was so fond of you.'

'And of Bea, too,' said George. 'Clare was always so good to her.'

'Bea has also been wonderful,' said Penharris. I don't know if he meant anything significant by it, but he was looking at me when he said it.

George smiled. 'She's a cracking lass, Bea.' He reddened. 'Sorry, Arthur, I...' He floundered, mortified.

Penharris didn't seem to notice. Finally, he said, 'A cracking lass, yes. And so like Clare.'

My pulse quickened. I was tight with fear. I scrunched my toes up inside my shoes.

George recovered himself. 'Have you decided what you'll do when term starts?'

Penharris gave a grim smile. His eyes watered. 'I've always loved my work. Bringing forth the young... I've always seen it as a privilege, an honour, but now I don't know if I can face being surrounded by other people's children.'

Even George was at a loss.

Penharris stared bleakly into the fire. 'I sound sorry for myself.'

'You've lost your daughter,' said George. His voice was hoarse, but full of kindness. 'We lost a child. We understand.'

Penharris filled our glasses. I was surprised that mine was almost empty. He picked up the packet of Woodbines. It was empty. He held it up to his eyes even, to see if one was hiding inside the packet. He stood up and felt his pockets, then scanned the room. He went over to a desk in the corner and opened a shallow drawer. He was terribly agitated.

'They sell them in the Lion,' said George. 'I could run out for you. It'll not take five minutes.'

Penharris sat down again and ran his hand through his hair. 'I don't know why I do it,' he said. 'It does nothing for the pain. I've allowed it to become some kind of crutch. Yes, George, please do. That would be so very kind.'

Then there was a sort of horrible pantomime, while Penharris tried to find some money to pay for the wretched cigarettes, and George said 'No, no', but in the end had to accept because he didn't have enough change, and I squirmed, just shrivelling in my chair at the thought of being left alone with Penharris. George had promised me faithfully... I couldn't very well remind him, now could I? If we'd only have agreed a code word beforehand.

'Take the brolly. It's proper pouring now,' I said. Rain lashed against the windowpanes.

No sooner had George left than Penharris looked at me with a cast in his eye.

'I want to adopt Bea,' he said. His jaw was set.

A screaming started in my head.

'It'll be a shock, of course, but she'll get used to the idea in time. We've become close in the past few weeks. She's just like Clare. She has a right to know that I'm her father.'

My mouth wouldn't work.

'I was happy to be connected to Bea through Sam and Clare. I thought I could get to know her gradually. I didn't want to rock the boat, to disrupt her, disrupt your family.'

I found my voice. 'Disrupt us? It'll ruin us. It'll destroy her. All her life, she's looked to George as her father. That's what he is. Her father. In every which way that counts. From the first moment he clapped eyes on her, he's loved her like he's never loved anyone else. Myself included, if you want to know.' I wiped the hot, livid tears that had sprung to my eyes. 'It's wickedly selfish, wrecking our family as you've none of your own.'

His face was as puce as the rage that tore through me.

'I've thought of that,' he said. 'It'll be hard on her at first, no doubt. But the young are very adaptable.'

'You can't ever be certain. She looks as much like Paddy as she does Clare. Do you want to claim him while you're at it?'

'There's no question in my mind that she's mine. When I saw her on her first day at school, I knew it. The first thing I did when I returned to my office was check her birthday against the date we—'

'Bea was born early.' It was a desperate lie.

'I don't believe you.'

'Yet you've said nothing until now? Now she's fifteen, you'll claim her? Now Clare's dead and can't judge you, you'll ruin us? You want to play happy families with someone who will hate you.'

'All these years I've kept quiet. I was afraid of what I'd unleash. Now I've nothing left. Nothing except her. I've come to know her. I can help her. She's talented. She could achieve so much with the right kind of tutoring, the right kind of guidance.'

'We've done right by every one of our kids. They've got us, they've got each other. George loves her. He's her father, in a way you can never be.'

I was standing, yelling at him, and was suddenly afraid of what George would see from the driveway when he came back. The Lion was only a few minutes away. Penharris was crying pitifully with his head in his hands. I sat down heavily in my chair, panting with panic and rage. His crying was pathetic. The fear he'd roused in me made me want to crush him.

'You're a selfish man, Arthur Penharris. All these years I've lived with what I did. With what you did to me. You took advantage of a mother frightened for her son. You're like a drowning man pulling us down. After all George has done for you. Do you think she'll ever look at you the way Clare did? Do you?'

I couldn't stand to look at him. His sobbing was so wretched. The fierce desire to hurt him left me. I suddenly felt exhausted.

I leaned forward. 'Please, Arthur, if you love Bea, you'll leave her be. You can see her all you want and not wreck everything. Please. We loved Clare like one of our own. You can do the same with Bea. There's no need to say a word. No need at all. It'll backfire on you, see if it won't. You'll make her hate you.' I sensed that he was listening to me. Finally, he took in a deep breath and he nodded. His sobbing began to still.

'George'll be back in a minute,' I said. 'Please, Arthur. You'll get the best of Bea by not saying a word about what happened between us. It was a moment of madness for us both. Don't ruin so many lives because of something we did so many years ago.'

He nodded and his breath came easier. Relief flooded through me.

'Bea told me that you read poetry together. She said that of all people, you understood how she felt about Clare. She got quite misty-eyed about it.' The steel coil in my chest loosened a little further. I put honey in my voice, like I did when putting my boys to bed when they were small. 'You've got a link with Bea because of Clare. You've got to start building your life up again. You've got us, you know. George said you're like family to us, and he's right. We would have had the same grandchildren. You've got to start thinking about going back to work. The school relies on you. So do the teachers and the kids. You can come over to us whenever you like. See us, and see Bea, with all her brothers around her...' I babbled away in the same vein until Penharris stopped crying.

He reached into his pocket for his handkerchief again, and he wiped his face and nose. He sat up and ran his hands through his hair. He looked resigned. I heard George's footsteps in the corridor. He must've left the front door on the latch.

'Brrr,' said George as he came in. He put a packet of Woodbines on the walnut table in front of Penharris, who reached for it and ripped off the wrapping.

'Thank you, George,' he said.

'George, you're dripping!' I said. 'Did you not use the umbrella?'

'I did, but it's biblical out there.'

267

His cheeks were flushed, his face was sodden. He mopped up with a hankie, then stood with his back to the fire.

'Nothing like a good blaze,' he said.

'I was just saying to Arthur that maybe he should take a leaf out of Sam's book and go straight back to work after the holidays. It's work that's getting him through the days.'

'True enough,' said George.

Penharris lit the cigarette that he had clamped between his lips, and inhaled it deeply. A kind of calm came over his face.

'I've been in touch with Helen Jackson,' he said. 'She's filling in for me. I'm lucky she's so capable. There're all manner of things that have to be done during the holidays, and I'm not in a position to do any of them. To even contemplate doing them.' He paused. 'But I told her I'd probably go back at the beginning of term. As I said, what else do I have to do?'

George and I could say nothing to this.

He carried on talking. 'It all really depends on how everyone adjusts.'

He looked directly at me, then at George. His jaw had set. 'If it's difficult for her, as I'm sure it will be, then I'll take time off. A sabbatical, if I have to.'

George shook his head ever so slightly. 'I don't follow you, Arthur.'

'I'm talking about Bea, George. She's my daughter.'

'No!' I screamed.

'Bea's my daughter,' Penharris repeated.

'He's addled in the head! Don't listen to him, George.'

'Haven't you ever wondered why she looks so much like Clare?'

'He's gone mad.' My voice trembled like a liar's.

'What you're saying makes no sense, Arthur,' said George.

'He's mad, George. He shouldn't say such things. He should—'

268

'Don't fret, Princess,' said George. 'You've nowt to worry about. Arthur, can't you see you're upsetting Edie?' He said this gently, as if afraid of inflaming a dangerous lunatic.

'Sixteen years ago, your son Patrick beat up a boy called Peter Wilkes. Do you remember that?' asked Penharris, voice like steel. He took in another deep puff from his cigarette.

'Of course I remember,' said George.

'Edie came to plead with me. I can't blame her for what happened. We—'

'George, don't listen to him! He's lying! He's mad, he's really gone mad.' I couldn't keep that tremor from my voice.

'Edie, shhh. Please,' said George. He turned back to Penharris. 'What were you saying, Arthur?' He said it as if Penharris were telling a joke, a nice little story, not taking an axe to a marriage that'd lasted upwards of twenty-five years.

'I can't blame her. We... it just happened. I can't explain it. That's not important anymore. What is important is that I have every reason to believe that... in fact I *know* that Bea is my daughter. She was born nine months later. The time between the two dates is just right.'

It took a while for the words to sink in.

'Is this true, Edie?' asked George.

I couldn't say anything, which gave him his answer. I couldn't look at him, so eaten up with shame I was. When I finally looked up, he'd gone.

'Where is he?' I hissed. Penharris made no answer.

I ran for home, looking out for George all the way. Drenched to the skin, I got home to darkness. He'd not come home. He could be anywhere. He could've gone back to the Lion Inn – he'd just had a terrible shock and he may have gone into the first place he could get a stiff drink. If I went out looking for him, he'd come home and find me gone. So I waited. I sat, wet and shivering, and waited. I had a bottle of cooking sherry in the pantry. I poured a capful for myself, then another.

George was not a drinker. He wasn't a pub man. He didn't turn to alcohol, as a rule. Maybe he'd gone back to Penharris's to thrash things out. I don't mean fisticuffs. Neither of them were the type. Maybe he'd gone to get the gory details. Maybe he was wandering the freezing streets. You never know how someone will react when they've had a shock.

I waited for hours. I walked from room to room, haunting my own house. No sign of him. Every now and then I topped myself up with sherry. Just before one, I heard voices outside. One o'clock was Bea's New Year's Eve curfew. I looked through the curtains of the living room. She was with Colin, who had his arm round another girl. The three of them were talking in whispers, and I heard a muffled giggle. Colin left to walk the girl home, leaving Bea at the gate.

She crept in, but I was waiting for her. 'Mam, is that you?' she said, then turned the light on. I was like a mole blinking in the sunlight. 'You right near gave me a heart attack. Mam, what's wrong? Are you all right?'

'If I'm all right it's no thanks to you.' My voice was unsteady, and loud in my own ears.

She looked at her watch. 'I'm not late home. What is it, Mam? Is Dad in bed?'

'I've no idea where your dad is.'

'Mam, are you... drunk?'

'No, I'm not ruddy well drunk.' My head was clouded with the sherry, but it was crystal clear that George leaving was her fault. From the day she was born things had changed. Meek as milk, she seemed, yet everything around us had shifted for her. I may have said as much.

'What have I ever done to you, Mam?' she sobbed.

'Go to bed, Bea. Go on. Just get out of my sight.'

As per usual, the sound of her crying riled me something terrible.

'Go on, Bea. Scarper!' I wanted to stay up for George,

but I needed her out of the way. Whatever I had to say to him was for him alone.

I heard a key in the front door. Colin, I thought, back from walking the little lass home. But it was George. With a glance, he took us both in.

'Blaming her still, are you, Edie?'

He looked at Bea with sorrow and longing. She rushed towards him and threw her arms round his neck.

'Oh, Bea,' he said, a world of feeling in his voice. His raised his arms to put them round her, then hesitated. His eyes were closed and his mouth was pursed, trembling with the effort of controlling himself. Like a robot, he awkwardly patted her on the back. 'You'd best get to bed, lass,' he said, unwrapping her arms from round him. 'Your mother and I have things to talk about.'

'What is it, Dad?' she asked. He didn't answer her. 'Dad, please,' she said, and sobbed pathetically. How could I save my marriage with her snivelling all night?

'I said to bed!' He'd never had a harsh word for her. Not in her whole life. Silenced, she went upstairs. I heard her door close.

'George, I'm that sorry,' I said. I could do nothing to stop my crying. 'A thousand times I've wanted to tell you. It's like it happened to someone else.'

'I wish to God it had happened to someone else.'

He marched into the kitchen.

'You'd best sit down, Edie.'

I did. I put my head in my hands and howled. 'You've no idea, George, what it's been like. I've lived with it for all these years. I'm sorry. I'm so sorry.'

'Sorry for yourself, you mean. Things are starting to make sense. I never could understand why you never loved her. You've blamed her right from the start.'

'I did it for Paddy, George. It was madness. Just a

moment of madness. It was years ago. So many years ago. I'm sorry. So sorry. Please, George, you've got to forgive me.'

'Everything I hold dear has been ripped from me because of what you've done. Every time I look into that poor lass's face I'll remember. I've been mother and father to that girl. She's your daughter, Edie, from your own body, yet you've been no mother to her. Now she's no father, neither.'

'You're her father, George. I swear it.' I looked up at his face.

He shook his head. His flash of anger was over. His voice was laced with misery, like he was sick in his soul. 'She really has no father. I've been so blind all these years to what's been staring me in the face. And Arthur can be no father to her either, whatever he thinks, the poor beggar.'

'Poor beggar! He took advantage, George. You've got to believe me.'

'Oh, Edie. You'd sell your soul for Paddy, and you threw in your body as part of the bargain.'

I was crying so hard I couldn't hear him any more.

'Please don't leave, George.'

'I can't stay.'

'Where will you go? George, don't go. We can fix this. We can be stronger than ever now. No secrets.'

'I'll take a few things now and come back for the rest later.'

'What will I tell the kids?'

He sighed heavily. 'Whatever you like.'

I heard him moving about our bedroom, then the bathroom as he picked up his shaving things. Their voices were quiet at first. Then George shouted. I held on to the kitchen door while I listened.

'Ask your mother why.'

She was hysterically crying.

'Don't leave me all alone. Not with her. Please, Dad!'

'Get a grip on yourself, Bea. Let go of me!'

I heard a slap. I held my breath. Silence. Then I heard him say he was sorry. Her sobbing got louder. On with the waterworks at every opportunity. He came downstairs with a heavy tread. He went straight to the front door. He opened it long enough for a gust of freezing air to blast in, as if he was hesitating on the threshold. But it closed, and he was gone.

I found Bea crouching on the floor against the bathtub. She was shivering. Her left cheek was inflamed.

'What's going on, Mam?'

'Shhh now. No more questions. You should get into bed and sleep it off.'

'Sleep what off? I've not been drinking, Mam.'

'You can't fool me, my girl.'

'Mam, I'm telling you I haven't. Where he's gone? What's got into him?'

'Enough! Stop plaguing me!' It's hard to explain how much she could rouse me. My husband had just left me. My heart was shredded; but everything revolved around her, as per usual. I shut the door on her sobbing.

I was just about to go to bed when I heard a key in the front door. Colin. I should've gone to bed. Instead I went downstairs.

'Mam!' said Colin. 'Every light's blazing. What's up?' he said when he saw my face. 'What's the matter?

'Your dad's left us,' I said.

He laughed. 'Don't be daft.'

'I'm telling you. He's gone.'

'Did you have a barney or something? He'll be back.'

He took me by both shoulders and looked down into my face. All my boys towered over me. Bea too, by then. Tall like her father, I thought bitterly.

'What happened?'

'Oh don't ask me, duck. I can't begin to tell you.'

273

'C'mon, Mam,' he said gently. 'Dad'll come round.'

I shook my head. Tears ran down my cheeks.

'Let me make you a cuppa.'

'Better make one for Bea. She's in a right state.'

'Why?'

'About your dad leaving.'

'Don't be daft, Mam.'

'It's true. He just left. He hit her and left.'

'Hit her? Come on,' said Colin.

'I'm telling you. He slapped her one. Right across the face.'

'Oh God!' said Colin. 'Where is she?'

Everyone worrying about Bea first, as per usual. He chucked the sugar spoon at the pot and missed. Sugar grains sprinkled all over the counter. He took the stairs two at a time.

'Mam!' he called from upstairs. 'She's not here.'

'What do you mean?' I fished a bit of tissue out of my dressing gown pocket.

'Her coat's gone.'

Colin wrapped up to go looking for her. I settled down to wait, then I thought I may as well take myself to bed. What harm could Bea really come to? If she was wandering the town like some tragic heroine, there was sod all I could do about it.

*** 

The next morning I woke to bright sunshine filtering through the window. I'd not shut the curtains the night before. The storm was over. I had a thick head and felt sick from the taste of my own bitterness. I felt filled with concrete. I rinsed my face in cold water and swilled my mouth out.

Colin's door was shut. Gingerly, I opened it. The room was dark and empty. Bea's room was also empty. As if I didn't have enough to fret about. Downstairs, there was no sign of anyone. The kitchen counter was still covered in scattered sugar grains. My empty mug was in the sink, and Colin's and Bea's stood on the counter, unmade, where he'd left them, a teabag in each cup. I wiped up the spilt sugar and put the teabags away.

I caught a glimpse of myself in the kitchen mirror, every line on my face etched deep. I'd squashed my hair flat on one side and it bushed out madly on the other. I didn't want George seeing me like that. I went upstairs to run a bath. I put in some bath oil that one of the boys had given me for Christmas. I shampooed my hair and used some of Bea's conditioner. After I'd combed it out, I went into her room to look for her hairdryer.

I opened her curtains. Light streamed into the tiny crypt-like space. I got down on my knees to look under the bed. There were all sorts of things under there, like books, papers and school folders. I saw the hairdryer cord, and pulled at it, which knocked one of the piles over.

A little notebook caught my eye. I opened it. On the first page, she'd drawn a lot of hearts in different colours and sizes with arrows in them. In each one, she'd written 'Bea 4 Arthur' or 'Arthur 4 Bea' in fancy lettering. There was a whole series of different signatures, each in different colours, getting progressively shorter. Beatrix Penharris. Bea Penharris, BPenharris, BPen, BP. On another day, I might have found it funny. I stuffed everything back under the bed and blasted my hair.

I put on a grey cowl-neck jumper and a green skirt. I didn't want to look like I'd made a huge effort. I put on some thick tights though, as it was that freezing still, and some heels. I tried out Betty's tricks and slicked on a bit of make-up.

Where in God's name was George? Where had he spent the night? Where were the kids? I looked around the kitchen as if seeing it for the first time. How much of my life had been spent in that room? Making meal after meal to the backdrop of the radio. Chopping vegetables, mixing sauces, stirring, baking, brewing tea, reading the paper by the warmth of the oven, the endless ironing, looking over the kids through the steam as they did their homework at the kitchen table.

Why had I never made the room nicer? I could've painted it a duck egg blue or a nice yellow instead of putting up with that awful beige. Even cream would be an improvement. I blinked back tears. My family was splintered, all because of something I'd done years back. My brain felt too big for my head. I held the side of the table and rocked myself back and forth as I cried, leaning forward to make my tears fall vertically on to the table so as not to spoil my cack-handed mascara. I'd already begged. I could do nothing else. I'd have to wait it out. Wait for him to get fed up of living on his own. He'd come round. He wasn't the punishing kind. He loved me. He loved our kids, Bea included. You couldn't just switch it off, could you?

Colin walked in. He looked like an unmade bed. Seventeen he was. Not yet shaving every day. His face was haggard and bleary, hair all over the shop like he'd not slept for a week.

'What's the matter?' I said. He was angry, so angry.

'I should ask you the same thing. Why did you not answer the bloody phone?'

'Language, Colin!'

'Bugger that. Bea's in the hospital. She jumped from the bridge into the river. She would've drowned if Mr Penharris hadn't saved her.'

'Penharris?' I said, stupidly.

'Aye. I looked all over for her. I was coming back here to call the police when I found him carrying her. Both drenched to the skin, they were. She didn't know her own name. Hypothermic. Him too, by the looks of things, but he insisted on going home. What pushed her to do a thing like that? What happened between you and Dad?'

'I-I can't say, Colin love. Don't ask me,' and I began to cry again.

'You may well cry. Your own daughter wanting to drown herself. What does that tell you, Mam? What does that say about us, that we can't keep her safe and happy? She'd not have lasted two minutes in that water if it'd not been for Penharris. I'm going to see him. Dad's—'

'You've seen your dad?' My nerves fizzed.

'He's with her in the hospital. I'd not have left her otherwise.'

My heart leapt with hope and fear. If he'd come round to her, he'd forgive me.

'Why did you not ring me?'

'I tried ringing a dozen times. Engaged, engaged, engaged.'

'The phone hasn't rung! I swear it!' I brushed past him into the hallway. 'It's been knocked over. It's off the hook.'

'Did you not think to wonder where the bloody hell we were?'

'I thought you were in your beds. I didn't know the phone was off the hook. I'm so sorry,' I cried.

Through my tears, I saw him looking at me, half maddened, half pitying.

'Oh, Col, sweetheart,' I begged. 'I can't take it from you on top of everything else. I swear I didn't know about the phone. I don't know why Bea did what she did. You know what teenage girls are like.'

'Yeah, I do. I'm at school with hundreds of 'em. As a rule they're not all out in force on a New Year's Eve trying to top themselves.'

'I can't think what got into her. It'll blow over, mark my words. I'll take care of her, see if I don't. Sit down, love. Let me make you a cup of tea and some breakfast. You look half-frozen to death.'

'I don't want anything. I'm going to see Mr Penharris.'

'Don't go, duck. He'll be wanting a bit of peace and quiet. You know.'

'I don't know anything.'

His face was granite. I put my hand on his cheek. 'It'll be all right, duck,' I said. 'What happened, it's between me and your father. He'll come back, you'll see.'

'If I knew what was going on, I could judge for myself. I'm going to Mr Penharris's.'

I wished to God Penharris would drop dead. 'Leave Arthur be, duck. He's... he's grieving. Your Dad and I, we'll go and see him later,' I lied.

'She'd be dead if not for him. It's the least I can do.'

What could I say? The days when I could tell him what to do were long gone. George had upped and left, but I was the villain of the piece as per usual. He was the one who'd slapped Bea. But oh no, he could do no bloody wrong. So much for how I looked. My make-up was smudged and the outfit was all wrong with walking shoes. I couldn't mess about though. I needed to catch George at the hospital.

I crossed the bridge on the way. Hundreds of times I'd crossed it without a thought for the distance between the bridge and the water. It must've been twenty, thirty feet. Colin was right. Leaping into that water on a wet winter's night was like signing your own death warrant. The river was known for its undertow. Bea was a good swimmer, but the current and the cold would have done for her soon enough, especially if she was weighed down by her coat. I shivered. I felt a needle of guilt. Every time I justified myself, an unwelcome thought popped up to judge me.

I'd kept my love from her. I never had felt the same way about her as I did the boys. I remembered the little scrap George had placed in my arms in the hospital. The same hospital I was going to now. Just a baby. A baby like any other, and I'd kept my love from her.

I took the lift to the ward. It wasn't easy to see where she was, as some of the beds were curtained off. An old lady was sleeping in the bed by the door. I tiptoed in so as not to wake her. It was a big ward, but I heard a quiet sniffling coming from one of the curtained-off beds. That would be Bea, I thought. Against my will, I felt a surge of irritation. Always bloody wailing. But it wasn't her. I found her eventually. She lay on the bed staring into space.

'Where's your dad?' I asked.

'He just left.'

'Where did he go?'

'I don't know.'

'When did he leave?'

'Ten minutes ago.'

I needed to find him. To make him see. I sat down heavily at her bedside. I fought back desperate tears.

'I've never seen you cry,' she said.

'What got into you? What made you do it?'

She pressed her lips together. They started to quiver. Fresh tears sprang to her eyes. She shook her head from side to side.

'Why's he leaving, Mam?'

I must say I was surprised. I thought he'd have said. If he hadn't told her, blowed if I would.

# CHAPTER TWENTY

Bea remembered that distant New Year's Eve with a shudder. The things her mother had said that night. Things Bea had never buried. 'You ruin everything. We were a happy house until you came. I've never understood how he can be so blind. He sees something when he looks at you that I will never see.' She'd grown up with the feeling her mother didn't love her, but that night, she'd had it ground into her face.

Her father had turned on her, suddenly a stranger. The pain of him leaving had cut her more deeply than anything her mother had ever done.

Arthur Penharris. The memory bit so hard she grimaced. She couldn't bury it. Sometimes she went for days without thinking about it, but it was always there, something she lived with, something she couldn't get rid of, like a stain.

After her father had left, she'd dragged on some warm clothes and crept downstairs, not wanting to alert her mother or Colin that she was leaving. She couldn't stay in that house. Not without her father. She slipped on the pixie boots Clare had bought her for her birthday, pulled on her coat and let herself out of the house without making a sound.

She went to Arthur's house. Arthur, Arthur, Arthur. She remembered murmuring his name to herself with every step up the hill towards his house. In the immediate shock of Clare's death, she had felt desperately sorry for him. Mourning had pulled them together. It had not taken long for different feelings to take root in her. Feelings that had nothing to do with pity. She couldn't pinpoint the moment when he ceased to be Clare's grieving father and became a man in her eyes. She had cherished the feeling, a feeling that had sprung from the sorrow of Clare's death, like an orchid emerging from a wasteland.

She was sure that he felt the same way about her. The way he hung on her every word. How he looked at her. In spite of his overwhelming grief, something wonderful happened to his face when he saw her. Compared to boys her own age, Arthur was like a work of Shakespeare next to the scribblings of an idiot.

Age didn't matter when it came to a soulmate. She'd help him see she was ready. More than ready.

She wanted to live with him. Her father had gone and her mother couldn't stand to look at her. No one would care. There was nothing they could do, even if they wanted to. She'd be sixteen in a few months.

She ran in the icy rain towards his house, sloughing off an old life and walking into a new one. 'I wish to God I'd never had you,' Edie had said. And now her father had gone. What was so wrong with her that he'd leave her?

Arthur didn't think there was anything wrong with her. She'd seen his face change each time he opened the door to her. She would do whatever it took to light up his blighted life. She'd make him happy again. They were two wounded souls who could help each other to heal.

As she crested the hill towards the house, she saw the drawing room lights were still blazing. Good. She'd not have to wake him. Her footsteps crunched on the gravel of the driveway. He wouldn't hear. Not through the rain and the wind. She saw him through the window. He sat with a pen in one hand, poised over a writing pad. His face was utterly desolate. He gazed ahead at the dying fire.

She wondered if she should knock on the window, but changed her mind. She walked round to the side of the house and rang the doorbell.

He took longer than expected. She bounced on her heels, as much from her jangling nerves as the cold.

'Bea!' he said, as he opened the door.

She didn't give herself time to think. She lurched forward into his arms. The door closed behind her, shutting out the rain and the wind.

Bea didn't know how long they stood in their embrace. 'Oh, Bea, my darling girl,' he said as he held her close. 'I'm so happy you're here.'

She nestled into his warmth. He smelled of clean linen and cigarettes.

His voice was filled with emotion. Through his tears, he said: 'I hadn't dared to hope you'd come to me like this. I thought perhaps your mother was right, that you'd—'

'My mother! Did you talk to her?'

'Yes, of course...'

Bea burned inside. Edie could be trusted to take a sordid view of something so beautiful.

'It doesn't matter what she thinks,' said Bea, her head against his chest, her arms about his waist. 'I don't give a damn any more.'

'And your fa— George?'

'He's gone.'

She heard his intake of breath. 'I'm sorry, so sorry,' he said.

'It doesn't matter.' And it didn't. Not just then. His arms were round her, and he was cradling her head against his chest. She raised her head for their first kiss.

He stooped to kiss her cheek instead. He was so kind. He didn't want to rush things. She turned her head to meet his lips, and took a step forward so she could properly melt into him. She knew just what to do. She'd seen it in a dozen films.

He froze.

'Bea, what are you doing?'

She stared at him.

'You're my daughter, Bea. My child!'

He grasped her by the shoulders and swung her round

so she was facing a mirror in the hallway. 'Just look at that,' he said. 'See? The image of Clare. You're my child, not theirs. My child!'

Bea could not look. A hot gust of shame rose up like a wave in her chest. It filled her head in a blaze. She trembled. She darted for the door, and escaped into the rain. She ran down the path towards the road, ignoring his calls.

She had no idea where she should go. She couldn't go home. That was no home. She couldn't bear to think about what had just happened.

Her mother's words came back to her. They didn't want her. She'd always been in the way. She ruined everything. Her father couldn't bear to be near her. The pain fought with the shame and she thought she'd implode with misery.

The idea came to her when she saw a group of drunken boys messing around on the railings of the bridge. She watched them from the far end, afraid to cross in case they hassled her. One of them pretended to fall, yodelling as he windmilled his arms. He grabbed hold of a lamp post and swung himself down. His friends laughed as they abandoned the bridge, making their way towards the centre of town. Once they were gone, the bridge was deserted.

The thought crystallised as she crossed towards the other side. The rain had died down and the wind was not as strong. She looked down at the dark river. It looked soft, velvety from where she stood. The water would deaden her to any further feeling. It would wipe out the disgust she felt for herself. Her mother had nothing but loathing for her. She had repulsed her own father. She pulled herself up onto the edge of the railings, her fingers clinging to the wet freezing metal. She draped an arm round the lamp post. She envisioned launching herself in a giant leap, but her foot slipped, so she fell very close to the bridge. She knocked the back of her head against a strut. Her stomach turned as she fell. The wind blasted past her, then was drowned out by the splash of her body hitting the water. Her ears were filled with the dull roar of the current. Her layers insulated her from the initial shock of the cold, but the water, like a thousand pinpricks, pierced through the fabric close to her skin. She let herself sink. It was terrifying beneath the surface. So dark, so murky. Something brushed against her face. Horrified, she panicked and raised her arms to protect herself. She didn't know how far she'd plunged, she couldn't see up from down.

Her coat was so heavy. One of her boots fell away from her foot. If she could only just let it happen, it wouldn't last long, she promised herself. Her lungs were burning. Be still, be still, just let yourself sink... if she breathed the water in, allowed it to flood her lungs it would be over sooner, but she couldn't make herself do it. Her limbs were leaden. Her lungs were about to explode. The dark water closed in around her and the roar dimmed as she sank.

Her heart pounded and her chest burned. The darkness around her was total. Her heart thumped to a crescendo and the burning spread to all her nerve endings. She fought the urge to breathe. She couldn't see a thing. She couldn't stand it a moment longer and she exhaled the poisonous air from her lungs. Her last breath. She burned with effort and pain. She struggled like a landed fish as she swallowed water. She felt the soft brush of reeds against her face. She knew she had to find the bottom to kick against it. She gave a weak kick against the reeds, which gave no purchase at all. She had wasted her remaining strength on a feeble effort. She would die angry and disgusted with herself. She had to try one more time. She let herself sink. She had to sink right to the bottom. She heard her own heart slowing. Then, as if a switch was flicked, her panic came to an end.

She found the stillness she'd been scrabbling for. She wasn't cold any more. She was weightless. The river was warm, soft and quiet. Flecks of light danced in front of her eyes. They multiplied in a silent explosion until they all joined together to dispel the darkness. She drifted, at peace, like falling into a cosy slumber.

She was violently pulled by an invisible hand. Feebly, she resisted. It was like being dragged from a warm feather-bed, back to the roaring waters she'd managed to escape.

Afterwards, Bea could not clearly relate what happened. That it was Arthur Penharris who had fished her out of the river was not in doubt. He had carried her back to the bridge. She didn't remember him covering her with his coat, but she was wearing it when Colin found them. They flagged down a car to take her to the hospital.

She and Colin were the last to see Arthur Penharris alive. His body was found downriver by a couple walking their dog in the early morning. A grisly find on a New Year's Day, she heard someone describe it conversationally a few weeks later.

Bea was in hospital for three days. The day she got home, the police came to the house.

'So you went out to look for your sister, and you found her on the riverbank with Mr Penharris, both soaking wet,' said Inspector Martin. His young colleague took notes.

'That's right,' said Colin.

'Then you managed to stop a passing car to take her to the hospital. Why didn't you just walk there? It's not five minutes from the bridge.'

'You should've seen her. She was blue, and hardly conscious. I didn't think she'd last much longer.'

'Why didn't he go with you?'

'I don't know. He refused, point blank.'

Edie weighed in: 'Are you trying to say my boy is somehow to blame for not forcing a grown man into a car? He knew his own mind. Is that not right, Colin?'

'I'm not trying to say anything, Mrs Newell. I'm just

trying to cover all the angles. Was there anything about him that struck you as odd?'

'Yes!' said Colin. 'He was soaking wet on a freezing winter night with a river weed sticking out of his ear.'

'No need to get sarky, lad.'

'Sorry,' said Colin, and buried his head in his hands. 'If you really want to know, I was more worried about my sister than about him. She needed to get into the warm. The cold didn't seem to be bothering him. He was fully compos mentis. Calm, actually, if you want to know.'

'Calm?'

'Look, I really tried. The driver—'

'I was going to ask you about him. Did you know him?'

'No. I was carrying Bea, and Mr Penharris stepped out into the road to stop him. There were no other cars around.'

'Did he know Mr Penharris?'

Colin looked confused. 'I don't think so. I don't quite see—'

'Like I said, we're just trying to cover all angles. It's quite unusual for people to stop for complete strangers in the middle of the night.'

'It was obvious it was an emergency. The driver told us to stop arguing and to just get in. He said he hadn't got all night, and he said neither's she, by the looks of her.'

'Meaning your sister?'

'Yes.'

'Anything else you can tell us? Anything at all?'

'Not really. Before we drove off, Mr Penharris told me to take good care of Bea, and to tell her—' He stopped abruptly. 'That was the last I saw of him. I went to see him the next day. His front door was wide open, but there was no one in.'

Inspector Martin listened in silence. The younger officer paused in his scribbling.

Presently, Martin said, 'He wanted you to tell your sister

something. What was it?'

'I don't see how it could be important,' said Edie.

'A man is dead, Mrs Newell.'

'He said he loved her,' said Colin.

'That's ridiculous!' said Edie. 'He couldn't have been right in the head.'

The officer ignored her.

'Why do you think he got back into the water?' asked Martin softly.

'I don't know.'

'Did he seem suicidal to you?

'I don't know. Looking back on it, there was something final in what he said. I wasn't paying attention though. I was just worried about my sister.'

'Would you be prepared to put all this in a statement?'

'Of course,' said Colin.

The officer turned his attention to Bea. 'Can you tell me what you were doing on the bridge?'

Edie's eyes burned into Bea, who didn't trust herself to speak.

'She fell.' This from her mother.

The two officers looked at each other.

'Is that true?'

Bea nodded.

'Can you tell us, in your own words, what happened that evening?'

She remembered the boys on the bridge. 'I was larking about.' She was not a good liar.

The two policemen looked at each other. 'Larking about. Was anyone with you?'

'No.'

'Bea, was anything going on between you and Mr Penharris?'

'No!' she cried. A fresh flood of shame washed over her

at the memory of their last encounter.

'Why would you ask her that?' Edie demanded.

'Bea was seen leaving his house, alone, in the small hours of New Year's Eve. Can you think of any other conclusion we should come to?'

Edie's lips thinned.

'According to the neighbours, members of this family were in and out of that house all the time.'

'Clare was engaged to our brother,' said Colin. 'What would you expect?'

'I don't expect a sane and rational man to jump from a bridge.'

'He did it to save me,' said Bea. Her voice was so quiet that the senior policeman asked her to repeat herself. 'Arthur— I mean Mr Penharris dived in to save me. He was leading me home when Colin found us. It's true, I swear.'

'Are you sure that's how Colin found you?'

'Yes!'

'What do you mean by that?' asked Colin.

'I might not be too happy finding a man older than my father pawing my sister.'

'I told you, it wasn't like that!' she had said.

'The first I've heard of anything between Mr Penharris and my sister is from you right now.'

'There was nothing between us!' she cried.

'We found a letter he was writing to you. Starting with "My Darling Bea".'

Edie took in a sharp breath.

'What did it say?' asked Colin.

Martin looked at the junior officer, who riffled through some papers in the notebook and read. 'Dearest Bea, I have loved you since I first set eyes on you. For so long I have wanted to tell you that you are my own darling girl. It will seem strange at first, but we will all adjust, even George and Edie.'

Edie put her head in her hands. No one said anything, until the silence was broken by Martin.

'Unmistakably intimate, wouldn't you agree?'

'What else did he say?' asked Colin.

The two officers looked at each other. 'That's it. He hadn't finished.'

Edie lifted her head. 'I don't like what you're getting at. It's as plain as day the man was unhinged.'

'You may be right about that, as there's something else.'

'What?' asked Colin.

'He made a new will a week after his daughter died. Got it witnessed too, so it's all valid. He's left his house to you, Bea. Apart from a bequest to the school and a few other bits and bobs to a couple of charities, he's left all his worldly goods to you. Why would he do that, do you suppose, if he wasn't sleeping with you?'

\*\*\*

What must they have thought of us? For years we'd been seen as a respectable family. Now we were a broken home, headed by a runaway father and a woman who couldn't keep her man, with a bridge-jumper for a daughter. They didn't believe she was larking about, not for a minute. They believed she'd been sleeping with Penharris. It was scarcely better having them think she'd tried to do herself in. They suspected Colin of chucking him over the bridge. What did that say about us? People still talk about it now. Not to my face, mind you, but I just know they do.

It was just Colin, Bea and me in the house. I could hardly look at Bea. Limp and wet as a dishrag as she was.

Sammy came back from Oxford for Penharris's funeral.

'Why didn't you call me, Mam?' he asked before he'd

put his bag down. It was hard to answer. Grief makes you selfish. I'd no room to think of anyone else. 'Where's Dad?'

Before I could answer, there was a knock on the door.

'I'll get it,' he said.

It was George. I looked a mess. Hastily, I smoothed my hair. I didn't want a scene in front of Sam.

He hugged Sam. 'It's a sorry time, lad. We can talk later. I've come to speak to your mother.'

'Steady on, Dad. What's going on?'

'I don't live here any more, lad,' George said. He put his hand on Sam's shoulder. 'Don't ask, son. Not now. I need a word with your mother.'

'Whoah, Dad. What's got into you two?'

'It's between your mother and me. Edie, come take a walk with me. Sam, go upstairs, lad. Go and see Bea.'

'Where is she?'

'In her bed,' I said.

'Is she sick?'

'Only in her mind,' I said.

'I hope to God you're keeping an eye on her,' said George.

'I'll go up,' said Sam.

'We'll not be long.'

We walked away from the house together in silence. My husband of so many years and me, facing forward, not touching. Rage pulsed from him.

'Why are you doing this, George?' I cried.

'The hurt you've done me is nothing to what you've done to that girl.'

'You'd just left me, George. She's a teenager having a strop. Excuse me if she wasn't the first thing in my mind.'

'That's just it,' George said, his voice laced with bitterness. 'She's never been the first thing in your mind.'

'George, please come home. I'll make it up to her.'

'You can never do that.'

'I could if you were with me.'

'I can't be with you.'

I cried so hard I could scarcely breathe.

'George, please don't tell the kids,' I said. 'I'd never be able to look them in the face. Not ever. I can't bear the shame of it.'

He turned to face me.

'I'll not say anything,' he said. 'But not to spare you. For Bea's sake I'll hold my peace. I'm ashamed of what I did. I turned my back on her. She didn't see that I was leaving you. She only saw I was leaving her with someone who can't stand the sight of her.'

'That's not true, I—'

'I never understood why you didn't love her like the others. She'd have walked through fire to get a bit of affection from you. She reminds you of something you'd rather forget. She's always looked to me as her dad. If I deny her again, she'll have no one.'

No sooner had probate been granted than Bea moved into Penharris's house, stoking the rumour mill even more. That was a big enough slap in the face without George moving in with her. He stayed in that house until he died. I'd sometimes catch sight of Bea in the supermarket, buying salad and olives and other fancies, and meat and beer for her dad and ginger biscuits, the ones he liked. It was like I was dead to them.

Colin stayed with me. Sometimes he'd come back home late and I'd know he'd spent the evening with them. I felt the loneliness of those evenings in my marrow. I didn't dare say anything, for fear he'd up and leave me too. Everyone I loved had left me by then, and him leaving was only a matter of time.

# CHAPTER TWENTY-ONE

Bea had had years to reflect on why Penharris had killed himself. He had fixated on her as a daughter figure, and her mortifying attempt at romance had destroyed his mad delusion. Her kiss had killed him, as surely as if her lips were poisoned. The shame she had felt that night, and the remorse that had lingered since... she had never spoken of it to anyone, not even David.

She crossed her arms over her stomach and rocked herself and the baby. She had fresh cause to be grateful that he'd saved her. She would give this child everything that Edie had denied her.

Lorena's venom circulated inside her. Bea needed to get out of the house. She gathered her phone and her bag and put her coat on. She wrapped a scarf round her neck and put the new set of keys into her pocket. She'd walk to Dorothy's.

The doorbell rang. She opened the door.

'Diana!' said Bea. A jolt ran through her.

'Were you going out?' Diana asked, as she took in the coat and scarf. 'May I come in? It won't take long.' Not waiting for a reply, she swept inside, wafting Hermès.

She stood beneath the overhead lights in the hallway and waited for Bea to close the door. The lights cast shadows across her lovely face.

'Can we sit somewhere? I have something to tell you that may be rather a shock.'

Bea laughed bitterly. 'Someone's beaten you to it. Come through to the kitchen.' She picked up the papers from the table and stuffed them into a drawer. 'Take a seat,' she said. 'Would you like some tea?'

'No. Thanks.'

Beneath Diana's immaculate make-up, her face was drawn, and her eyes shone with brittle intensity.

'I'll come straight to the point. I don't wish to bore you with intimate details, but I've been seeing your brother, Patrick.'

'Paddy? I had no idea.'

'No. I don't suppose you did. I hadn't the faintest notion he was your brother until I saw him at David's funeral. He was a bit stunned when he saw me there.'

So was I, thought Bea.

Diana continued: 'He said he hadn't known I was David's ex-wife when we met. He said he'd been trying to find the right moment to tell me that he was your brother. It shouldn't make any difference to us, he said.'

'Does it make a difference?'

'Not by itself, no.' She wrung her hands together. 'I expect you're wondering what this has to do with you.'

'Well yes. Paddy doesn't confide in me about any aspect of his life. We're not close. He isn't close to anyone.'

Diana put her hand to her throat. Her diamonds and her nail polish glinted merrily beneath the desolation of her face.

'Are you sure I can't get you anything?' asked Bea.

'Just a glass of water, please,' said Diana in a hoarse whisper. Tears sprang to her eyes. Bea filled a glass and put it in front of Diana. She took a sip, then put the glass down and laid her hands flat on the table. Bea was moved. She fought the urge to take Diana's hands in her own.

'I had hoped that Patrick and I...' said Diana, then changed tack. 'It's been a long time since the divorce. Whatever David may have told you, I loved him. It's taken an inordinate time to trust someone else. I should sooner have trusted a crocodile.'

'What has he done?' asked Bea.

'He's been having an affair with your cleaner.'

'Lorena?' It was a day for surprises.

'Yes. Lorena Carvalho.'

'Well, hasn't she been busy.'

Diana reached into her bag and pulled out a brown envelope that contained a stack of photographs. Some were not in sharp focus, but the two principals were unmistakable. There was one of Lorena and Paddy kissing. Lorena and Paddy leaving a club together. Lorena getting into Paddy's car. Another of Lorena and Paddy kissing, her hips pushed forward into his crotch. There was a theme to the pictures. The camera had captured the crackling sexual intensity between them, like the mating of two glamorous scorpions. Each shot had the time and date printed digitally in the bottom left-hand corner.

Bea's mind raced with the implications as she waded through the pile, looking at the pictures one by one. It was too much to think about. Lorena with Paddy. Lorena with David. So much for the great love affair between them.

'How did you get these?' she asked.

'After I saw Patrick at David's funeral, I hired an investigator. I've been seeing your brother about two years. I met him at the Hurlingham Club. He was always in the gym with a personal trainer, rebuilding his leg after his motorbike accident.'

'Motorbike accident?'

'Yes, you know...'

'Never mind. Carry on.'

'He's a little younger, but he seemed ideal. He's charming, clever, educated. He's attentive and he made me feel so...' Diana floundered. She took in a sharp intake of breath and sat up straighter in her chair. 'I fell in love with him,' she said. 'Or at least the idea of him. I didn't want to focus on the negatives, but after a while I found there were things that were hard to ignore. I've never been to his flat, for instance. In two years, can you believe. He's always been vague about what he does for a living. Most men can't stop banging on about their work. I've never met any of his friends, and certainly none of his family. If it hadn't been for David's funeral, I'd probably still be in the dark about his connection to you. The boys don't mind him, but Hilary can't stand him. It's actually beyond funny. Her hatred is... visceral.' Diana shuddered.

'Why are you telling me this?' asked Bea.

'I'm coming to that. I wanted things to become official between us.'

'Do you mean marriage?'

'Yes. Why not? We were in love. Or so I thought. We were free, and things seemed to be headed in the right direction, but his secrecy niggled at me. I asked him about it. He said we could go to his flat anytime I wanted, but it was spartan, more like an office as he worked from home. My house was so much more comfortable, that was all. He said he didn't talk about his work because it was dull and arcane, and he'd learned not to bore the pants off people. He said he'd lost touch with his family years ago, because they blamed him for a car accident.'

'A car accident?'

'Yes. A girl killed herself crashing her car, and the two families held him responsible.

'What did he say about it?' asked Bea carefully. Her skin prickled.

'He said she'd come to London to persuade him to attend her wedding to your brother.'

'Clare,' said Bea.

'That's it. They'd met for lunch. He said he'd ordered some wine to toast her and his brother, and she practically downed it solo. She was on a mission to get drunk and came on to him, but he sent her packing. He said he'd never do that to one of his brothers.'

Bea raised an eyebrow. 'What else did he say?'

'Just that she died on the way back to Hampshire.'

'It was Lincolnshire she was driving back to.'

'I know that now,' said Diana sadly. 'I've found out all about him, his little sabbatical at Her Majesty's Pleasure and a lot more besides.'

'Nobody blamed Paddy for the accident,' said Bea. Perhaps we should have, she thought.

'It appears he can't tell the simple truth about anything. I came here to warn you.'

'About what?'

'He's always shown a morbid interest in you and David. He's never been obvious, but when I think about it, I'm horrified how much I've confided. Anyway. After David died, Patrick encouraged me to sue his estate.'

'What for?'

'Some of my investments have taken a hit just like everyone else's. He said I had a right to make a claim for the sake of the children. The press described our settlement as generous, but it was entirely fair. We'd been married over twenty years. He worked and I looked after our three children. I could have probably made more over the course of my life by going for maintenance, but I wanted to get on with my life. I didn't want to have to depend on David for a monthly cheque, like some sort of minion.'

Bea said nothing.

'I was well within my rights to fight for a decent settlement. But going after his estate after he had died... it would have been mercenary, wrong, venal. I could only suppose that my enrichment was a benefit to him if we got married.'

Diana continued: 'I have much more than these photos. I have the transcript of a conversation between them, which is rather... humiliating, so I'd appreciate it if you just took my word for it.' She took another sip of water. 'They're planning to plunder the children's trust. It seems she's pregnant.'

'So she says,' said Bea, flicking through the photographs.

'So you know then. With David's baby.'

Bea looked up sharply. Her eyes filled with hot tears. She looked across at Diana. The twist of the knife must be sweet.

As if reading her mind, Diana said: 'If you expect me to be enjoying some kind of *Schadenfreude*, you'd be wrong. I don't take pleasure in other people's misery.'

'Did David cheat on you?' asked Bea.

'He decided to leave. That's a betrayal.'

'It's not the same thing.'

'What did he tell you?'

'That you'd grown apart. That you weren't close any more.'

Diana laughed. 'Did he tell you I didn't understand him?'

It had been a mistake to ask.

'I don't know if he cheated on me or not. It doesn't really matter. I'd have been able to bear it. God knows I loved my father, but he put my mother through the mill. He always came back to her, though. What I couldn't bear was that David left us.'

The two women were silent. Diana's voice took on a hard, pragmatic tone. 'You'll have to insist on a DNA test. Whatever he may have done to me is irrelevant now, but a test will give you your answer. I would regard it as a great favour if you said nothing about this to the children.'

'But if it's true...'

'Yes, then obviously they'll have to be told. I've been half expecting an announcement from you and David on that score for years. That would have meant an adjustment—'

'Not necessarily a hard one,' said Bea defensively.

'Not at all,' said Diana quickly, 'but this will be terrible for them. It puts David in the most appalling light.'

'You say it as if it's true!' said Bea.

'I don't know if it's true or not, but I don't want them stirred up unless this child is his, beyond a shadow of doubt.'

Bea looked down at the photos again.

'Have you reached the bottom of the pile yet?'

'No,' said Bea. Diana took the bundle from her hand and flicked through the remaining photos herself. 'Do you see this one?' she said, and put yet another picture of Lorena and Paddy together in front of her.

The picture was taken outside her house. Lorena was opening or closing the door. They'd been inside it. Together. Alone.

'Why are you telling me all this?'

'They've been playing us all, David included. I have no control over the children's trust, but you do. Baby or no baby, it's up to you to stop them.'

The truth had been eddying in the air around her since Lorena's visit, and was beginning to hit home. Diana thought it quite unremarkable that David had slept with Lorena. Didn't that tell her something? After so many years of marriage, she ought to know. She swayed on the chair and caught herself on the table.

'Are you all right?' Diana asked.

Bea was unable to respond.

'Look, I have to go, but you oughtn't be by yourself. Is there someone I can call? Somewhere I can take you? The car's outside.'

Bea trembled and fought to control herself before she said, 'My friend Dorothy. She lives a few streets away. I was going to go there when you arrived.'

She followed Diana to her car like a sleepwalker, slamming the door to the house behind her.

# CHAPTER TWENTY-TWO

Diana wasn't returning his calls. He'd overplayed his hand. Just as well. She had saved him the trouble of ending it. She wasn't useful to him any more. She bored him. She had a boring life stuffed full of boring people. She headed committees of do-gooding women with nothing better to do with their time than micromanage each other's fundraising efforts. The highlight of her week was her book club, at which she and a bunch of other harpies spent five minutes perfunctorily discussing some desperately uninteresting tome before settling in to the real business of the evening, which was bitching about their husbands, bragging about their children and gossiping about their friends. All over a civilised glass or two of wine. As for her interminable dinner parties... the table displays were considerably more glittering than the conversation. He'd had to keep a lid on himself. He'd have liked to tell her collection of Hugos and Arabellas to go and fuck themselves.

There was one person in Diana's life that Paddy regretted leaving behind. Hilary. How he would have liked to work on her a little.

The first time he'd bedded Diana had been undeniably thrilling. He'd had to work hard to get beneath those layers of cashmere. In the end, he took her out for yet another ruinous dinner and made sure she got properly wasted. Once the deed was done, she had been breathless, coy and clinging. What a huge deal she made out of a bit of sex. Like a Jane Austen virgin rather than a middle-aged divorcée with three kids. She insisted on romantic claptrap like candles, dinner, wine and kissing.

The things she talked about. The appalling standards of modern education. Kids these days. The client state. The corruption of charities. The rubbish on television. The difficulties of disciplining her children. He'd have liked to make a suggestion or two where Hilary was concerned. It was hard to decide what he wanted more: to fuck her or smack her.

Only once had a topic arisen at one of her gatherings that remotely interested him. Getting away with murder, prompted no doubt by some rubbish on Netflix.

He didn't seriously consider himself to be a murderer. Not really. Edie never let that baby out of her sight. He'd seen his opportunity and taken it. He'd felt so powerful. The feeling had lasted for days, and he'd been able to recreate it for some time afterwards by closing his eyes and replaying the scene in his head. Eventually, the memory lost its potency. Sometimes he wondered if it had really happened.

He hadn't meant to kill Clare. He hadn't slipped that stuff in her coffee to kill her, but that's what it had done. Paddy didn't consider himself to be a rapist either, but Clare needed a nudge. Certainly within such a short time frame. Given world enough and time, she would have been willing, he had no doubt, as Carol was.

On balance, he preferred a willing partner, but it had felt good to shag her. When she'd come to, she'd been disoriented and confused. She'd become agitated when she realised she was naked beneath the sheet he'd covered her with.

'What happened?' she'd asked.

'I bent you over the sofa while you were passed out and shagged you bandy.'

'You didn't. I—'

'Yeah, I did.' He held her knickers up, like a trophy. 'Trust Sam to pick a girl who wears white drawers. Marks and Sparks too.'

There was a dawning in her groggy eyes.

'Don't be like that,' he said. 'Not batting for the same side as old Borthwick, are you? I was hoping you'd stay the night. We could do it again.' He moved towards her. 'You might get to enjoy it this time.'

She shrank into the sofa. He held up her bra. Ostentatiously, he looked at the label. 'C&A. Very glam.'

'Give me my clothes.' Her voice quavered.

'Tell you what, I'll give them back to you if you suck on this.' He pointed to his crotch. 'I tried to stick it in your mouth while you were snoozing, but you weren't very cooperative.'

She'd thrown up on his rug. Now that had pissed him off. He'd loved that rug. He'd bought it from a stall on Portobello Road. Genuine Turkish. He'd developed an eye for beautiful things since leaving the dingy semi he'd been brought up in. No matter what he did with it, the smell had lingered, so he'd had to chuck it. The smell of her sick had outlived her by a comfortable margin.

'Now look what you've done!' he'd said. He'd wanted to hit her. He hadn't liked the pitch of his voice. Like a petulant maiden aunt.

She started to howl properly. He tossed her clothes at her. 'You should go now,' he said. Vomit had put an end to any thought of round two. The noise she had made. It had given him a headache.

She stumbled to the bathroom, clutching the pitiful bundle of clothes to her chest. It was difficult to be dignified when naked and afraid. She emerged in a flurry, gathering her bag and coat. She cried out when he left the flat with her.

'A gentleman walks a lady to her car,' he said. 'My mam taught me that.' He linked arms with her. 'Give my regards to old Borthwick, won't you, Clare. Tell her I miss our little chats. Tell her thanks for sending you along. It's been lovely. Also, give my love to Mam. On second thought, don't. You'll ruin her surprise. See you next week. Bit of a cheek, but I expect you'll be in white.'

Her teeth were chattering by the time they got to the

car. She struggled to fit the key to the lock. He took it from her and opened the door himself. He leaned across her and strapped her in. She shrank into the seat to avoid his touch. 'It's a bit late to come over all coy.' He smiled. He pecked her cheek. She shrieked. 'Don't be like that, Clare. It's time one of us redefined the terms of our relationship.' He shut the door on her. She stalled the car before she managed to jerk into the road.

'Drive safely!' he called after the bunny-hopping car. He was the last person to see her alive.

He didn't like remembering his father's death. His father had never loved him. George had made efforts to build bridges with the alien son, but Paddy, catlike, had known it was forced.

Paddy remembered an incident years ago, after he'd beaten up on one of the little kids, Colin probably. Soft brown stuff had hit the swirling blades. George had whacked him and Edie had got hysterical. The little kids thought it was Armageddon.

George had tried to explain after everyone had calmed down. 'He's smaller and weaker than you. That's why it's so wrong.' Paddy hadn't said anything. Of course he'd hit someone smaller and weaker. What kind of moron picked on someone bigger and stronger? George apologised afterwards: 'Whacking you was wrong, plain as the nose on my face. But why did you do it, son? You hit him, for no good reason, when you thought no one was watching. Why, Paddy? Why d'you do it?' Paddy was silent, knowing that George wouldn't fall for a lie and that the truth would do him no favours. Not like Edie, who lived on the lies he fed her. He could tell her dogs were cats and she'd make herself believe it.

The truth was he liked hurting the little kids.

What was so wrong with him that his father hadn't loved him? George used to look at him in a particular way. It had given him a sinking feeling in his stomach. He'd never cared what anyone else ever thought of him. Only his dad. George had looked at the other kids completely differently. He was indulgent, proud, loving. He hadn't known how to win George over, much as he tried. George liked his boys loveable, good-hearted, courageous, bright, fair in a fight. George valued intelligence, but did not appreciate Paddy's brand of low cunning.

He used to watch his father romping with the other boys, playing at pirates, knights, swinging them round, that sort of thing. Even with them, ten minutes was enough, before he wanted a bit of peace and quiet with the paper or watch the news.

Then Bea arrived, and the axis in the house shifted. Paddy remembered being swamped with longing when he watched his father holding Bea. Cuddling her close, crooning her asleep, jiggling her on his knee, singing to her, making her laugh. Before she could sit upright by herself, he'd loop his arms under hers in front of the piano. Her aimless plinking when tiny gradually evolved into primitive melodies as she grew, all under his loving care. His patience had been bottomless, even when she'd been so little and useless.

Edie did what was required for the baby and no more. George made up for her lack. Paddy had long known he could claim the lion's share of his mother's love. He had never respected her for it. The surfeit of love he received from Edie in such cloying abundance was evened out by George.

He remembered one Sunday Edie was in the kitchen, distracted, trying to rescue soggy crackling on a pork joint before visitors arrived. The smell of cooked pig filled the whole house.

Bea was upstairs asleep in the cot in George and Edie's room. All the other kids had had their turn in that cot except him. He could hear Edie clattering about in the kitchen and the mumbling of the radio. He looked down from the top of the stairs to make sure the coast was clear. He crept inside and pushed the door to. He stalked the cot warily, so as not to wake her. She was a fretful sleeper, as they all knew to their cost. He looked down at her. She had a halo of wispy blond hair through which her veiny scalp was clearly visible. What was it about her that George loved so much?

'What're you doing?'

Paddy started. It was Will.

'Nothing,' said Paddy, who remained quite still despite the fear and rage warring within him.

'Get out of here,' Will hissed.

'Or what?'

'If you go anywhere near her, I'll kill you.'

'I wasn't doing anything.' Paddy hadn't liked the way his own voice sounded. Plaintive. Feeble. That used to happen to him often, until he learned to modulate his pitch and tone.

When his father had moved to the hospice, he'd visited him almost every day. He used to go when his brothers and sister were not around. Even after all these years, it rankled how much easier George was around the others. The others did things for him. Bea had a light touch, a sense for knowing that he needed a tissue, a sip of water, a foot rub, whatever. Paddy's attempts to second-guess George's needs were politely declined as if he were a stranger. Paddy picked up on George's silent dismay each time he showed his face. George didn't like his visits, but he couldn't stop himself from going. He wanted to tell George that he loved him. Then somehow they'd achieved a breakthrough.

He had gone to the hospice to find his father dozing. He sat down silently, and waited for George to wake. He was in too much pain for any decent stretch of sleep. George's bed was tilted to allow him to sit up. His fingers had relaxed around a dark blue felt-tip, which balanced precariously against his middle finger. George's notebook had dropped to the floor.

Paddy picked it up, intending to put it on the bedside cabinet. Glancing at the top of the open page, he read: *'should never have let her send Jackie away. She regretted it, though she'd never say.'* His eyes darted towards his father's ravaged face, gaunt and hollow. His mouth was dry and flaking, and the thin turkey neck sticking out of the too-large pyjamas laboured up and down with each attempt to breathe. Noiseless, Paddy flipped the pages to the beginning and began to read.

*'Let sleeping dogs lie,' some say, but my time's almost up, so I'm going to give them a kick.*

*I first clapped eyes on your mother when she started work at Greenbaum's grocer's. I'd go in most days after work to buy my dinner. I'd no fridge, so I'd get what I needed every day. My landlady let me use her oven, so like as not I'd buy a pie and a bit of veg. They were huge pies made by Greenbaum's wife. I could eat a whole one, no bother. By the end of each day I was like a starving rat.*

*Your mother was a sight for sore eyes, let me tell you. Dark hair with blue eyes. She's always been a looker. She was beautiful as a young woman, and to my mind, as she got older, every wrinkle and new grey hair only made her more lovely.*

*In those days, the customer would stand at the counter and ask for each item and the shopkeeper would scurry about putting things in a basket. What a palaver everything was. Though you didn't hear me complaining when your mam was scurrying about for me. Mr Greenbaum was always hovering about.*

*She'd started to tease me about the pies.*

*'Hello Mr Newell. Pie again today, is it?'*

*'Hello, Miss Fell.' We Missed and Mistered in them days. 'I'll not be having a pie today.'*

*'Time to ring the changes, eh?'*

*'Aye. In fact, I'll not be buying me dinner in here at all. Not today, anyroad.'*

'Is that right?'

'Aye. I do want a bit of dinner though, and company while I eat it.'

Mr Greenbaum told me on our wedding day that he'd resigned himself from that moment to looking for a new sales assistant. He knew the signs, he said. He'd already lost two to marriage and one to trouble. He learned his lesson. The girl that took over from your mam was plain as a pikestaff.'

George stirred. Paddy darted a look at him. He slept on, although his frown deepened and his breathing became more laboured.

George had written in some detail about their early married life, the arrival of each child and his decision to set up in business on his own. It had been a big decision, and took up a chunk of the narrative. Paddy skim-read, knowing his time was limited. It was difficult, as George's handwriting went through phases of legibility. Abruptly, he slowed.

A lovely little chap, Timmy. I never knew what pain was until he died. Imagine how bad it was for your mother, who'd given birth to him. I thought she'd go mad with the grief. That was the start of where it all went wrong for us, your mother and me. We should've been united in our sorrow, but we splintered. It's not something I can put my finger on, but it's like she was hiding something. She blamed Jackie. I should never have let her send him away. She regretted it, though she'd never say. Your mother's not got a gift for admitting she's in the wrong.'

'Paddy, you've no right to read that.' George's voice was a croaking whisper.

Paddy looked up. 'I know, Dad.'

'So why do it, son?'

'You used to ask me that question all the time.'

'Pass me that water there, will you, lad?' George made a tremendous effort to sit up. Paddy put the notebook down and helped him. He held the plastic beaker to his lips.

'What did you think she was hiding from you, Dad?'

George sighed, and leaned back onto his pillows. 'It's all ancient history now. It was to do with you if you must know. After Timmy died... you didn't seem to care. God knows, Paddy, you were never like the other kids to start with.'

'How was I different?'

George paused, as if racking his brains for the answer. 'You never needed anything. You never cared about anything. I wanted your mam to have someone check you over. Get you some help. '

'As if I had a screw loose, you mean?'

George didn't respond. 'She wouldn't hear of it. Said you'd find your own way in your own time. She said still waters ran deep. I never believed it, though. Neither did she, I could tell.'

'You were right.'

'I've never understood how you turned out the way you did.'

'Me neither.'

'Not when all the others are... I should never have listened to your mother. I should have insisted we get help for you way sooner than we did. We waited for Arthur Penharris to force our hand.'

The mention of the name altered George's expression.

'Bea's father,' said Paddy.

'Jesus, Paddy,' said George. He coughed violently.

'I've known for years,' said Paddy as he leaned over to pat George on the back. 'It was a bit of a surprise that Mam had been putting it about. It wasn't just me who had a dodgy provenance. Colin looks a bit like that door to door bloke Mam bought her cleaning stuff from. Come to think of it, Will's a bit Heinz—'

'Don't talk about your mother like that!' George was seized by another bout of coughing. 'If you must know, she did what she did for you.'

'So she'd say, I'm sure.'

'How did you know about her and Penharris?'

'I heard them talking after the famous nativity play. He collared her about it.'

George coughed again, then slumped against the pillow.

'Who was my father?' Paddy asked.

George was silent.

'Come off it, Dad. I'm a grown man now. I don't need to be kept in the dark any more. You've protected Mam for so many years. For what? So she can hang on to some genteel image of herself? She's a prize hypocrite. No wonder you left her. I know I'm not your son. I wish I was, but I know I wasn't born into this family.'

'What do you remember before you came to us?'

'Mostly I remember being hungry and in a permanent state of warfare. There were a couple of older girls who terrorised the rest of us. It was hard going until I found a way to get them to leave me alone. After that it was easier.'

'What did you do?' George coughed again.

'Nothing you'd approve of, Dad.'

George didn't press it.

'So who was he? My father?'

George deliberated before he spoke. 'My advice would be to leave well alone, son.'

'That's like a red rag to a bull.'

'I suppose so. Leave it, son. It's not a pretty story.'

'Did she tell you?'

'Don't be daft. You know your mother. It was Jackie told me.'

'Jackie?'

'Aye, your Uncle Jackie, and only when he was deep in his cups.'

'Don't you think I've a right to know?'

'Maybe, but it's for your mother to tell you. When I met her, I didn't know she'd had a child. In those days things were different. I wish she had told me straight off, but she was too ashamed. She gave you up for adoption as soon as you were born. She needed to work, and there was no one else to look after you. She didn't know what else to do.'

'What about her family?'

'Her mother was dead. Her brothers all working.'

'And her father?'

George lifted himself off the pillow and gave Paddy a penetrating look. 'Her father was the last person she could turn to.'

'That fits. Nothing's more important to Mam than what other people think.'

George squeezed Paddy's hand with surprising strength. 'Don't judge her so harsh, Paddy. You've no idea what it was like. She did what she thought was best for you, and suffered for it. She thought of you every day. And she got you back.'

'When did she tell you about me?'

'Soon after Sammy was born. I woke up to hear her crying in the night. She was sat in the dark rocking him. One of the nurses at the hospital warned me that new mothers could be a bit teary. She kept saying "I want my baby." I didn't know what she was on about. There he was, in her arms, fed to the brim, fast asleep. Then it all came out. How they'd taken you away when you were just a scrap. The next day, I was at the council making enquiries about how to get you back. It was hard going, hitting my head against a brick wall at every turn. Eventually, I was told we were too late, that you'd been adopted already by a family who had a daughter, but couldn't have any more children.'

Paddy was suddenly assaulted by a memory, of sticking to the seat of a blazingly hot car with a girl trying to smother him with a stuffed bear.

'Your mother was beside herself, but after a while she seemed to accept it. She had Sammy, then Sonny, and she seemed happy enough, but often I heard her crying in the night, no need to ask why. Then they reversed your adoption. By rights we should never have found out. The woman at the council came to see me at work. She asked me not to say a word, as she could get into terrible trouble. Reversing an adoption was highly unusual, she said, but that was what was happening. She told me that if your mother and me applied to adopt a child, she would make sure we got you. You came to us just before you were five.'

'Why was the adoption reversed?'

'From the bits and pieces we were told, the daughter tried to do you a mischief.'

All Paddy had remembered of life before the Newell family had until then been being in care, but the memory of the girl in the car had set off other memories, all linked by a dread in the pit of his stomach and a furious desire to get his own back.

His visits to his father became easier, more relaxed. He moved into a bed and breakfast near the hospice so he could see him every day. His father even looked genuinely pleased to see him when he put his head round the door. He was careful to choose times when his siblings would not be there.

George seemed to accept whatever Paddy told him. 'What happened at Bea's nativity, Paddy? I had a feeling you had something to do with it. Did I misjudge you?'

Paddy laughed. 'I used the fluff inside rosehips. Homemade itching powder. We used it all the time at school. Her reaction though was proper allergic. I couldn't have dreamed it would work so well.'

George's eyes watered.

'You can't tell me it still bothers you now? So many years later?'

George nodded, overcome.

Paddy wasn't sure what to say. He took his father's hand. It was a gesture unthinkable a week ago, but they had a new closeness that Paddy wished they had fostered years ago. George seemed to relish the chance to talk, especially about Edie and Penharris, a subject he couldn't broach with the others.

'I was maybe wrong to leave your mother. She swore what she did with Arthur was a moment of madness, something she regretted every day of her life.'

'She only regretted it because she had a living reminder of her crime. And because she got caught. You were well out of it, Dad. She's a wrong'un, I'm telling you.'

The cancer had spread to George's bones. He had asked the doctors to stop all treatment, to focus their efforts on managing the pain, which was sometimes too excruciating for George to talk. When he recovered his power of speech, he seemed anxious to make up for lost time. He was eager to make amends.

'We should have got help for you, lad. I want you to know I'm sorry I listened to Edie. She didn't want to wash her dirty linen in public. I always let her have her way, especially when it came to you. I adopted you, which made you my son as much as hers. I wish I'd seen it then as clearly as I see it now. I'm that sorry, Paddy lad. If I could make up for it, I—'

'Shhh, Dad. I was beyond help.'

'Not at five. There's always help to be found.'

'I was different even from the kids in care.'

'How do you mean?'

'They cared about things. Teddies, dolls, about being adopted. Even the pair of tough-nut girls I told you about. As soon as you know what someone cares about, you can hurt them. I didn't give a shit about anything.'

'Self-preservation, though. It's natural enough.'

'No, Dad. It's not the same. I've done things that...'

'What things?'

Paddy hesitated.

George laughed. 'I'm a dying man, Paddy. If you're going to tell anyone...'

'You were right that Mam was keeping something from you. To do with Timmy.'

George gave him a sharp look. 'How d'you mean?'

'I smothered him with a pillow.'

'Paddy, you're sick in the head to say so.'

'It's true. Don't you remember the night Uncle Jackie left? The things he said? Will wanted to tell. Mam put the fear of God into him. She knew.'

George's face screwed up with concentration, with the effort to remember. 'It was cot death killed him,' he said, a plea in his voice. 'The heat... Jackie only said what he said to get back at your mam.'

'No, Dad. I did it. The doctor even said at the time that kids Timmy's age don't suffer from it as a rule. Mam knew what happened. So did Will. Mam blamed Jackie so you'd not look closer to home.'

'I heard what they both said, but I didn't believe it, not for a second. Not then, not now. Why would you lie?' George said feebly. He attempted to sit up.

Paddy felt dismayed at George's distress. 'Dad, it was forty-odd years ago.'

'It was a cot death,' George repeated.

'Dad. That was no cot death!'

This last was said with such conviction that George fell backwards on the bed, his puny frame racked with sobs. Paddy watched him, baffled, perturbed.

'Why, Paddy?'

'I wanted to. I saw my chance. That's all, Dad. Nothing more than that.'

The tears streamed down George's face. Paddy reached behind his father to plump up his pillows. George took a tissue from Paddy, and dabbed at his eyes.

'I did it to get back at Mam. I didn't give a stuff about the others. I never thought about you. I'm so sorry, Dad.'

'We should've—'

'Dad, it wasn't your fault. I did what I did to Timmy because I could.'

George seemed to slump into a depression full of despair and regret. Incredibly, he did not seem to have any rancour towards Paddy. It seemed only to confirm what he already knew. That he and Edie had failed their children.

'We let him down. We let you down. God knows, we let Bea down.'

The last week before he died, Paddy saw him every day. His sadness was still with him, but he had recovered some of his good humour, and was well enough to sit up and play chess.

'I've always wondered, Paddy, about what you do for a living. There's more to it than meets the eye, isn't there?'

Paddy nodded as he took a pawn.

'I launder money.'

'Not for terrorists?'

'For Albanians mostly.'

George was unnerved. 'How did you get into it?'

Paddy laughed. 'I met a couple of them in chokey. It's a good place to network.'

'How do you do it?'

'I set up fictitious businesses, with websites, mobile numbers and bank accounts. Then they pay cash in varying amounts with invoices to match, and it all comes out clean as a whistle.'

'What are they involved in?'

'Dad, you really don't want to know. Ugly stuff.'

'Such as?'

'Trafficking, prostitution, drugs, arms.'

'Sweet Jesus, Paddy. What if you get on their wrong side?'

'It's always a risk, but I have some insurance.'

'Why do you do it, son?'

'The money's good. And it's interesting. I mean seriously interesting. It relieves the tedium of being alive.'

'If that's true, Paddy, then I feel sorry for you.'

'I told you I'm not like other people, Dad.'

George had resumed his memoir.

'Will you write the truth about Timmy?'

'No, lad. Who'd believe it? I'm not sure I believe it myself.'

'Oh, they'd believe it, Dad.'

George's eyes had watered and his lip trembled. He said, 'You surely don't want them to know, Paddy?'

Paddy shrugged.

'Will you write about me? My father?'

'No, lad. I've told you. That's for your mother.'

George had called Paddy to him in the middle of the night. Paddy found him white and contorted with pain.

Paddy had called a nurse. 'For God's sake, you've got to give him something.'

'He's had the highest dose we can give him. He's not due any more for an hour.'

Paddy prepared to wait out the hour at George's side. George's body was seized with tremors. His breathing was laboured. He was trying to talk.

'Easy, Dad. Take a breath.' Reluctantly, Paddy asked, 'Do you want me to call the others?'

George shook his head. He took in a breath and put his claw-like hand on Paddy's arm.

'Help me, Paddy lad.'

'Are you sure, Dad?'

George nodded.

He reached behind his father for a pillow.

'Dad, are you ready?'

George nodded again.

It did not take long. The tremors stilled. He gently propped George up and put the pillow back behind his head. He smoothed his hair from his brow. He sat with his father's hand in his for a few minutes, perhaps longer. Then he got to his feet and tucked George's notebook into his briefcase. He turned at the door for one last look at his father.

'Goodbye, Dad,' he said, and silently pulled the door closed behind him.

***

Bea had decided to walk home from Dorothy's.

'Gordon will be back soon. He'll drive you, darling.'

'It's only a few streets away. I wouldn't mind the fresh air.'

'Take a taxi. I can't have you walking by yourself.'

'It's Kensington, not Kinshasa.'

'You wouldn't catch me on the streets at night.'

'I've never seen you walking anywhere.'

'That's because God made taxis, darling.'

Bea bent to hug Dorothy. It was like embracing the skeleton of a bird. 'Thanks so much for listening.'

'Anytime you feel blue, you know where to find me. Can't believe you resisted a drink. I was half squiffed on gin the whole time I was pregnant with Gordon. It was the only way to get through the whole ghastly experience.'

'Hence his name?'

Dorothy laughed. 'I prefer Bombay Sapphire myself. Gordon's father wanted another child but I put my foot down.'

Bea rubbed her stomach. 'It's the only thing that's

315

making life bearable for me.'

'Rather you than me,' said Dorothy. 'Thank the Lord those days are over. Now just remember – I don't care what those tests throw up. David loved you. I'm certain of it.'

'Thanks, Dorothy.' Bea's eyes welled up.

'She sounds like trouble, this Brazilian hussy. Don't hold it against him, darling. Men really are terribly pathetic, you know. Even the doziest of them have an eye out at the best of times. After so many husbands, I should know. She threw herself at him, in all probability. Then to have a fling with your brother... you have to hand it to her. If she manages to extort anything from you, she'll have earned the money.'

Once outside, Bea wrapped her scarf around her face and pulled her coat tightly around her. It was a blustery night. Dorothy had done her some good, but she felt a kind of numbness descend on her. She had too much to process. She carried two Davids inside her head. The familiar, funny man she'd loved so much and the stranger who'd betrayed her.

She crossed the road towards her house. A dark car pulled up alongside her.

'Excuse me,' said the driver through the open window. His voice was accented, Eastern European.

'Yes?' she said, pulling her scarf down from her face.

She heard a deafening crack and registered an unbearable burning in her side. She clutched at the wound and fell to the pavement. The baby, she thought. The baby, the baby, the baby. The car drove away at a sedate speed. She groaned and rolled into a ball. She heard doors opening, footsteps, voices, chattering, a scream. Someone held her hand and stroked her hair as if she were a sick animal. She was unconscious when the ambulance arrived.

\*\*\*

I had been in Will's study for days. I sifted through every detail of the past. I could manage getting up for the bathroom, but only with Sandra's help. She's a good nurse. I was so heavy, so clumsy, but she had the knack of helping me to move, taking all my weight, murmuring coos of encouragement as if I were a child. 'That's it, Edie. Lean on me, it's fine. There you go, almost there.'

I wasn't ill, that's not the right word. I didn't think I'd ever be myself again. I was lying in a slump staring at the stippled wallpaper when Will came in, flushed like he'd been given an electric shock. He sank to his knees by my bedside and took my hand.

'Mam, Bea's been shot.'

'What are you on about?' I was still angry with him.

'The police think it was a random drive-by shooting. They can't make sense of it.'

I sat up. The room spun around, like I was on a fairground ride that wouldn't stop.

'She's got a perforated kidney, Mam. If it doesn't respond to treatment, they may have to remove it. I bloody hope they know what they're doing.'

My mouth wouldn't work. I flabbed like a fish. 'Will she be okay?'

'I don't know, Mam.'

I'd failed her all her life. I shook off my company of ghosts and got out of bed. This time, I'd be there for her.

# CHAPTER TWENTY-THREE

## FOUR YEARS LATER

Damien Lillie slowed to a stop at the traffic light. After paying the congestion charge and ruinous parking fees, it would be cheaper and quicker to get the tube to and from the clinic, but he liked his time in the car. It still had that wonderful leathery new smell. It was a quiet cocoon, a bubble. It gave him a chance to think. Away from the shrews he worked with, away from his squabbling children, away from Steph and her demands. Always wanting more, more, more.

He was going home to his 'surprise' birthday party. Each year, Steph went mad ordering Krug and canapés for a hundred people he pretended to be delighted to see. This would be the last time.

He ran his hand through his hair. He could not believe he'd been so stupid. His nightmare had started with Julie, his new clinical assistant, knocking on his office door two weeks ago.

'Damien,' she had said. It grated on him the way she pronounced his name. Dye-me-in. She was a tall, beefy blond Kiwi mad about rugby, hired to replace Audrey, who had retired.

'Yes, Julie. What is it?' He had aimed for a busy, distracted tone. He rued the day he had ever hired the over-efficient cow. Audrey had always called him Mr Lillie.

'I got a call today from Mrs Bea Grahame.' Gry-am.

He had felt a flutter of fear at the sound of the name. He hadn't seen the Grahames for four, maybe five years. Something in Julie's tone put him on guard. The worry, long dormant, sprang to life.

'Yes. What about her?'

'Seems her husband died four years back, but he gave his consent for her to go ahead with treatment even in the event of his death.'

'Oh dear. How sad. Why has she waited so long? She must be forty-odd by now.'

'I don't know.'

'Well, make an appointment for her.'

'I did. She said we had six embryos.'

'Yes, I remember.'

'Well, that's the prob, see. She said six, the records say six. But I just checked, and there are only four.' Faw-ah.

Fear had gripped him. He had been convinced he had replaced the two missing straws. He need not fear they would be discovered empty, as the only person who would thaw them would be himself.

'They must have been damaged.' The pitch of his voice rose.

She had raised an eyebrow. 'You could only know that if you thawed them for use.'

'Look, Julie, I really don't have time for this. Perhaps they were damaged before freezing. I don't remember.'

'But you just said you did remember.'

'Four. Six. What does it matter? We wouldn't be implanting more than two anyway.'

'Of course it matters. It matters a lot to someone desperate for a child.'

'Are you quite finished?'

'For now, yes.'

Since then, he had the sense that Julie had started to count the spoons. A Kiwi Nancy Drew. All he bloody needed. Jesus, he missed Audrey. She was made in the old mould. Deferential, unquestioning. She, like him, had liked an easy life.

Just an hour ago, Julie had tackled him again.

'Do you remember the Nazaris? The ones who came in for treatment from Dubai shortly after I started?'

'Of course I do.'

'Well, I remember quite clearly that we harvested eleven eggs from Mrs Nazari. All eleven were fertilised, and we used the best two for immediate treatment. Three didn't take, and the remaining six we froze.'

'What's your point, Julie?' he sighed, taking off his glasses.

'My point is, that we've been charging them storage for nine, not six.'

He shifted in his seat. 'Are you sure?'

'Of course I'm sure.'

'Well... correct it then.'

'I already did. Thing is, I double-checked a couple of other cases where I was personally involved, where I absolutely remember the numbers that were frozen, and in all cases, we overstate the number taken. Which boosts the storage charges.'

'I'm sure there's a simple explanation.'

'Yeah. Funny you should say that.'

'I'm not sure I like your implication, Julie.'

'I'm not sure I like your methods. These people aren't scientists. There's no way they can find out if you store one or a dozen. I thought I'd give you a chance to explain. You've made a pig's ear of it. It's only fair to tell you I'm going to call the HFEA.'

His mind raced.

'I can see exactly what you're thinking,' she said. I've taken photocopies of the relevant records, plus the invoices sent out to the clients.'

He went grey. 'Please, Julie. They'll shut the clinic down!'

'Don't think I'm not sorry about it. You're bloody good at what you do, but I don't like rip-offs. I'd rather be out of a job than work for a crook.'

He turned in to his garage and cut the engine. The house was silent. They were all inside, lying in wait, Steph and the others, waiting to call 'surprise' the moment he opened the door leading into the kitchen. He sat as long as he feasibly could before he took a deep breath and got out of the car. Leaden-hearted, he went in to take his surprise like a man.

*\*\*\**

Bea took little George to the playground in the park almost every day, even in the rain. He thrived on fresh air and exercise, like a dog. She and George were known to all the regulars in the park, the parents, the grandparents, the nannies, the au pairs and of course, the children. Bea would sit on the corner bench with the paper or would chat with the other adults, warming her hands on bad takeaway coffee in a styrofoam cup from the nearby shack while the kids ran about. Conversation was constantly interrupted by children's commands to 'Push me,' or 'Watch this,' or the adults shouting out encouragement, instructions or warnings.

George was three years old. Bea never tired of watching him. She was often ambushed by an overwhelming love for him that made her eyes smart. She was allowed to snuggle him and cover him in kisses when they were alone, but he complained if she was too 'lovey-dovey' in public. Even when he had been tiny, he had wanted to do things for himself, and she had learned to let him try.

He was short for his age, but in all other respects he was a miniature David.

One day she would describe for him the circumstances surrounding his conception and birth. It would not be easy. She supposed she had years to plan how to do it.

'He doesn't ever need to know,' said Hilary. 'He's ours

and that's all that matters.'

'I'm with you there, duck,' Edie had said. 'Why do you want to tell him, Bea?'

'We all deserve the truth,' Bea had said.

Edie had said nothing.

After the shooting, she had been in hospital almost a month while they monitored her kidney. Miraculously, it had survived and healed, and she suffered no lasting physical ill-effects. Even more astoundingly, the tiny bundle of microscopic cells that she was fostering had survived. Regular ultrasounds in the following two months revealed that despite the trauma to Bea's body, the baby had apparently not been affected, and continued to grow.

Her mother moved into her house while she was in hospital, visiting her every day. The baby gave them some common ground, easing their habitual awkwardness.

'I'm so glad you finally saw some sense and realised that life's not all about work, work, work,' said Edie.

'Mam, we were trying for ages.'

'I had no idea. Why didn't you say?'

'You've never been an easy one to talk to, Mam.'

Edie looked down at her hands, chastened. Impulsively, she stood up and smoothed Bea's hair from her brow. 'Pot's calling kettle black,' she said softly.

Bea laughed.

Hilary came every day after school. Raw with grief for David, she had been so excited about the baby. 'It's brilliant, Bea. It's like a... goodbye present from Dad. I'll babysit all the time. I can move in and help you look after it. I hope it's a girl. Poor little thing not ever knowing her dad.'

Dad this, Dad that. Bea had to stop herself blurting that 'Dad' had maybe left behind not just one goodbye present, but two. She'd find out soon enough.

Dan came with Serena, or 'The Limpet' as Hilary called

her. Bea was never required to talk. Serena chattered about clubs and parties: '...and you remember Pete, don't you Bea? The one that came to your place for Dan's birthday weekend? He got so wasted and snogged this girl in Juju's who turned out to be some Lebanese princess who'd sneaked away from her bodyguards, and these two gorillas found them together and he had to scarper. It was hilarious, wasn't it, Dan?' Shopping: 'OMG I got some really cool stuff from the sale at Harrod's. It's normally full of really boring old-lady gear, but my mum dragged me in and I got this,' pointing at her purple tartan mini, 'and a load of other stuff, didn't I, Dan? When you're out of here I'll have to take you 'cos they've got some really cute stuff for babies, it'll be so cool if we could go together. You won't want to come, will you, Dan? The baby department will probably be like exquisite torture for you, haha!' The holiday they had booked to Magaluf to celebrate the end of their A levels: 'OMG Bea, it is going to be so mega, isn't it, Dan? Six of us in the clubs at night and on the beach in the day. I can't wait! I'm going to burn all my books, I swear to God. I wish I could tell that Mrs Connolly exactly what I think of her, but I can't 'cos my bitch of a sister beat me to it three years ago...' Dan never needed to utter a word.

Harry came with his mother.

'What a month it's been for you,' said Diana, who had brought a bouquet of beautiful yellow roses with a tasteful card. Harry was his usual silent and awkward self, but the ever-practical Diana had thought of a solution. 'He's brought his chess set. Do you play? Never mind, he'll teach you. I'll be back in an hour.'

The two of them focused on the game, a relief for them both.

Dorothy brought flowers and a hip flask of brandy, which she offered to Bea.

'I'm pregnant with a perforated kidney.'

'All the more reason, I say, but each to their own.'

She sipped from it while she chattered, and tottered resentfully downstairs whenever the craving for nicotine became too unbearable.

Then there were the police visits. They had a thousand questions and were armed with pages of mugshots for her to look at. She hadn't recognised the man, or the car, or been able to come up with any useful information. In the absence of leads, it was filed as a random drive-by shooting. She had the feeling they just wanted to park the file in a drawer and forget about it.

*** 

Four years now since Bea was shot. I never in my life met anyone shot outside of a war, then it happens to my own daughter. I tried hard with Bea those days in the hospital. It wasn't just because she was poorly. It's because the past had changed for me, and I wanted to change it for her. The baby gave us a link we'd never had before.

I was sitting with her in the hospital knitting green bootees when her boss came to see her.

'How are you, Bea?' He was clutching a bunch of pink carnations. They were from the gift shop downstairs. I knew the contents of that shop inside out. He waved them vaguely in my direction by way of greeting.

'Fine, thanks,' she said.

She'd been widowed and shot within a week, and found out her husband was unfaithful to her. I wondered what it would take for her to say, 'Not too good actually.'

It crossed my mind to leave the room, but he parked himself down and talked as if I wasn't there, so I didn't bother.

'You look a bit peaky,' he said.

'Yes, well. I'm hanging on to a kidney by the skin of my teeth.'

He looked at the tubes and paraphernalia around her bed as if seeing them for the first time.

'I came to ask you... well, first to see how you are, of course, but Bea, do you want to step down for a bit? You know, focus on getting well. Getting back to top form again.'

That was nice of him, I thought. She wouldn't be wanting to worry about work right now. Not at a time like this when she had so much else weighing on her mind.

'Are you firing me, Rob?' she asked.

He went red. 'No! Of course not! It's just that Martha—'

'Martha. I might have known.'

He looked down at his hands. 'She did a great job on the Sudan piece, you have to admit.'

'She changed a word here and there and put her sodding name on it. She can cover for me. I've done it for her a hundred times.'

'It's just that, well, after the last lot of botched IVF, she's decided to ditch the idea of having a baby. Decided to concentrate on her career, and she wants to take a turn at more serious stuff.'

'As if I've ever stopped her,' said Bea. I saw on the screen that her heart rate had spiked.

I stood up. 'Can't you see you're upsetting her? It's the last thing she needs.'

'You're right, you're right,' he said, desperate to get away. 'I'd never fire you, you know that, Bea. Come back whenever you're ready. So long as there's a mag there, there's a job for you. And when you have your baby we can fix you up so you're working more from home, you know, maybe get you to focus on more mummy-centric stuff. All the women I know with kids are bloody obsessed with them. Shit, Bea, I didn't mean that – you know what I'm trying to say. Anyway, you just concentrate on getting better. Put your health up there as your top priority.'

Red-faced, he said his goodbyes and scarpered.

Bea tried to sit up. She was shaking with rage.

'Bea, you heard the man. He's not firing you. He's giving you a chance to get well without having to worry about work. What with the baby and everything, you—'

'You don't understand! He's so spineless... he... I need that job.'

'You're right, I don't understand. You've a little one to think about. It's time you put your career to one side. It's not as if you need the money, thanks to David—'

'David be damned!' she cried.

There was no reasoning with her.

We'd never had much to talk about, Bea and me, then suddenly we had too much. Paddy, Timmy. Paddy and the hussy. David and the hussy. I still can't believe it of him. Tests can always be fiddled, can't they?

I did a lot for her, those early days of her pregnancy. It was healing for me, making my amends. I was so looking forward to a new baby, a little David. It was like being given a second chance. I could be useful again. I could be loved.

*\*\**

The bleeding started two months after she was released from hospital. A second trimester miscarriage.

'I'm really sorry,' said the nurse as she ran the ultrasound over Bea's stomach. 'The lining of your womb is definitely all falling away. You won't be needing a D&C.'

The pain was like being skewered. Her body was a useless shell. She was no good to anyone. She wanted to die. She remembered her teenage flirtation with death, that longing for oblivion, but she continued stubbornly to survive.

That summer, during a sudden hot spell, she had been listlessly sitting on the sofa looking out over the garden. It looked beautiful in its neglect. The roses were in full bloom, and the trees cast cool and inviting shadows over the overgrown grass. She was now so thin that she easily felt the slightest breeze, but even she had shirked off her cardigan in the stifling heat.

Martha had managed to edge her out of the magazine. Rob had been too craven to resist and Bea had lacked the stomach for the fight. No husband, no job, no child, no earthly use to anyone.

She and Edie rubbed along together surprisingly well. Bea thought about her dreams for herself as a child. Only in a far-distant alternative universe could she ever have envisioned herself as an unemployed childless widow, living with her mother.

She and Edie were going to New York. Sonny had been pestering her for months. 'I'll book it for you. Which dates are good for you?' Not that it mattered. Her diary was completely clear. She was as surprised at herself as any of her brothers when finally she not only decided that she would go, but she invited Edie to come with her.

She was contemplating going outside, lying on the grass with a book, and Edie was bustling about in the kitchen, when the doorbell rang.

'I'll get it,' Edie called out, and Bea heard her heavy tread, traipsing towards the door.

'And what in God's name do you want?' she heard her mother demand. 'Anything you have to say, you can say it through your bloody lawyer. Bugger off.'

Bea had never heard Edie swear. She picked herself up off the sofa and put her head into the hallway.

It was Lorena.

She wore a red tank top and a pair of blue denim maternity shorts. She was sweating, but her skin glowed with heat and health. Despite her enormous belly, her toenails were perfectly pedicured. She must be eight months gone, thought Bea, who was engulfed by a surge of jealousy so strong that for an instant she forgot to breathe. Suddenly, Lorena bent to put her hands on her knees, and took in a few deep breaths, clearly overcome by the heat.

'Come in and sit down,' said Bea.

'Are you mad?' Edie demanded.

'Don't you worry, Mam.' Nothing Lorena did could hurt her anymore.

Edie's mouth pursed. She kept her eyes trained on Lorena, as if she were about to spontaneously combust.

Lorena flopped into an armchair. Bea fetched her a glass of water and a dampened towel. Edie hovered uncertainly.

'Thanks,' said Lorena. She seized on the towel and mopped her brow.

'Are you feeling a bit better?' Bea asked.

'Yes. Thank you.'

'Why are you here? What do you want?'

'I heard you lost your baby,' said Lorena. 'I'm sorry.'

Astonishing, thought Bea. She actually sounds sincere.

'You didn't come here to tell me that.'

'No. I did not.' To Edie, rather sternly, she said, 'Please. I am not a wild animal. You should sit down or leave.'

'Don't tell me what I—'

'Sit down.'

Resentfully, Edie obeyed with a token tut.

Lorena ignored her, and addressed Bea. 'I am going to give birth in three weeks.'

'Congratulations.'

'I do not want to keep this baby.'

Edie emitted a kind of outraged snort. Bea gave her a look, and she was silent. Bea waited for Lorena to speak again.

'I swear it's your husband's, and a test will prove it. I am here to ask if you want to adopt the child. That way you will get what you have always wanted. It's a boy, by the way.'

'And what do you want?'

'I have consulted a lawyer already. It is illegal to pay money for adoption, and also for a...'

'A surrogate.'

'Exactly. It is illegal, but you are allowed to pay expenses. If I keep this baby, I will sue your husband's estate. I will be entitled to a quarter of the children's trust.'

'How do you even know about that?'

'I saw all your papers.'

Edie piped up: 'Don't listen to her, Bea. You should throw the thieving hussy out.'

'Shhh, Mam. So basically you want the money without the child, is that right?'

'That's correct.'

'Why should she take on your filthy little brat?' Edie screeched.

Lorena laughed. 'Because it is David's, you idiot. She is your own daughter and you do not know what she wants.'

'I'm not listening to this,' said Edie and stormed out of the room.

Bea and Lorena ignored her. They heard her thumping about upstairs.

'Where is the baby to be born?'

'In the Portland. By Caesarian,' said Lorena decidedly. In spite of the heat, she shuddered. 'I would consider it a favour if you paid the expenses.'

'If I agree, you will never see the child again, you understand?'

'I understand.'

'What will you do afterwards?'

'I will go back to Brazil. There is nothing for me here. And it is better if I get away from your brother.'

Bea became aware that Edie was hovering again,

listening.

'It is because of your brother that you were shot. He will not like me telling you this.'

Bea heard a sharp intake of breath from Edie. 'I don't understand.'

'He met some people in prison. Albanians. Kosovars. He did some work for them.'

'What kind of work?'

'He moved money for them. Opened accounts, issued fake invoices. But then he made an agreement with them that he did not honour. They threatened to hurt him, and he laid a trap with you as...' She faltered, but lowered her hand and rubbed her thumb against her fingers.

'Bait,' said Bea bleakly. 'Were you involved?'

'No. This I swear.'

'Why are you telling me this?'

'You need to know that he will always try to do you harm.'

Bea digested this and nodded. 'Yes. I know. I've always known it.'

'So why do you let him near you?'

Bea thought about it. 'He's my brother.'

After Lorena had gone, Bea sat thinking, for a long time. At last, she went upstairs to talk to her mother about what had just happened. She found Edie walking on the landing in a daze.

'Mam? Are you all right?'

'Ever since you kids were born I've let him get away with... with... murder!' said Edie in a feverish rush. 'Not anymore.'

'Don't you do a thing, Mam,' said Bea with steel in her voice. 'You leave him to me.'

\*\*\*

Prison life assimilated Paddy without incident. If he had been given to self-analysis or introspection, he might have appreciated how adaptable he was. He had managed to avoid the baptism by fire suffered by many of the new inmates. Having prior helped, but more importantly, Paddy knew how to be the grey man.

The cops had been given a tip-off about money laundering. They had raided his flat. Seized his laptop and his paperwork. They hadn't found anything. He kept nothing on his hard drive. He wasn't that stupid. But they had found a USB stick, his insurance policy against Fevze. They had found it hidden inside a soft toy, a rabbit that Paddy had kept for nearly forty years.

That can was now spewing out some very nasty worms. It would be interesting to see how the whole thing played out. They had even questioned him about Clare. He couldn't imagine how they'd managed to dig her up after all these years.

He had become a creature of habit. He woke at seven, and did a series of press-ups, sit-ups, star jumps and burpees for forty-five minutes. He meditated for fifteen minutes, showered at 8am and had breakfast at 8.30am. He looked forward to mealtimes. Not for the food, just for breaking up the day. He worked in the library until lunch. He was studying for a degree in computer science. It passed the time. It was interesting approaching a subject he was so intimate with from an academic viewpoint. He sometimes helped other inmates with their correspondence. Most had literacy problems. He knew how to be helpful without being ingratiating. He stored away favours like a squirrel.

He had a lot of thinking time. Things had turned out rather well for Bea. He would park that for the time being. For the sake of little George. He wanted to see the boy when he got out. He had to convince Bea he'd be a force for the good. It wouldn't be easy. She had declared she never wanted him near her or hers again. Edie had told him that if he tried, Bea would get a restraining order. He wouldn't much care if it weren't for the boy. She did not appreciate that if it weren't for him, little George would not exist. If he had any hope at all, it would be through Edie.

Edie visited him every two weeks without fail.

'You must be seventy-odd, Mam,' he'd said the last time she was with him. 'Why d'you bother coming? I'd enjoy what little time I had left rather than flog all the way over here every other week.'

'You're my son, duck. I'll not turn my back on you.'

'Two trains and a bus every second week, come hell or high water. It's pretty impressive at your age. I was just saying to Darren that if you skipped a visit it'd be due to dotage or death. Or decomposition.'

'Who's Darren?' she had asked.

'My new cell-mate.'

'You seem to get through them.'

He leaned forward and winked at her. 'Actually, Mam, they get through me.'

'Don't talk like that!'

'Oh Mam. Don't come over all prudish. Let's not forget your little adventure with that anaemic scarecrow Penharris. Not to mention Mystery Man, my father.'

'Don't start that again. You promised you'd not discuss it.'

'Come on, Mam. We don't have much to say to each other at the best of times. The least we can do is talk about real things rather than chit-chat about the weather. Who was he?'

'I'll never tell you.'

'I'll ask Uncle Jackie then.'

'You've a cruel streak, Paddy.'

'It's time you saw me for what I am. Dad saw it. So did the others. It was only you. You've only ever seen what you wanted to see.'

'I wish I still did, son.'

'Why won't you say? What have you got to lose after all this time?'

'It's not me with something to lose. It's you. Leave it alone, Paddy. I've already said too much.'

'What possible difference can it make to me?'

Edie trembled. 'You think you're a hard one, Paddy, but there are some things best left in the past.'

'That's what Dad said before he died.'

'He was right.'

'How would you feel not knowing your own father?'

Edie shuddered. 'I don't like talking about my father.'

Paddy stared at her. He felt a chill creep over his skin.

'What is it? You've gone white,' said his mother.

He shivered, as if shaking off crawling insects. 'I'm fine.'

She never stayed long, but no matter how much he baited her, she always came back. He was secretly pleased; her visits passed the time. Plus she always had pictures of little George and snippets of news about him. She now had a mobile phone, and had learned to take pictures with it.

He thought about Bea a lot. He wanted to be free of this desire to harm her. Feelings had never gone away in the past just because he wanted them to.

When he was free, he'd find Lorena. It was hard to accept what she'd done. She'd sold the child to Bea, like you'd sell a car or a house, and had cut him out of the deal.

Brazil was a big place. She could be anywhere, but Santa Ana was a good place to start.

Before his sentence started, he had begun his search. He had stumbled on a YouTube clip. He watched it again and again, and copied it in case it were ever taken down. It was a short, grainy film of a young girl running on a beach. It was called 'Odo corre'. It was of a girl running on a beach towards the camera. Her bikini top slips. She lets it fall away from her magnificent breasts. She does nothing to cover herself, running like an Amazon. It was beautiful. The young girl looked like Lorena. He watched it over and over. It was so beautiful it made him want to weep.

\*\*\*

The answer to the riddle continued to elude Lorena. She missed London. She missed her flat, her space, her freedom. She missed her clients. Married life did not suit her. Jorge had inherited the family construction business, one of the biggest in South America. Lorena had been gulled by the big houses, the swanky cars, the travel business, the company expense account, the helicopter, the beach house, the platinum credit cards, the memberships, the endless invitations, the dazzling parties, all of which required her to be coiffed, manicured and couture-clad in order to charm Jorge's associates, often with her excellent English. She never looked at price tags any more. It had taken all the thrill out of shopping.

She and Jorge had married after a whirlwind romance. 'Disgusting,' his daughter Luna had said. That girl was a big pain in Lorena's ass. She had finished school and was loafing around before deciding what to do with her life.

'Get a job,' Lorena said, fed up with having her underfoot.

'*You* get a job,' was the response.

'I have one. I fuck your father. What do you do?'

The girl had screamed in disgust and run to her room.

Jorge was always at work. If not physically, then in spirit, surgically attached to his mobile phone. As soon as he ended one call it would ring again. That didn't bother her. What bothered her was how often the phrase 'cash-flow problem' cropped up in his conversations. She found out the house was mortgaged, the car was leased, the helicopter rented, the businesses were in trouble and the continued enjoyment of all the accoutrements was beginning to look terminal.

She knew it was endgame when he started to pester her for money. 'Come on, *cara*. You know I'll pay it back. Just for a couple of months. To pay a few suppliers. A few wages.'

If Lorena was fair-minded, she might have seen that just as she had been blinded by the trappings of wealth, she had deceived him in exactly the same way. As far as Jorge was concerned, he had met and married a wealthy widow who had returned to the country of her birth after losing her English husband.

'It was terrible,' she had said. 'He had a heart attack in the middle of the night. While we were sleeping. I woke up to find him dead. I did what I could, but it was useless.'

Things weren't all bad. That morning, her new passport had arrived. Luna had gone to the beach with a friend, so she could pack in peace. She felt an excitement at the prospect of change. She was forty-two years old. She still had her looks. It was true her belly would never be what it had been. It had a pouch-like quality that no number of sit-ups would shift, plus a discreet Caesarian scar. Despite that, she could wear a well-chosen bikini with pride. She had enough money to start over again. She might not have the answer to the riddle, but she knew marriage wasn't it.

When she opened the safe in Jorge's office to get her jewellery, she saw the best pieces were gone; a pair of diamond earrings and a ruby necklace he'd given her for her birthday. Irritated, she scooped up the remainder: bracelets, earrings, necklaces and a brooch or two. She was tempted by a pearl choker left to Luna by her mother, but decided reluctantly against it. She would take what was hers and leave the rest behind.

It was a smooth run to the airport. She wheeled her

suitcase to the gate.

'Good afternoon.' The steward at the business-class counter smiled. 'Where are you flying to?'

'London.'

'And your name, please?'

She offered her passport. 'It's Carvalho. Odolina Carvalho.'

\*\*\*

Bea sat at the picnic table in the playground reading the *Evening Standard*. Little George was on the see-saw with a bigger boy, who liked to deliberately bounce hard when his feet hit the ground, so that George's bottom came right off the seat mid-air and he had to hang on to the handles for dear life. Bea had to bite her tongue. Expressing worry would only push him to further extremes.

It was getting dark. They'd be closing the park soon. She had some dried apricots in her pockets to bribe George into going home.

She had decided to try for another child. The odds were against her.

'You've nothing to lose,' Colin had said.

She knew that wasn't true. She had everything to lose. Once the remaining eggs were gone, they were gone. There was the death of hope and crushing disappointment when the treatment did not work. There was the indescribable pain when it worked, but you lost the baby anyway.

Edie didn't like the idea of IVF.

'Makes me think of Frankenstein. There are better ways of having a baby,' said Edie. 'Look to Gordon, Bea. He's a good man. He adores you. He'd marry you in a shot.'

Bea had laughed. 'Come on, Mam. Every second kid nowadays is a Frankenstein baby.'

'You never know what may turn up.'

'Even without IVF, you can never be sure what will turn up.'

Edie had sighed. 'True enough, I suppose.'

Bea noticed that the *Standard* featured a review of Rebecca Gladwyn's latest book, *The Hidden Influence of Birth Order*, but before she could read further, George's little adversary thumped his feet on the floor, sending George flying. His arms shot out to break his fall, as if he were diving into a pool. No sooner had he hit the ground than he scrambled to his feet laughing. He looked her way and grinned. He looked just like David, but at odd moments she also saw flashes of her father George in his face. She could not explain it, yet the resemblance was there, and she had not been the only person to notice it. There was nothing of Lorena in him, nothing at all. It was odd that a mother with such strong features and colouring would leave no stamp of herself whatsoever on her child.

'No mistaking his father,' Edie had said. 'But I could swear sometimes I see you in him too.'

'You know that's not possible,' Bea said.

'I'm telling you, I can see it.'

Edie's love for George was unbounded. Edie had moved back home but was a frequent visitor, often bringing Uncle Jackie with her. Bea did not press her mother for the story behind their reconciliation. If Edie wanted her to know, she'd tell. It was as simple as that.

Edie, of all people, had provided her with a kind of rough comfort about David's infidelity.

'You should forgive him. If only because what he did with that nasty hoor has given you so much happiness. People do mad things. Things they regret. He never got a chance to make amends.'

'It's not like you to be so understanding, Mam.'

'People change, duck. Sometimes, anyroad.'

'I'd cut my arm off to give him a chance to explain.'

'Sometimes there are no answers and that's that.'

Those close to Bea knew the story behind George's adoption. Lorena had claimed George's share of the children's trust. The deal had been brokered by Henry Armstrong, and the money had been paid into an offshore account he'd set up in Lorena's name.

As soon as the baby was born, Lorena had irrevocably ceded all parental rights to Bea in a closed adoption.

'The law is quite clear,' Armstrong had told her. 'It is not permitted under UK law to pay for surrogacy. However, Ms Carvalho is perfectly within her rights to make a claim against the Grahame children's trust. Following receipt of the money, she is also within her rights to give the child up for adoption. You, as his adoptive mother, are entitled to sue her for that money on his behalf if you're so minded to do.'

Of course, Bea was not so minded to do.

'Are you sure you want this?' Colin had asked her at the time. 'Are you certain you won't be reminded of Lorena and David every time you look at him?'

'I'll never blame him for it.' It was hard to explain to anyone, even Colin. However winding the route, she would finally have David's child. Her child, in every way that mattered.

The light was fading fast. She couldn't read Rebecca's review without squinting. She took a last sip of her disgusting coffee. 'George, it's time to go home,' she called, holding out his coat. She wanted to get home before Dorothy arrived. Dorothy was babysitting, as Bea had choir practice.

'In a minute.' He ran from the slide to the swings, dropping his scarf on the way. Her mobile rang.

'Mrs Grahame?'

'Yes, who is this?'

'It's Detective Inspector Hodge from Fulham and Chelsea Police Department.'

'Oh. Is this about the shooting?'

'Shooting? No, I got your mobile number from Mr Damien Lillie's files. I understand you and your husband were patients of his.'

'Yes, that's right. What's this about?'

'Well, it's a bit sensitive, and I'd rather not discuss it too much over the phone. Would you be able to come to the station? The one in Fulham.'

'Sure, but you must be able to give me some idea...'

'We're investigating Mr Lillie. We believe you and your husband were the victims of theft. A very special kind of theft.'

# ACKNOWLEDGEMENTS

To the original members of the Mug House writing group, and to everyone in the Chipping Norton Theatre Writing Group; thank you all for your sage advice and constant support. Thanks to my early readers: Rachel Morley, Caroline Brooman-White, Suneeta Ambegaokar and Rhiannon Hanney, and especially to Bruno Noble for his feedback and encouragement. Thanks also to the Unbound team, for working to incredibly high standards and for hiring Elizabeth Cochrane, who edited the manuscript with such forensic care. Three cheers for all my original patrons, who helped to crowdfund the publication of this book. Five years on, I still love the cover: Mark Ecob, you really know what you're doing.

A special mention to everyone at the Sea Club, where so much of this book was written, especially Jenny and Luis Cumberledge. Luis, Emma and Heather: RIP.

Thanks also to Jenny Dee, Festival Director of the Chipping Norton Literary Festival, for being such a pleasure to work with.

To all the authors who have entrusted their stories to me as editor of www.fictionjunkies.com; long may you continue to scribble.

Some credit has to go to every babysitter I've ever hired, except for the crazy one who nicked my underwear.

To say I had the support of my family is an understatement: Dad, we'll always miss you. Mum, thanks for not being anything like Edie. Arthur and Imo, I owe you a coffee, I think.

To the girls: Kitty, Ollie, Helena and Romilly for all the cheerleading... but the biggest hurrah of all has to go to my lovely husband, Richard, whose faith in me has never wavered, and who has always backed me to the hilt.

Printed in Great Britain
by Amazon